The Divine Bride Series: Book 1

These Shadows Become Her

Demi Clorissa

WHISPER
IN THE
WOOD
PRESS

Published by Whisper in the Wood Press.

Ebook ISBN: 978-0-6456822-3-6

Paperback ISBN: 978-0-6456822-4-3

This author would like to acknowledge the traditional owners on which this novel was written and she would like to acknowledge the elders past, present and emerging.

Cover created by Fay Lane (https://faylane.com/)

Edited by BLD Editing (https://www.bldediting.com/)

City Map masterfully created by Chloe The Cartographer (https://chloethecartographer.com/)

Character Art by amarnouille

*To those who fear those long, dark nights will swallow them whole.
Morning will come.*

The Cit
Western District
Rosda Manor
Lower District
Medicus Tower
Cau

Alderdeen
Valliss Castle
The Great Oak
Luc's Art Studio
Madame Diamonde
Temple
' House
Silva Forest
The Palisade
The Blacksmith
Moonshyne Markets
The Necropolis

Pronunciation Guide

Names:

Mia - Mee-AH
Kali - CAL-lee
Idris - Id-driss
Reagan - Re-GAhn
Sorcha - Soar-CHA
Wyn - Win
Mylo - MI-lo
Benny - Ben-KNEE
Henry - Hen-REE
Anne - Ann
Hartwinn - Heart–WIN
Maeve - MAY-eev
Mortias - Mor-TI-ass
Constance - Con-STAN-ce
Vivan - Vee-van
Alaric: AL-lah-ric

Gods:

Deus - DAY-us
Oryah - Or-YAH
Diabolus - Dia-BOL-ous

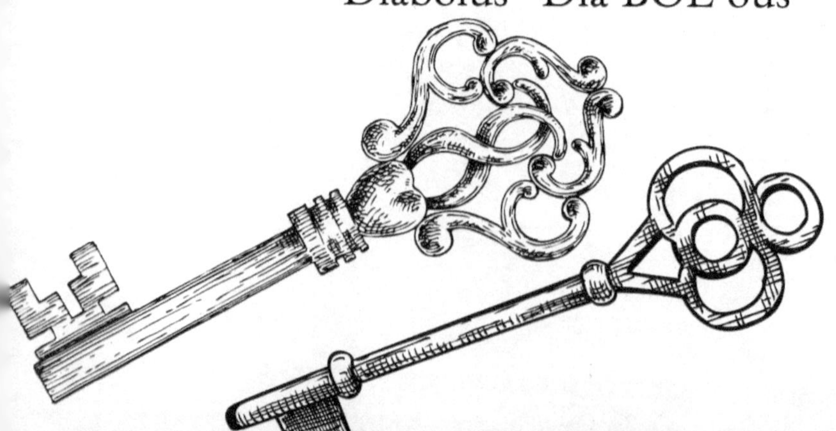

Countries:
Zeroth - ZER-oth
Moonmire -Moon-MYre

Cities:
Alderdeen - AL-der-dean
Vespera - ves-pe-RA
Goulrich - GOO-rick

Locations in Alderdeen:
The Medicus Tower - MED-uh-kuhss
Tower
The Palisade (the Pali) - Pa-luh-sayd
Valliss Castle - Val-LISS Castle
Silva Forest - Sil-VAH Forest
Moonshyne Market - MOON-shine

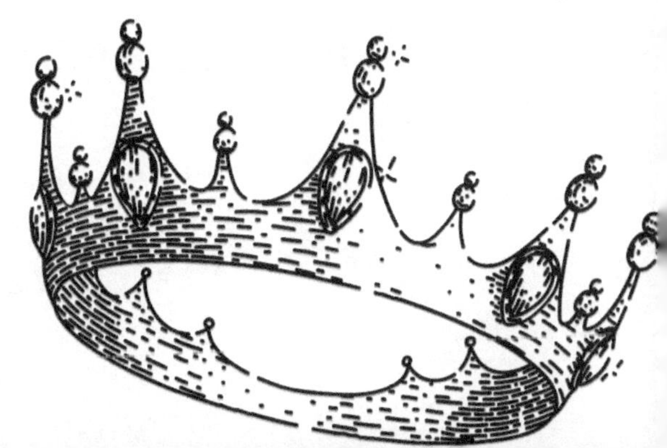

Content Warnings

These Shadows Become Her is not intended for those under the age of 18.

The following are the content warnings: *Swearing, graphic violence against women, descriptions of burning bodies, consensual sexual acts, alcoholism, and risky behaviours relating to alcohol use, slut shaming, sibling death, misogyny, on page sexual assault, discussion of previous sexual assault of the MMC (not by the FMC), gore, workplace sexual harassment, PTSD like symptoms (Panic attacks, and reliving the trauma), blood/blood Drinking/blood sharing, negative discussion of religion, and xenophobia (not towards FMC).*

Your mental health is important. Please reach out, and seek support.
Please remember you are *loved*.

PROLOGUE

The rotting, sizzling stench of burning flesh lingered on Gennifer's skin, in her knotty hair. Despite the fervent clawing at herself, she would never be clean, lest tear skin from muscle and flesh from bone. The feral writhing of her sisters against their pyres replayed in her mind. Orange flames danced up and over the soaked wood in search of the fuel-covered flesh. Gennifer's teeth scraped over her tongue, but the fatty, nauseating scent sank deep into her taste buds, filling her mouth with the rancid taste of kerosene that soaked into her clothing. Plumes of grey smoke dotting the horizon grew smaller, leaving the wild cries and whimpers in the distance. The carriage raced away as fast as it could from each of her sisters, burning.

Gennifer's hands shook, gripping the back of the bench so tightly her nails dug crescent-shaped indents into the leather. Her tear-filled eyes watched each puff of smoke disappear into the hazy orange sunset. A horse's panicked neighs and thundering hooves filled the air. She twisted sharply, meeting a pair of bloodshot brown eyes. Fear was all she could see beaming back at her, not for herself—a trained and seasoned queen's guard—but for the crying child bundled in a ratty blanket.

Ophelia.

Her soft blonde hair curled around her chubby face. A deep wound cut across her cheek, starting from the corner of her eye to the dip of her small chin, clotted but wet and oozing.

"Maeve—"

The world abruptly shifted sideways, tilting at an impossible angle as the carriage flung off the road, rolling and flipping. Heads, elbows and knees slammed into the unforgiving hardwood, and glass shattered, sending razor-sharp shards slicing Gennifer's exposed skin. Her ears rang, and blood dripped from her side, where a jagged piece of glass had lodged itself between her ribs. She grasped it, hissing as she yanked it free.

Ophelia wailed, her hair matted with blood and tears, mingling with the oozing wound on her cheek. Gennifer crawled over the broken glass towards her, hand grasping her side, glass crunching with each shift of her body. "Come now, witchling, dry your tears. We aren't scared of a little blood, are we?"

Ophelia continued to bawl, desperate for her mother.

Gennifer's eyes fell on Maeve, who lay splayed out, unconscious. Blood trailed from her nose and ear, running over the milky skin of her throat. With a trembling hand, Gennifer gripped her by the blouse, shaking her. Maeve groaned, and Gennifer let out a heavy sigh, relief flooding her. She was alive.

"Open your eyes, Maeve. We have to keep moving, for Ophelia's sake."

The child's little hand reached out, shoving her mother back and forth. "Mama! Wake up now."

Maeve's eyelids fluttered, her daughter conjuring her to consciousness. She struggled to her hands and knees, swaying with each movement, then sat heavily on her rear. "What in the Heylla happened?"

"We crashed. They will be on us soon. We must go."

A tug came from the edge of Gennifer's cloak. "Mama is bleeding. You have to heal her."

Maeve wiped her nose on the back of her hand, smearing the blood. She shared a small, calming smile with Ophelia, taking her hand. "Mama is okay, my heart. You and Gennifer have to go—and be quick about it. Mama has to stay so you have time to run from the men chasing us."

"Maeve—"

"I said, run!" Maeve commanded, her voice shaking. A solitary tear spilt down her cheek, but that smile never wavered, nor did her eyes leave her daughter. "You have to, Gennifer. You have to leave me to save her."

"Please, we have time..." she begged, shaking her head.

Maeve wrapped Ophelia in a tight hug, pressing a kiss to her crown. She looked at Gennifer, and desperation crossed her face. "I've stolen many moments from the great goddess, Oryah. Now, I fear it's time to pay up."

Tears rolled down Gennifer's face, her heart cracking in her chest. She was never to leave Maeve's side, born to protect her. It was the vow she'd made—and one she'd never break. But she watched as Maeve pressed another kiss to her daughter's forehead, wiping the blood and tears from her cheek. Gennifer knew the vow must be broken for the girl who shared her mother's eyes, who laughed like her father and who would one day rule her people.

"As you command, my queen. By the shadows."

Maeve searched Ophelia's face, eyebrows meeting with each desperate skim of her eyes. It could be the last time she would see her daughter, and that crushed the shards in Gennifer's chest to dust.

"By the shadows," Maeve murmured.

Gennifer scurried over broken glass, her hand clutched to her side. She rattled the door handle—stuck. She cursed, then turned to the half-broken window, kicking out the remaining glass.

"Come, Ophelia," Maeve said. "Gennifer and I will be right behind."

Gennifer helped Ophelia squeeze her tiny body through the window, and she disappeared from view.

Maeve's hand snapped out, gripping Gennifer's leather surcoat and dragging her closer. Her eyes were wild. Frantic. "Take her to them. That's where she will be safe. I can feel him. His darkness slips and slithers across the earth like a foul snake. He can never—"

A high-pitched scream pierced the air, sending the women scurrying out of the darkness of the ruined carriage. Gennifer's breath caught in her throat. Ophelia was pressed against the wood. Her brown eyes were wide with fear, while a man stood over her, a dagger held to her throat.

A wicked smile spread across his face. "Found you."

"You let her go, you scum!" Maeve screamed as she scrambled to her feet. She launched herself into him, knocking him down. He dragged her to the ground, fists flying. Gennifer grabbed Ophelia's elbow, pulling her away from the wrestling pair. A small silver blade appeared in the man's hand, glistening in the sunlight.

"Run! Ophelia, Run!" Maeve shouted as she fought for the dagger.

Gennifer heard Maeve's pained scream ring through the air as the blade buried itself in her side. Ophelia reached for her mother, her little hands stretched out, but Gennifer's grip was ironclad. Ophelia's begging sobs for her mother filled the clearing, a pained bleating. The man pushed Maeve off him with a grunt and rose to his feet.

He spat on her before kicking her in the ribs. "Stupid witch bitch..."

Maeve groaned, coughing up a wet puddle of blood. Gennifer paled as the man's attention fell to her. Magic swelled in her chest, a hot surge of warmth to her fingertips. She threw her hand to the ground, slamming it down and forcing her magic into the earth. Thick, fiery vines erupted from the dirt, capturing the hunter. For the moment, at least.

Gennifer swept Ophelia into her arms and sprinted into the forest. She knew they were close to the meeting point, but all she could see were blurred shadows and light. Ophelia's screams for her mother echoed over her shoulder.

She ran until the dizzying feeling of blood loss forced her to a stop, dropping the child. Her hand gingerly brushed over her side. Her shirt was soaked through, her fingers stained red. She cursed through a grimace.

"Y-you—said—b-bad—wo-word, Genni," Ophelia stumbled over her words through chest-heaving sobs.

Gennifer reached out and smoothed her hair. "Yes, I did, and I'm very sorry."

Faint black spots marred her vision as blood gushed from her, spilling down her side. She fell to her knees in front of Ophelia, who whispered words she couldn't hear. The frigid grip of Death wrapped his hands around her throat, squeezing the life from her.

"You have to run, sweet one. You have to leave me here. Go on without me."

"I'm not supposed to go anywhere without you, Mama, Papa or the queen's guard," she said with a heavy breath, reciting the words she'd told her every day.

Gennifer smiled through the pain, tears rolling down her cheeks. "You're right, Ophelia, but you're allowed to go without me. Just this once, all right?"

Ophelia's gaze flashed to something behind Gennifer, widening with pupil-constricting fear as a looming male figure reflected in the child's glassy eyes.

"We need to stop meeting like this," the witch hunter crooned.

"Go, now! Ophelia, now!" Gennifer yelled, her voice waking the little girl from her wide-eyed terror. Ophelia scrambled back, tears still running down her face as she dashed into the shadows of the surrounding forest, disappearing from view.

"Live, Ophelia. Live for all of us," Gennifer called after her.

She whispered a spell—words she knew would protect Ophelia—down the wind, right to the panicked little girl sprinting through the dense growth. She hoped it would worm its way into her ear, into her mind, hiding away the black plumes of smoke and raining ash of shadows and queens. Only to be uncovered when she truly needed it.

With the last of her strength, Gennifer struggled to her feet to face the man who would take her life. A man filled with hatred and disgust for her and her kind. He drew his sword, the cold iron glinting in the disappearing sunlight. Her lips curled back in a wild snarl. She would not be entering Oryah's great garden alone. She would drag his putrid soul with her. Her magic surged in her chest and flowed into her waiting hands, fiery and powerful.

I'm coming, sisters. Wait for me.

Her chin tilted to the sky as more tears fell from her eyes. She clenched her hands closed, her magic detonating like a bomb, incinerating herself and the lone witch hunter.

PART ONE:
Whisky Words and
Sober Thoughts

ONE

Mia could never truly create what she saw in her dreams, even with the rainbow of sticky oil paint smeared across the canvas. She held the paintbrush aloft, her head tilting side to side, scrutinising each brushstroke and dab of paint she had painstakingly placed.

The face of the man who haunted her every dream stared back at her.

His emerald green eyes shone through the darkness of the brushstrokes surrounding them. Something was familiar about his face, about him, but everything else was unknown. He came in flashes of wide, toothy grins and long, lusty looks. His face blurred at the edges, glimmering like the surface of a still lake. His image rippled if she reached out to touch it. Her brush met the rough canvas in tiny dabs of viridian green around the black–grey pupil. Her heavy-handedness wore away the flecks of gold she had placed the night before, making her grumble. She had been working on the piece for *weeks*. Layers upon layers of paint, and she still couldn't get it right.

"Mia!"

Her mother's voice broke her concentration, and a hurried knock rattled her small room, sending a jolt of fear through her. Her hand twitched, the pallet slapping paint onto her mustard-coloured dress and staining the white lace edging of her bodice. Mia stepped back, dumping the pallet on her paint-splattered table and cursing. Everything she owned was stained with paint, covered with charcoal sketches or buried under turpentine-stiffened rags. Her art consumed her room, her life and her every waking thought until Mia was nothing but dabs of paint on canvas with a lingering sense that she needed to be better.

Her adoptive mother, Anne, cracked open the door, her silken blonde curls catching the light from Mia's open window, her round blue eyes taking in her daughter.

"Good goddess, Mama," Mia grumbled, looking down at her paint-splattered dress. "I cannot be presented to court or to Master Luc with viridian smeared down my skirts."

Anne offered a tight-lipped grin and a rushed apology as she drew a handkerchief from her pocket. She dabbed but simply smeared the paint deeper into the delicate cotton. "You'll do just fine, Mia. Maybe Luc will be impressed with your dedication to painting. And besides, they won't be looking at—"

"At me. I know."

Mia's fingertips brushed the scar that cut across her cheekbone and down the corner of her mouth. Eyes would be on her adopted sister. The effervescent Kali Ashmore. *The gem of Alderdeen's court*, shining for all to see. Mia hid in the shadow of her sister, never able to step into that light. Not because Kali blocked her path, but because of the twisted, deep-rooted feelings Mia let grow in her rib cage like gnarled tree roots, curling around her soft heart. They squeezed out any joyful, soft emotion and turned it sour, heavy, laced with loathing.

Words she'd whispered in the mirror had morphed into a creeping, malice-filled voice slithering at the edge of her mind. She fought hard not to believe the voice, the lies it would spread, but sometimes she wasn't strong enough.

Anne cast her a sharp look. "No, sweet girl, they will be mesmerised by Luc's art. The portrait work is awe-inspiring *apparently*."

Mia glanced over her shoulder at the green-eyed man. Her stomach twisted, and hot nervousness washed over her. "Do you think he'll be impressed with my work? Or do you think it's immature or unrefined next to his? What if he hates my brushwork? Master Petra said it's great, but he is not—"

Anne rose, catching Mia's chin with her forefinger, stopping her anxious rambling. Mia struggled to meet her mother's concerned gaze. "Mia Ashmore, you were born for this. He'd be a fool not to see the talent standing in front of him."

She exhaled the emotion threatening to erupt from her chest and nodded.

Anne took her hand and led her away from the safety of her bedroom, down the stairs to the busy kitchen. She passed the cook brandishing a wooden spoon, yelling at staff, and pots bubbling with the day's meals. Polite smiles and well wishes were cast Mia's way. A stray hug and a ramble of soothing words came from Abigail, her mother's lady's maid. Mia gave her a tight-lipped grin, patting her on the arm.

Anne ran the tap over the corner of a stray rag, dabbing the paint away. "Your father will be home soon. Then we can all go to..." She prattled away, making Mia's mind wander to her painting and how she would perfect the sadness in his eyes.

A musical humming came from the stairs, a *creak* sounding with each step. Kali swanned into the kitchen, her striking violet dress skimming her curved body. A smile spread across her bronzed face, sending her azure eyes twinkling, her curly brown hair swept into a loose bun at her nape. She was effortless in every sense of the word.

Ever since Mia had wandered into Anne's rose-speckled courtyard with its crumbling walls at five years old, they had been joined at the hip. That was, until Kali was presented at court and swept into the endless balls, parties and gossip, leaving Mia to trail behind. She loved her sister, but deep down, envy bubbled.

"What do we all think?" Kali asked, spinning, skirts flaring.

She can't look anything but beautiful, Mia thought, turning back to the sink.

A thread of jealousy tugged in her chest again, twisting her lips into a sour pout. But it was soon snipped with love's sharp scissors. *It isn't Kali's fault everyone thinks she is beautiful,* she reminded herself.

A slither of a dark thought slid around the base of her skull. She shook her head and looked over her shoulder. With a smirk, Mia joked, "Is that what you're wearing? You look atrocious."

Kali narrowed her eyes but returned the smirk. "Don't be jealous, Mia. Green is an ugly colour on you."

"Kali Ashmore!" Anne exclaimed, fake shock echoing in her tone.

Mia threw a rude gesture over her shoulder, making the maids giggle into the bowls they were stirring.

"You girls will send me to an early grave!" Anne said as she dramatically fell into the chair, waving the handkerchief at the girls.

Kali sidled up to Mia, bumping her ribs with an elbow. "Are you nervous?"

Mia gripped the edge of the sink and exhaled for what felt like the hundredth time that morning. "What do you think?"

She stared back at the swirling water, her mind and stomach in tangled knots. She was nervous—*moist palms, unable to string a sentence together* nervous. And now she was paint-splattered and sweaty. Not the perfect apprentice.

"You'll be fine. We simply curtsy, bat our lashes and promise to be the best apprentices they've ever had. Simple."

It was anything but simple, especially for Mia. It was a tiresome process of awkward tests, painting lessons and late nights staring at blank canvases. It was now reaching the pinnacle.

The Delectu Processum.

At age twenty-one, the eligible men and women of Alderdeen were presented to the six guild masters—experts in their craft and eager to select the year's apprentices.

Mia and Kali had just turned twenty-one.

"Miss Kali, who do you think will choose you? You'd make a wonderful healer," a maid asked, bursting with excitement. It was an honour—a successful, anxiety-filled honour—to be paraded before a sea of stuffy, grey-haired masters. *No one asked me who would choose me,* Mia noticed as she wrung green-tinged water from the rag.

"A healer would be marvellous! But honestly, I have no idea," Kali said bashfully, waving her hand. Mia scrubbed harder, irritated at her sister. "Maybe the apothecary, but definitely not the Silver or the smithies. I fear I have no stomach or strength for that work. You know they have who they want in mind before we step into that room."

All except one—Luc Rennaik, whose selection was a tight-lipped secret. Mia wished and prayed to any god who listened that she'd be one of his secrets.

"You both will be *fine*. You're amazing women, and any of the masters would be lucky to have you," Anne soothed in her calm tone.

Mia turned to her, lip curling. "And the coin? Shall you take it and save it so Kali doesn't spend it all at the Moonshye Markets? Or are you giving it to the beggars on Seventh Avenue?"

"No, I will not take your hard-earnt gold. You will save it for when you need to provide a dowry—"

"A dowry?" Kali interrupted. "How *old-fashioned*. No man we know will ask for a dowry."

"I hope both of you don't know any men," Anne said, eyeing them with a narrowed, smirking gaze.

"Of course not, Mama," Kali said demurely, fluttering her eyelashes.

"Oh, good goddess, enough of this. I'd rather listen to Father Pristone drone on about Deus and his supposed greatness than listen to this anymore." Mia cringed, pushing away from the sink. A laugh escaped her, untwisting the knot a fraction.

The back door creaked open, and a pair of broad, muscular shoulders entered the kitchen. It was Henry, her adoptive father. His sun-bronzed face had only just begun to show the beginnings of age, with a deep furrow between his brows. He tucked a stray lock behind a pointed ear.

Fae.

Many fae had fled their lands as the human king war raged on, destroying everything in his path. They now mingled with humans. However, many felt uneasy around them, like something in their human body knew they were supernatural, otherworldly. Many even went as far as crossing the street to not come in contact with them. Not Mia. She loved Henry, regardless of the fact that he was a stubborn, rule-abiding man who was determined to ensure his daughters were respectable women in court. He showered her with the heart-swelling feeling as much as he did Kali. He was her father as much as Anne was her mother.

Bound in love, not in blood.

He smiled at Anne, pressing his lips to her crown, flicking his long black braid over his shoulder. "Hello, my lovely ladies. What are we discussing?"

Kali rushed to relinquish her father of his basket of goods, waving him into a seat. A grin twisted her face, setting down the basket. "Men—"

"Nothing, Father," Mia interrupted, casting her sister a sharp look.

Henry had one rule: *no men in the house*. Kali broke it any chance she got.

"We should be heading to the castle, not gossiping here. The guild masters wait for no one."

"Yes, Papa!" Kali said, snapping to attention, her fingers saluting him.

Mia pursed her lips, not moving. The knot tightened again, forcing her measly breakfast to rise.

Henry levelled her with a stern look. "You will be fine, Mia. Luc will select you."

Luc was the best portrait artist in their city, maybe in all of Zeroth. His art graced the stone walls of King Ewan's golden palace, and Mia ached to learn how he captured his subject's essence in their portrait. It was like magic.

"He has never picked a woman, Father. I don't think he will start now."

Henry shrugged, a smile playing on his lips. "You never know."

"Yeah, Mia. You never know. The Death Court may also choose you. You being a young, blonde—" Kali mouthed the word "virgin" at her.

Mia's face flushed, and her mouth snapped shut. She couldn't help the shudder that ran through her. The Death Court reflected its two vampyre kings: immortal, cold. Their predilection for blood was too strange, too visceral for common folk. So, the vampyres lingered in places with more shadows than sunlight. Mia knew little about the Death Court and even less about vampyres. Not that it mattered. The

Death Court only chose those with a flourish of magic for their presti-gious academy, the *Magicis*. Much to her disappointment, she didn't have a single drop in her body.

"Maybe they'll choose you, Kali. Your big head is full to the brim with magic."

She rolled her eyes, ignoring Mia. "Now, shall we go, family? I'm itching to see what Iris is wearing. I know it's going to be shocking."

"Wait, we have something for you both," Anne said, rushing out of the room.

Mia and Kali exchanged a confused glance at the sound of their mother rummaging through a drawer, shifting papers and trinkets. Kali shrugged. When Anne returned, she had two velvet boxes clasped in her hands.

A rare smile cracked over Henry's face. "A celebration gift for each of you, for being selected."

Mia swallowed her reply. The celebration was premature. Neither name had been called yet. But in a flash of hopefulness, she let herself believe Luc would select her, that everything would go to plan.

Anne handed them each a box. The material was smooth in Mia's sweaty, paint-speckled hands. She unlatched the golden clasp, but Kali's sharp exhale drew her eyes away before she looked inside. Pinched in her sister's long fingers was a bracelet of round emeralds and gold, gleaming in the morning sun and casting a green spectrum across her dress. Mia's eyes rose from the glittering gems to Anne's smiling face, who nodded at the box in Mia's hand. She swallowed, looking down to see a ring snugly placed in velvet. At its centre, fused to the gold, was a black opal. The stone shone as if fire were trapped within, creating flecks of red and orange. Mia brushed the smooth stone, heat radiating into the pad of her thumb. "This is too much," she said, her gaze lifting. "I cannot have this. Not yet."

She knew what it was—Anne's engagement ring.

"Not for you, my moon," Henry said through a grin. "And it is a fae tradition that I pass on something that brought me luck. For luck to find you."

"Put them on, put them on," Anne urged, smiling, clasping her hands in front of her.

Mia pulled the ring from the velvet, slipping it over her middle finger, the black stone stark against her pale skin. Kali slipped the gold bracelet over her hand, rolling her wrist in the morning sun and admiring the shimmering stones. "Now we're ready."

THE CARRIAGE RIDE WAS MUTED, SOLEMN, ALL OF THEM LOST in contemplation. Henry and Anne sat hand in hand, heads low, murmuring words to one another that were lost to Mia's ears. Anne's eyebrows met, her eyes narrowing at her husband's words. Her hand yanked from his, leaning back.

"Henry," she breathed, shaking her head. "You didn't."

"Mama? What is it?" Kali asked.

"Nothing, Kali," Henry answered sharply, leaning back from Anne.

The space between her parents grew, and tension bubbled in the quiet carriage. Kali sighed and sat back, chin in her hand and face pinched. Hidden under all the bravado, Mia knew she was as shit-scared as she was. She sighed quietly, resting her chin on her forearms. She watched the flickering green of the trees morph into the burnt orange mortar of the houses on the edge of her city. The carriage jostled over the cobblestones, indicating the change from their little world at the top of the hill into the sprawling city of Alderdeen. It spread through a deep valley, surrounded by tall mountain peaks. As the population swelled with refugees from wars fought in lands far away, so grew their little village. Bursting with life, noise and both human and not, lives mingled there. Families joined, creating something unseen before.

"*A true harmony*," Henry had once called it.

The carriage wound its way through the lower city, where homes jammed together, creating a haphazard pattern of rising and lowering tile roofs. The King's Road led to the looming castle, known as Valliss. Towering walls shielded most of the grey, ivy-covered stone from view. Those same walls hid the lord's court away from the wandering masses, making handshake deals and whispered trades.

Lord Hartwinn Novak and his three sons ruled Alderdeen as if they were the kings of the land. They only answered to the human king, Ewan, who was so far away, he may as well not have existed. Henry, an emissary of the Westryn Fae, spent his days bargaining for his people. Kali and Mia had spent their childhood playing in the courtyards and running down corridors. Happy memories of giggling and the cries of children flitted over her. Until Henry had shot Kali a heart-shrinking, chest-tightening, disappointed glare when she had been dragged, half naked, from a maid's closet with Lord Hartwinn's eldest son, Reagan, trailing close behind. Mia could still see the smug smirk spread across his face. She knew what he had done in those moments of sweaty release. He had trapped Kali in a golden cage, only for her to sing for him when he brushed a finger over those cold metal bars. And how well her sister would sing.

Kali reached out, slipping her hand over Mia's and squeezing. "Things are going to change, aren't they?"

She smiled at her. "Nothing's going to change. I promise, sister."

"Truth?" Kali asked.

"Truth."

Kali's face lit up, her tight-lipped expression transforming into a beaming grin, eyes crinkling and all. Mia turned away. Her sister needed words of promise and light, and she was never good at lying.

Deep down, she knew everything would change after that night.

Two

The Delectu Processum was underway when Mia and her family entered the tightly packed Valliss ballroom. The herald of the court's deep, baritone voice disrupted the soft lute music and the *clink* of glasses. He boomed Henry's name, announcing their presence.

A few cast glances over their shoulders, sharing knowing smiles, while others blatantly ignored him. Mia bristled, hands clenching at her sides. He'd been at court for longer than she'd been alive—longer than some members who now sat on Hartwinn's council. Henry had nurtured the city until it thrived, spilling gold into the pockets of nobles who only saw the bloody brute of a fae warrior who had walked off the battlefield years earlier.

"And, I cannot believe they let *those* people in," a fan-waving woman whispered to another who had the appearance of a withered dried apricot. "And Anne continues to flaunt her little *half-breed*."

The word was spat out as if it were bitter, foul-tasting.

Mia glanced at her sister, who had found a speck of invisible lint on the velvet of her skirt, jaw clenched. Mistrust ran deep, like a fissure in the earth, for King Sundryl, who had done nothing but simply defend his people from the crawling war machine of King Ewan.

Anne's spine straightened, hands fisting. Instead of walking away with her chin held high, as she would have instructed Mia to do, her mother leant in, ready to spew vitriol over the crusted, ancient, cobwebbed woman. Henry caught her elbow, pulling her to him. He pressed his lips to her ear, whispering. A sickly sweet smile spread on Anne's face, and glee awoke in her eyes.

"I do not believe—"

"Believe it," her father cut in, a smile playing on his lips.

Anne looked both women up and down before snorting a laugh. Henry ushered them forward, but leant in and placed a kiss on Anne's temple before they were swallowed by the crush of bodies.

Families encircled well-dressed young people who nervously glanced around, looking for the masters. Untouched food was spread across tables as bubbly wine was poured into shining crystal glasses. Mia's head darted back and forth, searching the walls crammed with golden frames of art, splattered with Luc's work. She spotted the whitewash frame of her art halfway down the wall, tucked between masterpieces. The urge to pull from her family to inspect each and every painting was almost too powerful. A speck of her wanted to flee the nervousness working its way up her throat to somewhere more comfortable—to be alone with the art.

Kali's hand settled on her elbow, and she leant in to whisper in her ear, "Steady on, Mia, you'll get to see them. Wait for Uncle Hartwinn's speech. Then you can scurry off."

Mia had been dragged to too many parties, balls and soirees for them to be anything but normal. But that day, Hartwinn would shake her hand and congratulate her, sharing that smile he saved for those close to him. She could see it all as a glimmering mirage. Kali dancing, a blue ribbon in her hair, marking her as a healer's acolyte. Hartwinn giving her parents a back-slapping hug, demanding they share a glass of whisky in his office. Herself standing in front of that damned portrait, the sadness exactly right as if it were real.

Hushed female voices whispered in her ear. Too soft to understand, but enough for her to turn, searching.

Nothing.

The people surrounding her were too engrossed in shaking Henry's hand or smiling at Anne to speak to her.

The doors swung open. It wasn't Hartwinn who entered, but a tightly packed group of nervous-looking fae. A scandalised whisper spread through the crowd, ladies muttering behind fans, and fathers whispering into their sons' ears. It was the first year the fae who were born in Alderdeen had been invited to the Delectu Processum, and Henry had spearheaded it. He'd insisted that it was only right to give *all* children of Alderdeen the opportunity to better the city.

Henry straightened his surcoat and raised his hand, capturing their attention. The crowd split, scurrying back, allowing the fae to cross the room. Mia grinned at them and gave a small wave, but turned her attention to the closest painting—a small landscape of Alderdeen, signed by Samuel Salvatore. The brushwork was heavy-handed, lacking the finesse that a delicately painted landscape needed. She knew Samuel from days spent in Master Petra's studio. He was a smirking, pompous arsehole— her least favourite kind of noble's son. He'd stolen her first kiss in those years of awkward adolescence with a flurry of tongue and clash of teeth, only to cast words of disgust at her for years after. Words she didn't deserve.

Murmuring returned to the crowd for just a brief moment before the boom of a horn made all conversations cease. It was so silent that Mia could hear the heavy doors creak and swing open, then, the scuttle of slippered and booted feet parting once again to let the lord of Alderdeen stride through. Hartwinn wasn't a tall man, nor was he hulking with packed muscles. Instead, he was made of fine, lithe ones. His size didn't dominate the space. His presence, pragmatic and capti- vating, did. A short-clipped blond beard hid his aged face as his twin- kling, youthful grey eyes searched the room. Unfortunately, his hawklike gaze rarely missed a thing. Mia had felt the sharp edge of that look after being trotted out as a child to be reprimanded for the mischievous games she and Kali played. However, Hartwinn was less of a distant ruler and more like family. Anne had been his father's ward until her twenty-fifth birthday, and they had grown up together. Scandalously, there had been whispers that he had loved her, but Anne only ever had eyes for Henry.

The masses tracked Hartwinn as he made his way to the front, nodding at nobles and ladies on the way past. He winked at Mia and shared a coy smirk. Her heart picked up pace, and she returned a nose-crinkled wink. He bowed deeply to Anne, who waved him away with a hand and grin. Hartwinn turned to the crowd and clasped his hands at his front.

"Shall we begin?" he asked, before the guild masters appeared at the door.

THREE

Mia's cheeks ached from the forced grins she'd shared with the rough-handed blacksmith, who said her arms were too soft for swinging a hammer and her lady skin too smooth for the rough work. She politely agreed. Then, the milky-eyed master librarian swept her into a soft, murmured conversation, his sun-weathered face adorned with wrinkles deeper than crevasses. He'd reminded her that her literacy skills lacked the comprehension to devour and dissect the ancient texts in the library. Mia hung her head and confessed that she'd rather face the heat of the blacksmith's fire than spend the days with her nose in a book, making the frail man howl with laughter.

She glanced over her shoulder at Kali, who was surrounded by two masters—apothecary and the grand master of the healers, both vying for her attention. Her wide eyes and nervous hand waving made Mia stifle a giggle and wander away from the librarian.

Two figures lounged in chairs tucked away in a dark corner. Long, pale hands gripped chalices of ruby-red wine—or so Mia hoped. Both men were handsome, with black hair and dark eyes, their faces chiselled from stone. They were so similar in appearance they could have been brothers—twins, even.

The vampyres.

Mia stepped forward, swallowing the ball of unease. No apprentices lingered around them—not that she expected them to. At the last Delectu Processum, the vampyres selected no one before melting back into a flurry of velvet and darkness.

"Good afternoon, sirs," Mia said, curtsying. A pained smile spread across her face. "How goes the hunt for apprentices?"

The one on the right tilted his head, sizing her up. A voice to her left rumbled, "Lacking."

"How disappointing. I do hope—"

"You are lacking. I can feel it radiating off you. The Death Court shall not be choosing you, girl."

Mia's cheeks warmed, her stomach twisting tighter. She opened her mouth to reply, but nothing came out. The heat of their glares scurried over her skin, making her step back. The vampyre on the right leant over, shaking his head, gripping the glass tighter. "No. This one has his mar—"

"The answer is *no*."

Mia wished for the earth to open and swallow her whole. "I shall leave you to discuss your chosen apprentices, then, sirs."

He waved a pale hand. "Go. Your misplaced desperation to be selected by these humans is suffocating me. These men are below you, and you aren't even aware of it."

Confused, Mia dipped into another wobbly curtsy, then fled into the crowd, seeking the relief of the masses. Words flitted around her, but her ears pricked up when she strayed closer to the knights of Alderdeen, the keepers of law and order.

A rough, accented voice spoke. "No. I will not be discussin' the deaths of the women—"

Someone cut in, words swallowed by the noise of the crowd. Mia pushed closer, seeing the flash of silver armour.

"It's an open investigation, ya see. I cannot—"

"Sir Mylo, I heard it was bloody—"

"Firstly, it's lieutenant. And it's too awful to be spoken about with this many women about, boy. Now, do ya want to hear the pitch, or will ya end up in the Medicus Tower, dabbing sweat of birthin' mothers?"

That shut up the questioning young man, making him snap to attention.

Mia caught one of Luc's pieces in the corner of her vision, bound in a gilded, swirling frame. She wandered from the crowd, hands clasped behind her, eyes growing wider as she leant closer to the piece, a soft exhale leaving her lips. Her gaze danced over the small, worn nameplate —*The Burning of the Witch Queen*, by none other than Luc Renniak.

Mia couldn't find a place to settle, skimming over the exposed, milky skin of Queen Maeve and across the ripped velvet, right to her bound wrist and down to her clenched hand. Blood-red wood was stark against the dark background, against her pale skin. The flames licked at her feet, the smoke billowing around her. Mia couldn't meet the gaze of an anguished knight, crying at the feet of the woman, hands reaching for his queen. Instead, she found herself enthralled by the soft, serene look of the woman who was burning. Her face revealed a sad resignation, as though she knew nothing could save her or her people.

Something flared to life in Mia's chest, so small that she hardly noticed it.

She leant forward, bewitched by the scene. The scent of wood burning was strong, invading her nostrils like the painting had caught aflame and was burning in front of her.

"Now, you seem to have excellent taste. This is a wondrous piece," stated a male voice from beside her, snapping her from the painting and returning her to the busy room and its overwhelming sounds.

Ignoring the voice, Mia tilted her head in the opposite direction, attuning her eyes to the dabs of paint and pained brushstrokes. "It's simply more than wonderful, sir. It is a masterpiece of balancing light and shadows. The colours...Oh, good goddess, the glorious colours. The redness around Maeve's eyes shows that she was crying, but no tears were shed on the pyre. And the muted background brings the observer's eye right to the flames—and Maeve, of course. Everything was selected on purpose to evoke emotion."

A body settled closer to Mia, clothing brushing over her arm. "What do you feel?"

"Sadness, but something else. Not the gleeful destruction of Diabolus—the great evil one—as others have shown, but maybe bravery? Going to the pyre without shedding a single tear would be a great feat."

"Bravery?" the man repeated, voice clipped with interest. "I've never seen the lack of tears as brave, but as a woman too stubborn to let a man have the last word."

"But—"

"But?"

Mia lowered her chin, still not turning to the man. "Maybe I shouldn't."

"Go on," he urged. "I wish to hear it."

She pointed to Maeve's breast, exposed by the ripping of her bodice. "The nudity, the ripped clothing. It doesn't fit. If he wanted the observer to see Maeve as a brave, compelling queen, why debase her with nudity?'

"I never thought of that when I was painting her. I was more thinking she was once this object of great, dignified beauty. Now, torn and exposed, she is none of those, but simply a witch going to the pyre."

The man's words made a clammy sweat spread over Mia's skin. She stiffly turned her head, finding Luc Renniak standing only a breath away from her. His face of hollowed cheekbones and thin lips was alight with amusement. His deep-set onyx eyes burnt into her bare skin before turning back to the painting, searching it. "I'm glad a woman of your class can appreciate a fine piece of work. It may be my favourite."

A hot flush crept up Mia's neck, staining every inch of her décolletage. "I think the portrait of Lady Seanna that you did for Lord Hartwinn is much more inspiring, sir. May she rest in peace."

Luc's gaze slid to her, his grin widening. "You know my work?"

She arched a brow and smiled back. "I think everyone knows your work. Let's not be modest here."

He chuckled, gaze dropping to the splatter of paint across her skirts. "Emerald?"

Mia's hands spread over her stain, her cheeks burning. "Viridian, actually..."

Luc turned on his toe and offered her a bemused smirk over his shoulder. "It is wonderfully mixed, from the remnants I see. Are you an artist?"

She nodded, suddenly flustered with the ease of conversation. "My art is here on the wall somewhere, but it's a simple piece. I'm Mia Ashmore."

Luc clasped his hands behind his back, rocking on the balls of his feet. "Well, then, Mia Ashmore, you must show me you work. If it is mixed like the paint on your skirts, then it will be quite a sight to see."

"It is nothing like your mastery of portraiture," she sputtered out, her hand raising to cover her mouth to stop more gushing compliments from leaving her.

"Well, we all start somewhere, don't we?" He chuckled. "Now, oil on canvas?"

Mia nodded, letting out a nervous exhale. She needed to impress him, almost desperately so. She launched into a passionate, albeit boring speech on the merits of using walnut oil over safflower oil when finishing a painting. Luc nodded, adding in measurements of the oils that Mia had never thought of doing.

With each step, he absent-mindedly brushed a finger over her forearm and down over the dip of her wrist. A stray hand lingered on the small of her back when he leant in closer to joke about fraying paint-brushes—which Mia giggled at, but didn't find very amusing. The blond strands falling across his cheekbone hypnotised her. The curled smirk he flashed when she agreed that oil was preferable over water-colour made her heart race. *He's attractive. Almost heartbreakingly handsome. And young. He's only a handful of years older than me. But, more than his flesh and bone structure, he's brilliant. An exceptionally bright artist, rising through the Artist Guild's ranks before his thirty-fifth birthday—*

"Am I to be your next portrait, Mia? You seem to be contemplating my measurements," Luc said, interrupting her rambling thoughts.

Mia was so eager to please him that she would have agreed to anything. "I would love to sketch you." *But my hand would probably tremble too hard for the drawing to come out any good,* she added silently.

A finger brushed over hers, and she felt cold gold slip over her knuckles, then a tight hand gripped her wrist. A stray brush of lips over her cheekbone led right to the curl of her ear. "Maybe I can draw you... with a few of these stained, frilly layers off."

Luc's words simmered in her mind for a moment, making the tips of her ears burn. Her eyes rose to his, lips parting. Her heartbeat picked up speed, threatening to smash right out of her rib cage. Mia giggled, unable to find the words to either reject his brazen offer or let him down more gently.

"My art is behind you, Master Luc, if you wish to see what I can do."

He searched her eyes, giving her a squeeze. "I can only imagine what you could do."

Mia gently took his arm and turned him, pointing to her own small portrait of Henry. The rich, buttery tones of his skin gleamed in the soft morning light, capturing the strength in the planes of his face. Her father's stern face glared at her from within the curling frame, dampening the tension brewing between her and Luc. But his eyes never never left her face. They bore into her with such intensity that Mia wondered if she was a rabbit stuck in a snare, flying around, the hunter standing over the trap.

She gestured at the wide strokes, then the flecks of lighter colours—a mimicked attempt at what Luc had done in most of his artworks. "You see, I used the same technique," she paused and added on quietly, "as *you*."

Only then did Luc's eyes finally leave her to glance at her art. A swell of pride, edged with self-doubt, filled her chest. She had even spotted a section she wished she had gone over again with varnish. He cocked his head, drawing closer to the portrait. Then, after a tense moment, he huffed a laugh and nodded. "Not bad for a woman. Your blending needs work, however, and remember where your light source is coming from."

Mia nodded, memorising his words, ready to dissect later.

"Not bad at all…" he repeated quietly.

"Does that mean you'll take me on as an apprentice?" she asked, words falling out before she could stop them.

A look of complete bewilderment spread across his face, followed by a confused grimace. Mia took that as a good sign that she'd guessed his secret list, and her name was on it. Some may have called her delusional at that point, but she didn't care. A horn boomed out, indicating the start of the Delectu Processum choosing.

Luc cleared his throat and straightened his silver coat. The air was suddenly awkward, strained. "Good luck, Mia. I shall see you again soon."

"Luc, I want you to know I'd be—"

"I have to go."

And with that, he disappeared into the sea of hopeful apprentices and their nervous parents, leaving Mia alone and confused. She cast one last glance at Henry's portrait and merged with the crowd, ready to face her future.

FOUR

The Delectu Processum was to be witnessed in front of the entire court, so nobles remained accountable. Years had passed since the scandal of bribery and shady dealings of a few nobles. It had thrust the ceremony out of the sandstone guild chambers right to Valliss. The eligible young people had been rounded up and lined up outside in the hallway to chat nervously amongst themselves. Mia hurried up the line to find Kali, hearing her musical laugh before seeing her. Her boot caught on the raised end of the stone tile, making her stumble forward, sending her heart into her throat as the ground rushed towards her.

"Look at her. Can't even keep on her two feet. No wonder no one invites her to parties. At least Kali is good to look at," a male voice said, earning a chuckle from those around him.

Mia would know that grating voice anywhere. Samuel Salavatore. He angled his sharp chin down, glaring down his nose at her. His chestnut-brown eyes took her in with a hint of disgust. With his curled hair and flecks of freckles across his tanned skin, she would have thought him handsome if it weren't for the air of arrogance that surrounded him—and the fact that he could only paint boring landscapes.

Mia turned on her toe, hands in fists. She glared at Samuel, lips curled into a frown.

"Yes, Mia? Finally have something to say, or are you going to run home to Daddy and tattle on me?"

"You should..." Her words faded, the insult lodged in her throat.

Samuel mocked her with sputtered words and cruel laughter.

Mia scurried back from him, cheeks burning, Samuel and his cronies' cruel laughter mixing with the hard thumps of her boots. She found Kali surrounded by friends, an easy smile cut across her face. From just the way her eyes glimmered, Mia knew she'd seen Reagan. But before she could question her, the line moved, propelling her forward. Kali slipped in first, leaving Mia frozen at the entrance, hand on the doorframe. The line milled around her with excused passes and shoulder bumps. She watched Kali take to the stage, chin high, beckoning her in with a sharp wave of her hand. Mia swallowed the hard lump in her throat, urging her feet to step forward. Nervousness flooded her, causing a thick layer of sweat to form on her palms and drip down her spine.

All you have to do is wait for your name to be called and allow the guild masters to decide which one will want you. But Luc will call your name, and your future will be decided for you. Truly nothing to worry about. Simple, really, Mia thought to herself in a half-hearted attempt to settle her nerves that only made the muscles around her knees twitch. The slither of the negative voice unfurled, stretching. She exhaled once, ignoring the uneasy feeling, and stepped through.

Her heavy footfalls cut off the man speaking—the master of all masters, the guild chief. Robbert was a wrinkled man with deep-set frown lines. His faded blue eyes fell on her, cold and angry. The gazes of the apprentices shifted on her, then each one of the guild masters, making her want to slink back into the shadows like a scorned dog.

"Good of you to join us, Mia Ashmore. Take your place next to your adopted sister," Robbert commanded.

Mia pursed her lips. *They never let me forget that Kali and I share no blood, do they?*

She rushed across the space, tucking a free strand of blonde hair behind her ear and swallowing the sharp remark that threatened. Mia seemed to always do that, never truly saying what she wanted to. She wanted to snap at the man, to tell him that Kali was her sister, even if they didn't share a single drop of blood. They were bound by something stronger than blood. Love.

Mia found herself at the end of a long line of men and even fewer women. Eyes raked over her, assessing her, considering her. Her cheeks burnt hot under their scrutiny. Her gaze settled on the golden swirls in the marble under her boots, tracing over them, deciding whether they were a genuine gold or simply a bright yellow.

"Now that we are all here, we shall begin," Robbert announced.

He listed names in a seemingly random order. Men and women stepped out of the line, and a guild master would call their name. The masters from the Death Court picked apprentices with a rise of a pale finger, not a single word spoken. A cheer would erupt from the family, a hearty handshake would come from Hartwinn, and they were then led to the garden.

Mia raised her gaze to the masters, going down the line and skipping Hartwinn, who looked almost bored. Then she landed on Luc, who lounged in a tall back chair, chin resting on his paint-stained fingers, legs crossed. He caught Mia staring, causing her to straighten and share a polite smile. His lips smoothed into a flat line in response. She dropped her gaze, eyebrows meeting in the middle as her smile formed into a tight purse. *Did I just do something wrong? I shouldn't have been so forthcoming with him, sharing my thoughts so openly. Should I have agreed to let him sketch me in nothing but my underthings?*

"Kali Ashmore."

Her sister stepped forward, her hands clasped in front of her. Her chin lifted, meeting each pair of eyes, a strained smile on her face. Mia smiled through her pursed lips. *Kali is unapologetically herself. It's something I've always loved about her. She knows who she is, whereas I'm lost in splashes of colour and the stench of turpentine.*

Voices raised as masters argued for Kali. Her brows rose almost to her hairline, her head jerking with each voice.

"She is—"

"Mine." The grand master healer let her narrow, curled in shoulders forward, cutting everyone off with a sharp command. "She was born to be a healer. You all know this. Now, let me have her."

"Please. It would be an utter waste to send her to the Medicus Tower," a deep voice cut through the arguing chatter, right from one of the dark-eyed vampyres. "Give her to the Death Court so we can educate her to use her magic effectively at the *Magicis*."

Kali glanced over her shoulder, meeting Mia's gaze. Desperation flared in her blue eyes. She shook her head slightly as if to say, "*Please, anyone but the Death Court.*"

"Let the Ashmore girl choose and be done with this. We have plenty of apprentices to get through," Robbert commanded.

Whispers echoed amongst the apprentices and through the crowd. It was unheard of, unprecedented. No one got to choose. Ever.

The vampyre leant in, his eyes narrowed, his hands gripping the arms of the chair. Tension had built in the room as everyone, including Mia, held their breath.

Kali lowered her eyes, brows meeting in consideration until she raised her chin, taking a step forward. "I choose...Her Ladyship, Grand Master Healer."

Disappointed sighs and exasperated exhales followed.

The healer leapt from her chair with a joyous cry, beckoning Kali over with a wave of her ancient hand, cutting Hartwinn off. Kali strode over to her and was personally escorted through to the garden.

Only five apprentices remained: Mia and the four fae. Her heart pounded with each name called, knowing she could be next. Soon, she was the only one left.

"Mia Ashmore."

Luc stood, straightening his surcoat and pushing back his hair. Mia's heart jumped to her throat, a tight smile curled on her face. She took a small step forward, anticipating the words already falling from his lips.

"I have no interest in this one," he announced. "The Death Court can have her. That's if she's got any magic in her."

Her stomach dropped to her boots, and her jaw fell open. She took another step, her hand reaching out for him. "Sir, I can prove myself. I swear, I will."

Luc paused, just turning his face to hers. "You are not apprentice material, girl."

He left the room without a second look, taking with him her hopes and dreams.

Complete silence met Mia when she turned back to the masters, head hung. The warm, nauseated, sweaty feeling of humiliation washed over her. Tears pricked. She bit the inside of her cheek until the rush of copper coated her tongue and took her mind off the mortifying situation unfolding.

Everyone had been selected but her. That wasn't the way. Everyone who was invited got selected. This had never happened.

A Death Court master leant and whispered to another. The urgency of the head shakes caused a flicker of hope to flare in her chest. But neither made a move, a sign or a shift of a pale, knobbly finger.

Not even the vampyres want me.

"You may go." Robbert dismissed her with a wave of a hand.

Mia was glued to the spot on the hard marble, feet refusing to shift. Her mind could not accept that she hadn't been selected. Chatter came from the crowd, the swirling words filtering to where she stood, but she could only hear the blood rushing in her head and the pathetic *thump* of her heart. A singeing sizzle of an invisible hot poker burnt right between her breast, through skin, fat and bone, right to that useless thudding organ. Each digging stab allowed a harmony of whispers to ooze out of the melted flesh.

"By the shadows, free us."

Frightened, Mia took a stumbling step backwards as if the whisper were a swinging fist. Her eyes hurriedly shifted over the blurring faces, seeking the owner of the voice. But she was totally alone, standing with her hands gripped in her skirts. Gazes crept over her skin, pulling the cotton and lace from her skin, to tear at her flesh and what they found was lacking.

"You've been given an order, child. Leave," said one of the vampyres, breaking through her panic. "No wonder you weren't chosen. You cannot follow a simple command."

Mia nodded absent-mindedly, tears leaking from her eyes and down her red cheeks. She turned towards the exit, where the others had left.

"Not that way. The way you came," Robbert said flatly.

Hartwinn stood up, head shaking, glancing up and down the line.

"Now, that's unnecessary. Fellow gentlemen and ladies of the guild, I'm sure Mia would make a fine addition to any of your programs. I can personally vouch for her. She is a smart and bright young woman who is an exceptionally hard work—"

"She has not been selected, Hartwinn," Robbert cut in, silencing the murmuring down the line of masters. "This is the will of the guild. We took on the fae younglings. Don't push us to take on this one, too."

Words cut deep, but the ones Mia was repeating to herself cut to the bone. Her jaw shook, forcing sobs down. Her footsteps were loud as she descended the stairs towards the crowd, her palm pressing right where she burnt.

The masses of bodies parted as if she were sickly, contagious. But one couldn't catch what Mia was: a failure. She could hear Henry call for her, and Anne saying her name. She couldn't raise her chin from the swirling marble on the floor, nor could she bear to have Henry's disappointment land squarely on her shoulders, forcing her to her knees. She ran from the room, escaping the cool gaze of the masters behind and losing the shred of dignity she had left as it floated through the air.

As soon as Mia stepped through the threshold of Hartwinn's castle walls and into the busy street, she broke into a sprint. She ran around corners, down alleys and past marketplaces, hot tears rolling and bouncing with each pound of her boots on the cobblestone. Her hair was loose, flowing in golden waves over her heaving shoulders. Her legs dragged to a stop, and she scrubbed the tears from her face with her sleeve, smudging the delicate kohl around her eyes. Raising her head, she found a pub—The Cauldron. A chipped and sun-worn cauldron was painted on the sign, matching the outside paint, exposing the brick underneath. She heard loud laughter from inside and smelt the sharp stench of burning liquor and hops wafting out to her. Mia clenched her jaw and pushed through the swinging doors with a sniff.

She was going to get rotten drunk.

FIVE

INSIDE THE CAULDRON WAS WARM AND INVITING, WITH THE rumble of voices and shouted laughter. A musician strummed a lute in the corner. Curious gazes fell on Mia from the spattering tables, scanning her from top to bottom. Their expressions twisted into looks of disappointment when they found the scar on her face. She wondered for a split moment if she, herself, actually hated her scar or if it was the disappointed looks and whispered words she had endured that had distorted her mind.

Mia stared into the half-filled glass of whisky melting on the worn, dented bar for what felt like hours. The ache in her rear from sitting on the hard stool only confirmed that night had indeed passed into early morning. Customers had filled in and stumbled out, leaving only her and a handful of the wine-addled barflies left.

"I think it's time to close up your tab and wander home, miss. It's getting late," the barman said, wiping the bar beside her.

Mia's chin rose to the man, taking in his golden, russet skin, gleaming with sweat, and the smile spread on his thick lips. His woodsy brown eyes gleamed with a strange mischievousness as he waited for her to spill the gold she owed across the countertop.

"I think you should think twice about telling me what to do, Benny," she said sharply.

"I was merely making a suggestion, Mia," he countered, leaning his stocky frame on the bar, his brawny forearms crossing over his chest. "You have a long walk up to Rosda Manor, and I can tell you that cobblestone isn't as soft as your feather-filled mattress."

"Or I can stay here forever!" Mia slurred, shooting back the whisky with a cringe. The burning chased away the feelings threatening to erupt from her. She was straying too close to the reason she sat at that pub, her arse aching. She didn't want to think. She wanted to forget about it all, especially that unnerving, whispering voice.

"I don't think the boss would like that. Not at all," Benny murmured to himself, topping up her drink.

"Who own—"

"And what is a beautiful woman doing in a filthy bar like this?" The stranger's deep voice was smokey and rough, but skimmed over her exposed skin like a brush of the softest velvet. A foreign accent clipped his speech—a telltale sign of an older century.

Mia turned from the bar, her movements sloppy, her mind hazy. Her body felt light but heavy. Her hooded gaze worked up the tall, muscular man, tracing over the straining dark material that gripped his broad shoulders. The sleeves of his shirt were rolled to reveal ropy, tense muscles. Her fingers flexed, wanting to trace the deep groove under his scarred, tanned skin. She had to drag herself from his distracting forearms to his firm jaw, dancing over his prominent cheekbones. Her eyes dropped to his full, kissable—*very* kissable—lips. When she finally met his lusty gaze, glittering emerald with the thinnest rings of gold around his blown pupils stared back at her.

Mia wet her own lips, tasting the sharp whisky. "Getting drunk. Isn't that what one does in a bar like this, sir?"

His hand went to his chest, right over his heart. "Sir? Do I look like a sir?"

Mia made no move to answer him. She just allowed her eyes to roam over him, biting down on her lip. *No. You look like a mighty good time, however,* she silently replied.

"Call me Idris."

"Idrissss," Mia mouthed, dragging out the final syllable.

She ran a finger around the thin edge of her glass. Those emerald pools tracked each movement. Hungrily, he stepped forward, encasing her in those muscular arms, each hand gripping the bar. His scent—rich whisky and ash, blended with clean leather—swirled around her. It was abhorrently masculine, like everything about the handsome stranger. He oozed masculinity. Mia had to fight to drag him deeper into her lungs like the hot, spiced smoke of firebud.

"You're looking for trouble, looking like you do, acting the way you do."

"Maybe I am. Are you trouble?" she asked, her words slightly slurred.

A crooked grin spread across Idris' face, pushing up a cheek, showing a dimple and making her breath hitch. *Of course he has a damn dimple.*

He leant in, his large body taking up any space left between them. His lips brushed the curl of her ear as he whispered, "I can be anything you want. Your salvation...your destruction."

A shiver shot down Mia's spine, making her feel flushed as the heat pooled deep in her lower belly, turning her desire molten. She twisted in his arms and downed the rest of her drink, the heat of the whisky burning her body more. Slamming the glass down and tapping the bar, she allowed Benny to slosh two more fingers of whisky into her glass before casting a glance at the handsome stranger.

"Does that line work on the other poor women you accost?" she asked over her shoulder.

A soft chuckle escaped that smirk. His hands gripped the wood tighter, narrowing around her body until his forearms brushed her arms and his solid chest met her back. Surrounding her with flexed muscles, he leant in close again. "Unlike other men, I rarely have to resort to lines of poetry."

Mia exhaled, running a finger through the condensation rings, smearing the wetness across the worn countertop. She wanted to do something—anything—with her hands but trace his scarred knuckles.

"Hey, Benny, I'll get one for my new friend." She glanced over her shoulder to see Idris staring directly down at her, that same hungry look in his eye. "Whisky, or something else?"

"Just whisky."

Mia leant an elbow on the worn wood of the countertop, her finger swirling into the melting chips of ice and the last few drops of the alcohol left in the glass. With bated anticipation, she watched Idris lift yet another glass to his lips, swallowing the whisky in one fluid shot. The hard centre of his throat bobbed with each gulp of the amber liquid. He ended it with a satisfied exhale, his tongue flicking out, catching any drops left on his lips. Mia bit down on her own to stop the sharp gasp from leaving her. The sensual sight awoke the tingling throb of arousal between her legs.

"In a rush?" she asked, releasing her lip.

"We have somewhere to be."

"We?"

"Yes. You and I."

Mia reached over and, with a cold, wet finger, dragged down the column of his neck to the open collar of his black shirt, over his warm skin. Her roving finger found the first button of his shirt, then the second, then the third, curling around each one. His eyes tracked each touch, lips curving into a more devilish grin until he returned that hungry gaze to her flushed face.

Good goddess, I can even feel the heat in his gaze.

She had never felt so in control yet so wild at the same time. The damn alcohol burnt away any sensible thought that rattled around in her mind, but she didn't want sensible thoughts. And in that drunken, tense moment, she craved to feel the handsome stranger's body pressed against hers on any bloody surface they could find.

"And where do you and I have to go?" Mia murmured quietly in the loud dim of the bar. Her hands spread out across his chest, feeling the fine linen of his shirt and his thundering heart under her palm.

"I'd take you anywhere you fucking want. A bed, a castle, in a dark alleyway."

His rough-skinned fingers skimmed over her arm to settle on her jaw. He thumbed her lips open. Without a single thought, Mia sank her lips over his thumb, tasting the clean flavour of icy water mixed with the saltiness of his skin. She captured his gaze as her lips popped, making his lips part and his eyebrow arch. With an unsteady step, she closed the space between them and pressed her curved body against his. She pushed onto her tiptoes, straining her neck to brush her lips against his in a fleeting kiss.

"Let's leave this filthy pub then, Idris," she breathed against his lips, allowing their mouths to touch for the briefest moments, sparking something to life.

Something so deep inside her, she didn't even notice it.

The frigid night air woke Mia, taking the dull edge off the swirling intoxication that made her head spin. She stumbled up the road, tripping on her feet. Idris' hand slipped over her womanly hip, spreading a hand over her soft stomach, righting her. He pulled her closer to him, allowing the heat of his body to seep into her chilled one.

"By the gods, what a body you have hidden away," he murmured to himself.

Mia blushed at his words, ducking her face into his chest. "You're not so bad yourself."

A snorted chuckle came from Idris as he pulled her to a stop outside a darkened house. In the dim of the midnight light, she could only see the shadowy façade.

"I..." She blinked up at the two-storey building, confusion bunching her eyebrows. "You brought me to your house?"

He dug in his pocket for a key. "Where did you think I was taking you?"

Mia's lips pursed. She hadn't had a clue where he was taking her, but to be brought to his house felt slightly anticlimactic. "Somewhere more—"

"Dirty?" Idris finished, unlocking the door with a *click*. He nodded to a dark alley. "There is an alleyway over there if you'd prefer this to be rough and quick."

Mia rolled her eyes, pushing past him into his house. She turned on her toe, casting him a mischievous grin. "I'd actually prefer this to be slow and gentle. I want you to take your time with me."

She didn't wait for his reply before delving deeper into his house. Each room was dimly lit, and a fire had burnt to embers in the lounge room. Lanterns burnt low in the hallways, letting shadows seep out. Mia's eyes searched, sliding in their sockets, making out paintings on the walls, plush rugs and leather furniture. A staircase swirled, leading to the second storey.

Not another soul resided there, but it well was lived in by one. *Idris.*

Mia rubbed her arms. The buzzing feeling of intoxication had already begun to fade, allowing the ebbs of apprehension to surface. She had gone to a complete stranger's house, drunk and shamelessly flirting, to do gods knew what. But deep down, she knew what she had gone there for.

A moment of blissful forgetting, to lose herself for a handful of moments in a man's arms.

Mia levelled a hooded, drunken look at herself in the hallway mirror, struggling to make eye contact. The caramel that surrounded her pupils had almost darkened to a woody brown with lust. Her cheeks flushed, making the stark white scar on her face almost illuminate. Pink patches splotched her freckled décolletage, running into her ample breasts and spilling from the tight bodice. She haphazardly pushed her blonde hair back from her face.

She felt powerful—*beautiful*, even.

"You're drunk," Mia muttered to her reflection, poking herself in the mirror and leaving a smudge across the glass.

Turning, she leant against the small wooden table under the mirror to find Idris watching.

"Are you going to take me to bed or what?"

His smirk curled higher, deepening the dimple. "In a rush?"

Mia huffed a laugh, narrowing her eyes playfully. Idris advanced, making her take a step back. Her hip bumped into the sharp corner of the table, shaking a porcelain vase. It toppled, rolling off and hitting the rug with a *thump*. But his eyes never left hers, beaming that hot, hungry look of desire at her.

"Mia, Mia, what will I do with you?" He breathed, softly and slowly, causing her to exhale.

Her back found a solid wall as Idris' looming frame encapsulated her, his forearm bracing the wall above her head. Her chin craned, determined not to lose that honeyed, desire-filled eye contact. Idris' head tilted, leaning down. His warm, whisky-infused breath cascaded over her skin, pebbling it. Mia pushed up on her toes until the tips of their noses touched.

"By Deus, I need to kiss you..."

"You can do much more than kiss me, Idris."

"Thank fuck," he murmured, smirking.

"Then what are you waiting for?"

He leant down, pressing his lips to hers. Within one bated moment, their kiss turned frantic, hurried. The tip of his tongue brushed over the seam of her mouth, then crashed into hers. She matched each press of lips and swirl of tongue with the same hungry intensity.

No one had ever kissed her like that before.

Never had chaste, sloppy kisses dragged the air from her lungs and sent the bundle of nerves between her legs pulsing in time with her rapid heartbeat. His leg had inched between hers, allowing her to roll her hips against it, seeking any sort of friction. His fingertips dug into her flesh, grinding her down even harder against the firmness of his thigh. She pulled Idris to her bare throat, allowing him to breathe in her scent in one big inhale. Teeth scraped over her thundering pulse, sending her skin pebbling. The thumping transformed into a pounding, sending the ache of pleasure through her.

Her hands roamed his body, feeling every inch of powerful muscle, edging closer to his manhood. His fingers tangled in her hair, yanking gently and breaking the bruising kiss.

"Slow, Mia. I thought you wanted me to take my time with you. You're rushing to the end."

Her tongue curled around his name as she crooned, "I don't think you want to go slow. I think you want to be sunk deep into me."

Idris closed his eyes, swallowing hard.

"I have not done this in a long time." He paused as if to catch his breath. "Slow may be best. If you wish for this to last longer, then a prayer to Oryah."

Mia let loose a giggle, resting her head back on the wall. The room spun too fast for her, nearly allowing a drunken confession to fall from her. She'd had kisses and wandering hands under skirts, but she had never gone that far with a man. Skin on skin, completely bare to each other. And, by the gods, she wanted to—with him, the mouth-watering stranger.

Mia's hands flew to his shirt, yanking it from his pants. She needed to see him, bare and glistening. Her fingers struggled with the buttons on his shirt, and she grunted in frustration. He pulled his shirt over his head with one hand and a grin. It fell in a puddle of cotton at their feet, exposing the peppering of dark chest hair and honed muscle. Mia almost moaned at the sight, her eyes roaming his torso eagerly. A deep scar ran across his heart, the pink flesh puckered and warped. Her fingertips brushed over his hard abdomen, feeling the roughness of his body hair.

Finding his belt, Mia made quick work of his buckle. Her hand rushed up to his nape, pulling him down into another hurried embrace. Her hips ground against his, feeling his hardened manhood press into her stomach. Chasing the promised release, a lusty moan slipped from her parted lips, making Idris smile against her.

"Shall we move this to the bed, or are you so desperate for a release that you want me to take you here on the wall, then on the floor, then against each damn surface in this house?"

His hand swept up from her hip, meeting the swell of her breast, his thumb swirling her hardened nipple, poking through the thin silk of her blouse.

Her skin felt flushed—too flushed.

The muttered word "bed" was all she could manage. Her head swam as the hot, sickly feeling of her stomach turning filled her chest, the rush of bile rising in her throat. Before she could stop it, she heaved up the half-bottle of whisky and the measly breakfast she'd had hours earlier, covering the plush rug, his shirt and half the entranceway with vomit—sickly, chunky vomit.

Idris darted back, eyes widening with shock. Mia's hand clamped over her mouth so no more vomit, rushed, embarrassed words *or* the remaining contents of her stomach could spill out. With a mumbled apology, she pushed him away and rushed to the door.

"Mia, are you—"

She couldn't hear the rest of the sentence over the embarrassment screaming in her head as she ripped the door open, launching herself through it and into the night.

Six

A splitting headache cracked Mia's skull in two with each painful *thump*. Her mouth felt both dry and sticky, a bitter taste of bile coating her tongue. Cracking open an eye, she saw the hot beam of sunlight cutting across the stained wooden floor, heating her room with a smothering, feverish feeling. She groaned, pushing up off the bed. Her head spun, making her stomach contents rise again.

A disapproving click of a tongue came from Mia's high-backed velvet chair. Her sore eyes found Kali, lounging with a medical book in her lap. Her fingers flicked pages, her glazed eyes not taking a single word in.

"What time is it?" Mia croaked.

Kali's gaze flicked up from the book, her fingers still turning. "Two o'clock—in the afternoon."

"Two?!" Mia exclaimed, standing. She squeezed her eyes closed, demanding the world to stop spinning.

"You didn't stumble home until five in the morning."

"Father—"

"Is not happy," Kali cut in. A grin stretched across her face, sending the sky blue of her eyes twinkling. "Finally, it's your turn for the stern talking to. The 'I'm not angry, just disappointed' talk. I never thought I would see the day. The perfect Mia coming home drunk, stinking of a man!"

Mia's hand found the buttons on her dress, undoing them with trembling fingers. "Of course he is going to be disappointed, Kali. I wasn't selected by a master. Not even the bloody librarian wanted me."

And I've lost my godsdamn mind because of it, Kali. A voice from the shadows is telling me to let it be free, she added on silently.

Kali closed the book, her smile fading. "That's..."

Mia shook her head, slipping the dress from her body, leaving herself only in her thin cotton undergarments. She felt dirty, not from the sweat and the splashed whisky that coated her skin, but from the thick, slimy feeling of shame at almost falling into bed with a complete —albeit distractingly handsome—stranger. Those strict rules of Hartwinn's court made her head thump a fraction harder.

"You know how he will be, Kali. He is quietly angry, and I don't know what's worse."

"He loves you, Mia. He cannot be angry about the masters' decision. You had no control over it. But coming home drunk as a fae on Starmorn and waking every man and his dog up in this house? That's what he will be angry about."

Mia shot her sister a narrowed look. She was not convinced.

Kali raised her arms, shaking the book. "'Think of your reputation, girls! How will this reflect on the family? How ever will you find husbands?'" Kali growled, an imitation of their father's deep, monotone voice.

A laugh left Mia, then another as Kali continued on pantomiming their father's cross face and concerns about their future marriage proposals. She crossed the room, gathering clean clothing as she passed. "How was the celebration?"

"Oh, you know. Stiff, boring. Nothing really happened," Kali replied, her gaze on the book as she toyed with it.

Mia cast a sharp look over her shoulder. "Kali, you don't need to lie on my behalf. Truth?"

"Fine...truth."

Kali launched into an exciting story of spilt drinks and scandalous kisses, her hands animated as she spoke. Mia smiled to herself. Kali was happy. She deserved to be happy. Even so, Mia felt nothing but the twisting of her stomach. The heaviness of disappointment had slid across her shoulders, weighing down each step. She splashed her face with cool water, washing the drunken memories from her skin and scrubbing the lingering embarrassment away with the smudged kohl.

"And then Reagan turned up..." her sister continued hesitantly.

"Reagan was there?"

"Yes," was all she said.

Mia's hands braced on the stone wash basin. He had made her sing for him again, tempting her with a finger along those cool metal bars only to snatch his hand back when reality showed its face in the creeping of the morning sun. Marriage loomed for him in the spring. It was not to Kali, but a faraway princess, daughter of King Ewan.

Kali was chewing her lip as Mia re-entered her bedroom dressed and feeling a fraction more human.

"He's not worth it, you know. This heartache."

Kali blinked at her. "Whatever are you talking about?"

Mia sighed, rolling her eyes. "Kali—"

Her sister raised a bronzed hand, cutting her off. "If you'd ever been in love, you'd know it's worth it."

Her words cut deep, deeper than Mia allowed her to see. She hadn't been in love—not counting the girlhood crushes she'd had on the brawling knights of the Silver, or on Wyn Neverclove, Lord Hartwinn's captain.

"I don't want to be in love, if this is how it is," Mia snapped back, only to add quietly, "that is, if anyone would want to love me."

Kali raised her chin at her, piercing her with a frowning look. "Never say that, Mia. You give others an excuse to say it."

Mia squished her lips together, not wanting more self-loathing to spill from her. She had drunk the dismal words down with each sip of burning alcohol, allowing them to fester in her stomach until she found herself in a man's arms, spewing across his house.

"Sister, I went home with a man last night—"

"Mia!" Anne's voice thundered through Rosda Manor.

Kali's eyes widened and her jaw fell open. "You did what?"

"Mia Ashmore! You come downstairs *now!*" their mother called again.

"You *must* tell me. I want all the details!" Kali whispered, turning to follow her through her bedroom.

Mia hesitated at the door, briefly lost in how the firm wall of masculine muscle had felt against her body. She found her sister, half out of the chair, a sly smile spread across her face. "He was *something* else, Kali."

THE STRAINED VOICES INSIDE THE METICULOUSLY decorated dining room were loud enough for Mia to hear through the crack in the door. They were arguing about the Delectu Processum and, even more embarrassingly, how she wasn't selected.

"I cannot believe you, Henry. Out of all the things you have done—"

"No one was going to select her. Robbert told me himself. For weeks, they have been volleying her to each other. None wanted her."

A sharp sting sliced through Mia's chest, awakening the slithering, dark male voice that curled around the shell of her ear.

Even Daddy Dearest thinks you're worthless.

The hairs on her neck shot up, sending a wave of unease down her body. It wasn't the pleading whisper she'd heard while dying from embarrassment in front of the entire Alderdeen court, but one that had haunted her for years.

Great, now I'm entirely sure I have gone howling-at-the-moon mad, Mia thought

"So, flashing about gold is what we do now?" Anne asked, her tone sharp with anger. She was rarely angry. "What do you think that does, Henry?"

"It puts her on an even field. There were whispers of what she—"

"It does *nothing* but sully her reputation and destroy any love she has for you. How do you suppose she'll react when she finds out you bribed Luc and he still didn't select her?"

The dining room, with its vaulted ceilings, the scattered trinkets and Mia's own paintings lining the walls, tilted and became fuzzy around the edges. The only noises Mia heard were a piercing ringing, the distant sounds of chairs sliding and the door creaking open. Her gaze fell on Henry, half standing and eyes wide, glassy. Anne was already to her, steadying her. Mia's gaze never left her father, who sat heavily in his chair, head in hands.

"Is it true?" was all she could say.

The silence was deafening. Neither of her parents made a move to answer her question. So, she asked again, her jaw trembling with each word. "Is it true?"

"Yes, Mia," Henry answered softly.

A cry burst from her, a soft wail filling the emptiness. One she had suppressed, drunk down with each mouthful of whisky. She wasn't sure if that same drink had stripped her of all her defences or the lingering thump in her head, but she felt ripped raw. Those two words flayed into her skin, allowing each venomous, self-loathing word she'd whispered to seep from her like black, oozing blood. And with those two words, she believed every single one.

Mia pulled from her mother's soft grip, scrubbing the tears from her face. "Why?"

"You had your heart set on Luc. I couldn't let you be embarrassed like that—"

Mia's scoff cut her father off. The hot, sweaty rage of betrayal was a powerful emotion, but the gut-twisting shame that filled her body was stronger. It coated her insides with a sticky, molten tar, spreading on each twist of bowel and over the curve of her stomach, filling her with the hot, bubbling liquid, threatening to spill. No wonder Luc cast her to the streets without a second thought. She had no chance, even if she was Zeroth's best painter.

"Do you think so lowly of me, Henry? You thought I couldn't do it myself, that I'm not enough for them? For you? Maybe I'm not. You should have believed in me."

Her words made him raise his head, cheeks wet when he finally found her. "Mia, I do. My moon in the night sky, I do. You are wonderful—"

"But not enough, apparently," she spat, stumbling back from his lies, each stabbing her in her guts. She couldn't hear the words spill from his lips anymore. Only the sharp hiss of the malevolent voice who spoke the truth about her—who always spoke the truth.

"You had to...for Kali, right? That's why they argued for her?"

A tiny bloom of hope filled her chest, knowing that she could at least share the hurt with the one person she trusted the most. They could hold each other until the wound wasn't a stabbing pain, but simply a twinge. Henry's eyes sank to the table, eyebrows clenching together. She took a trembling step towards him, pushing past her mother and her concerned look. Mia's head shook in disbelief, breathing the same question over and over. She gripped onto his sleeve as she had when she was a child, when the world terrified her.

"Please. Tell me, Father. You had to for Kali too?"

Henry looked straight, his gaze never falling on her. But his jaw ground, lips parting then pressing together. That hopeful bloom was dragged down into the burning tar with his silence.

"Not for Kali, no."

"Of course not. Not for Kali," Mia retorted, her own voice coated with the same sticky venom of the man who would whisper to her. Something cracked in her chest, and a frigid sadness seeped out. Her whole being trembled with the cold. She could hardly contain the frosty spread of that deep, chest-aching sadness. It turned the tar solid, weighing her down.

A gasp came from the doorway, snapping her attention from her father. Mia's eyes raised to Kali, and silver tears shone back at her.

It's all suddenly too much.

Mia scrambled from Henry as fast as her feet could take her until her back hit the sharp corner of the doorframe. She swallowed the words she wanted to scream at her father with each gulp of air into her unwilling lungs.

Henry followed her, hands out pleadingly. "Mia, as your father, I've had to make some hard decisions on your behalf, but you've got to let me explain."

Her tear-filled gaze rose to his. Sobs punctuated each word that spilt from her. "*Nothing.* I have to do *nothing* for you, Henry. You're not my father. I don't think I recognise the man standing in front of me."

His face crumbled as if she had struck him. "Please."

Mia shook her head, tears flinging. "No. I don't want to hear it. It will just be lies."

"Please, there are things you don't know. Let your father explain," Anne pleaded, her voice soft.

"No," was all Mia said, before turning on her heel and storming from the dining room, barging past Kali and slamming the front door on her way out.

SEVEN

Days blurred into weeks, and the whisky burnt a little less with each sip. Mia's body roved down shadowy streets, her mind lost to the dangers of the dark nights and lonely alleys, her purpose lost to the splashes of vomit and tears shed.

She had nothing left; her future dashed, her reputation sullied with the swirling rumours of gold exchanging hands. Even her old teachers turned her away with sullen shakes of their heads. The quiet refuge of her art had brought nothing but bitterness, making her slash canvas and scrunch balls of paper.

Worst of all was Henry's face, his words humming and transforming into a dark harmony he sang to her, haunting her. She never thought she'd be the type to snap in two, but something deep within her cracked open. All the self-loathing she had pushed down all those years spewed from her, flooding her with such hatred she could barely look at herself in the mirror.

And that melody of voices never whispered again.

Having slept throughout the day, Mia hardly saw the hot rays of the sun, only to storm from her home when dusk fell to find a dark corner and that sweet abyss. The Cauldron was simply the best hole in the wall she had found. Alcohol free-poured until Benny—barman-turned-friend—worked out how much she could tolerate before she'd fall from the stool. It wasn't much.

Mia stared at the swinging doors, waiting for something that would never happen—for that green-eyed stranger to saunter through. Muttering into her glass, she shot it back. The warm liquid filled her bones with a lashing of courage and not much else.

The man who whispered was on her tail. She had outrun him for the past few nights, drowning herself before stumbling home. That night, however, whisky alone wouldn't suffice. She turned on the stool, her drunken gaze skimming over the dimly lit bar to find a pair of dark eyes watching—no, not watching, *devouring* her, pulling off her silk-wrapped layers with each dip of his eyes until she was simply bare in front of him.

Her finger dragged down over her lips, parting them, skimming over her thudding pulse and down over the laced edge of her bodice and directly between her breasts. He watched her with a dark intensity, tracking each movement.

The stranger leant forward, flickering lantern light capturing his features. Shadows cut in his cheekbones, covered in a thin layer of stubble. He was handsome in a roguish way. She knew he'd smell of sweat, leather and all things not good for her. And she'd know that devilish smirk anywhere.

Wyn Neverclove.

Her father's former best friend, and the captain of Hartwinn's guards.

Wyn raised his eyebrows once—a silent hello—and dragged his tongue over his bottom lip. He ran a hand through his hair before bringing a pipe to his lips and lighting it with a snap of his fingers.

Fae.

Mia would recognise that wild, otherworldly magic anywhere. Born of the dirt, of the trees, of the air, of the stone deep in the earth, given by the great goddess herself. The elemental magic was a sharp contrast to the seductive, mysterious magic the vampyres held close to their chests. Human bodies contained no magic, yet King Ewan, who was simply a man, held all the land in a choke hold. That was more powerful than any magic.

Wyn drew in deeply, only to blow out the thick firebud smoke in a billowing wave. She didn't know if it was the whisky or the raging fire burning only metres away, but Mia was flushed, molten in places she'd only experienced pressed against that green-eyed stranger.

"Mia, that is a very bad idea," Benny warned, eyes tracking hers to the smirking Wyn.

She flashed a grin over her shoulder and said, "That's the point, isn't it, Benny? He is an awful idea."

He shook his head, tongue rolling around his teeth. "You know he's not a man you should simply tumble with. He comes with attachments—serious attachments."

"He has no wife or children." But she knew what Benny meant. He knew who her father was. He'd known since the first night she stumbled into The Cauldron. That, and she sent her drinking debts straight to Henry's coffers.

"He's tangled with your father. That means he shouldn't be tangled with you. Wasn't he his best friend?"

That tidbit of information didn't slow the desire building in her, nor make her drop the impressive staring contest they were having across the busy tavern. It only spurred her along and steeled her resolve, knowing it would piss Henry off. She was almost gleeful at the idea.

"Then he is the best idea I've had all night. Maybe in all my life."

"Mia, no—"

Ignoring Benny, she slipped from the stool. She cast a wicked grin at the barman, finishing the half-filled glass of whisky. "I'm simply saying hello to an old family friend, Benny. Nothing more."

"You'll face a world of hurt if you take him to bed, Mia."

She turned on her heel. Little did Benny know she was already hurting, and nothing could make that worse, especially not tangling in the sheets of a man she'd thought attractive since she was fifteen. Her slow, deliberate steps took her across the room, right to him. Her hands spread out on the table as she leant forward, a half-smile on her lips.

"Hello, Wyn Neverclove..."

"Well, hello, Mia Ashmore. My, my, how you've grown," he crooned, his voice rough, deep, settling right between her legs. His eyes lowered to her flushed décolletage, then dipped a fraction more. He flicked his gaze up and held up his pipe. "Smoke?"

Mia nodded, biting her lip, watching him take in a lungful of the spiced smoke. She leant over the table, right over his half-drunk ale until her lips were a fraction away from his, drawing the smoke right from his exhale, deep down into her lungs, blowing whatever was left over his head. She'd never been so wild, so reckless. It was intoxicating, and she was drunk on the exhilaration.

"Do you want to make some terrible choices with me, Wyn?"

THEIR BODIES COLLIDED, LIPS PRESSED TOGETHER, HANDS roving. The room in the closest inn to The Cauldron was threadbare, desolate. A bed with thin sheets waited for their sweat and moans. It wasn't a place of romance and candles, of thrown flower petals. It was a place of cold, detached bodies. Certainly not a spot you'd want to have sex for the first time. But Mia was chasing more than a release. She was seeking the abyss, to be lost in something more than the tangled mess of her mind. But deep down, under all the hurt and self-loathing, she yearned to be needed in that sweaty, skin-to-skin moment.

Wyn's lips dragged down her throat, his tongue sliding over her skin. His hand tangled in her hair, and he yanked her head back, baring her to him and allowing himself to bury his face in her neck. She was right—he smelt *delicious*. Sweat and the spicy musk of a man sent her frantic, hands roving over hard muscle, linen and leather. His fingers tugged at the ribbons of her bodice, pulling it from her body. She shimmied it off, along with her skirts, leaving her curves adorned in lace underwear.

"*Fuck,*" Wyn breathed, eyes tracing over her to the roundness of her hip. "Good goddess, you've become a beautiful woman."

The curse awoke a soft fluttering between her legs. Mia shook her head, her finger dragging over the sharp edge of his jaw to his lips, silencing him. "There are no gods here."

"Good. I'd hate to hear you moan anything but my name."

Mia laughed, her hands greedily pulling at his clothing, undoing belts, then the dull *thud* of metal falling to the floor. Long, lithe muscles and spatterings of dark hair adorned his scar-ridden body. Their lips met again, hungry to taste each other, then a tangling of legs sent them tumbling to the mattress.

Wyn encased her with his arms, his eyes searching hers for something she wished only to shove away. His lips parted to speak, but Mia devoured his words with a kiss. A hardness slid over her stomach as his hips lazily undulated against hers. Her own hips worked in time with the swirling of tongues, creating the lick of pressure where she desperately ached to be touched. Their lips only left each other to drag over skin, swirling around hardening nipples, dragging soft moans out of parted mouths.

He leant back on his heels, clutching her ample inner thighs. Mia swallowed the nervous giggle that almost erupted from her. She was at her barest, spread before a man who she should have never fallen into bed with. However, her mind was the clearest it had been in weeks. No slither of a voice lurked, nor the hurt. He wanted her—at least for the next handful of moments.

He spat on his fingers, spreading his spit over her centre and forming a devilish slickness over her sensitive bundle of nerves. He circled and curled, creating a delicious sensation that radiated throughout her body. Mia writhed and panted as he watched with a dark intensity. Wyn continued to stroke her until she was teetering on the edge of her release, her moans coming in short, sharp gasps. Then his hand left her, leaving her begging for it to return. Something hard but velvet-soft slid through her and firmly pressed against her entrance.

"You want me, don't you? Desperate for it," Wyn crooned, his rough words striking her in the chest. But they did not dampen the desire thumping in her veins. Rather, they added fuel to the flame. "Does Daddy know you're out here, begging to be bent over by a man you shouldn't?"

"Are you going to lecture me about the complexity of your relationship with Henry, or are you going to have me moan your name? Your choice, Wyn." The bellyful of whisky bolstered her confidence, so much so that she reached down and gripped his manhood. She gave him a firm pump, then another, pulling a deep groan from him. A smirk curled on her lips as she pumped him faster, drawing out his pleasure. "Now, do you want to talk, or do you want to..."

The way he grinned down at her, the tip of his tongue skimming over his top teeth, and the wicked gleam that emerged in his steely blue eyes, had Mia's heart racing with anticipation.

"You're going to wish you'd spoken nicer to me."

Mia smirked up at him. "Oh, really—"

The sharp, splitting pain radiating from her core wiped the words and smirk from her lips, making her gasp—and not from pleasure. He'd thrust into her without warning, filling her to the hilt. The painful stretch of delicate skin was nothing as she had expected, nothing like lying in bed with her fingers between her thighs. She almost wiggled right out from underneath him to escape the throbbing and burning in each deep thrust.

Wyn groaned, eyebrows brunching.

Mia lay dead still, worried that if she moved with him, the pain would get worse. When she began to pray, Wyn paused his exploration of her insides and glanced down at her, seeing her sweaty and teary-eyed.

"You're a virgin, aren't you?"

"No," she lied, then sputtered, "I guess not anymore, and I don't wish to speak of it."

Wyn stared at her for a long moment, cogs turning, then cursed. She worried he would stop, that he'd cast words at her that dripped not with desire but shame and disgust. Instead, he reached over with a thumb and brushed a strand of hair off her face. Out of all the things they had done, that felt the most intimate. Too intimate. She slapped his hand away. She didn't like the feeling bubbling to the surface.

"You should have told me, Mia. I would have been more gentle."

"*Gentle*? Good goddess, I don't want that. Not a single bit, Wyn."

"Well, I could have made sure you"—he pinched her nipple between his forefinger and thumb, sending a thrill to her throbbing centre, making her let out a soft moan—"And this perfect, tight cunt was prepared to take me. Gods, I could have showed you how fucking amazing your body can feel with just my fingers and my tongue."

"And what would you have done to me?" she asked, dripping with desire.

It was a dangerous game of promised words and drunken feelings mixing in her chest, with one feeling slipping through the hurt: want.

Wyn leant down, close enough to brush his lips with hers. "How about I show you? I've never been too good with words."

Those rough, callous covered fingers slid over her swollen nub, building that tormenting ache of pleasure again. Her back bowed off the bed, his name slipping from her lips. Her thighs clenched together, trapping him to her body, desperate for release. Wyn's hips drew out as he carefully slid back into her. His thrusts were languid, but they created a diabolical friction—one she needed more of. But the burn of him stretching her seared any pleasure away.

"Breathe, Mia. The sting will only last a few moments. It'll feel good soon, I promise," Wyn said, voice softer than it had ever been. His lips brushed her forehead, his fingers sliding between hers, making her breath hitch.

Mia expected it to be a lacklustre moment of thrusting and groaning. A flare of pain. Not this. It was all too soft. She'd rather he call her a whore, cover her in bruises and make her ache in places she'd never ached before. She wanted anger, indifference. Not the gentle, soft caress of a lover or the honeyed words slipping from him. It stripped the confident bareness she'd fallen into his bed with and made that uncomfortable vulnerability press against her skin. Hurt and desire warred in her head. But she wasn't aware of the swords being drawn. She was too lost in the blissful silence and the deep throbbing of her release building between her legs.

"That's it, take all of me..." Wyn whispered into her throat as he bottomed out.

Soon, the pain and everything else melted away, and pleasure was all Mia felt. It radiated from her core in hot, creeping waves. Her muscles tensed, then loosened. A deep moan ripped from her, fingers digging into Wyn's spine.

A release erupted from her, sending stars shooting through her vision.

The feelings she'd been fleeing from welled in her and slid down her face in salty tears. With each lash of pleasure opened a wound much more painful: shame. That sticky, hot emotion. Mia relished in it, wanting to feel anything but the stomach-tightening feeling of disappointment.

If Wyn saw her tears or noticed her sudden change, he said nothing, nor did he stop. His thrusts, suddenly wild and untamed, sent her deeper into the lumpy mattress. His hand flashed to her breast, gripping her so tightly that she knew she'd bruise.

"*Yes, yes, yes,*" fell from her.

His face contorted, and with a hissed curse, he spilt a warm stickiness over her stomach, pooling in her belly button.

Wyn quietly slid from her, panting, sinking to the edge of the bed, head in his hands. Mia curled to her side, gripping her rib cage, her shoulders shaking with smothered tears. Wyn's hand found the dip of her ankle, thumb brushing over that bony protrusion. The rush of her fading release and his hands on her body, mixed with the dimming of her intoxication, became too much. Suddenly, even breathing, the shift of her sweaty skin and the dark slither of the voice returning was all too much.

The mattress shifted, and Mia heard the rustling of clothing being pulled on as footsteps moved away from the bed she was curled in. Her underdress was placed next to her. She snatched it up, pulling it over her head, shimmying it over her hips. She flopped back, her tears drying on her face, heart slowing.

"We can never tell Henry. *Ever.*"

"Obviously, Mia. He'd skin us both alive. I..." His words faded off with a clench of his jaw. The door unlatched. Then, a quiet sigh. Wyn met her eyes from across the room, his face unreadable. Gone was that soft gaze that skimmed over her curves, a lingering hardness in his blue irises in its place. It made her push up onto her elbows.

"Take it from someone who has lived a lot longer than you, Mia. You won't find a cure for your pain in a dingy inn's bed with more men between your legs than you can count. You've got to let yourself feel it, and realise it cannot hurt you as much as it threatens to."

Each word slammed into her, echoing around the darkness of her mind. A sudden realisation crept over her skin. In those tangled moments in threadbare sheets, exploring bodies, Wyn had seen each twisted, aching part of her. And he didn't baulk, nor did he splash her with harsh words. He simply saw her. And it terrified her.

The thick spill of panic rushed up her throat, and with it, the stinging venom of her words. "Do you normally give the women you lay with a mouthful of unwanted advice after you finish, or is that something you reserve for your friends' daughters who you deflower?"

Wyn's only answer was to slam the door behind him.

Mia rose from the bed, sticky with body fluids, a dreaded hangover looming. Wyn's warning burnt in her mind, but it wasn't his words that swirled. Their sweaty actions had formed a barrier—a shield—because as soon as they stumbled through the threshold and their lips joined, right to when he tossed her into her release, that dark, menacing voice hadn't spoken once.

EIGHT

Soon, nothing—not even the sweet oblivion of a whisky-induced blackout—ridded her of the whispering. The cruel taunts seemed to grow louder with each sip, not quieter. But other things allowed her mind to drift. A man's hand up her skirt was one. They all promised pleasure, and she would follow them to beds and alleys as they painfully took parts of her she'd never get back and gave her nothing but brief moments of soothing silence.

Mia drank down the feeling with yet another gulp of cheap whisky as the dim of The Cauldron filled her ears for yet another night.

"You might want to ease up, beautiful," a male crooned in her ear, his stinking breath making her cringe. "You'll want to be conscious when I take you to bed."

Her bloodshot eyes slid across the bar to a blond-haired man. His attempt at a roguish smirk showed a pointed canine. *Vampyre.* He had been trying to persuade her to fall into his bed for the past hour. She wasn't convinced.

"Piss off, bloodsucker," she muttered, finishing her drink.

His smile faded to a sneer. "Excuse me?"

Benny's eyes flicked from her to her companion for the evening. Then, a grin curled on his lips, stifling a laugh, busying himself by shining the same glass over and over. He had become her only friend during those blurred weeks as she drank herself stupid, peeling her off the bar and dragging her back to his ramshackle apartment, only to shove the heel of bread into her mouth and send her on her way home to pass out in her own bed.

The whispering, negative voice lurked. She could almost feel the slithering at the shell of her ear. Mia pushed herself away from the bar, turning to the vampyre. Her gaze danced down over his slim body and his neat clothing. Not a single thread was out of place. His pale face was flushed and round, not hollowed. *Well-fed and reasonably handsome.*

She took an unsteady step forward, closing the space between them. Her mind scrambled to find the god-awful things he'd been whispering at her. Taking a stab in the dark, she plucked words from her fuzzy memory. "What were you saying? Something about a coin?"

That slimy grin spread on his face—her jab had found flesh. "If I flip a coin, what are the chances of me seeing your frilly little underthings?"

The confidence he dripped over his words made her inwardly cringe. He had lost the point of the joke in his desperation to impress her.

"How does one become one of you?" Mia asked, not wanting to leave the safety of The Cauldron. Not just yet. "Does it involve blood and bodies pressed together, writhing in pleasure?"

"Oh, we can get bloody if you desire, lovely," the vampyre chuckled, his hand sliding over her waist, dragging her closer, hip to hip. "But no. It starts as sickness, burning from the inside, years after we are born. Then, we slash our palms over some sacred ashes and send a prayer to Deus before we are swallowed whole, only to be reborn. After, we must feed and fuck, as our body demands it."

"I'm curious," Mia muttered, her fingers dragging over the gold stitching in his doublet. She had never taken a vampyre to bed. There was a certain rush to it; being so close to the sharp edge of danger.

"Curious about?" he replied, leaning closer, wafting the strong spice of the wine he was drinking over her.

"About the feeding part," she answered, her voice a soft purr. "Does it make the fucking part better?"

He exhaled, nodding. "If you think you've felt pleasure, think again.

You'll be begging for more. Now, shall we go find a bed to fall into together?"

"We don't need a bed. There's an alley just outside..." Mia gripped him by the front of the shirt, dragging him closer to her. "You better not disappoint me, vamp."

"My name—"

"No names. You don't need to know mine. I don't need to know yours."

His grin widened as he leant in, lips brushing over hers. His hand snaked out to grip her waist tightly, making her gasp. Benny straightened a fraction, concern flashing in his eyes, but Mia's giggle made him return to the glass. The vampyre's tongue parted her lips, sliding in and searching her molars. He tasted wrong, but she kissed him back, hoping a spark would fire. But nothing warmed her core. Nothing.

He brushed his lips over her cheek to her ear. "You know, I won't be gentle with you. I want you crying and shaking."

Mia turned to hide the pinched grimace that emerged on her face. Her hand gripped a handful of his shirt, dragging him towards the door. His hand slipped over her rear and gave it a tight squeeze. He leant in and whispered, "I cannot wait to taste you."

A throat cleared in front of her, catching her attention. Kali stood at the doorway, arms crossed, a deep-set frown on her face. "Mia Ashmore, you let go of that vampyre and come home. Now," she commanded with every ounce of authority an older sister should have. Even though they were the same age.

Mia's grip on him tightened as her eyes narrowed. "No."

The vampyre's hands slid from her body, pulling from her. "Wait, you're Henry Ashmore's daughter?" He pried her hand from his shirt. "No way. I can't do this, not with you. He would have my fucking throat."

Mia turned her glare on him. "You're scared of my father?"

"If you knew what he was capable of, you'd be scared too."

He backed away with his hands raised. Gone was that lusty look. Suddenly, fear—genuine fear—flared in his gaze. He edged around her and pushed through the doors, escaping into the night.

Mia grunted, rolling her eyes. "What do you want, now that you've ruined my evening?"

"What do I want?" Kali scoffed, shaking her head. "I want you to come home at a reasonable hour. And not stinking of this place, or the men you've decided to—"

"What? *Fuck*, Kali? Good goddess, you can slink around with Reagan, dragging him into any bed you find, whenever you want, but I can't?"

Kali's eyes narrowed to slits, her hands bunched into fists. It had been a long time since they'd had a fist-flying scuffle, and by Oryah, Mia was looking for it. Instead, Kali took a deep breath and smoothed her hand, much to Mia's annoyance.

Her sister reached out and took her hand in hers. She didn't pull away, letting her sister turn her hand over, tracing the lines on her palm with her forefinger. "I'm worried about you, Mia. You don't come home for days at a time, and when you do, you're half the person you once were. Spending your days in bed, in the dark, only to fill yourself with whisky and men. And I am absolutely sure that you haven't even touched a paintbrush in what seems like forever. "

Mia's eyes didn't rise from her sister's tracing finger. The truth fought its way out, spilling from her like an upturned glass. "I can't. Not anymore. Nothing is right, nothing works. Not painting, not drawing. Not even fucking splashing paint on a canvas. It's all ruined." Her voice cracked on the word. Quietly, she added, "I'm *ruined*."

The word settled in her chest, roots twisting around the hurt. She'd tried to create, but it only ended with the ache of disappointment, the harsh slither of the dark voice reminding her that she—and her art—was worthless.

"Please come home, Mia. Please."

Mia glanced over her shoulder to the empty barstool waiting for her to return and the sweet call of the abyss. She knew Kali could see the hesitation written across her face by the gentle squeeze of her hand. She wouldn't—*couldn't*—escape the feeling in her chest by fluttering through her home, painting and casting Henry a cheerful smile. But the soft plea of her sister tugged at a string she'd thought was hidden away.

"The whisky and the men won't mend the hurt you feel, Mia," Kali said softly. "This won't heal you."

"I guess you'd know, right? Being an acolyte and all?" Mia bit back, her words not as sharp.

"No, I wouldn't have a clue. They have us in droning lessons and scrubbing cauldrons. Not the life I thought it would be."

"Neither of us really thought about the life we would have after we stepped out of Hartwinn's ballroom. We just dreamt and hoped for the life we may have deserved."

Kali's eyes rose to hers, those lines of worry creasing her forehead, but she said nothing. She didn't need to. Mia knew her sister as well as she knew herself. Kali—glowing, shining Kali—was worried. Terribly and stomach-twistingly worried.

"Kali, is everything—"

"Now, come, let us get some food in your belly. You don't want to face Father smelling like cheap hops and even cheaper cologne."

"I don't want to face Henry at all," Mia muttered, tugging her hand back.

Reality crashed down, snapping the thin thread of her sister's plea. But Kali refused to let go, making Mia drunkenly stumble, her eyes downcast and unable to meet her sister's determined look.

"I want you to stop this feud you've worked yourself into with him. Let him apologise and grovel at your feet, Mia. Demand he buy you that fancy charcoal set you've always dreamt of, or let you turn the sunroom into a studio. Anything." Kali paused and took a steadying breath. "You know, I heard both of you cry that night. Both of you."

Mia raised her chin. She'd never seen her stoic father shed a single tear. "Truth?"

"Truth," her sister replied.

Kali pulled Mia away from the darkness of The Cauldron and into the busy, lantern-lit streets, travelling deeper into the city, where more bodies packed together. The stores were finer and gold was more frequently spilt. Mia was drunk. Her head spun as the light streaked and flared in her vision.

"We need something to soak up that cheap whisky you seem to like," Kali said, pulling her stumbling sister closer.

"It does the job," Mia slurred. "You should try some. It's not all bad."

"I don't need to. It seeps from your pores," Kali joked, waving a hand in front of her face.

Mia unceremoniously sniffed herself. She did stink of whisky and men. Not a specific man, and certainly not the emerald-eyed stranger and his smoke-and-whisky scent. Her mind seemed to wander, more than she cared to, to that chance meeting of hands on body and lips on skin, even though she knew nothing about him. She should have pushed him from her mind and forgotten about him, but for some reason, she couldn't.

Kali dragged her into the beginnings of the Moonshye Market; a bustling street of brightly coloured tents where all manner of creatures sold all manner of things. The scent of charcoal-grilled meats wafted down the street, filling Mia's nose. Her stomach grumbled impatiently, wanting something more than the scrap of bread Benny had made her eat and the bottle of whisky she had drunk.

Two fae men walking side by side leered at her, dragging their eyes up and down, then doing the same to Kali. Mia waved her fingers at them, a haphazard smile on her face. She blew a kiss at them, making them turn and walk backwards, grins on their faces.

"Mia, stop that," Kali snapped, dragging her away. "You know, you shouldn't entice men like that. Not at this time of night."

"Come on, Kali," she moaned, rolling her eyes. "First, we are in a public place. I can see two silvers leaning on the wall over there, so we can scream bloody murder if anyone dares to lay a finger on us." Mia pulled from her sister, a smirk curling on her lips. "I know for a fact that these men aren't as rough-handed as those at The Cauldron. This one time, I thought the stone of the building was going to give away from how hard this man was taking me..."

Her words faded away as those lines of worry re-emerged on Kali's face.

"Mia, have any of them hurt you?"

She blinked at her sister. In a way, they had—those painful moments of stripping pieces from her soul in unready, fumbling touching—but she'd wanted them to. None could steal what she was freely giving away. None had continued when she demanded them to stop. None had forced her. Rough and indifferent, sure, but never violent and cruel.

"Not in the way you're asking. Never in that way."

Kali reached out and tucked a loose strand of hair behind an ear. "I'm glad to hear that, Mia, truly. You've found something in these men's beds. But—"

"But?"

"Precautions? Have you been taking precautions?" Kali asked in her utmost serious voice.

Mia blinked again, then a rumbling laugh spewed from her, causing her to double over, gripping her sides. Laughter came in heaving giggles. She didn't really know why those words from her sister's mouth made her giddy. "Once a healer, always a healer, hey, Kali?"

She crossed her arms, pouting. "Well, I feel like I'm much too young to be an aunt, and Father would blow a blood vessel if he found out you were with child."

Mia straightened, locking her arm around her sister's for support. "Worry not, sister. There will be no screaming babies up in Rosda Manor. Not yet, at least. Abigail has been slipping me the contraceptive tonic for weeks now." Her voice lowered in volume a fraction. "And the final eruption usually happens outside of the...ah, body."

Kali shared a soft smile at Mia, chuckling at her lewd comment. But something akin to fear flashed in her eyes, if only for a moment.

"Hot, steamy wedges! Get 'em while they're hot!" a rough female voice called out.

Mia squealed and dragged Kali to the vendor. A friendly-faced woman took her drunken order with a grin, who turned and nodded to her sister. Kali rolled her eyes and spilt silver coins across the table. She handed them back a paper box full to the brim with hot, salted potato wedges. A spiced seasoning coated each of the crispy edges. Mia let out a deep groan at the sight of steaming deliciousness. Kali pulled her to a lump of grass, sitting her down and demanding that she eat. Mia shovelled the hot potato in her mouth, chewing dramatically.

"You know, I've heard Father and Mother arguing about the bills you're racking up. You spent ten gold coins in one night. Ten! That's almost two months of my wages."

Mia narrowed her hazy eyes at the bustling street. She had little idea of the money she'd spent, simply sending the tabs to Henry to make right. The Cauldron, though, had charged her less and less. Until, during the last few nights, she'd simply begun drinking for free.

"Ten? That's impressive. Next time, I'll try for twenty," Mia laughed, eyes widening.

Kali giggled, popping a steaming, fluffy potato into her mouth. "That vampyre. I've seen him at court. He is a pest, Mia. I cannot believe you'd even fathom the idea of letting him touch you, let alone drink from you."

"He was not all too bad. However, the lines he was spouting nearly made me want to take a vow of chastity," Mia answered between chews. "Not like..." Her words faded off. She'd told no one about Wyn, and wasn't planning on unloading it on her sister at that moment.

Instead, she sighed Idris' name. "Now, he was something else."

Kali grinned, stealing a potato wedge and crunching down. "Now *that's* a name. Tell me everything, sister!"

"Well, I met him at The Cauldron, and we went back to his home. His actual home."

"Where did you think you'd go?"

Mia chewed while she thought. "I don't even know. I didn't think that far ahead. We just kissed, then I left."

"You just left?" Kali repeated, unconvinced.

"Yes, I just left. Nothing of note happened." *I definitely didn't empty my stomach across his entire house.*

Kali wiggled her eyebrows at her. "Nothing of note, hey?"

Mia waved a potato wedge at her, her head mimicking the movement. "I would have woken you up and told you the gory details."

"Was he at least handsome?"

Mia moaned loudly, flopping down onto the grass, her belly full and soaking up the lingering alcohol. "Good goddess, Kali, yes. Like, *throw your entire life away and run into the forest* handsome."

Kali laid down beside her, crossing her ankles. "Is that why you go back to that hole in the wall? Hoping he will come sweep you off your feet and carry you off into the sunset?"

Mia's eyes narrowed at the twinkling stars above her. "What else am I supposed to do now that I'm deemed unfit by the guild, by Luc? Go get married, then fat with a child? That seems wrong, like a path I'm not supposed to walk down. Not yet, anyway."

Kali took her hand, squeezing tightly. "Then you do whatever the fuck you want. If a group of stuffy old men and a pompous artist don't see your immense worth, fuck them. You're worth more than the stars in the sky and the gold deep in the earth. You lost nothing in that room —you were freed."

"I don't feel free. All I feel is that I've lost everything, Kali. I'm simply in the dark, fumbling for a lantern, not knowing that a monster lurks in the dark with me."

"You haven't lost *me*, Mia. I'm still here. But promise me you will move past all this anger, this sadness, because I can't lose you to that darkness, or the monster, or the drink."

Mia turned to look at her sister to find her searching the night sky, eyes glassy. Kali bit down on her lip as if to stop the tears from free-flowing. Mia pushed up onto an elbow, gripping her sister's hand tighter. She'd do anything to stop that sadness from tightening on her face, to not see a single tear roll down her cheek because of her. She would even make a promise she wasn't sure she could keep.

"Hey, Kali, I promise. Only happiness from here on out. Now, let's go home."

NINE

The space between the single step into Henry's office and the hallway felt like a mountainous crevasse opening up. Mia stood on the edge of the swirling chasm with the wind slamming into her. Across that dark abyss sat her father, hunched over his desk, scribbling away. She knew she had to take the plunge and free-fall into the rift, but the hurt froze her in place, rising in her chest and constricting the air from her lungs.

Betrayal had slithered into her belly and made its home there.

They had only shared a handful of strained words over the past few weeks. She'd mostly spat venom at him, and he took it all with a stoic grimace.

From where she stood, she could see the small portrait she had painted of her family smiling back at her. He had never moved it, even with their strained relationship. That meant more than she'd expected. Mia glanced out the bay window, blinking the tears away, to Anne's meticulously kept garden of hedges, flowers and rows of ruby red roses. Henry needed a near-constant connection to nature. It was one of the only undoings of the fae—one that King Ewan took complete advantage of by razing each fae forest his army took, stripping them of what made their magic powerful.

"I can feel you watching me, Mia. What is it you want?"

"Kali has demanded we both walk her to the Medicus Tower now that I have returned home."

"And for how long will that be? Days, weeks? Until you decide you'd rather stare down the neck of a bottle again and send your mother sick with worry?"

Mia bit down on her lip and stepped into his office. She'd hurt more than herself in those weeks of nothingness, bruising the tender bonds that kept her family tethered.

"I never wanted either of you to worry about me, Henry."

Straightening, he gently placed the owl feather quill she'd brought for his last name day. His thumb traced over the white-speckled edge. "I will always worry about you, Mia. As long as I breathe, I will worry."

A tentative rope was thrown across the void, but she let it slip, falling into the abyss. "Is that why you did what you did?" she asked, her voice soft, no longer full of venom.

"I cannot apologise enough for my mistake, Mia. Please forgive me."

She crossed her arms as the pain in her chest cut into her. "I haven't found it in myself to..." She wanted to say, *"forgive you"*. Instead, she swallowed the words and said, "You didn't answer my question."

"Mia, you're an incredible woman, but you were born for more than that life. Much more."

"Well, I should have chosen that. You should have let me choose, Henry. All you did was snatch that away, making both of us look like fools."

Henry stood, hands braced on wood, pinched face upturned to the window. "I'm used to feeling like a fool, Mia. When I came to this court, I knew nothing but how to command men and fight. I fell on my face more than once. All these years later, these men don't respect me. I've never been their equal. Always an outsider. Even after Hartwinn gave me a bloody title. I just wanted you to be seen as I see you: radiant, intelligent. Not some brute of a fae's adopted daughter."

"And now I will never be seen as anything but that."

Henry turned, his eyes shining, jaw trembling. "And I will forever regret it."

Mia forced herself to meet his gaze, and when she did, the soft words she wanted to stay nearly slipped out. She wanted to throw her arms around him and hold her face tightly to his chest. To forgive the only father she had ever known for trying to force the hands of fate by lining the pockets of the guild master with gold. Instead, she gave all she could give—an inch.

"Kali and *I* want you to escort us to the Medicus Tower, Father. She wants us to walk her to work."

MIA WAVED FURIOUSLY AT KALI UNDER THE TALL ARCHWAY that led to the looming, grey stone tower. The Medicus Tower was a feat of impossible engineering, with its tall spire and flung open windows, allowing the soft autumn air to flow through. A low stone wall surrounded it with arched walkways, allowing apprentices and healers to slip through and hurry off to tend to patients.

A grin stretched across Mia's face as she beamed at her sister. Her simple, sky-blue dress cinched the smallest part of her waist, flaring around her booted feet. All acolytes wore the same blue, signalling their medical training to all. Strips of coloured material would be bound to her waist as she rose through the ranks. Only the masters wore pure white.

With her book bag slung over her shoulder, ribbons braided into her dark hair, she was the perfect vision of a young apprentice.

"Have a good day. Have fun scrubbing those chamber pots!" Mia called out.

Kali shot her a sharp look over her shoulder, poking her tongue out. Her shoulders rose, then sank down as she took a deep breath and pushed into the mass of blue cotton.

"Mia, leave her be, " Henry said, elbowing her. But his eyes never left the door. "She is nervous."

"Or are you?"

His unimpressed gaze slid to her. "You are too perceptive, daughter."

"Father, this is Kali we're talking about. She was born to be a healer."

Henry's gaze travelled up the cobblestoned road leading to Valliss, a strange longing flickering over his face. "Want to join me at court today? It's going to be awfully boring with the discussions of more settlements of refugees in the Westryn District, but I could teach you..."

An awkwardness settled as they stepped back and forth between how it used to be and how it suddenly was between them: strained and tense. Mia sighed. He was *trying*. Trying to throw ropes over that chasm, only for her to let them slide into the abyss with each toss. At least she didn't cut it with harsh words.

"I can't today, Father. I have something I need to do. Something to make right," Mia replied, reaching towards him. She squeezed his forearm once. "But thank you for the offer."

Henry cast her a small smile, running a hand over his braid. "You are always welcome to come to court whenever you wish. I was thinking—"

"That is a dangerous habit, Father," Mia cut in, already turning away from the archway.

Her shoulder clipped another, knocking a pile of books from the stranger's arms. Pages fluttered as heavy tomes thudded to the ground. "Oh, goddess. Sorry," Mia sputtered, reaching down for the books.

A blue-clad healer with an emerald sash crouched in front of Mia, already gathering the books and stacking them in her arms. Her mass of curly, rust-orange hair wildly sprang out from her face, obscuring most of her features. She batted Mia's hands away, her annoyance apparent. "No bother, girl. Just watch where you are going next time. These books are worth more than you are."

Mia bristled. *This healer can't be more than a handful of years older than me. How dare she call me a girl?*

The woman rose, flashes of green and hazel eyes glaring back at her and lips pressed into a thin line. The books more haphazardly piled in her arms, she blew a curl from her face and stormed off.

"You should really watch where you're going, Mia," Henry joked, chuckling.

"Shouldn't you be at the castle discussing boring things like grain harvests and what flowers Reagan is going to have at his wedding?" Mia snapped back, but her lips curled upwards at the corners.

Henry's laugh echoed down the street as he turned on his heel and walked off. She wondered if the hurt she felt overpowered the love she had for him. When he disappeared from view, she realised that love and pain were on a scale, and what had happened between them tipped the balance towards pain. Was all she needed a feather of hope to balance out the hurt he had caused?

She couldn't tell.

Her grumbling sent her forward, her boot catching on a book and sending it skidding over the cobblestones. A forest-green tome lay flat on the ground, the golden words shining in the morning sunlight.

Guide to Witches' Bloodlines: Vol. Four.

Mia scooped the book up and flicked through a few pages. Words described important witch covens and their centuries-long bloodlines. Her eyes traced over royal family trees—*Magntai, Delvaux, Beauchamp*—elegantly scripted into sprawling oaks, inked into the eggshell paper. Mia's finger brushed over the Magntai family tree, swirling over one name—Maeve, the last of her line—her mind wandering to that grand painting of her burning. She turned and strode down the street, still lost in the pages, not noticing the flap of feathers or the sharp caw of the raven flying overhead.

TEN

Luc Renniak's art studio was a single-storey building made of dark brick with two gleaming windows big enough for Mia to peer inside. Not a speck of dirt marred the glass, reflecting her tense face. She was nervous—even more so than when she had been standing in front of the cold guild masters. In her arms, she clutched her leather portfolio of sketches and small paintings to her chest. Her best work.

She had thought of her master plan in a drunken haze, and Benny had cautiously agreed. But as the buzz from the whisky fizzled away, so did her courage. A bell jingled as customers entered and left the store, spurring her into action.

"Now or never," she told herself. *And I would much prefer it to be now.*

Straightening her green bodice and tucking a stray hair behind her ear, Mia pushed through the door. The overpowering smell of art making slammed into her lungs—a strong, earthy scent of linseed oil and the brutal slap of turpentine. Sunlight beamed through the clear glass, capturing the colours in long fingers of light and casting shadows where the paint had clumped. Her fingers itched to drag over the dried pigment. To feel the texture. To allow each emotion brushed onto the canvas to soak into her. She ached to create the same feeling in someone else's chest.

Nobles browsed, nodding and whispering to each other as men in stiff white coats stood in corners, faces severe. Art making in that building was as serious as those inspecting each piece to spill gold. More gold than she could ever fathom.

Mia approached the counter, her fingers drumming the glass countertop.

"Can I help you, miss?"

Her eyes flicked up to find a middle-aged man with salt and pepper hair standing in front of her. His silver eyes inspected her to see if her clothing could give away how much gold she had to spend. She raised her chin and said, "I'm here to see Master Luc."

The man arched his brow, a smile edging his thin lips. "It's a touch early for a private appointment with Luc, miss. Maybe I can assist you? We have an affordable few posies left, done by one of his apprentices, to decorate your bedroom."

Mia didn't want the half-heartedly painted flowers—pieces she could do herself in a matter of moments with a dash of paint.

"No, sir. I'm not here for an art piece. I'm here to enquire about employment. A job. If you can assist with that, then go right ahead. Assist away."

The man's brushy eyebrow rose to meet his other. "You want a job here?"

Mia's mouth twitched into a strained smile, her fingers gripping the leather of her folio a fraction tighter. "Yes, sir. Right here in this building. Now, please, if you can direct me to Master Luc's office, I would be very grateful."

His head cocked, his smirk fading. "Show me what you've got in there, girl, and I'll consider it. My name's James. What's yours?"

Mia's smile tightened, her hand bunching into a fist. She wished people would stop calling her *girl*. She was a woman with a reasonable head on her shoulders and a sliver of talent, not some silly girl with dreams of grandeur. She slammed the folio down much harder than she intended to, the loud *thwack* disrupting the peaceful murmur of the studio.

"Mia. Mia Ashmore."

James sighed, lazily flicking through her art. Brows rising higher with each piece, his eyes roamed each sketch, then flicked to her, then back to her art. Disbelief lurked, making irritation simmer in her guts. He scrubbed his jaw. The scratching of his bristles set her on edge.

"Luc isn't going to give you a job here, Mia, even if you can paint, draw and mix colours better than some of his fourth-year apprentices."

Her smile faltered for a moment as the hot wave of rejection flushed her skin with sweat. She stomped it down, clearing her throat. "Well, that is Master Luc's decision, I presume? Please take me to him so I can present my art."

"If that is what you wish, then please, come right this way. Luc is going to love this."

James motioned her to follow him with a wave of a hand. Mia could see the other men holding back snickers behind snarky sneers. She bit her tongue, swallowing down the sharp words. She followed James down the narrow hallway, past studios filled with pine easels, half-finished paintings and more men in white coats, holding paintbrushes aloft and staring intently into their work. A firm rap on a closed door, then a muffled shout to enter came from the other side. The door to Master Luc's office cracked open. A sliver of morning light beamed through, showing glimpses of mahogany, leather and bookshelves.

"I have a girl here looking for a position. She wishes to see you," James called into the room. "What was your name again?"

A chair scraped on the ground, and Luc replied before she could answer. "A woman? James, you must be joking."

The door swung open wider, and Mia came face to face with Luc. His smirk faded into a displeased grimace. "You."

"Me."

James glanced between them, his eyebrows bunching in confusion. Luc sighed, pinching the bridge of his nose.

"I've come here for—"

"Yes, Mia. I know what you've come here for. Come in. I'd rather not break your heart again in the corridor."

She strode into his office, chin held high, summoning Kali's attitude as much as she could. It was, however, fake and half-hearted.

Luc closed the door behind her, and with a *click*, she was alone. Very alone. Her hands grasped around the soft leather of her cluttered portfolio to hide the tremble in her fingers. Her eyes found expensive furniture, trinkets and a large wooden desk strewn with papers and bottled pigments.

"I wish to be hired here, apprentice or not," Mia announced, pulling a piece of parchment with her scribbled speech on it from her pocket.

With an exhale, she began reciting the names of artworks she had sold, where her portraits hung in Valliss Castle and what her teachers had reported. Right to her passion to create, rambling about the honour it would be to learn from him. She nervously shoved the crumpled paper in her pocket. Opening her portfolio, she showed him the sketches and small strips of canvas.

Luc just watched her with an amused smirk, his gaze casting over her flushed face and dipping over her body. But never at her art. Never once at her art.

"...and I think it would be remiss of you not to hire me," she ended, closing her folio with a sharp *snap*.

Luc leant on his desk, crossing his arms. "Now, I appreciate your tenacity to come here, prepared with a speech and not awful art, but I already have my quota of apprentices, Mia. I stand by my decision."

"There has to be a way, sir."

"Unfortunately not."

Mia couldn't take no for an answer. She stepped forward, closing the distance between them and shaking her head. "Please, Master Luc. I will work hard—every day if I need to—and prove myself worthy. I promise I will do anything you need me to do."

Luc's eyes dragged down her body slowly—painstakingly slowly. "*Anything?*"

Mia swallowed, eyebrows bunching. Her thumb brushed over the warm opal adorning her pointer finger. They were playing a risky game of twisted words and promised terms. He wouldn't speak the terms, but he didn't need to. The hungry, lusty look in his eye was enough to understand what the word *anything* meant to the man.

Yet, Mia pushed on, for she had never wanted for something more.

Not a dress or a fistful of diamonds. All she wanted was this, to spend her days hunched over canvas, paint-splattered and full to the brim of ideas, all under Luc's keen eye. She had nothing else. Her life was hollow, empty. So, when the next words fell from her, she barely cared for the consequences of the handful of syllables.

"Yes, Master Luc. Anything."

He pushed off the table, his finger hooking under her chin. Luc dragged his paint-stained thumb over her scar, causing an uncomfortable shiver to spread over her, like his touch repulsed even her nerve endings. The scurry of her skin crawling sent her nails digging into her folio, leaving crescent-shaped indents forever imprinted in the soft leather. A small part of her wanted to rage against his casual touch—not to bend to his will, but to bite the hand that dared to touch her.

"Who did this to you?"

"I..." Mia paused, blinking. She hadn't expected him to ask her that. "I had an accident when I was a child with a stray ball and a shattered window."

He hummed a response, then a soft, almost kind smile spread on his face, brightening the onyx pools of his eyes and making her relax a fraction. His hand dropped away, but he didn't step back. "It makes you more striking, Mia," he breathed.

"Thank you."

"And it seems I'm in a generous mood this morning. I will make you an assistant to James and the others. Maybe, if you prove yourself, I will make you an apprentice."

Her gaze flashed to his as a smile worked its way across her face. "Truly?"

"Truly. But you will not touch a brush or tube of paint without James' or my direct supervision. You're not here to create as you see fit. You're simply an assistant to wash brushes, stretch canvas and do whatever else I desire until I say you aren't, or I will punish you. And you don't want that, do you?"

She shook her head.

Luc cocked his head and wet his lips with a sweep of his tongue, making her heart slam in her chest. With a shift of his feet, he had invaded the remaining space between them, until there was simply clothing between their bodies. Nothing more. "If I ask you a question, I require an answer, Mia."

Her stomach dropped, and for a split second, she wondered if it was worth it. But the sharp smell of turpentine and fresh pine had her head spinning and words slipping from her. "No, Master Luc. I understand. I won't give you a reason to punish me."

He leant into her; a strange scent flowed off him, like the stench of a wet dog mixed with a mouldy rug. His lips skimmed across her cheekbone until he found the curl of her ear. "You have much to learn, Mia, and it will be my pleasure to teach you."

"And, it will be my honour to work under you, Master Luc."

Pulling back, his gaze fell to her lips, his own parting.

A kiss to seal their deal.

Mia's body froze, each muscle tensed. "Master Luc…"

"Yes?" he answered, chest rising and falling, bumping into hers with every inhale.

"If someone were to walk in, they would believe us to be in a precarious position, and I wouldn't want—"

"To *tarnish* my reputation?"

Mia nodded again, dragging her portfolio between them as a leathery barrier. He shot her a quick, apologetic smirk and slinked back. A soft exhale left her as relief made her shoulders sag.

"How considerate of you. Now go. I expect you to be here at seven sharp tomorrow. Don't be late." He turned to his desk, shuffling papers. He called over his shoulder, gaze meeting her own. "Oh, I shall instruct you myself, in our own private lessons. I need to ensure you are up to scratch with the others."

Mia backed towards the door. She shared a small smile with him, clutching her art to her chest almost protectively. "I would greatly appreciate that. You won't regret this. I promise."

A soft, lopsided grin spread on his face, contrasting with the darkness in his gaze. He returned to his desk, his voice following her from his office. "Oh, lovely Mia, I don't think I'll ever regret this."

Eleven

The worn stone bench was warm under Mia's rear, soaking in the day's last light. She had agreed with Kali to meet in their own secret sanctuary. A hidden place on the ancient, crumbling fence edging Henry's property—the invisible line between their quiet existence and the bustle of Alderdeen. Mia exhaled, the leftover nerves buzzing in her chest in the soft dusk air. She knew what she had agreed to, and she would be a fool not to understand what the lusty looks and overfamiliar touching meant.

Have I promised too much? Agreed too hastily? Were the moments of thin-lipped discomfort worth the lingering shame to create, to learn under his masterful hand?

There were too many thoughts swirling, making her cast her gaze from the tufts of grass to the shimmering horizon. The last of the sun's rays shone over the tilted roofs and threading of cobblestone streets. Mia decided, with a bite of her lip, that if she had to grin and bear the moments of discomfort, she would. However, a stray thought stuck to the sticky sides of her skull. *How is this different from Henry bribing him? Gold and flesh are interchangeable.*

Mia sat with the thoughts running through her head, tangling even further until she couldn't find the ends. She hadn't heard a whisper of the malice-filled voice for a day or two, but the creeping up her spine proved he would speak to her eventually. And the abyss of men and whisky wasn't an option. Not anymore.

She spotted her sister's curls before she saw Kali stomping up the road, skirts in her fists. Reagan followed right on her heels, his black hair flopping with each step, his frowning face flushed, eyebrows nearly meeting in a bushy line. His hand snapped out, grabbing her roughly by the elbow and spinning her around. The harsh movements made Mia straighten, narrowing her eyes and dropping her folio to the grass. Reagan spoke to Kali so closely that Mia could see the specks of spittle as he hissed his words at her sister.

He shook her once, making Mia launch off the fence and rush down the road as fast as her legs could take her.

"You will do as I say—"

"No. How many times do I have to tell yo—"

"Let go of her, Reagan," Mia called out, drowning out the rest of the conversation.

His icy blue eyes, ringed with the tiniest sliver of amber, slid to her, spreading a chill over her skin. His lips screwed up in a scowl, his knuckles whitening on Kali's elbow. "Mind your own business, Mia."

She stepped closer, her hands fisted by her sides. "I said, *let her go.*"

Kali yanked her arm away and pushed Reagan square in the chest, sending him stumbling back. "Don't you ever grab me in anger *again*, or you'll regret it."

Reagan's face softened, but his gaze betrayed the rage he held tightly onto; a contrasting battle. He closed his eyes, his jaw clenching and unclenching. "Kali, my love," he began, his voice more controlled, softer. "I'm sorry. I shouldn't have grabbed you, but you weren't listening—"

"I have ears, don't I?" Kali cut in, crossing her arms. "I was listening, but that doesn't mean I have to agree with you."

Reagan's face hardened a fraction at her unimpressed tone. "We need to discuss this further, and in private." His eyes flashed to Mia, who glared at him. "Tomorrow? We could go to that bakery you love. Please. You know I cannot sleep if you are angry at me."

Mia fought the urge to cringe. Reagan's words always felt forced. Sugarcoated, but rotten in the centre.

Kali exhaled, pout edging into a smirk. "You better buy me at least two sweets. But that's if I ever want to see you again."

"I'll buy anything you want, my love," he replied quickly as he straightened his coat. A soft smile spread over his face—one that held tension at its corners.

Mia watched as Kali's eyes rose to him, then dropped to the dirt under her boots. "You know what I want, Reagan."

He sighed, turning from the women. Eyes cast to the horizon, hand in his hair, he was a man torn. "One day. I promise, Kali. One day."

Mia slipped her arm around her sister's, drawing her closer. Hope radiated from her. Reagan had dragged his fingers over the bars, waiting for her to sing for him.

"You cannot make a promise like that to my sister, Reagan. We all know that."

Kali looked away, a sullen frown pulling the corners of her lips down. Her brief spark of hope was smothered by Mia's words.

His glare snapped to her, and the bitterness brushed over her skin, making her stomach tighten. "Kali and I don't need anyone to speak for us. Especially you."

Especially me? I have every right to defend my sister, you pompous arsehole, Mia thought, adding to the tangled mess of her mind.

"Anyway, Mia, don't you have a seedy bar and a filthy man to run off to? Kali told me what—or should I say *who*—you've been doing," he said, dripping with smugness.

The slimy feeling of shame heated her cheeks. Mia dropped her sister's arm, stepping back. "You told him?"

Kali's blinking gaze flashed to her, shaking her head. "I was worried about you. You were coming home so late, so drunk. Sometimes you were covered in bruises, your clothing ripped. I didn't know what to do. So, yes, I told Reagan. He offered to help. To talk to Robbert for you."

A smirk flashed on Reagan's face. "Yes, Mia. I'm happy to talk with Robbert. I'm sure the Death Court requires another apprentice, or *meal*."

Mia raised her chin. "That is unnecessary, Reagan. Master Luc has employed me as an assistant. He's agreed to take me on as an apprentice when I prove my worth."

Reagan's brow arched, but Kali spoke first, confused. "How?"

Mia crossed her arms, holding in the unsettled feeling. "I simply asked. Now, are we going to drink this wine, or are we to attend prayers with Mother, Kali?"

And Kali only, Mia added silently, hoping her frosty glare would scare Reagan off.

Kali and Reagan shared a somewhat strained embrace. There was bubbling tension in their farewell. With a final scowl at him, Mia turned on her heel, not bidding him goodbye or even waiting for her sister.

"Good night, Mia. Let hope Henry isn't made a grandfather tonight," Reagan called after her.

Mia flung a rude gesture over her shoulder. She wouldn't risk either of them seeing the tears well in her eyes as that malice-filled voice whispered, *Disgusting, ruined creature.*

MIA SLID DOWN THE STONE WALL, KNEES TUCKED TO HER chest, finger tracing the crescent-shaped indents in the leather of her folio, the sting of her sister's betrayal making her grimace. Kali huffed and plopped herself next to her, stretching her legs out and rolling her ankles.

Neither spoke. They just stared in opposite directions, both letting the hurt fester. Mia could hear Kali dig through her bag, the *thump* of books being discarded on the grass, then the soft *tick* of fingernails on glass.

"How could you?" Mia muttered into her knees. "How could you tell him about me? That was mine, and mine to share. You knew he'd only cast it back in my face."

Kali exhaled, shifting closer until their arms were flush. "I'm sorry, Mia. I shouldn't have shared a secret that wasn't my own. But I was just so worried about you. I couldn't go to Mama or Papa, or even Hartwinn. Reagan was...*is* the only person I trust, aside from you."

Kali sniffed, a telltale sign that she was holding in tears. "I felt like I was losing you, Mia, slipping between my fingers like sand. Honestly, I had no idea what to do or how to help you. I wanted to make it better."

Mia still couldn't look at her, the hurt drawing its jagged nails across her fleshy insides, deciding where to dig its claws in. Her hand bunched into a fist as tears threatened to spill. Mia struggled to find the words to tell her sister—*I forgive you, of course you should have told someone*—but they all felt hollow. None rang the truth.

"There was nothing you could do to help me, Kali. Nothing was there to fix, because nothing could fix me. I'm not sure I will ever be whole again."

"Mia, you don't mean that."

She sighed, finger tracing the stitching on her skirt. "Something broke inside me that day. And then the betrayal of what Henry did forced its ugly fingers into the crack and yanked it open, allowing something to be set free."

"You're free, Mia—"

"No, Kali, I'm not. That room of old men and women may have opened that cage, but I simply fluttered around until someone else closed it."

"Luc."

A silent tear escaped. "I don't wish to speak about him."

"Mia, I do not believe you simply asked him for a position and he gave it to you. That is the most ridiculous thing I have ever heard."

The words, *gold and flesh are interchangeable*, slammed around her mind, cracking against her skull.

Mia pivoted, meeting her sister's concerned gaze with a tear-filled sneer. "Like you and Reagan? I don't believe for a second that he'd ever be truthful to his word. Maybe when we were younger, but I don't recognise him now."

"He has done nothing to deserve this ire from you. He loves me, Mia."

"Truth, then? He has done nothing?"

Kali paused, then looked away from her. "Truth."

A lie.

She knew it. Her sister was a great many things, but a liar, she was not.

Mia's eyes fell on the sea-green bottle of fae wine in her sister's lap, a wooden cork holding the bubbling contents. The giggling elation was only a handful of moments away.

"You aren't angry at Reagan," Kali said gently. "That is obvious. You're angry at what he represents."

Mia scoffed, shaking her head. "And what's that?"

"A world you've been forced into, only to be forced from."

Silence rang loudly as Mia blinked at her sister. The uncomfortable truth punched her in the guts.

"One you've so easily found a place in that you glided into it without a stumble," Mia said, adding on, her voice barely a whisper, "One you so readily left me for."

Lines of worry formed as the tips of her sister's brows lifted. She looked speechless. Totally and utterly speechless. Mia swiped the tear that escaped with the truth. Kali's hand found hers, gently cradling it to her chest, those ocean-blue eyes searching hers. Love edged with flecks of hurt beamed at her.

"I have never left you behind, and I never will. You are a part of me, as much as I am part of you. Bonded with the ties of love, not in blood. I am nothing without you, my sister."

"Then why do I feel like nothing next to you?"

Kali's hand slipped from her, only to grip either side of Mia's face, forcing her to face her own crumpled reflection in her sister's glassy eyes. Her lips opened to speak, but nothing came out. There were no words she could say. No soothing, elegant analogies of being worth more than gold and the stars in the night sky. Words were beyond them, beyond Mia's broken heart. Nothing was going to heal what had broken in her that day.

"Am I worthless, Kali?" she whispered, voice shaking.

Her sister let loose a soft gasp, then threw her arms around her neck, dragging her close. The bottle of fae wine slid to the grass with a thump.

"I love you, Mia," was all Kali said before sobs stole her words.

Mia allowed herself to melt into her embrace, feeling each shake of her sister's shoulders. Out of the tangled mess of emotions spilling out of the women, a single thread of buttery gold was shining—one Mia could untangle through the loops and knots. It led from the slow, rhythmic beat of her own heart right to the strong thudding of her sister's.

They were bound. Nothing would drag them apart. Not angry words or secrets spilt. Not even death itself.

Mia's hand found her sister's hair, smoothing her wild curls. She wanted to escape the feelings brewing in her chest, but not cast herself into the abyss. And maybe that was a start.

"Now, shall we have this fae wine? Henry will know we will have swiped a bottle. We might as well drink it."

THE BUBBLY FIZZ SPILT, SPLASHING OVER THE COBBLESTONE and leaving drops of fizzing wine on the toes of their boots. Kali gazed at the bottle with a strange, pensive look, then took a deep swig with her eyes screwed shut, finishing the last dregs. A giggle escaped Mia's clenched lips. Joy bubbled in her chest. A boisterous laugh emerged from Kali as she danced across the cobblestone with an invisible partner. Their delight leaked into the shouted cries of stall owners and the indistinct murmur of chatter in the packed streets of Alderdeen's lower city.

A side effect of the fae wine—unabashed, pure elation.

The soot-encrusted lanterns burnt above them, lighting the darker corners of the city, scattering the dimmed light over the grimy streets. The same dingy inns Mia had lost herself in dotted the street, with folk streaming from them and merging into the flow of people. Danger lurked in flashes of iron as purse strings were cut from unsuspecting bodies. Fear should have filled her stumbling steps, but she found that it quickened her pace. She wandered through alleys and down streets, past painted women wrapped in shawls, hungry-looking children whose hands readily took the coins she spilt, and those who wished for the same abyss she had once sought.

Something brewed there that Hartwinn's looming mass of marble and vine didn't contain. *Life.* That cruel, twisted curse.

"This wine has gone straight to my head," Kali slurred, a sloppy half-smile plastered on her face. "I know why Father doesn't want us drinking this stuff. It's too good!"

Mia broke away from her sister and spun, her skirts flowing out in ribbons of soft cotton, chin cast upwards to the blurred lantern light. Her cheeks ached from the grin she had worn for the past few hours. Kali watched her with a poorly hidden sadness that hung in her eyes. Her sister was fighting the elation of the fae wine, and she was losing.

"Mia, where are we going?"

"To my favourite place." She hiccuped. "In this whole city."

Pushing through the mass of bodies, Kali grumbled and complained about her feet hurting. Mia yanked her closer, travelling swiftly along the packed street. Her shoulder bumped into a burly knight of the Silver, almost teetering over. A warm hand settled on her spine, steadying her. The familiar ash and leather scent surrounded her.

Idris.

When she turned, the soothing touch had slipped from her body, and the scent was replaced with hot spices from the cooking meat from a nearby vendor, mixing with the stink of bodies. She scanned the crowd for those glittering emerald green eyes set in that face made of angles, finding neither.

Kali gripped her arm, dragging her away. "Take me to wherever this place is, or home."

"Not much further," Mia mumbled, her gaze still glued over her shoulder, searching.

THE FIELD WAS ABANDONED, WILDFLOWERS GROWING AND the grass cut short only to prevent rat infestations. In the centre was a glorious maroon oak tree, stretching to the twinkling night sky, indicating the shift of the bustling, grimy downtown to the flashy, golden upper city, where rubbing shoulders with the nobles of the city was an artful dance.

Mia dragged Kali across the grass, right to the rough bark. The oak's impressive branches twisted above them, allowing the silver rays of moonlight to filter softly through the leaves. Roots erupted from the dirt in gnarled twists as if even the earth couldn't contain the strength of its growth.

"You brought me to a tree?" Kali asked flatly, pouting. "I'd hoped it was to The Casserole Dish, so I could see this Idris for myself."

Mia rolled her eyes. "It's The Cauldron. And I told you, Kali. He never came back. Now, stop that sulking and climb."

Kali scoffed, stumbling back, her head craned to the dizzying heights. "No way. I can't climb a tree. I can barely see straight."

Mia grumbled at her sister, then jumped to reach for a limb. Her hands missed, shooting a sharp *clap* through the air. She landed, teetering on the balls of her feet, then fell straight down on her rear. A laugh escaped her, then another. Her contagious laughter sent Kali spiralling to the dirt next to her.

"You're my best friend, you know that?" Kali asked through fits of chuckles.

"What an honour you bestow upon me, sister!"

Kali wiped tears from her cheeks, a smile finally meeting her eyes. "Why did you bring me here, of all places?"

Mia wiggled until she pressed her back against the hardwood. Her fingertips traced the patterns in the rough bark. "This tree meant something to someone. It's important."

Kali squished next to her. "You're not making any sense. It's just a tree."

Mia rested her head on her sister's shoulder. "No, Kali. It isn't a normal tree. This one is different. I can't explain it, but I feel it in here." Her hand spread across her chest, feeling her slowed heartbeat. "I can feel it as if it grew a mouth and spoke to me."

Kali's eyes glazed as a memory replayed. Her gaze shot to Mia, lips parting. "I have something to tell you—"

"You and Reagan are together again, aren't you?" she cut in, a sloppy grin on her face. "And still arguing about getting married, aren't you? You should just run away and get married in the forest by a wood nymph. They'd braid flowers into your hair and make a bouquet of weeds for you to carry down the aisle. Then Uncle Hartwinn couldn't deny your love, as it was sanctioned by Oryah herself. Even if I think Reagan's a pompous arsehole, and you deserve better."

Kali returned her smile, gaze rising to the night sky. Mia wiggled closer for warmth, her eyes finding the glittering twinkling of the stars. Her sister leant down and pressed a gentle kiss on her crown, then rested her own head on Mia's and whispered, "You're right, Mia. I do deserve better."

TWELVE

Mia stood in the corner of Luc's studio, her hands clasped tightly behind her rod-straight back, lips pressed into a thin line. Instead of the starched, crisp white coats the others wore, she donned an apron edged with soft lace, bound around her waist over the sensible navy-blue skirts she had nervously chosen that morning. Not a single customer glanced at her or spoke to her. She was invisible even to them.

The apprentices gave her narrowed, side-eyed looks and a wide berth. Not that Mia cared. She wasn't there to make friends. James, the grumpy second-in-command, was the only one who bothered to speak to her. He was positively surprised when she turned up at the back door thirty minutes before the seventh bell. He showed her around with sharp words and sharper movements, then sent her out of the studio.

She answered with a distracted nod, eyes locked on the spread of half-finished works—landscapes, portraits and still life peered at her. She itched to pick each up and inspect it. Instead, she clasped her traitorous hands together and allowed James to shove her in the corner to be bored and alone.

"Mia! Come in here now," he called.

She sprang into action, her skirts swishing with each rushed step. She found him out in a small offshoot of the main studio, leaning on a sink full of brushes. Rainbows of colour strained the white bristles, paint drying in fat globs.

"What is it, sir?" she asked eagerly. "Do I need to get my notebook and quill to write notes?"

James gave her a confused, long stare.

"Unless you need to note about how to wash these, then no." His hand waved behind his head. "Scrub these until they are spotless, and clean off any leftover paint."

She didn't move. "How is this supposed to teach me—"

"Teach you, girl? You won't be learning anything here. You're nothing more than a scullery maid for those who are actual artists. Well, until Luc has his fill of you and puts you out on your pretty arse."

Mia clenched her jaw and shoved him aside, stepping towards the sink. "We shall see."

With a hard face, he leant over her. "Luc will never allow a woman to be an artist here or in any of his other establishments. His views on women aren't as progressive as the rest of the guilds. This is a waste of your time and talent."

Mia held his gaze as she picked up a wide, flat brush with two fingers and dropped it into the bucket of water. A handful of boiling hot liquid splashed out, catching James across the lap. He jumped back, hissing.

"My apologies, sir. My talent seems to be overflowing."

"If they don't shine, Luc will know, and he won't be pleased," he said, clenching his jaw.

"As you command," she muttered before getting to work.

Mia leant against the doorframe, her apron sopping wet. Her fingers were red and pruned, but the brushes and pallets that stood drying sparkled. The store had closed an hour ago, and the apprentices had filed out with a mountain of homework set by the grumpy James. She watched him work, his skilful hands gathering, mixing and grinding pigments to mix into paint—a stunning alizarin crimson.

"What are you working on?"

His gaze flashed up, then down. "A painting for Lord Hartwinn."

"What are you painting for Lord Hartwinn?"

"If you have time to gawk, you have time to sweep."

Mia bit her tongue and grabbed the broom, her focus not leaving his hands, nor the ingredients. She noted each colour he picked up, how much he gently tapped into the small pestle. Repeating it over and over until she could write it down.

"Eyes on your own work, Mia," Luc crooned from the doorway.

Her gaze dropped to the straw bristles of the broom, embarrassment heating her cheeks. Luc's boots clicked on the stone as he approached her. His ruby-ringed finger slipped under her chin, lifting her face to his. His free hand slid around her wrist, holding her in place.

"Master Luc—"

"Why do you want to work here?"

Her gaze flicked from him to James, who continued to work, ignoring the scene unfolding in front of him.

"Look at me, Mia," Luc quietly demanded.

"I have always felt drawn here, to create with my hands. To help them feel happiness, sadness, joy. Just feel *something*. Anything."

"Why not ask to become a healer if you want to help?" Luc asked, his blond brow raised.

She shook her head. "I don't want to be a healer."

"Then why, Mia?"

She hated the sight of blood. Even the smallest drop made her faint, but she would not confess that to Luc. Instead, she said, "Because they're not *you*."

That curling smirk stretched across his face. "Go on."

"I wanted to learn from the best. To be the best, and I can only do that here with you."

Luc puffed his chest out, satisfied with her answer. "Well, then, are you ready for your first lesson?"

"Already? On what?" Mia asked, squeezing the broom handle until the rough splinters dug in her palm. His touch left a twisted, sick feeling in her stomach. She wanted to step back, to create the space between their bodies she desperately needed, yet she was so desperate to learn from him that she remained locked in his grasp.

The creeping male voice whispered, drawing out each syllable. *Now, creature, you sold yourself, and now you hesitate to settle your debts?*

"The girl is still cleaning, Luc," James said, finally speaking. "I don't want to be here until the tenth bell tolls, tidying up after useless apprentices. Isn't that what she is here for?"

Luc's smirk faded, gaze flicking to James in a silent challenge. James seemed unfazed, cocking his head, waiting for his master to answer.

"Send her to me when you are done with her."

Luc strode from the room, his fingers ghosting down her arm, trailing a creeping feeling over her skin.

A beat of silence went through the studio until James broke it with a sigh, saying, "I know what you promised him. He is going to pursue you until you give in, Mia, and when you do, he will not be kind."

Her fingers relaxed, bubbles of blood pooling in the lines on her palm. Her eyes didn't leave the paint-splattered grey slate floor, a sickly shame coating her body in a hot sweat. "I promised him nothing I wouldn't give away freely."

"Well, I hope it's worth it, Mia. Now, come. I wasn't lying when I said I have things for you to clean."

"Go home, Mia," the weary James commanded.

Her gaze flashed to the hallway leading to Luc's office, pursing her lips. Her fingers found the end of her apron strings, fiddling with the end. "Are you sure there is nothing more I can do for you?"

James dismissed her with the wave of a hand, shrugging off his coat. "Go. I will inform Luc of your departure."

"You'd do that for me?"

"I suggest you go before I change my mind."

"Thank you, sir."

"James. Please call me James. And there won't be a next time."

"Well, thank you, James."

Mia ripped off the apron, gathered her belongings and rushed through the back door. Her bag *thumped* with each hurried step. Kali was waiting for her, and she was late. Very late.

She made it to the worn stone seats just as the sun disappeared for the day. But Kali wasn't there. Exhausted, Mia sat and waited and waited as the moon crept across the sky.

Something is wrong. Kali hasn't come.

Mia could feel it in her chest like a heavy weight sinking deep into her guts. A bell droned in her skull in apprehensive tolls. She stood, fumbling around the stone wall, trying to remember where they'd left each other notes when they were children. One slid from the sandy mortar, revealing a scrap of parchment. She snatched it up, opening to reveal a rushed note in her sister's swooped handwriting.

Too busy for your own sister, hey?
I've gone to The Cauldron. Meet you there.
Kali.

Mia shoved the note into her pocket and raced back down the hill. Her boots slapped against the cobblestone. Her legs demanded she move faster, breaking into a sprint.

Panic flooded her, making her movements sloppy and rushed.

Eyes watched her as she launched herself through the streets, bumping into people, stumbling over gaps in the stones and through the stretched shadows cast by lantern light.

Mia skidded to a stop in front of The Cauldron, panting and sweaty. Rowdy voices flowed into the night air from the dingy pub. Her trembling hands found the rough wood of the swinging doors, shoving them open. Mia knew she was overreacting. Kali would be there. *Why wouldn't she be? Kali will laugh and tell me I am being ridiculous.*

As soon as her boot found the worn, stained wood, Mia began searching for her sister's twinkling blue eyes. But Kali was nowhere to be seen. She rushed over to the bar, calling out for Benny. His eyes shot to her from the customer he was serving. His smile disappeared the moment he saw her sweaty, dishevelled appearance. Concern flashed across his face. "You all right, Mia?"

Her head swivelled, looking down the bar, still not finding her sister.

"Has Kali been in here today?" she asked, her voice rising above the inaudible murmurs. "Have you seen her?"

"Nah, Mia. I haven't seen your sister since she dragged you off that slimy vamp. Is everything all right?"

She met his concerned gaze, shaking her head. "I don't know, Benny. Something is wrong. I can feel it."

"You can feel it?"

Mia's hand rubbed the centre of her chest, heaving. "Kali must have gone home and not come here. Or maybe she is with Reagan."

Benny held aloft a half-drunk bottle of whisky, sloshing the amber contents. "Drink, Mia? I've missed my friend, and it looks like you need one."

She dragged herself off the bar, barely hearing his voice, and left the pub. Her mind was already on route to the castle, planning what she'd say to Hartwinn, when a glint of an emerald caught her eye from the dark corner of the alleyway that skidded up the side of The Cauldron. Mia froze, and a sharp gasp left her lips.

Thirteen

Blood pooled in each divot of the cobblestone alleyway, running red rivers around the stones. Resting just above her head was her slack hand, reaching out to Mia. Her skin, once flushed and warm, was a waxy white, losing all the warmth as her life force fled her body. The soft cotton of her dress was ripped from her. But what caught the breath in Mia's chest was her eyes. Open but abandoned. The fire that had danced was extinguished.

Mia's wide eyes dragged down over the splatters of red on her chin to her throat, a mangled mess of torn flesh and blood exposing the sickening viscera underneath. Blood flicked carelessly around her.

Kali was dead.

A hooded figure was crouched over her sister's lifeless body. Long fingers gingerly poked at her ruined flesh as if they could connect the wound like a sick puzzle piece.

Mia's bag slid from her shoulder, falling to the ground and spilling her belongings across the stone. The only sound she could muster was Kali's name, repeated over and over in a panicked mumble. The figure lifted their head to the noise. The world spun, making Mia bend at the hip. A flushed sweat broke out over her skin, bile rising in her throat.

Not Kali, not her. She can't be...dead. Not her.

Mia scrambled, desperately clawing at the pull of unconsciousness. All she could smell was the hot, metallic stench of blood, mixed with the faint scent of leather and ash.

"You shouldn't be here," was all the hooded figure's deep male voice said.

Mia recognised the voice, yet she couldn't place it. Her mind was a swirling gale, leaving nothing but that howling inside her mind.

"What have you done?" she asked, voice wavering, tears falling down her cheeks. "What did you do to her?"

"Nothing. I have done nothing to this poor woman."

An icy breeze picked up strands of Mia's hair, sticking them to the pooling saliva at the corners of her mouth.

"Liar," she gritted out.

She took a stumbling step closer, blood and muck splashing over her boots. A gag slipped from her, barely holding in her stomach contents. If she could reach Kali, maybe she could do something—anything—to bring her back.

"What did you do to her?"

The hooded man rose from Kali's body, head turning. "I simply found her."

He stepped away from her body, revealing more spattered gore. Mia's hand found the comfort of the stone wall, keeping her upright. Her breath was coming in sharp gasps, ending with a wet sob. Tears ran rivers down her face. Desperate prayers fell from her.

Not Kali. Please, Oryah, please don't take Kali. Please, not her. Take me.

"You should really go. Whatever killed this poor soul may come back."

Mia's eyes snapped to the man. With every ounce of venom she could muster, she spat, "The thing that killed her is standing in front of me."

He cursed, whirling around, his face shrouded in shadow. "I had nothing to do with this—"

"Stop *lying!*"

Something cracked in Mia's chest like a fracture in a teacup, leaking out a hot sensation that ran down her arms to her outstretched fingers. She threw her head back, a scream ripping from her mouth, forcing that crack to widen to a chasm. Every muscle in her body strained, fighting.

Words slipped from her mouth.

Words that were whispered to her late at night.

Words spoken in her dreams.

Words that she could just hear on the breeze.

Words that begged to be freed when she was full of anger, joy, excitement or sadness.

"By the shadows, be free!" Mia screamed into the alley.

Magic poured from her flexed hands, conjuring thick ribbons of darkness from nothing, unravelling like reels of silk, slipping and slithering across the bloody ground and directly towards the hooded figure. Tendrils of shadows lashed out, wrapping around the man's wrists, binding him. He made no move to fight the black shackles.

"Calm down, girl, before you expose yourself and end up on a witch's pyre."

Mia's scream forced more shadows out of her hands, extinguishing every light in the alley. Even moonlight struggled to beam through the mists of shadows. Her hair rose, cutting across her face with each gust of magic she conjured. Tears sizzled out. Her palms ignited, spreading warmth up her forearms and heating the pain that suddenly clawed at her insides, adding fuel to her magical fire until her whole body was ablaze.

The man stood in the centre of the blast, unmoving, unfearing. Shadows slipped over him, spilling into the dark alley corners.

Mia waned and wavered.

The fire inside her died to smouldering ashes, leaving an icy cold void in its wake, freezing her right down to her toes. The only warmth came from the line of blood dripping from her nose and down over her lip. Her legs gave way under her, and she collapsed to the ground. An awful, agonising pain was all she felt as her heart was ripped from her chest and discarded across the stone to lie with Kali's body.

The shadows dissipated, allowing the moon to cast its rays down on the gore-filled alleyway.

The man strode forward with his long legs, eating the space between them. He crouched down, slipping his finger under her chin and forcing her gaze to shift from the spattered blood to the darkness under the hood. A pair of glittering emerald eyes rimmed with gold stared back at her.

"Hello, Mia. We meet again," Idris crooned.

PART TWO:
Lost to the Nothing

Fourteen

Tears that had stung her eyes earlier had dried to nothing. She couldn't force herself to cry even if she wanted to. An unfamiliar numbness engulfed her. Each painful emotion was suddenly rounded, no longer sharp and pointed. The grief scratching at her chest was a horrible, heavy ache, weighing her down, demanding that she lie down and never rise. She fought and battled against that swirling darkness as it latched onto her, digging its jagged claws into the soft flesh of her heart.

Kali was her single lantern light, but she had burnt out, leaving Mia alone in the pitch-black.

Many had come to their house to leave flowers, food and condolences, heavy words of sorrow and sadness. But none spoke of the absolute joy her sister had brought to every life she touched. Only that she would be missed, and they were sorry. None of them were really, truly sorry. It was a dance of bows and curtsies, of hugs and firm pats on the back. A dance Mia was forced into, but she didn't know the steps.

Reagan turned up on their doorstep, dishevelled and red-faced. He knelt at Anne's feet as fat tears fell down his cheeks. He uttered a speech expressing his love for Kali and his wish that it were he who was taken. Mia stood at the doorway, watching him scrape and weep. It felt like an act. Even his words felt rehearsed...hollow. She had to leave, to escape to the quietness of her bedroom before words she couldn't take back spilt from her mouth.

The entire house softly sighed as she forced her window open, letting the cool air brush against her skin. A voice murmured on the breeze, too soft for Mia to catch. Leaning on the windowsill, she forced a long, shuddering breath out. Her fingers turned the opal as her gaze vacantly skimmed over the tubes of colours, jars of paintbrushes and her paint-splattered rags.

No joy was found in the dabbing and broad brush strokes on canvas.

Nothing worked. Each stroke was wrong.

She had even splattered red from a stray tube across the handsome stranger's face, making herself hiss a curse and hide it away. But she knew, deep inside, that she wanted to bury it. She could not stare at the sadness, that soft longing in his eyes, knowing it reflected in her own like a glimmering emerald mirror.

But another painting sat on her easel.

A portrait of Kali.

She had painted it for her birthday—her sister's only request. But it was only half completed. Mia's fingers brushed over the dried paint, the swirls of blue and rich dabs of brown and tan. Her face lacked depth; the richness of her skin, the gleam of her blue eyes, the soft pink of her lips. Mia dug her fingernails into the thick oil paint, peeling it away, leaving gouges across Kali's smiling face.

Flashes of blood and gaping wounds played over her vision.

She stumbled back, clawing at the buttons on her blouse, forcing the bile down. Everywhere she turned, Kali was there. In a smile, a laugh or her vacant, empty eyes.

"Get out..." Mia mumbled, backing up further. "Get out of my head!"

Warmth spread from the centre of her chest as something awoke to the panic building in her. Shadows slipped from her fists, spilling around her ankles. She scurried back from them, slamming against the door.

"What are you?" she whispered, her voice tight. "What am I?"

"*Rare,*" a soft female voice whispered—no, not one singular voice, but many. A chorus of women. "*Someone we've been waiting for.*"

"Fucking Heylla," Mia cursed, hand going to her mouth.

They didn't speak again, instead watching and waiting. For what, she couldn't tell, nor could she even begin to understand. Her mind was too full of Kali and the nightmares that haunted her to piece anything together.

Mia turned sharply, fleeing from the lurking shadows and the ruined artwork. She thundered down the stairs, ripping open the front door to launch herself from the muted sadness of her home into the bright, warm outside world. She sprinted past the perturbed onlookers as they stepped out of her way, not casting a single glance at any of them. Her eyes remained fixed on the gravelly dirt road, her mind firmly set on where her feet were racing to.

THE FIELD WAS EMPTY. NO CHILDREN PLAYED ACROSS THE grass with their gleeful shrieks, nor did lovers lounge in the sun, lost to each other. Mia was the only soul in the great expanse of untouched land. Stray rays of sunlight glinted down onto her as she rushed through the park, right to the maroon oak. With trembling fingers, she reached for the trunk, smoothing her hand over the rough bark. She hoped it could pull the wallowing sadness from her chest and hold it for her until she was ready to feel it. A soft sigh of the wind and a brush up her spine was all the tree could do to soothe her. Because, like Kali had said on that night of truths and fae wine, it was simply a tree.

Mia stretched up and pulled herself onto a tree limb, then another, venturing higher and higher until she reached dizzying heights. She towered over the roofs of Alderdeen, peering right into the lush garden of Hartwinn's castle. Sage green hedges and rainbows of flowers opening their blooming faces to the sun swayed in the soft wind.

She hugged the trunk, face pressed to the bark. She spied the light blond hair of Hartwinn stepping through the vast garden, his back to her. He lifted his head, gazing at something above his eyeline. He was speaking, but there was no one around to hear his words.

A chill crept down Mia's spine, straightening each hair on her neck.

A stray caw from a raven came from the branches above, causing her to jump and slip on the trunk. Her chin dipped to the shuddering height she had climbed to. The ground seemed to race up to meet her, forcing her to grip the tree tighter. A ball of fear lodged in her throat, making her swallow. Hard. Her eyes flicked up at the whisper of her name. Hartwinn was staring directly at her, his hawk-like gaze burning as if he could see her hidden in the branches.

She scrambled from her hiding spot at an alarmingly fast pace. In her haste, her foot slipped on the branch and sent her spiralling from the tree. Before she could reach out and grip onto anything, Mia slammed into the ground. With the breath knocked from her lungs, she wheezed and rolled onto her side. The soft cushioning of the grass did nothing to dull the pain ricocheting down her back. A giggle escaped her, then another until she was clutching her sides. Laughter poured from her, sending the cackling into the air.

Great. I have fallen from a tree and subsequently lost my mind.

Mia couldn't stop the erupting mirth until it turned into short, sharp, gasping sobs. Her grief devoured any speck of happiness and spat out the bones, leaving only chest-tightening sadness. She brought her knees up, curling into her body. Soon, her skirts, covered in dirt and stray leaves, were soaked with tears.

"I miss you, Kali," Mia murmured, squeezing her legs tighter. "I think I will miss you forever."

FIFTEEN

Mia thought her mother's muffled sobbing in the stillness of their home had been the worst of the whole fucking thing. In the dim of Alderdeen's necropolis, a forgotten city with its crumbled, vined walls and lost foundations, Anne's heaving sobs shattered whatever remained of Mia's heart.

Death's invisible fingers caressed her as the dead converged to take Kali's soul to the afterlife. The thin, golden-edged white dress was not enough to keep that unsettling chill from prickling Mia's skin. Running her hands over her forearms, she commanded Death to leave her be—she'd given enough to him. But Death always demanded more, taking and taking until there was only a shell of a being left, filled to the brim with pain. That harsh reminder of being alive. The one thing that joined them all, human, fae or vampyre—Death would come for them.

All of them.

Mia's hair was loose, the blonde strands cutting across her vision. She'd refused to wear the mourning veil, casting it to the wind. *I will not hide my grief away. All will bear witness to my pain. And I'll be brave in the face of Death, not wilting under his gaze.*

Anne stood hunched between Kali's friends, each holding an elbow and steadying her. Her own veil shrouded her crumbled face as she brought a tear-stained handkerchief to her cheeks. Her mother's own bright, kind light had diminished to just a tiny flicker.

A slow hum of a hymn came from her left, signifying the beginning of the end.

Morose-faced priests, dressed in simple, long white robes, carried Kali's shrouded body under a crumbled archway. Father Pristone followed them in his full priestly garb, an intricately sewn cape of green and gold covering his plain robes. On his head, he wore a large, pointed mitre with the same swirls of green and gold. And in his arms, he held his tattered tome of Deus' writings.

Her parents had argued in terse, raised words about how Kali would be sent to the afterlife. Henry wanted to intern her body to the cool, soft dirt to be consumed by the worms, surrounded by her father's family, as was the Westryn Fae custom. But Anne demanded her daughter be scattered to the trees, to the soft wallowing of the dead of the necropolis. Close to her home, close to them. A place for them to visit, to be with her. For Kali's soul to linger, and watch them age and eventually have their own ashes scattered across the cracked stone. Finally reunited.

Mia watched them lower Kali's linen-wrapped body onto the stacked funeral pyre, tossing wildflowers over her, the rainbow of colour stark against the bright white of her burial shroud. Nothing of her could be seen. Not the curl of her lip or the twinkle of her eye, or even the wound that had ended her life. Nothing of her was left. Her soul had escaped that alley of horrors, leaving Mia behind.

A sea of serious faces stood around Kali's pyre. Much too serious. She wouldn't have wanted tears and frowns. She would have wanted laughter and smiles—the way she lived her life, every second of it. Mia met Reagan's gaze across the stacked wood. He didn't weep, nor did he throw himself at the edge of the pyre. He simply stood stoic, jaw set. Mia narrowed her eyes at him, lips forming a firm line, finding it suspicious. Just as she was about to speak, Anne's loud sob interrupted her.

Henry had emerged from the sprawling forest, stone-faced, eyes red-rimmed. His long black hair was gently floating in the wind, drifting across his face in inky streaks. His torso was bare, but he wore white, gold-threaded pants. Three fae males stood guard around him to protect him from any lashings of misery, but she knew they were also there to soothe him; a hand on his arm, a grip on his shoulder and firm bodies behind him.

All to hold him upright until he got to the edge of the pyre.

Wyn—of all the men in the world—was amongst them. His eyes met hers, his eyebrows bunched, and he mouthed her name. She shared a small, pitiful smile with him. Out of all the things that could have reunited them, she was sad this was it. And she wanted nothing from him but for his powerful body to hold her father up.

Mia had prepared herself for what was coming, but the uneasy feeling still churned in her guts. Henry dropped to his knees, letting out a pained wail from deep in his chest. His hand slapped his bare skin over his heart again and again until the skin turned a mottled purple. The loud thwacking of skin sent her own prickling. Mia cringed at his anguished screams, each one ringing in her ears. A sound she would never forget.

The fae males began their chant in their mother language, their baritone voices rising and falling as words curled from their tongues, drowning out her father's pained howling. Wyn grabbed a handful of Henry's hair and, with a silver flash of a blade, cut it from his scalp. Each man chopped until only a sloppy, close shave remained.

Henry's hair was sacred to him, a symbol of his connection to the goddess, Oryah. It was only cut when a child was born, and when someone left the earth to journey to the afterlife. The beginnings of life and death. A sacrifice to the great goddess.

He raised his head as two tears rolled down his face. "I shall pay the price for my daughter, my bright sun in the day. My Kali. The second love of my life."

Anne sobbed at his words, bending at the hip. Hands grasped her tightly so she wouldn't collapse to the ground. Her heaving breaths sent Mia's bottom lip trembling. She held the whimper in, her hands clenched so tightly around her skirts that the material became crumpled and sweat-stained. A hot shot of copper coated her tongue as her teeth cut into the soft flesh of her cheek.

Through tear-blurred vision, Mia watched as the men laid hair in Henry's waiting hands. He rose, reaching up, and placed the bundle on top of the flowers. Tears began running in salty rivers, flooding his face.

He backed away from the stacked wood and his daughter's body. Together, they stood in the undulating darkness, allowing their sorrow to mingle with one another's.

Someone handed Henry a lit torch of flickering and spitting flames. The heat seeped into Mia's chilled skin. Her father held the torch aloft, frozen in place, eyes not leaving Kali's linen-wrapped body. The muscles in his face twitched, a heartbreaking sadness etching its way between his brows.

Mia forced herself to stand beside her father. Reaching out, she grasped the wooden handle just above Henry's hand, making his arm flex. "Let me, Papa. I can do this for us. For you and Mama."

Henry's bloodshot eyes never left the pyre, but one by one, his fingers released the torch, letting Mia hold the heavy burden of setting her sister's soul free.

Father Pristone's voice droned in the background, words merging. Mia knew his sermons only brought comfort to those who believed in his twisted views of the afterlife. Deus, the all-seeing male god of humans and vampyres, would grant one eternal life in his godly land after a life of pureness, of holiness, of abiding by his rules. And if ever one committed a devilish sin, they'd be sent to the Heylla pits of Diabolus, his cruel brother. Father Pristone was Deus' mouthpiece, spewing the words across the air.

Mia didn't believe in it. She never had.

Henry had told them stories when they were children of the goddess Oryah, whose wonderful garden was welcoming to all, where souls were reborn back into the chaos of life. Mia hoped that was the truth. She'd even prayed until her head hurt, wishing that one day, hers and Kali's souls would reunite in whatever life they found themselves in next.

"Until the next life, sister. I promise to live my life. I promise I will live enough for the both of us," she whispered, so softly she wasn't sure if her lips even parted.

With one last look at Kali, she tipped the torch down, lighting the oil-soaked wood. The pyre caught alight with a sudden *whoosh*, drowning out Anne's choked sobs. Flames played in Mia's eyes as a single tear rolled down her face.

And I vow to find out who did this and end them.

Mia and Henry stood side by side, silent in their last goodbyes to Kali, watching her ashes float away in the chilled night air. The pyre had burnt to blackened logs, but Mia couldn't shift a single muscle. Not until that final orange ember died out.

Mia's cool hand found her father's, warm and calloused. "It all seems so stupid now. The fighting. The jealousy I would feel. That longing to be just like her. All pointless."

Henry's reddened eyes slid from the embers to Mia. "Jealousy?"

"I was always *so* jealous of her, Papa. From her beauty to the way she lived her life," Mia confessed. She spoke in a gentle voice, scared to disturb any of the lingering ghosts as the hard truth slipped from her. "That your love for each other created her. She was your miracle child, after all. I always knew you'd love her more than me, more than a child who simply stumbled into your life—"

"You've never been so wrong, Mia."

She sharply turned to him. She wasn't finished. Words formed on her tongue that needed to be spewed out like a night on the whisky. Henry reached down and cupped her face. His ancient eyes searched hers, beaming a soft, wondrous look at her. From that gaze alone, she knew he loved her with all his heart.

"My heart is held by three women. Anne, Kali and you. The love I have for you surpasses the blood in my veins. It surpasses whatever brought you to me. I am your father, and you are my daughter, and there is nothing that could change that. Not words, not actions. Nothing. Oryah blessed me the day you stumbled into my life. You made our family complete, my lovely Mia, my glowing moon in the night sky. You completed us."

Her father had never spoken so openly, so emotionally before.

Mia launched herself into Henry, his strong arms encasing her. He pressed a kiss to her crown, resting his chin on her head. Tears wet her cheeks as apologies bubbled out in sobs.

"I have always been so proud of you, but today I am especially proud. You set Kali's soul free. Not me, not Anne. You. Something I couldn't do. That took strength."

A man called Henry's name, and with one last squeeze, he left her alone. With a sniff, she scrubbed her face with the heel of her palm, her gaze returning to the last of the dying embers.

"Mia."

She whirled around to see Idris step out of the shadow of a crumbled pillar. Her heart thundered in her ears as a cold sweat poured over her skin. A solemn frown pulled his lips down, eyes not on her, but on the smouldering embers. A moroseness hung in the muscles of his face, like he had stared into the same ashes.

Not that it mattered.

He'd killed her sister, and now he had come to see her float away in the wind.

A scream for help worked up her throat, clawing its way out.

Mia took a wobbly step back, making Idris close the space. His hand flashed out, covering her mouth as his other gripped her nape, squeezing her. She bellowed against his rough palm, the sound spilling between his clenched fingers. She slapped at his chest, her blows bouncing off the rigid muscle. His gaze searched hers, not with the depraved madness she thought a killer would have, but with a softness. A pleading desperation bled from his eyes.

"Hush, Mia. I need to speak to you without the hysterics. Now, if you promise you won't scream, I'll let you go."

She nodded against him, her fight fading until her arms fell to her sides.

He lifted his hand, allowing a breath of smokey air to be dragged into her lungs.

"Help!" she bellowed, pushing him away. "Help me!"

Idris cursed under his breath, advancing on her. "Your sister's murder is not the only one in this city. There is blood being spilt on the streets, Mia. Blood of those forgotten by the nobles in that marble palace."

Mia scrambled back, shaking her head. *Why should I believe a word that slips from his lips?* All she let out was another weak yelp. The soft, waxy smell of clean leather fought against the smokey wind. His cloak had shifted, exposing a sword strapped to his hip. A human skull cast in worn iron adorned the pommel, lines crossing to make a star formed a strange rune, stamped into the forehead of the skull. One she had only ever seen in history books, hidden deep in Hartwinn's library—a witch rune.

"Mia—"

"I suggest you leave her alone, boy," a deep voice rumbled behind her. She glanced over her shoulder, finding Wyn standing with his arms crossed, a cool glare on his face.

"We shall see each other again, Mia. I promise you that," Idris whispered, his breath skimming over her cheek.

She turned to find him gone, disappearing into the same shadows he had appeared from. A clench of her heart let loose a slip of a feeling—one she couldn't name. Was it regret? Had she wasted drunken moments fantasising about a man who could take a life so brutally? Her eyes slid back to the smouldering ashes, hand gripping the long, tangled mess of blonde strands. She couldn't find the answer in the fading orange. But she knew with full certainty that she needed to make her own sacrifice for Kali's soul. A payment to the great goddess, in hopes Oryah would allow their souls to be reunited.

"Hello, Wyn."

He settled next to her, his finger brushing over hers. That tight squeeze of shame swept away the kernel of that nameless emotion. She turned from him to hide the grimace tightening her face.

"Hello, Mia."

Silence fell between them. Heavy, weighted silence. His fingers brushed over hers, and with a soft nod, he slid between hers until he was holding her hand, palm to palm. A sole comfort in the chill wind.

"She will be missed."

"She..." Mia had been spouting the same line over and over, and it felt insincere to say to Wyn. They had shared something deeper in that threadbare room. Instead, she said, "When will it be safe to feel again? You said it can't hurt me, but there is a dagger being held at my spine, and the tip is digging in."

Wyn sighed and squeezed her hand. "I can't tell you, Mia. It's something you will just know. If you need an escape, or someone to talk to—"

"Do you have a blade?" Mia cut in, letting go of his hand.

It was then or never. She needed to do it before Oryah turned her eye away.

Wyn arched a brow at her but didn't say a word as he yanked a dagger from his belt. Mia's trembling fingers grasped the hilt and stepped closer to the pyre. Her tongue slid over the words, unfamiliar in her mouth. Wyn's voice caught the fumbling vowels and began whispering with her. She gathered the thick bundle of her hair and, with a quick flick of her wrist, cut it off, shearing through until the blunt ends just brushed the tops of her shoulders.

Wyn's hand caught her own as she cut off the last of her hair. "You're not supposed to do this alone. Let me help you."

Mia shook her head, pulling away. "This is mine to bear alone, Wyn."

Her fingers released her hair, allowing her shining blonde tresses to be captured in the wallowing wind, spreading over the black ashes. Wyn was talking, but she couldn't really hear the words. Mia lost herself in the sight of her hair burning away, hoping it was enough. She would have bled herself dry to appease Oryah, but really, she was doing it for Kali. She would do anything for her sister.

Sixteen

As days, then weeks crept by, Mia worked quietly in Luc's studio, stretching canvas until the hammer slipped from the wood frame and struck her thumb, blackening her nail. Then James ordered her to scrub paintbrushes. She numbly watched the rainbows of watery paint swirl down the drain. Soon after, she was kicked out of the small washroom because she left splotches of mustard yellow on a brush, ruining one of Samuel's lacklustre landscapes. So, she'd stand, listless and numb in the gallery's corner until James cast her narrow-eyed looks of pity and allowed her to watch him craft for moments between her duties. With each whispered instruction from him, another murmur chorused from the apprentices.

"Luc's little plaything," they crooned at her with shit-eating smirks.

They all knew what she had promised.

It wasn't hard to deduce, with Luc's wandering hands and his lingering looks at Mia. She took it all with a sad indifference. Their words did not strike the soft flesh of her heart, nor did a lick of heat emerge from Luc's touch.

Mia would return home every day to collapse on her bed as if simply existing was exhausting. Sleep was elusive, with sheet-tangling night-mares of gaping wounds and pale, gaunt monsters. The soft siren's call of The Cauldron, the urge to lose herself in the burning whisky, was almost too strong to resist. Instead, she forced herself to remain staring at her velvet-backed chair until the sun rose, demanding Kali's ghost to appear. But she never did. Mia couldn't bring herself to feel the sharp, cutting edge of emotion, so it was replaced with a dull numbness.

She couldn't decide what was worse: bleeding out from the cuts, or feeling nothing.

Mia walked the muted hallways leading to her parents' room.

A draughty gloom had lowered over Rosda Manor. Once a place of light and laughter, it was suddenly filled with muffled cries and choking darkness.

She could hardly stand the sight of the smiling portrait of them hanging high above her, resisting the urge to slash the canvas. She could remember the heat of the room, the stiff ache of her back. Above all, Kali's musical giggle echoed in her ears. Each shake of her sister's shoulders cut into her, slicing into already bleeding flesh. Her fingers reached for Kali, but the horrors of that alley flashed over Mia's vision. Her sister's grin turned into a slack, gaping mouth, splashes of gore across her skin.

Mia scampered back from the portrait, running from the ghost haunting the halls.

She found herself in the doorway to her parents' bedroom, combating the tightness of her bodice. A panicked nervousness had emerged in her chest, and the damn boned cage wouldn't let her breathe. Anne sat propped up with a mountain of soft cushions, her hands holding a cup of tea. She had barely left her bed since the funeral, curled deep in the sheets. Lost to the outside world. Lost to her grief. Henry had spent more time there than ever, reading to her, making sure she ate, holding her while she wept.

"I'm off to the studio now, Mama," Mia announced.

Anne looked up from the steaming tea, a smile curled on her lips. The lines on her face seemed deeper, as if she had aged in the handful of weeks since Kali's funeral. However, a slight colour warmed her cheeks, and she was at least dressed for the day.

She was finally having a good day.

"Have a great day, Kali."

"It's Mia, Mama."

The corner of Anne's smile twitched down, and her hand trembled. The porcelain clattered together, falling from the bed and spilling the dark contents across the rug. Mia rushed in, picking the cup up. Dragging a handkerchief from her pocket, she dabbed at the spill. She glanced up at her mother. Anne's hands covered her face, and Mia could hear the deep huffs coming from her.

"Mama—"

Anne dropped her hands into her lap and let out a deep sigh. Her lips had thinned, and her brow furrowed. She almost looked disappointed in herself. "Of course it is you, Mia. My Mia, my moon in the night sky. I've been out of sorts, not my right self. I didn't even notice you cut all your hair off."

Mia tucked a loose strand behind her ear. "I did it for Kali..."

Anne's smile edged up, relaxing the muscles in her face. "She would have been so angry at you for cutting your hair. She always wanted your shining blonde locks. We always seem to want what we cannot have."

Mia rose, placing the empty teacup and the sopping handkerchief on the bedside table and ringing for Abigail. She cast a half-hearted smile over her shoulder and said, "She would have been downright furious."

"We would have never heard the end of it either," her mother added, a soft laugh coming from her.

"Never."

"Be safe, my Mia. Now, don't be late home. Your father said the Silver has instilled a curfew for women. They're to be out no later than the ninth bell."

"Only for women?" Mia mumbled, biting her tongue. *What if the monster has a taste for men? What if that monster has a taste for me?* Idris' soft, pleading face flashed over her mind. She cast it away, steeling herself.

"Why hasn't the curfew been put in before now? I heard that women in the lower city have been going missing—"

"And who have you been gossiping with?" her mother asked, flicking the blankets back. "You know you shouldn't believe everything you hear. Hartwinn is determined to keep his people safe from this monster. All his people, including those in the lower city."

"And the Silver?" Mia threw her hands up. "What are they doing? What have they found out about Kali?"

"Hartwinn has commanded the best lieutenants to be put on your sister's case. He wants to solve this as much as we do, Mia. Don't forget how much he loved her."

"Then why wasn't he at Kali's funeral?" His absence was only missed as her ashes had settled.

Her mother's shoulders tensed, her hands gripping the edge of the mattress. She took a long, strained breath and released it with a sigh. "Hartwinn had his reasons not to attend. Ones that hound him. Just know, he regrets it. There is nothing like fear, Mia, to make you work out what you want to fight for, or flee from. And Hartwinn chose to flee. Now, you better run off. I would hate for you to be late to the studio."

A look of steely determination had spread across her mother's face as if she were facing a deadly enemy on a battlefield. And as Mia thundered down the stairs, she realised Anne was facing an enemy that Henry couldn't battle for her. Her mother had begun the hard slog through the bloody mud and pelting rain, maybe not back to who she was, but back to who she thought she could be without Kali. As she stepped into the warm rays of the morning sun, Mia wondered if she had even glimpsed the same battlefield yet, or if she was still miles away, marching to her death.

Mia stood in front of the busy studio, gripping the leather strap of her bag. She couldn't bring herself to push through the door, to tie that starched apron and avert her eyes from Luc's leer, to hide from his passing gropes. She itched to create, to take charcoal to paper. However, she knew all she would create would be the flashes of her nightmares, and she had seen enough of those.

Nightmares. Nightmares for a disgusting creature. You deserve every last one, he whispered, making Mia clench her jaw.

Go away, you cretin, she whispered back, banishing the dark thoughts to the corner of her mind.

She turned on her heel and pushed her away into the bustling streets. Her legs took her far from the gold-lined streets of the upper city and into the sprawl of the lower city, past bars and those establishments the lonely ventured into.

Mia found herself at the only stretch of farmland Alderdeen could spare.

The homes, not made of brick and terracotta but wood, fell from the surrounding Sliva Forest. Even the cobblestone had faded to a simple dirt road. Rainbows of flowers and buzzing bees surrounded homes, with fae children laughing and squealing as their little legs took them over the lush grass. Fae refugees had populated the lands, mixing in the periphery of the city. A safe haven from the horrors of war. All thanks to Henry and his dedication to his people.

As she wandered down a skinny lane, her fingers trailing over the rough wooden walls, Mia wondered if he felt some sort of guilt for his hand in the disastrous battle that had cost him everything. She only knew snippets of his life before Alderdeen—well, before Anne. A warrior born of noble blood, without his royal father's name. A bastard. What broke Mia's heart the most was that he'd been married before, and she had tragically died in their marital bed, pushing his child into the world while Henry was battling King Ewan's armies. Neither survived. Mia admired how he had managed to put one foot in front of the other and not crumple completely.

She smiled and waved at the fae she knew, ducking her head at those who looked worried that a human was walking their streets. She made her way to a low wooden fence, letting the soft breeze pick up strands of hair. Leaning an elbow on the wobbly fence, her eyes danced over a simple house with an oak tree shading the wooden slats of the roof. The thick roots erupted from the dirt, and whoever lived there had planted flowers in the crevices, doting the earth with colour. Mia itched to capture it. She'd do anything to be able to mix colours so close to those she saw in nature.

The tree rustled in the breeze, harmonising with her sigh. Determined to push through whatever was blocking her, she dug through her bag, pulling out her leatherbound sketchbook and a pencil. She smoothed the paper with her hand, her pencil poised, ready to draw.

A scream ripped through the serenity of the day.

Mia's pencil skidded across the page as she jumped directly out of her skin. Her heart roared in her chest as she whirled around, searching for the source of the scream. Her legs moved before a single reasonable thought emerged between her ears. She skidded across the dirt, all care for her safety forgotten. She needed to reach her before more blood was carelessly spilt. Before another family had to stare into the funeral pyre. Her shoulder slammed into the wood, taking the brunt of her fall.

Mia was too late. Far too late.

Behind a barrel, a pair of slim legs splayed out, and a sickening amount of blood oozed in a thick, viscous pool. Mia's world shifted sideways, and her own scream joined the last of the dying's echoes. As her head hit the ground, her eyes rolled, searching for the green-eyed stranger. But she only found the gory fuel to etch more nightmares into the backs of her eyelids.

Seventeen

A knight of the Silver slammed his hand on the table, the sound reverberating around the small stone room deep in the cold, grey Palisade—or Pali, for short. If anything else, law and order reigned supreme. Mia woke from her dazed stupor with a jump. Her chair skidded behind her, scraping loudly as she attempted to flee from his hard gaze.

She had nothing to hide. She had done nothing wrong.

Just like the first time, the rough-handed knights shoved her into a cold, sparse room and asked her questions upon questions. She could answer none, only heaving frantic words. But this time, she kept her mouth shut and the lid on her panic.

Mia's tear-rimmed eyes rose from the table to the knight. She pinned her foulest glare at him, but her cheeks were flushed and tear-stained, and her bottom lip wouldn't stop wobbling. He didn't baulk, only cocking his head, like he was trying to work her out. Her gaze dropped to the stitched white lines that sat on his leather tunic, over his heart, signifying his high rank.

Anne was right. Hartwinn has really assigned the most experienced to Kali's case.

Mia scrubbed her tear-stained cheek with the blanket around her shoulders, pulling it over her hands. "I don't know what to say, Lieutenant Mylo. I just heard a woman scream."

"Just Mylo. Why do I keep finding ya standin' over dead bodies, miss?"

She shrugged. "Why do you keep letting women die in your city?"

He scoffed, sliding his hand back, slumping in the chair opposite her. "I don't do anythin'."

"That's my point," Mia replied flatly. "Why are you wasting your time talking to me when there is a deranged monster out there?" *And his name is Idris.*

"I don't think this is a waste of my time."

"I do, and I wish to go home."

"Not just yet, Miss Ashmore. I still have a few more questions. Why were ya out in the Westryn District?"

She squirmed in her chair, tucking a lock of hair behind her ear. "I..."

I can't say I was avoiding my groping boss.

Mylo noted her hesitation. "Yes?"

"I just went for a walk to get out of the upper city for some fresh air. Is that against the king's law?"

"No. It's not—"

"Then I will go wherever I please."

Mylo leant back in the chair, hand threaded in his lip, ankles crossed. A fake air of ease surrounded him as if he wanted her to mimic him. Mia scoffed at his attempt. She'd never feel comfortable within the cold stone walls of the Pali.

"Ya know how suspicious it is, right?" he asked, arching a brow at her. "Bein' at both scenes?"

Her gaze snapped to him, her lips pressed into a firm line. "One of those scenes was my sister, lieutenant, and I am aware of how it looks."

Mylo raised his hands in apology. "I'm stumped, Mia, honestly. These women keep dyin', and there isn't much in the way of evidence."

"What about...the others?"

His eyes hardened as his tongue worked around his mouth. "Nothin' aside from the bodies. It's like a phantom, a ghost doin' the killin'."

"There has to be something? Witnesses? A scrap of material? Anything?"

Mylo shook his head. "Nothin'."

"Nothing? You have to have something! Who has found these bodies, aside from me? What did they see?"

Mylo cleared his throat, shifting uncomfortably in his chair. "That's not for a lady's ears."

Mia stifled the urge to roll her eyes. "I've heard worse, Mylo."

"Care to enlighten me with any information ya have, then?" he asked, a smirk pushing up his mouth.

She quirked a brow and sat back. "Well played, sir, but like I said, I have nothing to say. Only that I'm sorry for the families of those who died, and may Oryah take care of their souls."

"Mia, I'm serious—"

A loud scuffle of feet and shouting voices came from beyond the door. He stood, muttering to himself, and cracked the door open. Mia caught glimpses of men wearing silver armour scuffling with a man in leathers.

"I demand to know the meaning of this," Wyn's deep voice boomed through the small room. "You have taken Lord Henry's daughter in for questioning without a chaperone? Have you lost your godsdamn mind?"

"Captain Wyn, you have no right to barge in there," a knight said from the hall.

"Like Heylla I don't," he snapped. "Mia!"

"I'm in here!' she called back, pushing away from the table, the blanket slipping off her shoulders.

Mylo's head snapped to her, a narrow-eyed glare skidding over her skin. "Ya called for Wyn Neverclove? Are ya fuckin' serious?"

"Better than my father, Lord Henry Ashmore."

The forceful shove of the door sent Mylo stumbling back into the wall. Wyn burst through, eyes searching for her. He exhaled when he found her and turned on his heel. He smoothed his coat, tucking a hair behind a pointed ear as if attempting to simmer his temper. "You. What is your name? Rank?"

"Mylo. Lieutenant, sir."

"Well, Lieutenant Mylo, I hope this isn't a new position, and you've reaped all the benefits from it. You'll be out back mucking stalls when I speak to Commander Dayvis about this terrible lapse of judgement."

"Wyn, there is—"

"That is Captain Wyn to you, boy, and you're lucky I haven't yet informed Lord Hartwinn about this. His Lordship cherishes Lady Mia."

"There is no need to involve the lor—"

Wyn's hand flew up, stopping Mylo spluttering. "Enough. Now, come Mia. We have somewhere to be."

Mia strode to Wyn and took his outstretched elbow. She cast a grin at the flushed lieutenant. "Pleasure, Mylo. I do hope we never see each other again."

Mylo had recovered enough of his dignity to smirk at Mia, and replied, "Nah, Miss Ashmore, we will see each other again. I can promise ya that."

Eighteen

The noisy tavern deep in the Westryn District was bustling with life. Tankards slammed down and satisfied sighs filled the tightly packed space. Fae laughed, slapping each other on the backs. Joy saturated the air, brushing over Mia's skin. Many cast wide grins and shook Wyn's hand with such vigour that she thought his arm would loosen in the socket.

She found it strange.

Death had roamed those streets, snatching away a life, but that wondrous thing filled each one of them. Life. It was abundant in the room, flowing freely like the ale being poured. Those people didn't fear Death. They drew him ever closer in a lover's embrace.

Mia slid into a booth hidden in a dark corner. Wyn soon followed, a frothing ale in each hand. He slopped it down in front of her, foam spilling down the sides. "Now, Mia, do you want to tell me what you were doing in an interrogation room in the Pali, and why I had to save your arse?"

She stared at the fizzing bubbles, lips pushing to the side. "I found another body," she whispered.

Wyn's gaze snapped to her as a soft curse left him. His warm, calloused hand fell on her wrist, thumb rubbing circles on the bony divot.

Mia exhaled, leaning back from the table. "I was too late, Wyn."

"You couldn't have done anything."

"Because I am a woman?"

"Good goddess, no. There is nothing like a woman cornered, all teeth and claws. But you had no weapons, Mia. No training. No way to defend yourself."

She scoffed. She had nervously avoided the sweaty, embarrassing training with Wyn by complaining of some strange ailment which seemed to only occur when she was ordered to go. Adolescence had made her awkward, giggly, and most of all, obsessed with him. Not much had changed in the years since.

"I suppose you're right," Mia grumbled, not pulling away from his touch. "I didn't think, Wyn. I just ran, hoping to get to her before Death snatched her away."

"That poor soul in the alley, or Kali?"

She shot him a withering look. He was right in more ways than one. Maybe something in her wanted to protect someone, to combat the horrors that filled her. But that was pointless. Nothing could save her.

Mia exhaled, melting away the tension in her shoulders. She took a small sip of the bitter ale before she answered. "It's like there's a disconnect between my mind and body, Wyn." She tapped the side of her head and then covered her heart with a hand. "One knows Kali is gone, but another doesn't want to accept it."

"Grief is a cruel mistress."

Silence stretched between them, both contemplating the floating words. Wyn's hand travelled up over her shoulder and settled at the base of her skull. His thumb dragged up and down the tense muscle. "Why did you call for me, Mia?"

She leant into his touch, smirking at him, the abyss of sweaty pleasure in a fingertip's reach, luring her to dip her toes in, seeking the relief she had once found. "You were a better option than having Henry storm the Silver, demanding demotions for sullying my reputation—wait, you did that."

Wyn chuckled, each ale-infused breath wafting over Mia. His fingers slid over her jaw, tucking that annoying strand of hair behind an ear. "Are you…"

"What?"

"Worried about sullying your reputation?"

Her smirk curled higher. "Are you going to sully it?"

All it took was one brief look down to his lips to make Wyn close the space between them. He brushed his lips over hers.

A silent *yes*.

Her fingers tangled in his dark locks, pulling him closer, knees bumping as he forced her against the worn leather of the booth. He gripped her rib cage tightly, cupping her just under her breast, thumb caressing the soft fabric of her blouse, sending sparks right to her core. Her tongue slid over the seam of his lips, diving in.

He tasted like yeasty ale and all things bad for her.

She devoured it.

A hand from the abyss glided up over her foot, slowly tracing her ankle as if the caress would be convincing enough for her to throw herself off the edge right into the murky darkness. Perhaps Mia was ready to fall again and have the air ripped from her lungs. To be lost to pleasure.

He broke the consuming kiss, chest heaving.

"Fuck, Mia," Wyn breathed into the space they shared. "Do you actually want me, or is this another attempt to escape the shit in your head?"

Her fingers dragged over his tensed thigh, swirling around the silver buckle of his belt, inching closer to the hard bulge developing in his pants. "Can't I want both?"

Wyn sighed and leant back. "We should…"

"Get out of here?"

"No, Mia. I don't think we should be alone again."

She snatched her hand away and flopped back hard into the booth. Rejection sent a hot poker through her stomach, searing through her soft, squishy innards. Right to the place that she kept hidden, piercing it with a fatty sizzle. The cruel whispering played in her ear. *Ruined, disgusting creature.*

Her words came out harsh, wobbling with emotion. "Don't want me now that I'm used?"

Wyn's face pinched at the word. "*Used?* I don't give a fuck how many men you've had, Mia. I'd bend you over and take you on this table until you couldn't form a coherent word if I had my way. But..."

Mia crossed her arms, closing herself off to Wyn and the desire building in her lower belly. "It's Henry, isn't it?"

"We have just mended the hurt from the past, Mia, and I don't wish to—"

"Fuck it up over a woman?"

"Did he ever tell you why we fought in the first place?"

Mia shook her head, not trusting her own venomous words.

"Over a woman. But not any woman. My sister, his beloved bride. Kitra. I held such anger for him when she died in his bed, while he was off trying to prove his worth to his piece of shit father. Regardless, Mia, you are not just some woman. You are his whole world."

She exhaled, eyes falling on the amber fizzing ale. Annoyingly, he was right once again. Falling into bed for a meaningless tumble—well, it meant more than a meaningless tumble to both of them—would be disastrous. She forced down the rejection with a deep gulp of ale, trying not to let that whisper slither over her and ruin what friendship had developed between them with venomous words.

Wyn reached over, tilting her jaw up with his forefinger. His face had softened, lips parting. "Trust me, my mind rarely lingers on those I spend time with between the sheets, but you, *M'eudail Mia*, I cannot seem to forget about."

Mia's tongue curled around the fae words—*my darling*. He called her his darling. Her cheeks heated at the simple phrase.

"It was something, wasn't it?"

He grinned, huffing a laugh. Leaning his elbow on the table, he traced his finger over the condensation rings. "You seemed to enjoy yourself...quite a bit."

Mia took a deep swallow of her lukewarm beer, finishing the foamy froth, then winked at him with a smirk. "Don't worry, Wyn, your love-making skills are up to scratch."

They had strayed close again, even as their bodies leant into each other, fingers creeping over the cracked leather. Desire was consuming, intoxicating. She knew the feeling after being drunk on it for weeks. But she didn't know how to enjoy it with restraint.

He nodded at her empty glass. "Want another one?"

Mia wiped her lips across her sleeve. She couldn't play that game with Wyn. Not with a friendship blossoming between Henry and him. "I better get going. The curfew starts soon, and I don't wish to be dragged to the Pali again."

As she slid from the booth, Wyn grabbed her wrist, stopping her. "What I promised you at the funeral stands. I will always be here for you. I'm always here to get you out of a jam."

Mia's hand slid over his, her thumb circling. "Thank you, Wyn. Maybe you'll be my knight in shining armour one day, rushing out to save me."

That made him laugh, throwing his head back, eyes crinkling. "No, Mia, you won't need me. You'll save yourself."

"Thank you, Wyn. For all of it," Mia said, leaning forward. Without hesitation, she pressed her lips to his cheek, then fled into the night.

Nineteen

Mia splashed through the muck-filled puddles pooling around the slick cobblestones, her hands shoved into her armpits, feeling the unseasonable chill in the air. The lanterns were doused, leaving the street cloaked in darkness. She kept peeking over her shoulder, convinced the echoes of her boots were another set following her.

She cursed herself for not asking Wyn to walk her home.

The dark streets of Alderdeen were dangerous. Now that the curfew was in full force, no women roamed the city. Only those lurked who had let the night strip them of the last shreds of whatever made them human. Rowdy laughter echoed from a street over, and the sound of glass shattering caused her heart to quicken. Her legs drove her faster as shouts followed her. She glanced over her shoulder to see a group of drunken devils lit by moonlight, readying to snatch her.

"Hey, girl, what are you doing out so late?" one of them called out.

Mia clutched herself tighter, biting down on her tongue only to stop words spilling from her.

Just get out.

Just keep going.

Don't make a fuss.

Don't make them angry.

A hand gripped her shoulder, yanking her back and wafting the harsh stench of cheap whisky over her.

"Do you need help? We can help you, can't we, lads?"

His question earnt a chuckle from the other men.

"I'm quite all right. I don't—"

Fingers skimming over her rear made her scurry backwards. Her gaze worked over each of the rough-faced, leering men, letting their faces sear into her mind.

"Let us walk you home. Don't you know there is a monster snatching girls off the street?"

"No, the monsters are here with me," she mumbled.

One narrowed his eyes at her. "What did you just say?"

Her hands bunched into fists. "I said, I am all right, and I don't need help from you."

The one who'd had his hand on her stepped forward, a frown cutting across his ruddy face. "Bit mouthy, are ya? Maybe we should show what we do to mouthy girls."

Mia's hands flashed out, pushing him the square in the chest and making him stumble back into the others. Her boot slipped on the slick cobblestone as she twisted away, but by some miracle, she stayed upright. She hurdled towards an alley, breath strangled, hot sweat covering her. The sounds of scuffling feet and demands for her to stop fought to catch up with her. Without a glance back, she careened down into the maze of laneways of the lower city, hoping to lose the men. She could hear them yell for her, their words bitter, angry. "You stupid bitch. I hope the creature gets you!"

Mia braced against a moss-covered wall, leaning her forehead against the dampness. She clasped her hands over ears, fingers digging into her scalp, squeezing her eyes closed. That warmth emerged in her chest, releasing a slip of shadowy mist. Velvet wrapped around her wrist. Another wave of panic crashed into her, sending her throat tight.

"Get away from me, whatever you are," she demanded, cracking an eye open.

They turned their unseen gaze on her, watching her. *"Ozul,"* the shadows whispered. *"We Ozul."*

Mia didn't care what *Ozul* was. She wanted them gone. With a hiss and a wave of her hand, the shadows misted away.

The sharp screech of metal against metal had Mia straightening, peering down the alley.

"Hello?" she called out.

The sewer lid had been pushed free and discarded on the cobblestone. She took a cautious step towards it, body tensed. A flash of a pale body darted in her periphery, making her whirl around, finding nothing. But another flash made her jerk away.

Something was edging closer, ghostly fingers brushing over her skin, hot breath on her neck and a pair of eyes creeping over her.

Mia's heartbeat thrashed in her ears, sending the panicked thudding around her skull. She took a wobbly step back, her heel snagging on the edge of the iron sewer lid. Then she was falling. Two hands caught her, dragging her to a solid chest before she could crumble and fall to her death down in the sewer system of Alderdeen.

"I got you, Little Witch," Idris breathed into her hair. "Now, you have to be quiet—"

The terrified screech she'd been holding in reverberated around the stone, piercing her eardrums.

Idris is going to kill me.

She thrashed against him, his arms encircling her like iron shackles. His hand clamped over her mouth, allowing her scream to spill between his fingers. He dragged her back, legs flaying. Ozul slid from the dark corners, swirling in the air.

"Good goddess, do you want that thing to rip both our throats out?" Idris hissed in her ear. "Calm down. I'm not going to hurt you."

In the struggle, his hand slipped over her chin. Mia was feral, determined to get away by any means necessary. She bit down on the fleshy part between his thumb and pointer finger. Her teeth tore into him, blood coating her tongue. It tasted strange, bitter and herbaceous.

Idris yelped, dropping Mia to her knees, blood pooling in the corners of her mouth.

Her eyes rose to the tiled roof above her. A person—or so she thought—was crouched down on the edge, long fingers curling around the gutter. She could only make out the silhouette of a man in a threadbare cloak waving in the wind, but something was wrong about him. He twitched and rolled his shoulders, as if he weren't contained in his skin.

"Thank you," he called out, his voice cracking with manic laughter. "I wasn't entirely satisfied after my delicious little appetiser earlier, and now you've given me a main course."

Idris growled and took a step forward, the silver of his blade glinting in the moonlight. She hadn't even noticed he had drawn a weapon, but the monster who'd slayed her sister didn't use a sword. He used his teeth and claws, tearing skin from muscle and ligament from bone, leaving a gory mess.

"Come down here and try to take a bite, then," Idris yelled.

"I don't think so. Not with your shiny little needle out."

With that, the creature scrambled back and disappeared from view.

Mia sagged to the cold, wet road, exhausted, only the dregs of whatever made her heart race and hands tremble left in her. Jamming her fingers in her ears, she curled tighter as if the world could simply disappear. But it never did.

In the distance, cries for gods who were not watching filled the night air, waking barking dogs and shouting mothers, calling for the Silver. She braced herself for that last drowning scream as those devilish men who stalked her with dark thoughts met another type of monster—one that craved blood, chaos and death.

Twenty

A letter sat on her bed, basking in the afternoon sun when Mia returned home from yet another mind-numbing day at Luc's studio. The envelope had her name written across it in swoops and dips. Her finger traced the dried ink, and she muttered, "Beautiful."

She slumped onto her mattress, yanking off her boots. Days had passed since Idris had swept her into his arms and carried her home. During the arduous trek back to Rosda Manor, his only words were, "Do you believe me now?"

His words plagued her mind, forcing her to replay every sentence, every glimpse of the creature over and over. Until she could do nothing but numbly watch the grey sludge of the murky paint water swirl down the drain, taking everything she knew with it. Once, late at night, she had whispered, "Yes." But then, in the same breath, it was, "No".

Mia groaned, flopping back.

She still didn't have an answer.

Gripping the letter, she ripped into the envelope, careful not to tear her name. A simple note was inside.

Mia,

You need answers and I can give them to you.

The Cauldron.
Tomorrow night. Seventh bell.
Ask for me.
Idris.

She sat straight up, studying each letter, hoping for words that would help her confused thoughts. But he had only added to them. She glanced out the window at the lowering sun. Yet another day had passed with the monster who took Kali from her roaming free, and she remained frozen, still.

Not anymore.

Mia poised to scrunch the note up. Instead, she folded it and slipped it into her pocket, turning to the blank canvas. Her eyes trailed over the stark white material, seeing where colours could go, where shadows could stretch. Her trembling fingers brushed over the wooden handles and the rough hog bristles, to the smooth tubes of paint. With a steadying breath, she picked up a brush and dolloped a velvety purple on her palette, then allowed herself to spill across the canvas.

"Just a drop of ivy green. Not a smidge more," James instructed the next day, squeezing a fat blob of green right next to a bright yellow.

With his palette knife and a flick of his wrist, he blended the colours together to make a lime green. Then, taking a minute amount, he flicked at the base of a landscape he was instructing the students to paint.

Mia loathed landscapes. She found the detailed painting of small parts of a building mind-numbingly boring.

Each apprentice nodded appreciatively, murmuring amongst themselves. Silver from palette knives gleamed, paints mixed and the studio filled with quiet concentration.

Mia paused her sweeping for just a moment, forcing herself to remember the instructions James had barked. Samuel angled his chin over his shoulder, his murky brown eyes taking her in with a hint of disgust. She hated that Luc would clap him on the back and give him praise for work that was bland and boring.

"What do you think you're looking at?"

Her gaze dropped to the bristles on the broom. "Nothing."

"Then get back to work. I think I see a windowsill that needs dusting."

"Enough, Samuel. Leave her be," James snapped, eyes never leaving the canvas.

Samuel turned to her, a sly smirk cut across his face. He leered at her, making her skin crawl. "What, James? Does she suck your c—"

The broom handle slammed into his guts, causing him to double over. Gasping for air, he wheezed the word "slut" at Mia.

"Call me that again," she demanded, bending over and forcing him to meet her furious glare. "I dare you."

"Mia Ashmore! Did you just strike one of my apprentices?" Luc's voice boomed.

Mia's stomach jumped into her throat, causing her to step back. Her eyes flashed from Samuel to James, who was scowling into his work, then, ever so slowly, to Luc. He stood in the doorway, brows raised, his arms crossed.

"She was just—"

He held a hand up, silencing James. The command that shot him was hard. "My office, Mia. Now."

"Yes, Master Luc."

She pushed the broom into Samuel's chest and followed her master.

THE DOOR CLICKED CLOSED, THEN A BOLT SLID HOME, locking her in with a man she'd been avoiding being alone with since they had struck their bargain. Her sweaty palms looped over and over, twisting with her stomach.

Luc settled next to her. A stray hand brushed over her rear, his warm breath spreading over her. He was closer than he'd been in days.

"You can't go around striking my men, Mia, or the offer of apprenticeship I drafted will be destroyed. Do you want that?"

Mia's eyes snapped up at him, her stomach coiled tighter. "No, Master Luc. It won't happen again, I promise. I didn't think, I just..." She paused, collecting herself. "Samuel was being crude."

His fingers crept over her wrist, trapping her in a tight grip. "What did he say?"

Mia swirled the crass words around her mouth. With a sharp tug from Luc, they spilt from her, heating her cheeks with each mutter.

"Now, never mind what that idiot said. Have you ever let someone between those lips, or is that something I'm going to have to teach you?"

A smirk spread across his face, but his onyx eyes lingered on her lips.

Mia flushed even hotter at the intensity of his question. Hazy memories of tasting salty flesh, fingers threaded through her hair and the hard stone cutting into her knees surfaced, coating her insides in that hot, sticky tar of shame. Her chin dropped to her chest, brows bunched, and in a quiet voice, she said, "I don't think we should be speaking of—"

"Oh, yes, my *precious* reputation," Luc cut in with a hint of mocking in his tone. "You haven't always been a good girl, have you?"

Mia's gaze rose slowly, finding him staring down at her with a lusty, dark look. Deep down, she enjoyed being looked at with desire—that feeling of being wanted. But not from Luc. There was malice in his gaze. And, like a rabbit trapped in a hunter's snare, it made her nervous.

A small shake of her head. "I wouldn't say I've been especially good or bad."

Luc laughed, his chest bumping into her arm. "You're a surprise, Mia. A very welcome one."

A splash of relief swirled around in her chest, taking the sticky shame with it. Her shoulders drooped, as her hands loosened around her apron. "So you will not punish me?"

Luc's grin widened, showing off a set of crooked white teeth, shaking his head. "You won't be facing any punishment today. Quite the opposite. It's time for a *lesson*."

Mia exhaled and let a relieved smile stretch across her face. "Thank the goddess. You know, I couldn't bare to watch Samu—"

Luc leant down and pressed his lips to hers, stealing her words.

Nothing.

She felt nothing.

Not the heat of arousal, nor the stomach-churning, skin-creeping feeling of revulsion she had expected. Mia didn't know what was worse. She should have felt something—anything. But she had poured herself out over the cobblestone, in those mens' beds and across the worn bar of The Cauldron.

She simply had nothing left.

He stepped her back against the door, tongue invading her mouth. He tasted bitter as if he was coated in poison.

This feels wrong. All of this feels wrong.

His hand slipped from her face to her skirts, yanking them up and brushing higher over the clasps of her stockings. He found the edge of her lace undergarment slipping under. He circled the crease between her thigh and her core in haphazard strokes, only a finger's distance from where he intended to touch her. Mia's eyebrows met in the middle, confused.

I've never had a man not find my entrance, nor miss the sensitive bundle of nerves. Yes, brush it for a matter of moments, not drawing any pleasure, but never miss it completely.

His lips left hers to drop to the swell of her collarbone, sucking and biting her flesh. She froze, not whispering a single word. She let him keep rubbing the wrong spot, coaxing something that would never come.

"God, you're so wet for me, aren't you?"

No, that's sweat. "Yes, Luc. So wet."

"Come for me, Mia," he whispered roughly. "I want to hear you fucking moan."

Her eyes flashed to the ceiling, biting down on her lip. "Luc—"

"Come for me. Now."

A loud, exaggerated fake moan slipped from her lips. She shut her eyes, gripping his tunic as if she could feel the radiating pleasure. All she did was pray for it to be over.

"Good girl. You've done so well for me." His hand dropped from between her legs to the buckle of his belt, retching it apart. "You'll be ready to take me now."

Mia's hand snapped to his wrist, mind scrambling for an excuse—anything—and what came out her mouth shocked even her. "Luc, I've never gone this far with a man. We should slow down."

A rotten lie.

She had been with men, in every sense. Yet, she knew those words would stop him, that he'd take some sick satisfaction in thinking he was the first man to touch her.

And she was right.

His eyes lit up like she was a sort of rare art, and he was a desperate collector.

"You're a virgin?"

"Yes," she lied again.

Luc pressed his lips against hers tenderly. His hands slid up to cup her face, resting his forehead against hers. "You're right, Mia. We should slow down and not get carried away with our want for each other. I don't want you to lose that precious gift against this door."

Mia schooled her head into a tight-lipped nod, and not the grimace that nearly emerged at the words "precious gift". She hadn't ever considered her virginity a gift, nor had Wyn when he took it from her during those moments of sweaty bliss. Mia realised she didn't lose a single thing when she was tangled in those sheets, seeing stars, but she had gained something. Command of her body, of her own pleasure, and that was power.

Luc was talking, but her spluttered words cut him off.

"Luc, I think you have the wrong idea. I don't want to do *that*. Not here, not with you."

His hands snapped tightly around her cheeks, squeezing her lips apart. "Do you want to be an apprentice here or not, Mia? Do you wish for you and your pathetic art to fade into obscurity? You need me, girl. I don't need you, or the inexperience you'd bring to my bed. It'll do you a world of good to remember that when you speak so brazenly to me again," Luc spat, the light fading from his eyes, chilling her.

The carrot he dangled in front of her was the only thing Mia had.

She wouldn't let that slip through her fingers. Even so, she couldn't meet his gaze when she mumbled, "Yes, Master Luc."

He dragged her closer until their noses touched, until her own fearful expression reflected in his eyes. And she knew that was what he wanted. He craved that trembling fear leaching into her flesh, so he could taste it when he devoured her, body and soul.

"Then you will do as I ask. And if that's on your back with those legs spread right here in this fucking office, then you will do it."

That warmth brushed along each rib, coaxing her to free it, to not allow a man to speak to her like she was nothing but a warm body to rut into. She clenched her fist, feeling the soft velvet squish in her fingers. The shadows. Her hand slid under her apron, hidden away. But she didn't silently demand they leave.

Luc shoved her away with a grunt, making her stumble back into the door. "Now get out, Mia. I presume there is a paintbrush for you to wash."

Twenty-One

Mia scrubbed her lips with her sleeve, erasing the rancid taste of Luc's kiss. Her fist crumpled Idris' note as laughter from The Cauldron leaked into the street. She silently cursed. She did need answers on how to end the monster before anyone else faced those sheet-tangling terrors that haunted her every step. But what she needed even more was a stiff drink to pluck up the courage to face Idris.

When Mia pushed through the swinging doors. Rough men—human, fae and everything in between—occupied the tables, laughing loudly and shouting words that would make even the roughest knight of the Silver blush. Leering gazes turned sour as they skimmed over the scar that cut across her cheek. She knew that not a single one would care once she dragged them into that alley. None ever did.

Her fingers found the rough edge of the scar, covering it as she shouldered through the packed bodies to the worn wood of the bar. Her hands spread out over the nicks and dents, calling Benny's name. His gaze found her, a wide grin spreading across his face.

"Mia! You're a sight for sore eyes."

She smiled back and said, "You're a welcome one."

He held aloft a bottle of whisky, the brown spirit splashing around the bottle. Mia wet her lips, almost tasting the abyss it would bring, but shook her head.

"Water...just water," she gritted out. *I guess I'm doing this sober.*

Benny arched a brow and placed a glass with a splash of water and three ice chips in front of her. She swished the clean, crisp taste around her mouth, washing away the bitter poison that Luc had left in her molars.

Benny leant on the bar, brawny arms crossed, eyes hooded. "I heard about your sister, Mia, and I was very sorry to hear it. I lost my own sisters. Bloody Heylla, it'll be going on seventeen years now." He scrubbed his stubbled jaw, then continued, "If you ever need to talk to someone who knows...that ache in your chest, I'm a good listener."

Mia stared into the swirling ice cubes, allowing his words to soak into her mind. She looked up at him, the same sadness she saw in the mirror reflected in his eyes. She bit her lip, stopping herself from spilling across the bar.

Not tonight. Tonight, I'm here for Idris.

"Benny..." She didn't know what to say.

He sighed, pushing off the bar. "It's hard to find words, Mia, isn't it?"

"Words are easy. You can say things without meaning. But actions, Benny, they are much more powerful."

With a nod, a tight-lipped smile appeared on his face. "Right you are, Mia. Now, down to the business of the evening. I presume you are looking for Idris. He is waiting in the back office for you."

Her eyebrows bunched in confusion. "How did you know I was here to see him?"

"He may have told me to expect you, and he is kind of the boss around—"

"He runs this bar?"

"No, Mia. He *owns* this bar."

Her mouth fell open, and a shocked splutter left her mouth. He had been there the entire time, only a room away. And Benny had known. He'd known as she poured herself out over the bar for days in drunk, slurred fantasies, detailing each and every thing she'd let Idris do to her with waggled eyebrows and exaggerated moans. But more mortifying was the fact that he'd been there when she'd taken men by the hand and left. The urge to launch herself at the barman and strangle the life from him was almost too strong to resist.

"You knew this the whole time," was all she said through a clenched jaw.

Benny held his hands up, his grin spreading into a mischievous smirk. "I can make it up to you."

Mia's eyes narrowed. "Go on."

"Something expensive, and old, and it would piss Idris off to no end."

She returned a devious smirk. "Now I'm listening."

WITH TWO GLASSES IN ONE HAND AND A DUSTY, ANCIENT sea-green bottle with a peeling label in the other, Mia swung the door open to the office without knocking. She found Idris leaning back in a worn leather chair, ankles crossed at a wide, dark wood desk, thumbing through pages in a book. Her eyes flashed up the spine. *Guide To Witch Bloodlines.* Her book. She hadn't realised she'd lost it in the flurry of her bloody discovery. He flicked a page, eyebrow arching. "Interesting reading material. Are you researching your kind?"

"All witches were exterminated, burnt to extinction years ago, so no," Mia replied flatly. "And hello to you, too, Idris."

"Hello, Little Witch."

She placed the glasses down with a *clink* over the top of scrawled letters and bills. Yanking at the crumbling cork, a fruity, spiced warmth hit her nose. She glugged the dark maroon liquid into each of the glasses, spilling fat drops onto the scattered parchment. "I would prefer you call me Mia, thank you."

His eyes dropped from her to the glass, then to the bottle, his nostrils flaring. "That's—"

"*Expensive*, I would presume. And old, considering the layers of dust on it."

Mia pushed the half-filled glass towards him. Curling a hand around her own, she snooped against her better judgement. Her steps took her around the small room, fingers undoing the button on her collar. Her eyes swept over each painting, book and trinket. Despite everything being meticulously placed, the room still felt as lived in as his home had.

Mia sipped the wine, allowing the deep berry taste to explode on her tongue. Spicy heat radiated down her chest. With each tiny sip, the flavour developed deeper into a ripe plum taste. It was delicious.

She glanced over her shoulder to watch Idris consider the fading label with a strange intensity. His eyebrows twitched inwards, his only sign of annoyance. "Now, the murders—"

"Who are you?" she cut in. Her finger traced over a worn, yellowed map over ancient divides that no longer existed; King Ewan's ruthless conquering of the land had destroyed them. He had dominated the land, but the Northryn Fae had slowed him down, sacrificing hundreds of their own to do so, years before even she was born. Yet, the fae and the humans still had spats over land, sheep—anything, really. King Ewan's desire to rule the entirety of Zeroth knew no bounds.

His eyes snapped from the bottle to Mia. "Me?"

She flashed an eye roll over her shoulder. "Yes, you. I presume you're not a sergeant in the Silver, nor is this an official investigation."

He didn't answer her, instead taking a long swig of wine. "Who I am is not important, nor is the legitimacy of this investigation. The creature attacking women is, and how we end it."

Mia hummed in agreement, finding a seat across from Idris. The worn leather sank under her weight, but she resisted the pull into its comfortable leathery depth, instead perching on the edge. "What now?"

He tilted his head and gave her a slow, considered look. "You've already agreed to help me? That didn't take a lot of convincing."

Mia squirmed in her chair, clutching the glass a fraction tighter. She was deciding on what truth to let slip, or was it a tale she wanted to twist? Mia decided on a truth—a singular truth.

"I need to find whatever killed my sister, and I want to stare it deep in its eyes"—she took another sip—"and send it back to Heylla."

Idris softly exhaled. "Revenge isn't always the answer, Little Witch. It plants something dark deep inside you and feeds off the bitterness that revenge eventually brings."

Mia's eyes rose to his, straying too close to that choking emotion. She cracked half a smirk and cocked a brow. "Or maybe I'm trying to see if you slip up so I can haul you to the Silver myself. After all, people have described me as charming."

Idris laughed, a smile stretching across his face, dimples divoting his cheeks. "'Charming' isn't the word I'd choose."

"Well, pray tell, how would you describe me?"

"Clumsy and weak-stomached," he murmured into his wine glass.

She narrowed her eyes. "Excuse me?"

"Oh, nothing. 'Charming' fits," Idris replied, finishing his drink.

A satisfied sigh rumbled somewhere deep in his chest, causing a spark to dance at her core. She crossed her legs, demanding that it stop.

"I told Ben never to open this," he said, peering into his empty glass. "This was a special bottle."

Mia took the tiniest sip. She couldn't lose her edge. Not with the call of the abyss so close, tempting her with promises of sweet nothings. Idris sloshed the wine into his glass, then lifted it to the low lantern light, admiring maroon fractures of light through the sea-green bottle.

"This is vampyre wine, Mia, and a fucking rare one at that. It's made in barrels infused with magic, allowing a plain wine to become something more exquisite. It's allowed to ferment for years—centuries, even. Soaking in flavour, but steeping in the magic."

"Does it have any effects?"

He swirled the alcohol, coating the glass with a red sheen. "Effects?"

"You know, fae wine makes you elated and giggly. Human wine makes you sad and sloppy. What does this rare vampyre wine do?"

His gaze dipped to her pulsing artery, then lingered on her cleavage, exposed in flashes of silk and lace. The tip of his tongue slipped over his top lip at an agonising pace. Mia's eyes never left his face, searching for answers about who he was. Or maybe it was to take in each wrinkle, freckle and scar that lined his face.

When his gaze returned to hers, that honeyed desire stared back at her. "It makes you taste divine."

Mia bit down on her lip as heat flushed her chest, leaking into her cheeks. Her breath fought to even out. He leant forward and discarded his glass. She rose from her chair, curling her hand around the edge of the desk.

Something beyond Mia's understanding drew her to him, forcing them together. It was like a firm hand on each of their spines, pushing whether they liked it or not.

Like some timed dance, they leant in until their heads tilted in opposite directions, lips only a fraction apart, smelling the warm berry on one another's breath. The memory of how his firm thigh felt between her legs lit a flame, turning her core molten. He breathed her in in a deep, chest-expanding breath. Her hand slipped over the papers, brushing her fingertips against his, waking him.

Idris sat back heavily in his chair, breaking the tension, growing the air with a snap of his fingers. He left Mia standing, her chest heaving and her body hot with arousal.

"Idris—"

"The other night? That was a lapse in judgement, Mia. It cannot be repeated. This cannot be repeated," he interrupted, his voice hard but wavering as if the words were hard for him to say.

A flash of cold, sweaty embarrassment washed over her, making her sit straight down. Her spine was stiff and her shoulders tense, poised to run.

Idris was speaking, but the whispers of the dark voice drowned out his words. *See? Even he doesn't want you. Nothing. Worthless. Unlovable. Scarred freak.*

"Go away," Mia whispered in such a small voice, she could hardly hear herself.

She barely caught the end of Idris' sentence. "—you work at Luc Renniak's art studio, don't you?"

Her hands clenched in her lap. "Yes, I do."

Idris gave her that furrowed, cocked head look again. Confusion. "How? You didn't get chosen by a guild master."

"I didn't realise one of the most embarrassing moments in my life had spread to the dark, dank taverns of Alderdeen. I used my charming personality," Mia replied drily.

A realisation dawned in his eyes and he sat back, gaze dragging down her body. But this time, instead of lust, judgement flicked. That simple look made anger bubble in her.

"Didn't know you were the type."

"The type?"

"Someone who uses their charms—"

"First, you know nothing about me. You haven't even bothered to try."

He straightened, opening his mouth to speak. Mia continued, her tone cutting. "Second, if I use my body for anything, it's none of your business, and I will not be shamed by you."

"Mia—"

She held a finger up, silencing him with a snap of his jaw. "Third, we are here to find my sister's murderer. That is all. So keep all this friendly chitchat to yourself. Now, where do we start?"

Idris stared at her for a moment, lips clenched tight until she motioned for him to talk with an annoyed wave of her hand. "At the beginning, Little Witch. At the site of the first murder."

Twenty-Two

Mia's fist slammed on the door, sending the sound of thumping down the peaceful, misty street. The morning sun had just risen, casting rays of pink and orange over the sandstone building, cutting through the lingering fog, waking the sleepy city and its inhabitants.

She knocked again, her impatience clear with each *slam* and shift of her feet.

Mia bundled herself deeper into her cloak. It wasn't heavy enough to stop the early morning chill from seeping into her flesh. "Hurry up, Idris. It's freezing," she muttered.

A dishevelled, shirtless Idris cracked the door, squinting at the light. "Goddess, what time is it?" he croaked, voice thick with sleep. "And how do you remember where I live?"

"How I wish I could forget, but it's seared into my mind. Now, are we going to do this or not? I cannot be late for work."

As Idris opened the door wider, exposing more of his bare chiselled torso, Mia's eyes were fixed on the elaborate swirls carved into the wood rather than the line of dark hair that trailed down from his navel into the lowly slung waistband of his pants.

"Do you want to come in?"

"No. I want you to show me where the first murder was. Now get dressed," she snapped, turning away, adding under her breath, "It's distracting."

Idris chuckled and closed the door.

Mia kicked at the rocks with her worn boots, scuffing a toe. Her brown trousers hugged her thighs and gripped her hips, but the blue, billowy blouse she had pulled on hid most of her body. She'd decided she should dress as the men did so she was taken more seriously. But she knew, deep down inside, that a pair of pants wouldn't ever change their opinions of her.

The door clicked closed behind her, making her glance over her shoulder. Idris stood in the doorway of his house, wrapped in a forest-green cloak, squinting at the rising sun. Mia pulled him from his stoop. Their gazes dropped to her hand, gripping his sleeve, and she let go of him as if he'd burnt her.

Careless, Mia. That was careless, she thought to herself.

"The sun is somehow brighter this morning," he groaned, hiding in the shadows of his hood. "And there is an awful thumping in my head from that damn vampyre wine."

"I told you..." Mia crooned, tapping her pouted lips with her index finger, turning to him. "What did I say exactly? Oh, yes, that you'd be sorry for finishing off that bottle."

Idris' hooded gaze slid over to her, burning his unimpressed glare into her. She knew his eyebrows had twitched together. "Now, if someone hadn't opened a four-hundred-year-old bottle of wine on a whim, only to drink a mouthful, I wouldn't have had to finish it and then get put to bed by my own barman."

Mia whistled and then flashed him a toothy grin. "Four hundred years old, hey? No wonder it was a bit vinegary."

"Vinegary? You thought a priceless rare wine was vinegary? You simply haven't developed your taste yet, but with age—"

"So you're old? That's one thing I've learnt about you. You're just a grumpy old man," she cut in, screwing her nose up at him.

Idris grumbled a curse. "You speak as if I'm this decrepit elderly man, when in actual fact, I'm quite young for a —"

A laugh slipped from her, spilling onto the street. She gripped her sides, letting that light feeling dance around her rib cage. Mia couldn't remember the last time she had laughed. He watched her with a strange intensity, then turned his face away. She swore she saw the bright white of his teeth from under the hood.

"Ah, I see. Benny offers that service to all his customers. There were times he just brought me to his apartment when I was too belligerent to walk all the way to the manor."

"No, Little Witch, only those who are important to him."

Mia felt her smile waver and fade away as she remembered why she walked those streets with Idris, why she knew Benny at all. The amusement was squeezed from her, dying at the sharp claws of grief.

"How far away is it?"

"Not far. Maybe three blocks."

She nodded, eyes on the slow waking up of the city. Stall owners pulling up their canopies, stacking their shelves with their ware for the day's oncoming customers. Storekeepers flipping open signs, stretching in the soft tendrils of the early morning sunlight. There was a quiet safety in the empty streets, fog-laden and silent. A sereneness—one only seen when the sun had just begun to show her face.

Mia exhaled, suddenly realising that was how she chose to remember Alderdeen, rather than in the dark night, when groups of men whistled or chased her into the burning light of a shop front.

For once—maybe for the first time—Mia craved to paint a landscape of pale yellows and burnt oranges, of mortar and roofs, of the lightest greys of the soft, lingering mist and the deepest forest greens, of Idris' swirling cloak. She fought to sear the image in her memory, but the sharp, nutty allure of a vendor dragged her down a side alley. She veered off, leaving Idris behind and following the scent like a bloodhound. She could almost taste the bitter chocolate flavour on her tongue. Mia sighed when she found the elderly human woman—the same one Kali had always gone to—hunched over her stained cast metal pot full to the brim of the warm, black elixir.

Koffee.

Kali had pushed the first cup into her hand, and then she had been hooked. Her heart clenched at the vision of her sister curled around a hot porcelain mug, sleepy and dishevelled, wearing a faraway look. Mia wanted to live in the memory where Kali was safe, alive. A stray tear leaked down her cheek.

"Now, I didn't think I was so ugly that I'd bring young maidens to tears," the woman grumbled, humour lacing her tone.

"No, no," Mia said, wiping the tear that had escaped away. "My sister loved your koffee, and she's now..."

"With Deus?"

"No, she's in Oryah's gardens."

"Well, wherever your sister is, I do hope she knows she has fantastic taste."

Mia huffed a laugh through her nose, digging into her pocket for her velvet coin purse, finding nothing. She cast the elderly woman a strained smile and took a step back.

"I'm sorry, I must have forgotten my—"

Silver coins flashed in front of Mia, tumbling across the bench. She glanced over her shoulder to see Idris' hand slipping back into his pocket.

"Idris—"

"Order your brown sludge."

Mia blinked at him for a moment, her lips parting. An uncomfortable feeling emerged in her chest, a mixture of face-warming gratitude and sorriness of her ire towards him. He was being kind to her, and with the scattering of silver, he had both shattered and mended her heart simultaneously.

"Thank you, Idris."

"It's just a cup of koffee. Calm down," he said stiffly.

Her gaze dropped from his, uncomfortable with the feeling tightening in her chest.

Mia cleared her throat and turned back to the koffee vendor, ordering by holding up two fingers. The woman cast her knowing smile, wrinkling the corners of her foggy eyes. She hummed a soft song as she busied herself pouring the koffee into two small ceramic cups. Splashing cooling milk, she dropped a chocolate nub into the swirling liquid. "Now, dry those tears, girl, and go enjoy that handsome man."

Mia's cheeks heated, denials spilling out as she quickly scooped up the mugs and muttered her thanks. Holding one out to Idris, her heart fluttered with the brief touch of skin.

He pushed his hood back, sniffing the liquid with a cringe. "You like this?"

Mia nodded, taking a sip. The warm bitterness, mixed in with the sweetness, made her smile around the cup, warming her cold fingers. "My sister, Kali, always loved this vendor. I think it was the chocolate, and that she would often forget to charge her."

Idris opened his mouth to speak, but instead, he took a small sip. His face screwed up, lips smacking. "It's far too bitter."

"Even in your old age, it seems you still have to develop some taste. Now, finish up and let us get going before the noon bell rings."

IDRIS LED HER TO THE EASTERN CORNER OF ALDERDEEN, where homes were so squished together that walls nearly brushed against each other. Neighbours lived on top of each other—figuratively and literally. Each building had been converted to have two families live in the one home; the population had swelled so quickly that builders couldn't keep up with the demand for housing.

Alderdeen's streets of luxury and spilt gold were miles from that pocket of poverty.

Mia could feel the thickness of the air coat her skin, leaving an unpleasant taste on her lips. Her gaze found the soot-hazed windows of a tall, skinny home with tatty white curtains pulled tight, stopping the warmth creeping into their bedrooms. She paused, watching the curtains move. The small face of a child popped up between the two strips of lace, wide-eyed and dirt-smudged. She waved her fingers, smiling. The little boy grinned, waving a tiny hand at her, and disappeared. Stray cats slunk around the waking streets, hopping over puddles of water and human waste.

Life endured there, without the glitz of Valliss Castle or the riches the velvet-wearing occupants had. Maybe it even thrived, whereas it perished within those grand stone walls.

Idris had pulled to a stop at the mouth of a narrow, plain alleyway when she caught up to him. The cobblestones petered away, turning into muddy dirt. "This is where they found the first body," he said, crossing his arms. "A woman—a fae—maybe thirty years old. She hadn't faced their *deas* yet. Same...injuries."

Mia peered around him. "Any other evidence?"

"She had a note screwed up in her hand. Directions to a farm out in the Westryn District. But that led to nothing. She was a refugee from the war."

Mia's gaze rose to Idris. His features were hard. "She was new to the city?"

"Yes. She was to start work here, on one of the farms."

"No family?"

"No family," Idris replied a fraction too sharply. "All died in one of the many wars King Ewan has waged, leaving her by herself in the world."

Mia searched his unreadable face for an answer to the sharpness of his voice, finding none.

"How scared she must have felt, wandering these streets," she whispered. "I can't ever imagine being that alone."

Idris' eyes widened, something flaring in his pupils, but he turned away before she could read further into it.

Mia lingered at the opening into the alley, hands in fists. The dirt showed no signs of the brutal murder that had happened on top of it. Not a puddle, nor a mark.

Nothing.

It was simply an alley.

Mia pursed her lips as nervousness edged up her throat in a hard ball. As soon as her scuffed boot stepped onto the hard earth, her world spun. All she saw was Kali's body, mangled and lifeless on the cobblestone. Her ears rang with the harrowed scream that fled from her, alerting the Silver. How rough their hands had felt when they dragged her, fighting, from her sister's corpse, only for Henry's face to flash over her eyes, pale and distressed, when they had to identify her body.

Mia's lungs refused to draw in precious air as the alley walls began to close in on her. Her knees trembled so hard, making her almost lose her footing. She ripped the cloak from her shoulders, casting it to the dirt. She shoved her sleeves up, hoping the cool breeze would calm the panic burning under her skin.

Her frenzied memories were strangling her breath from her.

"Mia, what's wrong?"

"It wa-was a m-mistake to come here...I ca-can't do this," Mia spluttered. "I can-cannot be here...not again. Not with he-her ghost haunting me."

"*Let us be free,*" Ozul demanded.

Warmth emerged at her fingertips as fire licked at her veins. Shadows spilt from her outstretched fingers, curling in the air and around her. Idris' dominating body shielded her and the shadow magic from curious passersby.

Idris said her name, sternly and seriously. "Nothing can harm you here. Not a ghost. Not memories. Nothing."

"All I do is get hurt by memories. They are barbed, Idris, cutting into my flesh until I am nothing but a mass of raw flesh and blood."

His hand gripped her elbow as if to ground her to their realm, but the sudden skin-to-skin contact spooked her. Her shadow-entangled hands snapped out, shoving Idris square in the chest. He stumbled back, his skull making a sickening cracking sound as it collided with the rough stone wall. He slumped to the dirt, leaving a smear of bright red blood in his wake.

Mia muttered the words, "I'm sorry" over and over, sharp with panic as she scrambled to the ground next to him.

He made no reply to her, nor did a breath escape his lips. He just lay hunched, chin to chest.

Mia gripped his shirt and shook him. *Great. I've gone and killed the only man I've actually ever wanted.*

"Wake up, you sack of old bones," she demanded with another shake.

"Stop calling me old," he groaned.

His eyelids fluttered as he dragged a wheezing breath in. He leant forward until his forehead hit her shoulder. She peeked at the mass of blood and split skin. The sight turned her stomach, forcing bile up her throat. His hands found the expanse of her thighs, gripping on. She resisted the urge to wrap her arms around him and draw him closer still. Instead, her fingers travelled from his shirt to cup his face, feeling his sharp, prickly stubble on her palms, lifting his heavy head. "I shall call you whatever I wish. Now, open your eyes for me."

Idris cracked one eye, showing her a singular blown-out pupil surrounded by golden emerald green. A crooked smirk spread on his face, dimpling his cheek. "You're stronger than you look, Little Witch."

Mia breathed out a sigh of relief and allowed a small smile to play on her lips. She patted his cheek once. "Oh, thank the goddess you're alive, Old Man. I didn't particularly want your death on my conscience."

"How caring of you," he replied drily.

Idris appeared a little dazed, his eyes drifting in his sockets. But when they both realised how close their lips were, his pupils quickly sharpened. Mia was subconsciously drawn to him with each passing moment. *All I would need to do is push forward—*

He pulled from her grip, twisting his face away. His hand gingerly ran up the back of his neck, careful not to touch the wound. The blood had dripped down the thick column of his throat in a viscous river, pooling in the collar of his shirt.

"We need to get you to the Medicus Tower, Idris. You're losing quite a bit of blood."

"It'll heal," he said with a grunt. "Don't like blood?"

The heat drained from her face, blanching at the word. Blood. Her thumb caressed the warm opal. "Not particularly. I've never been good around it. Now, let's get you to the healers."

He shook his head. "I will be fine, Mia. I promise."

She rose, tucking her hair behind an ear, her hand extended out to him. "I won't accept a no, Idris. I would feel awful if you died in your sleep tonight and Benny lost his job. That man isn't made for anything but shining glasses and gossiping like a courtesan."

He gazed up at her from the dirt floor. The morning sun caught his cheek bones, casting shadows down to his jawline. A bemused look spread across his features, but it didn't meet his eyes. A hurt pooled in his emerald gaze—not from pain from the throbbing wound, but an old, aching twinge. Something that lingered in every movement, like the man from her painting.

She searched his face, trying to memorise the sea of colours the golden light had captured, how his brow had inched closer and how that look made a chest-tightening emotion squeeze at her ribs.

"You know, it's rude to stare, Little Witch."

Mia rolled her eyes, flicking her fingers at him. He took her hand, and she yanked him to his feet with a strained grunt, pulling him close, her arm around his waist and his over her shoulders. Mia's mind was firmly set on how she had painted Idris before she had ever met him.

Twenty-Three

The Medicus Tower loomed over them, its windows pulled shut to the frosty morning air. The thwacking sound of a flag snapping high above them synced with her pounding heart. Mia heaved Idris under the healers' archway, dragging him across the empty courtyard. Sweat pooled in her armpits and dripped down her spine, over her aching muscles.

"Help! We need help!" Mia called out, her voice echoing back at her.

"I'm not dying. There is no need to shout," Idris said, wincing. "Like I said multiple times—"

"Good goddess, will you just let me help you?" Mia flashed him an annoyed scowl. She took a breath and allowed another truth to tumble from her. "I hurt you, Idris. Accidentally or not, I *actually* hurt you. The idea of it creates this awful twisting in my stomach."

He cast that chest-tightening, sad look at her again, then let her name slip from his lips. Softly, delicately, as if he were saying a prayer.

Mia set her eyes on the door, not letting her mind linger on how right her name felt falling from his lips.

A bright orange-haired acolyte stuck her head out from the door, her braid slipping off her shoulder. Her eyes widened when she found Mia and Idris, blood-stained and sweating, causing her to rush from the door. Her sky-blue dress was smeared and crumpled as if she had been awake all night, tending to the ill and injured.

"My name is Sorcha. Let me get you both inside so I can examine you," she said, voice gentle but firm.

Her hands hovered over Idris, waiting for permission to touch him. Idris clenched his jaw and nodded. Sorcha launched into a calm, practised movement, swinging his arm over her shoulder and her arm around his waist, bracing with her knees instead of her back, lifting him off Mia's strained body. She leant over, her hands on her knees, gasping for air.

"Sorcha? That's a fae name," Mia said through heaved breaths.

The healer averted her eyes, her slim brows meeting. "If that is too tricky, then you may call me—"

"No," Mia cut in, shaking her head. "Sorcha is just fine. My father is fae. Their words are not as tricky as others make them out to be."

Sorcha glanced at her from the corner of her eye and nodded for her to take Idris' other arm. Mia slid her body close to his, hands gripping the material of his shirt.

They stumbled through the large wooden door and directly into the heart of the Medicus Tower. Mia quickly introduced herself and the half-dazed man, harmonised by her quick footfalls. With soft commands and pointing fingers, Sorcha led the pair through corridors, under hand-carved archways of benevolent women tending to men, right into an expansive room with a handful of long benches.

Mia dumped Idris down, wiping the sweat from her brow with her sleeve. Dragging a lungful of fresh air, she tasted the spiced citrus of the cleansing potions they splashed around to clean the blood and grime from the stone floors.

The Medicus Tower wasn't simply a spire for healers to study and carve up cadavers. It was Alderdeen's place of healing for the sick and injured, and for those who had left the world. Their bodies lay on chilled marble slabs deep in the dungeons of the tower. However, the dead and dying weren't all that filled the halls. Precious life was pushed into the world there, allowing those first cries to soak into the walls.

Life and Death were bound there, like lovers, long fingers skimming over stones as they walked hand in hand.

Mia straightened, groaning. "You weigh a bloody ton."

"I didn't ask you to drag me halfway across town, nor did I demand you bellow and screech for help as if I'm dying."

"What happened?" Sorcha asked, cutting into the tension. Her keen hazel eyes methodically inspected Idris from the top of his crown right down to his worn leather boots.

"He...fell over and struck his head against a wall."

Sorcha nodded and crouched in front of him, tucking a stray curl from her face behind a pointed ear.

Fae and a healer. That is almost unheard of, Mia thought. *Besides, Ewan has outlawed any use of the fae healing magic. Nevertheless, she must be impressive for* Alderdeen's guilds, who welcome only a few fae who found a home here.

Whispers emerged of a new way, a new life. It made the nobles of Alderdeen nervous, filling them with resentment.

Sorcha held a slender finger up, moving it side to side. Idris' eyes tracked it sharply. The eye rolling daze had left him, much to Mia's relief.

"It's just a nasty cut. It'll heal. Your wife is especially panicked, so how about you allow me to examine you, just to make sure you're fighting fit?" Sorcha soothed, casting a soft smile at him.

Mia coughed at the word *wife* as if it choked her.

Idris turned to her, a sly smirk on his lips. "Yes, my wife."

She rolled her eyes. "You really hit your head hard, didn't you?"

"I hit it hard when I fell for you, my Mia."

She turned her entire body away from him, crossing her arms, a frown cutting across her face. "You must have knocked all the sense out of that thick skull as well, Old Man. I'm not his wife, Sorcha."

A pretty pink flushed the healer's cheeks directly under her speckled freckles as she shot up. "My greatest apologies. I thought with the ring, your panic and just the way you look at each other..." she sputtered awkwardly, palms waving in front of her. "Regardless, let's bring you out the back, Idris, to cleanse and stitch your wound."

Sorcha helped a swaying Idris up with a flurry of hands and muttered words. She motioned towards the closed door, hovering over him. Mia followed close behind. So close that she bumped into Sorcha.

"Patients only, sorry."

Idris waved his fingers at her, that crooked smirk on his lips. "See you soon, wife."

Mia glared at the space between his shoulder blades, muttering under her breath as she watched the door close. Leaning against a stone pillar, her fingers found the opal, allowing the gold to slip over her smooth skin. A group of yawning acolytes strode past her, books in their arms and hair braided, crisscrossed with pale blue ribbons.

Kali had tied her hair with the same ribbon the morning of her—

Mia pushed off the wall, a sudden need to move overcoming her. Emotions had crept in, causing welling tears and a scratchy sensation in her throat. A drop of Idris' blood had fallen on her sleeve, making that feeling turn into a strangling ball. Scrubbing at it, she only smeared it in a long, bloody stain. She strode over to the bench, sitting right on the edge, her leg bouncing as more chattering acolytes passed her. Her eyes rose to the door Idris had gone through. Something in her wanted to follow them and be privy to their conversation. A smaller part of her wanted to make sure that annoying, smirking fool was safe. The idea made her leg still. *Why should I care for a single second about his safety?*

She was getting too close to something she was afraid to consider. Even so, she couldn't name it in the darkness of the night while wrapped in the safety of her blanket, let alone in a deserted room of stone and wood with her sister's ghost on her heels. She quickly peered up the corridor, dashing to the door. Opening it, she slipped through, leaving just a singular thought on that bench: *Maybe he had nothing to do with Kali's death.*

THE CLICK OF MIA'S BOOTS WAS LOUD IN THE COLD, STERILE hallway. The walls were bare, not a single painting adorning them. She passed empty rooms with beds in the centres and not much else. She kept glancing over her shoulder, expecting a stern-faced master to grab her by her ear and toss her out on her rear. But no one came.

It unnerved her, causing each hair on her neck to rise and her ears to prick at each sigh of the tower.

Mia rounded a corner, hearing the deep rumblings of Idris. She found a secluded spot to press herself into, face against the cool stone.

"It will heal, Sorcha. Don't mind the girl out there. She isn't used to the sight of blood," he said, a hard edge to his voice. "Just stitch it up and send me on my way."

"Just stitch it up? It will heal at a human rate..." Sorcha's voice faded away.

Mia crept closer, her hands running over the stone.

"...another blow, and you're done for, Idris. You must feed. Your kind cannot go without it for this long..." Sorcha's voice grew faint again as she strayed further from the door. "You must be in horrendous pain..."

"I am fine," he repeated sharply. Too sharply. "I can withstand the urge. I have for a long time."

"You need to—"

"I don't need to do anything, Sorcha."

"You won't simply feed, Idris. Your hunger won't be sated with a mouthful of blood. You will drain and kill whatever—whoever—you feed from. You will be ravenous."

"Ravenous?" Mia whispered into the wall.

"Why would you do this to yourself, Idris? You cannot survive without blood. It is the curse of your kind," Sorcha said earnestly. "Is this some sort of twisted self-punishment?"

Mia's mind raced to piece together the information she\'d just heard, her eyes working in their sockets with each bounding thought.

She pushed off the wall, leaving any sensible notion behind in that dark corner. Her sister's mangled throat flashed over her open eyes while Sorcha's words stuck to the insides of her mind.

Drain. Kill. Ravenous. Blood.

Each word was like a fly drowning in honey, buzzing and buzzing, fighting a losing battle.

Mia's fingers gripped the door handle, swinging it open. She found Idris sitting, his shirt unbuttoned. He met her gaze. Confusion bunched his eyebrows, but concern radiated from his pupils.

She had found the monster who had ended her sister's life. *Idris must be that giggling creature's master. This was all a ploy, a game.*

With that thought, Mia brazenly launched herself towards him. She found anything she could latch on to, yanking him from the table with all her might. She dragged Idris a few steps until his hands snapped to her wrists, locking her against him. Soothing words left his lips, but she cared little for them. They began a tug-of-war, stepping and pulling for control.

"I know what you are, Idris," Mia said, her voice hard. "I know what kind of monster you are."

Shadows seeped out of her linen-bunched fists, curling around her tensed forearms like vipers, readying to strike. A sharp gasp came from Sorcha, her hand smacking over her lips. Her wide hazel eyes didn't leave Mia's shadows.

"And what is that, Mia? What am I?" he spat, words puncturing the tension between them, stabbing at her.

She squeezed her jaw closed before the words came rushing out. The low lanterns flickered, then fizzled out with a lash of the shadows, shrouding them in darkness.

Idris' emerald eyes glowed, boring into her. "Braver in the dark, are you, Little Witch? Or do you fear yourself so much that you can't stand to look at them?"

"I fear—"

"If you say nothing, you're a rotten liar. You fear *everything*. Even yourself, what you are. Now, tell me what I am. You seem convinced that you know the monster that dwells in the darkness with you."

A curse was poised on her tongue. "You—"

Idris scoffed, shaking his head. "Prick? Arsehole? Come on, you're above these petty insults. Or, I thought you were, at least."

"You don't know me at all, Idris. Stop presuming you do."

"I'm presuming? You burst in here. Over what? A half-heard conversation and your own mistrust of me."

"I know what you did, what you are," was all Mia could say. She refused to let his words weaken her resolve.

"Then say it, Mia. You seem to have a lot to say about things you have no fucking clue about. You've merely dipped a toe in, not dived in as you thought. You're nothing but a rich brat who—"

Mia shoved him back, ending his angry tirade. His words hit her harder than she'd expected them to. Her anger, sadness and absolute despair fuelled the magic pouring from her, causing the shadows to pour out of her in drumming beats until nothing but numbness and an awful empty feeling in her chest remained.

Sorcha muttered a prayer from behind her fingers.

Idris' eyes never left her. Not a single drop of fear emerged in his emerald pools. "Say it," he demanded.

"You're the blood-sucking monster that killed my sister."

Twenty-Four

A tense silence filled the small healers' room as the minutes dragged into what felt like hours. Mia's knees wobbled as the warmth that burnt her skin left her with the icy coolness that only a winter's storm would bring. She refused to let her legs give way, to collapse at Idris' feet or allow the venomous glare she cast at him to falter. Even when the hurt of her accusation flashed in his.

"By Oryah, Mia, I will say it once more, and only once more. I did not kill your sister. I wished her no harm. I just found her body, as it was in the alley next to The Cauldron, for fuck's sake. Do you think that if I had killed her, I would have allowed you to live? I know the Silver took you in. Why didn't you tell them? Why didn't you give them my name and address?"

"I don't know, Idris! I make no claims to know the mind of a killer, to play a sick game with your prey. Was I to be your next victim?" Mia asked, her voice teetering on hysterical.

Panic engulfed her. She struggled to grasp on to herself, causing her breath to come in heaves and her vision to narrow.

"Mia—"

"Why did you do it?" Her trembling hands flattened on his chest. She couldn't stop. The rambling words had escaped her. "Kali was innocent, destined for greatness. Why didn't you just take me? I'm worthless, nothing. I doubt if anyone would care if I was gone."

That sad lonely truth, demanding to be said.

"Mia, take a breath," Sorcha's voice came softly from the corner. "The vampyres have many well-kept secrets, but as a healer of the Medicus Tower, we know a vast majority of them. One is they cannot lie. Yes, bend the truth, but they cannot outright lie. Idris, did you murder Mia's sister, Kali Ashmore?"

All he said was, "No."

"Truth, Idris?" Mia asked, her voice wavering. A warmth dripped from her nose, seeping into her dry lips and spreading the copper taste over her tongue.

"What? It is the—"

"When I say, 'Truth,' you reply, 'Truth,' if it is so."

She couldn't explain the intricacies of Kali and her childhood game of something that had spread right into their adulthood. It felt too personal, too close to the oozing wound in her chest.

She glanced up at Idris to find him staring directly at her. That furious anger had seeped away, leaving only earnestness.

"Truth."

Mia's hand fell away from him, allowing herself to take a deep, steadying breath. The shadows retreated, slithering to dark corners. His eyes dropped once, right to the line of ruby red blood leaking from her nose, then over her shoulder. To Sorcha.

"You know what she is, don't you?"

Sorcha's hazel eyes were wide, glancing around the room, piecing what she saw together. Her gaze finally rose to meet Mia's.

"A witch."

Mia paused, sleeve still half-dragged across her nose. "A what?"

Her body had a strange reaction to the word; a feverish tremble, and then a horrible tightness in her chest. Words whispered to her, not from the male voice of malice, but from Ozul. They called to her, to the warmth spreading to her fingers, to the shadows that gushed from her across the stone.

"*Let us be free.*"

Mia yanked at her blouse, pulling the first two buttons from their delicate stitching, sending them clattering to the ground. "Witch hunters hunted them to extinction on orders of King Ewan. Every child in Alderdeen knows this, and how he allowed not one soul to survive. He even burnt their queens. The elders said they could see the pyres from miles away. How could I be a...*witch*?"

Idris was still, so still that he barely inhaled. The only thing that moved was the fine tremble in his fingers. His eyes glazed over as if he had lost himself to memory.

Mia took a tentative step towards him, then another, until she was flush against his arm. Her hand slid around the divot in his wrist to slip her palm against his, threading her fingers through his. Calloused and rough against her silky and soft, she stared at their joined hands for a moment, then up at him. His name came as a soft whisper, waking him. He didn't leap from her like she was a burning flame, but held steady.

"Some must have gotten away, Mia. King Ewan couldn't have killed each and every one," Sorcha said, adding quietly, "Even though he tried, that warmongering arsehole."

Mia knew King Ewan wasn't loved as much as he was feared. But hate ran through many for the man who simply let his army destroy their homes.

"You're adopted, Mia, aren't you?"

"And no one lets me forget it," she answered flatly.

Idris pulled his hand from hers to button his shirt up, eyes on his task. He hadn't said a word since Sorcha sprouted nonsense about witches. Mia found it strange and unnerving, but what was more unsettling was that her hands ached to be back in his.

Sorcha began to pace backwards and forwards, her forefinger and thumb stroking her chin. "Mia cannot be some common witch. Those shadows—"

"The shadows are witch magic?" Mia cut in, shaking her head. "I have been tested. I have no magic."

Sorcha stood across the room, feet taking her a fraction faster as her mind worked. "The test is only for fae or vampyre magic, not banned magic, Mia. They would have missed it. In my research of witches, there was a coven—"

Idris tilted his head, stopping Sorcha mid-sentence. "You're researching witches?"

The healer's eyes dropped to the floor, twisting the tail of her stained apron. "Well, not officially, vamp. But I'm mostly researching healing magic...amongst other things."

Mia arched a brow at the vagueness of her answer, but that damn book flashed in her mind. "*The Guide to Witch Bloodlines.* That was yours, wasn't it?"

Intrigue lit up Sorcha's face, making her take a step towards Mia. "You found my book? See, now, that's interesting. Some say those books call to those written in the pages."

"But I'm not a witch. I'm human, as were my parents," Mia said, repeating the words over and over as if they could surround her and hold her from the panic quelled only moments ago. "I'm a human, not a witch."

Idris' gaze fell on her. She presumed she was more interesting than buttons now, but she was edging closer to true unruly hysteria. A soft remorse hung in his emerald eyes, like he was sorry for something. But his lips pressed together so as not to spill truth across the shining stone floor.

Mia stepped away from him and his unsettling gaze, heading right towards the door. "I have to go, Idris. I'm late for work."

He was quick on her heels. "You can't just go—"

She raised her hand, stopping him mid-sentence. "I can and I will. This talk of witches and shadow magic isn't getting us any closer to the creature that killed my sister."

"This has to be linked, Mia. The deaths. You. All of it."

Mia tensed, fist curling by her side. Idris was right. It could not be two isolated events, waiting to collide. They were already clashing like ships in a harbour. Wood cracking under the forward force, spending splinters into the rolling water.

"I cannot..." she murmured, glancing at him. "I cannot be the cause of her death."

His gaze dropped from her, taking her stomach with it.

"You think I had something to do with it, don't you?" Mia poked him in the chest. Disbelief cut through her tone as she continued. "I had *nothing* to do with these horrific killings or the death of my sister."

Sorcha cleared her throat, flashing a look at Idris. "Of course you had nothing to do with your sister's death. But Idris is unfortunately correct. These things correlate, even if we cannot stomach the idea. Let me help. I can look through the archives about your magic, and maybe even whatever this creature is."

Their gazes found each other, the healer's full of earnestness and hope.

"You would do that? Why?"

Sorcha raised her narrow chin. Determination flared in her features. "Kali was a daughter of the Tower, and we furiously defend our sisters. In life or death."

Mia exhaled and nodded to her. She turned, glaring at Idris, his face filled with remorse. "I'm glad you'll make it through the night, Old Man. Come find me when you locate the sense I knocked out of your head, and we can end this monster."

Twenty-Five

The boned corset was too tight on Mia's rib cage, making her breaths shallow and uncomfortable. Her gloved hands yanked on the bodice with a sharp impatience. The pins that jammed into her scalp didn't help her mood, either, nor the fact that she'd have to scrape and curtsy to the nobles of Alderdeen for an evening instead of gathering more evidence with Idris.

"These things are of Diabolus' making," she muttered to herself, giving the material a final yank. "A torture device hidden in silk and ribbon."

Henry shot her an annoyed look, then glanced back up the dirt road. Her family had been summoned—more like painfully coerced—to court for the unveiling of Reagan's new bride. However, their carriage was late. *Or not coming,* Mia thought.

Every noble worth their gold would be in attendance. Her father was one of the handful who got a written invitation, inviting him and Anne. But her mother was having yet another bad week of soft sobbing and refusing to leave the safety of her bed. Forcing her to attend court seemed cruel to Mia, so she offered herself up, much to her own irritation.

Henry tapped a toe on the dirt, running a hand over his cropped hair. Only brief words had been shared between them for the past few days. Not because of bubbling anger, but the fact that neither of them really knew how to comfort the other. They had spent the morning in relative silence but kept gravitating towards each other as if all they needed was each other's presence.

"Where the bloody Heylla is this carriage?"

"We could just walk…" Mia's words faded off when her father shot her an annoyed look.

He glared down the road as if a battalion of raging soldiers were charging up. "It's not proper to 'just walk in.'"

Her hand fell on his arm, making him stop his frustrated groaning. "Who cares about looking proper? We are Ashmores. We rarely do anything proper."

Henry huffed a laugh, tension seeping from him. "We shall walk, then, and fast. We cannot be late."

✦ ✦ ✦

Noble men and women filled each nook and cranny of the vast Deus' Temple, an impressive building of vaulted ceilings and glimmering rainbow stained glass of priests in their finery, praying at the feet of a kind, benevolent Deus. People stood squished shoulder to shoulder, hoping to glimpse the faraway princess. Carefully chosen members of the court were allocated seating to the nauseatingly perfumed and tight-lipped unveiling ceremony.

As the custom of Deus demanded, Reagan would unveil his bride, running an inspecting eye over her, and take her hand, vowing to marry her before the court.

The entire event left Mia feeling uncomfortable. It simply made the woman seemingly only worthy if a man found her so. He would know nothing of her merits, her charm. Only how her skin stretched and formed over a bony skeleton. Only the vain and vapid reasons. Mia's fingers itched to cover her scar at the mere thought.

Henry pushed his way through the mass of bodies, parting the crowd. All the while, Mia apologised to the guests she bumped into. He paused at the front, straightening his doublet and nodding to Wyn, who slouched against the wall on the opposite side of the temple, his armour worn, dull. He hadn't bothered to polish it, making Mia smile.

Henry found his seat, name slashed over a crisp white page, and sat down, Mia slumping next to him. Reagan's raven-haired brothers, Tobias and Brimm, sat a few seats down, bored and arms crossed, whispering between themselves.

The dark eyes and high cheekbones of Luc flashed in her periphery. Mia stiffly turned in her seat, casting a strained smile at him. He waved his paint-stained fingers, smirking. Her gaze dropped to the swirling marble floor at her feet, cheeks burning as a pinched expression emerged.

Henry's elbow caught her in the ribs, bringing her attention back to the stuffy, perfume-stinking room. "I know you hate these things, but can you at least not look like Kali..."

He cleared his throat as if her name got stuck, choking him.

Mia's hand found his wrist, squeezing. "You can still say her name, Father. Kali would hate for us to never use it again."

Henry considered her for a moment, then cast his eyes to Deus' altar. The smallest smile curled on his lips. "You are correct, my moon. She would've hated it."

"Almost as much as I hate these stuffy, boring events," Mia added with a grin.

A murmured hush went through the room as the cascade of footsteps split the crowd in two, ushering in Lord Hartwinn. He wore an expertly tailored, deep maroon doublet embossed with gold stitching down the sleeve and across his chest in a weaving pattern. A belt of black leather with a matching gold buckle was slung over his hip over fitted pants. Even his boots gleamed. The costume was more for the gawking masses than for the princess, who still hadn't arrived.

Reagan followed behind him, the spitting image of his late mother, Lady Seanna. He dressed in a stunning royal blue attire, a sword around his hips. A gold ring embellished his little finger, and much like his father, a gleaming ruby sat in the centre.

"Of course he swans in here looking handsome as ever," Mia muttered almost silently. However, she could see the cracks in the façade. The dullness of his skin and the chewed quicks around his nail beds, down to the awkward way his clothes didn't fit him, like they were a fraction too big.

With hands clenched, she watched him grin at the crowd, shaking hands with men and bowing to women. Playing the part of a lord's son, eager to see his new bride perfectly. Not a single hint of grief was in his eyes or across his broad shoulders. It was like he had simply moved on and forgotten all about Kali and their supposed love.

I have never hated anyone more than I do Reagan. If he loved her, he'd have begged Hartwinn to postpone this sham of an event. But he asked for it to be brought forward. I can't fathom why.

Hartwinn found his place in front of Deus' overflowing altar—food, wine and other offerings given to the god for luck and good fortune—hands clasped. He looked tired, purple smudged under his bloodshot eyes. Reagan jogged up the stairs, casting that toothy grin at Mia, who returned a cool glare.

"Welcome, ladies and gentlemen of Alderdeen! We are gathered here today to celebrate a joyous occasion. My firstborn son, Reagan, and his marriage to Princess Constance, daughter of our brave and kind King Ewan. As per tradition, she must be presented and deemed worthy before they are wed."

Mia held back an eye roll, but a poorly timed grumble slipped from her when the court quietened for a moment.

Henry's elbow dug into her again. "Mia..." he whispered—a quiet caution.

She spread a tight, pained smile on her face and cast it to Henry and those around her. Directing his eyes to the ceiling, he muttered a prayer, then shifted his attention back to Hartwinn's speech. Mia allowed her gaze to dip to Hartwin's hand; a ruby wrapped in old, thin gold gleamed from his pointer finger. Leaning forward, she cocked her head. The stone throbbed as though it had a pulse. Long fingers of a ghostly touch brushed over her skin, turning her stomach.

Something was wrong with that gem.

When Lord Hartwinn's hand disappeared behind him, the pull broke, leaving Mia sweaty and nauseous.

"Now, shall we begin? I believe we would all rather be celebrating out in the garden than in this stuffy room."

A few chuckles came from the crowd. He took his seat, crossing his legs, chin in hand. Mia locked eyes with him across the room. He cast her a small smile and a wink. She returned a nose-scrunching wink.

She'd always liked Hartwinn.

Father Pristone took to the stage dressed in his priest finery, much like he had been for Kali's funeral. Henry stiffened beside her, hand clenching in his lap. Mia's hand rested on his forearm, allowing his hand to relax.

The priest cracked the well-read tome in his hands and began reading. Mia instantly tuned his voice out. She rarely took any notice of what he was saying. His words were full of obedience, meekness and tolerance for women, but valour and bravery for men.

The doors groaned open, silencing Father Pristone mid-word and making a sour, pinched look emerge on his face. Mia turned in her chair, craning her head for any glimpse of the woman.

"Can this be done with? I know Hartwinn will have the good wine out tonight," Mia whispered to Henry, who didn't share the same eagerness as her for sweet bubbles.

She knew she'd only sip, then discard whatever was left in the cool soil of the garden bed. She wouldn't fall into the abyss. Not then.

"Only one glass, Mia," Henry replied sternly.

"'Only one glass, Mia,'" she mocked in a deep voice, rolling her eyes.

Henry refused to meet her gaze, but arched a bow.

She had sufficiently annoyed him, much to her own delight.

The crowd had parted enough for her to finally see the woman whom the court couldn't stop speaking about: Princess Constance, King Ewan's firstborn daughter. A short, waif-like woman stood in the doorway with a pout on her face. A veil of gold, edged with fine lace, brushed over the top of her pursed lips. Her shoulders were too tight, her back too straight.

Lush royal blue velvets made up her gown, elaborate lacing crisscrossing over her bodice. It cinched tightly at the waist, flaring out to sway with each step she took. She matched Reagan, right down to the gold trim on her skirts. She clasped her gloved hands so firmly at her front that she crushed the stems of the wildflowers. It was a careless arrangement thrown together at the last minute, as though ripped from the earth of the palace grounds on the way to Deus' Temple.

Women dressed in simple blue cotton gowns surrounded her, all sharing the same tense face. One even had tears shining in her eyes. And judging by the way she bit down on her lip, they weren't tears of joy.

Princess Constance's footsteps were neither hurried nor painstakingly slow as she made her way up to the altar. Murmurs carried around the room, but the princess never lowered her chin. Reagan bounded down the steps, a serene smile cut across his face. He held a hand out to her.

She considered it for the briefest of moments. Then she simply sank down onto the plush cushion. Reagan cleared his throat, straightened his doublet and knelt next to her. Mia smothered a laugh with her palm and thought, *that will stab at his over-inflated ego.*

Father Pristone took his position in front of the kneeling couple, one hand raised and his tome open in the other. His droll voice recited a hymn, echoing around the room. Then, a sudden silence, and a nod to Reagan. The entire court held their breaths as he reached out and flipped her veil. Her narrow face was all soft curves and long eyelashes. Her icy blue eyes burnt bright against the deep amber tone of her skin.

She was beautiful—and absolutely furious.

"Do you deem her worthy, son?" Hartwinn called out, standing.

Reagan took her in with an almost cold calculation. He lifted his hand as if to brush it over the soft angle of her cheek. Instead, he tugged on a stray curl, causing the princess to narrow her eyes and clench her jaw. She dared not bat his hand away.

With one single word, Reagan could declare her unworthy, and they would send her back, shamed and embarrassed. He let it go with a spring and sly smirk. Then, he abruptly snatched her hand up, making one woman step out of line. A touch on a wrist was the only thing that stopped her.

Reagan pressed a kiss on her knuckles. A strained, uncomfortable smile spread across her face.

"Yes, Father. Princess Constance is more than worthy. I vow to marry her," Reagan announced.

Not that either of them has much choice, Mia thought bitterly. Alliances tied their families together. Not love, or even like. It was all just a painful, awkward show.

A mighty cheer flooded the tightly packed room as people threw rose petals in the air, showering the couple with soft pink flutters.

Mia was unable to stop herself from imagining Kali dressed in her own wedding finery with her wide smile, her bright eyes shining with tears of joy. But that illusion soon turned sour with nightmarish images of mangled throats and cold, dead eyes. She couldn't shake them. The ghost of her sister remained, haunting Mia's every breath, thought and beat of her broken heart.

Twenty-Six

THE CRESCENT MOON WAS SHARP IN THE NIGHT SKY, casting its soft, silver rays across the rugs and wooden floors of Mia's bedroom. She'd lain awake for what felt like hours after she and Henry returned to Rosda Manor, tangled in her sheets, tossing and turning.

Sleep hadn't come.

She couldn't shake the flashing of Kali in her mind. Not even emptying herself onto a canvas in dark greys and blacks had helped.

A flurry of pebbles struck her window.

Tap.

Tap.

Tap.

Mia pulled herself up, frowning at the sound. Her feet found the plush rug as another *ping* shook the glass. She tiptoed along the floor, peering over her windowsill.

Idris stood below the window, surrounded by Anne's carefully tended garden, with a handful of stones, arm poised to throw another one. She yanked the window open, letting the cool night air suck out any warmth left in the room.

"What do you want?" Mia hoarsely whispered down to him. "It's the middle of the night."

He shot her a grin, dumping the pebbles at his feet. "I've come to ask if you'd run away with me—"

Mia scoffed a laugh, rolling her eyes. She leant her forearms on the windowsill and called back, "You know, I'd need to actually like you to even consider the idea, and I seem to just tolerate your presence. Go, Old Man, before you stuff it up and say something stupid."

The impressive glare he shot up at her made her grin widen further.

"Now, what do you really want?"

"To discuss our investigation, obviously, Little Witch. I wouldn't be standing out here freezing my bollocks off if this were a social visit."

Mia glanced over her shoulder at her bedroom door, her smile fading. Henry only slept a few doors down, and his blasted fae hearing would hear their quiet murmurs. Not wanting to rehash old arguments, she turned back to the window, sticking her head out. "My father will skin us both alive if you're found in my bedroom this late at night."

Idris cocked an eyebrow, and that damn dimpled smirk spread on his lips. "Found in your bedroom, or your bed, Little Witch?"

Her pulse spiked at the simple thought of Idris splaying her open on her bed, dipping that honeyed gaze over her until he found that devilish heat pulsating at her core, leaning to taste her...She shook her head, demanding her traitorous thoughts to leave her.

"Good goddess," she murmured to herself.

"Hurry up and decide, Mia. It's freezing."

"I'll come to you."

In a flurry of activity, she pulled her boots on and yanked a lace shawl around her shoulders. Dragging her fingers through her sleep-knotted hair, she rushed over to her vanity, plucking a pot of pink rouge and dabbing it on her lips. Her finger stilled as the realisation of what she was doing dawned on her.

She was making herself pretty.

As if the midnight visit was a romantic tryst between lovers and not a discussion of senseless murder. Slowly, she screwed the lid back on and placed it down. Leaning on the solid wood, she hung her head. *He doesn't want me like that. He said so himself.*

Mia couldn't understand why the simple thought made her heart hurt.

She raised her eyes to her reflection. The rough scar cutting across her cheek glowed in the silver light. It was like a blemished flower in a bouquet; still beautiful, but spoilt.

The male voice, which had been subdued, almost silent for days, whispered in her ear, *He could never want you, disgusting creature. Only I will want you.*

Mia turned from her vanity. Those words had crushed any elation like a bug under foot. She didn't even bother telling the voice to go away. She believed him.

She cursed under her breath, dragging herself back to her window and peeking out. Idris remained in the spot where he had been planted. With little thought, Mia discarded her shawl and climbed over the windowsill. Her boot found the lattice. Kali had used it as a ladder, sneaking out and sneaking Reagan in. Mia had never dared to, not trusting the rickety wood and thin vines to hold her weight.

Not until then.

She preferred to scale the side of her home in just her nightgown and not much else, rather than face Henry and his ire.

Carefully lowering herself down, she clung to the lattice. In the moments it took to finally find solid ground, her muscles ached, and a layer of cooling sweat covered her body.

"You know you have a front door, right?" Idris asked, his eyebrows inching together as she landed on the hard dirt with a huff.

Mia shot him a grin, trying to hide the tremble in her fingers behind her back. "Ah, but where is the fun in that?"

He grumbled something under his breath, casting his eyes to the twinkling sky, annoyed.

Mia was drawn to the sharp cut of his cheekbone, drawn forth by the moonlight, right to the parting of his lips, then to the soft point of his ear.

Half fae.

Her fingers itched to track a line from his jaw, over his cheek, right to that point.

He was striking in the daylight—and even by candlelight—but he was breathtaking in the moonlight. As if he were a cursed prince to exist in the moon's cast, only to be forgotten by sunrise.

Mia bit down on her lip, tilting her head. Flashes of emerald and sadness emerged in her mind. Her painting was of him. She was sure of it. But she cared not, as she wished to draw him then, as he was. To take charcoal to paper, to capture his essence. Only for purely selfish needs, to gaze at when she felt the hot rush of arousal.

"Why do I have to keep reminding you it's rude to stare at people, Little Witch?"

Heat warmed her cheeks.

She had been so lost in her own thoughts that she didn't realise he was giving her a brow-arched look.

Mia gripped his wrist, careful not to slip her hand into his, and dragged him from her window. "I've just never seen a man so young and so old at the same time. I'm simply staring at the oddity that you are."

THE HEDGES OF BLOOMING ROSES SURROUNDED THEM, roots cutting through the cracked pavement. A low stone bench seat was the only lonely piece of furniture.

The warmth radiating from the manor had dissipated with each step, making Mia painfully aware of the night chill. Her skin goose pebbled, and the thin material of her nightgown strained under the peaks of her hard nipples. Her arms crossed over her chest, a futile attempt to hide the effects of the cold.

"Where are you—"

"Somewhere more private. And away from listening ears. Our staff are much too curious for their own good, and they love to gossip."

"About what?"

She turned away from him, rubbing her arm with one hand, then using the other to flap around in the air. "Me sneaking out to see a man."

"You don't do that often, I presume?"

She shot him a pointed glare over her shoulder. "Your presumption is incorrect, Old Man."

"The way you wobbled down that lattice proves otherwise," he murmured.

A full-body shiver clattered her teeth together. "Excuse me?"

There was a shift of fabric, then a warm cloak enveloped her, spiced with ash and wood from whisky barrels. Her skin instantly warmed, but not from his body heat.

"Thank you," she murmured, yanking his cloak tighter.

"You looked cold," Idris said, sitting.

Mia strode over and plopped next to him on the bench. "This better be good. You're disturbing my beauty sleep."

"Good thing you don't need it, Little Witch."

Mia openly gagged at his sugar-coated words. Now that she was closer, she could see a day's worth of stubble had grown on his jaw, and purple bags hung under his eyes. He looked as she felt: tired.

"Shall we go over what we know, if this is what you've dragged me from bed for?"

Her gaze dropped to the laced edge of her nightgown, peeking out from the cloak. The lace cut off an inch above her knee. Scandalously short. Idris' gaze travelled with hers, skimming over the flashes of bare skin. He cleared his throat. "The first murder was a fae woman."

"Was the next human?"

He looked away. "No, it was a female youngling."

"Youngling?"

"A young vampyre, not having yet reached their time for the rebirth," he explained.

Mia humphed a response, her lips pursing.

"What?"

"I thought your lot were immortal."

"We live long like the fae—longer than humans, or witches, even—but we are not indestructible."

"How old are you?"

He raised an eyebrow at her. "I may never wake you this late again, Little Witch. Did you lose your manners as well as the rest of your clothing, coming down here?"

She exhaled, casting attention to the roses. "How is this supposed to work if you dodge every question I ask about you? If we are to be partners, I need to know something about you."

He stilled next to her, taking a deep breath and letting it loose into the night. He didn't speak for a long while, as if he was looking for the right words but fell short.

"Because I don't matter, Mia, not really. Not a single drop of blood in my worthless body matters. I have nothing to offer this world. Not anymore. No purpose outside of kicking drunks to the street." A heavy sigh left him. "Once, I had a purpose, but like all the valuable things in my life, that was ripped away. Maybe stopping more women from getting hurt by this creature is enough for someone to see that I am worth something. Make me feel less...I don't know. I just want to help, instead of hurting, because that's all I seem to be good at."

A soft breeze swirled hair from Mia's surprised face.

She was speechless.

She'd expected honesty, but the sorrow in his voice shocked her to silence. He believed every single word he said was true. Her own broken heart—each shattered piece—throbbed in her chest as his truth settled around them.

How little he thinks of himself...is mirrored in me. I wonder if the same man who torments me haunts him too.

"You're wrong, Idris. So wrong. You matter," Mia whispered, worried she would spook him. She blinked and a tear escaped down her cheek.

Idris cast her a sad smile. "Truth?"

She scrubbed her face with his cloak. "Truth."

The silence of the night surrounded them.

Idris' hurt had hooded his eyes and made his jaw twitch. He has given too much, shared too much. *Or have I?*

"How does one kill a vampyre?" she asked, changing the subject.

His boot kicked at the cracked pavement, looking everywhere but at her. "Ripping their throat out before they can complete the rebirth usually does the trick," he replied, his voice hard. "But usually, capture them, starve them and cut their heads off."

Mia paled, her body shivering even with Idris' body heat warming her. "Did you know her?"

Idris shook his head and draped his arm across the back of the bench, his fingers close enough to brush over her shoulder. "I don't get out to court much, Little Witch. I rarely see my kind outside splitting up the occasional bar fight."

"It was a fae woman next, wasn't it?"

"Yes. She worked at a tavern in the lower city. The same wounds, and nothing left at either crime scene." Idris scrubbed his jaw. "Human, then more Fae. These women were people who, sadly, no one would miss. No one would look for them. There is more to this. We are missing something. It cannot be merely senseless attacks."

"We are missing everything, Old Man. Kali doesn't fit with the other victims. She is—was—lord's daughter, loved by the court."

"You're right, she doesn't fit. Did she have any enemies, someone who wished her harm? Jealous ex-lover? Angry lady?"

He had asked the same question the night of the vampyre wine. But a faded memory rose to the surface from the weeks of whisky: Kali's biceps littered with yellowed and deep purple bruises as if someone had gripped her hard. Arguments she'd overheard stumbling into bed, and the sadness that lingered in her sister's eyes.

"Reagan."

Idris' gaze flicked to her, brows meeting. "Lord Hartwin's firstborn son? That pompous, snobby prick?"

"The one and only," Mia replied drily, stretching her legs out. The silver rays of moonlight caught the constellation of freckles across her milky skin. "You know, he wasn't always this...unbelievable arsehole. He was kind, but something switched in him."

"Power does that," Idris said soberly.

She huffed a laugh. "Reagan has no power, Old Man. He doesn't even sit on the council. Hartwinn has made sure of it. Henry said something about him not being yet mature enough to sit in on the meetings."

"He's what...twenty-eight? Why isn't he on Hartwinn's council? That's strange."

Mia shrugged. She had never bothered to consider it until then. "Reagan is twenty-nine, and how old does that make you?"

Idris side-eyed her and exhaled. "I'm thirty-six."

"And how long have you been thirty-six?"

"Long enough," Idris replied drily.

Mia hummed a response, biting her lip around her grin. She'd gotten a minute piece of information. Thirty-six. Half fae, half vampyre, a bar owner and not an awful kisser.

Idris said, rubbing his eyes, "We saw the creature, and it didn't resemble someone wrapped in about a hundred gold pieces' worth of velvet or carrying the air of lordling arrogance he carries."

That sick laughter had wormed its way into her consciousness, playing on the edge of her dreams.

"No, Old Man, your eyesight hasn't failed you yet. Reagan wouldn't debase himself by getting his hands dirty."

He grunted, still not convinced.

Her mind worked faster, trying to jam the pieces of information in places they didn't fit. One stuck out—one that fit seamlessly. "That thing must have a master."

"I agree. But Reagan? I don't know. Feels far-fetched to even me. Does he even have magic?"

Mia groaned, all but forgetting the strained celebration dinner they all had suffered through with Kali and Reagan smirking at each other all night. It was only days before Reagan trapped her in that golden cage to make her sing whenever he wanted. However, Mia did remember the strained smile and the stiff pat on the back Hartwinn gave him at the end of the dinner. She had questioned her parents about it incessantly, but had never gotten a proper answer.

"He has fae magic. A lot of it."

"How? I presume his lineage would be traceable, being nobility and all. How did fae magic slip into his veins?"

"When it was announced, there were whispers of Reagan's paternity, but it was all swept away with..."

"With?"

"Two days later, Kali and Reagan were discovered in a maid's closet...entwined."

"I see. You think their entwinement was to cover something up?"

"No." She shook her head, sighing. "No one in the court would ever speak out on this. Not after Lady Seanna."

"Mia, I'm not up to date with goss—"

"She died in childbirth a few years ago, and the twins—two little boys—soon followed their mother."

"Oh," he breathed.

"She left three sons behind, and Hartwinn never recovered. I think the worst part was Anne's crying. A sad, harrowing sound, like a part of her soul was ripped from her."

He sighed, lips parting. "How devastating. The gods are cruel."

Mia glanced at him from the corner of her eye. He was searching the twinkling night sky. A moroseness hung around his neck, weighing his shoulders down. She'd hoped for some wise words or elegant piece of poetry to fall from her, but all she said was, "The gods have forgotten about us, Idris. They care not for the cruelty of the life they have cast us to."

"Not all of us, Little Witch. The gods remember a few among us, the pawns in their divine game."

His fingers slid from the bench, skimming over her rib cage, splaying over her soft stomach. She let herself lean closer, drawing him into her lungs.

"Maybe Reagan is a changeling, stolen from his crib and replaced with a fae child."

Humour edged on his lips as he pulled her in a fraction tighter. "Now, that's a story. One I believe someone entirely made up to scare human children from running in the woods at dusk. The fae are quite protective of their offspring, considering their difficulties in conceiving."

"You know, my parents had trouble conceiving Kali. It took them years. They were going to give up, but then she was born. Their first miracle, a gift from Oryah herself."

"What was their second?"

Mia grinned up at him, one that crinkled her eyes, bunched her cheeks and showed nearly everyone of her teeth—her first genuine smile in maybe weeks. "Me."

Idris let loose a soft exhale, wafting the faint heat of whisky over her. His eyes danced over her face, taking in each inch of freckled skin as if he was trying to capture the way she looked to lock it in his mind.

"And what a wondrous gift you are," he murmured.

She squirmed, uncomfortable with his praise. It fought the self-loathing, malice-driven words of the voice. They clawed at each other, twisting, falling into the darkness.

"Do you have any children?"

"No, Little Witch."

"With the way you pick up women at The Cauldron, are you sure there are no tiny Idris' roaming about the land?"

He chuckled, shoulders shaking. "I can assure you that you were the only woman I've ever picked up at any bar, and look how that ended."

She laughed, elbowing him in the ribs. "I will never live that down."

"Never," he replied, grinning.

It wasn't a lopsided smirk, but a smile that deepened the dimples on his cheeks that made light dance in those emerald pools like sunlight reflecting off the water. It washed away the heartbreaking sadness in the muscles of his face.

It was beautiful.

Then, it was her turn to feel breathless and flushed. Her own grin faded as grief clawed its way from the darkness, leaving bloody tracks up her insides.

Idris cleared his throat, shifting. "So, Kali and Reagan. Tell me more about them."

Mia's fingers found the edges of her cropped hair. Tiredness had begun its slow crawl through her body, weighing her down. She slumped back, dragging his cloak around her tighter. "They loved each other, apparently."

"Apparently?"

"One moment, they loved each other, the next, they fought with words full of anger, loud voices and raised hands. All she wanted was to be his wife, but that would never happen."

"Sounds complicated."

"Doomed to fail is more like it, Old Man."

"How do we get even close to him?"

Mia grimaced at the thought that flashed through her mind. "The engagement ball, just before the wedding. Henry has been droning about it for weeks. I even have a dress."

The tips of his fingers mindlessly drew circles over her stomach, searing heat through the soft cotton of her nightgown as if he were brushing bare skin. All her senses honed to that simple brush of his finger. Mia spread her hand over his, pressing his hand to her softness, feeling the small scars that criss-crossed his knuckles.

"What colour is your gown? We should match."

"Why would we need to match?" she asked, hoping her voice remained even.

Idris bit his lip, a smirk glimmering around a pointed canine. "Because we are going together, Little Witch."

Her heart picked up speed, fighting the tiredness. "Are you asking to escort me to the ball?"

"For the case only. There will absolutely be no dancing, nor will I be toted around like some jewel all night."

Mia laughed, shouldering him playfully. In doing so, she slipped deeper into his embrace. She gazed up at him through her eyelashes. His face was only inches away. As if timed, both their eyes dipped to each other's lips. Idris reached up and captured her chin, tilting her face a fraction closer to his parted lips.

A bated moment passed.

Neither pulled away, nor made a snide remark to cut the tension. They only needed to cross that damned bridge that was stopping them from devouring each other.

"Nothing more," Idris whispered, each word a feather touch on her lips.

"The ball is in a month…" she whispered back, hand sliding over his thigh. "We should track him and see if he slips up. Catch him bloody-handed."

"Agreed."

"Mia Ashmore! You get inside right this instant," Henry's baritone voice rumbled through the garden.

Mia launched herself from Idris, his cloak pooling at her feet. He leant forward, head in his hands, chest rising and falling.

"I will be—"

"Go, Little Witch."

Mia frowned at him and took a step towards him, reaching for him, but she only found air. He had leant away from her touch, and that sadness had returned to the muscles of his face.

Without looking at her, he said, "Please, Mia. Please go."

With a quick turn, she fled into the night, tears welling in her eyes and those sharp claws digging into her heart, leaking precious lifeblood out, engulfing her with each thump.

TWENTY-SEVEN

"WHAT IN THE GODDESS' NAME DO YOU THINK YOU ARE doing?" Henry thundered as soon as the front door closed behind Mia. "And what are you wearing?"

Her hands gripped the edge of her short nightgown, yanking it down, raising a furious glare at her father, tears drying on her cheeks. "What am I doing? What are you doing? Bellowing for me like I was a lost child."

Henry glowered right back, his hand pointing towards the gardens. "You were out there with a—"

Mia stepped forward, her arm stretched out wide. "A man? What about it? I'm a woman, Father, not a little girl. I'm allowed to do what I wish."

"I am very much aware of that. And you've been running rampant down in the lower, haven't you? You think I didn't know what you were doing, all the while you were neck-deep in a bottle? You think I don't know what the hourly-charged inns are called?"

Henry's eyes dropped over her, his words leaden with unsaid meaning. And for the first time, she saw a flicker of something like revulsion. It made the cracks of her heart scrape against her chest, that sticky tar of shame seeping out.

Mia's arms fell to her sides, her jaw trembling, unable to deny it. She had let men tear parts of her, devour them and leave her ripped raw. Back then, she hadn't cared. And by Oryah, she wished she had.

Henry took another step forward, reaching for her. "I didn't want to believe the whispers at court, Mia. Until I saw it with my own eyes. Drunk in some waste of space's lap. This isn't you. That definitely wasn't you."

Mia let out a shaky breath, cringing. He had seen her when she could barely see herself.

"I don't think I know who I am. I don't think you know who I am."

"Mia—"

"But you don't get to throw that back in my face, Father. You don't get to shame me for trying to heal from the hurt you caused."

"We have moved past that, Mia. You have forgiven me."

"Then why can't you let me try to forgive myself for what I did?" Mia asked, her voice cracking, tears escaping down her cheeks.

Henry's face crumpled, but he didn't speak.

The truth was overwhelming her, and she was powerless to stop the wave of rumours, secrets and truths from pouring from her open mouth like disgusting, murky river water.

"I was hurting, and I couldn't run to the person who has only ever made me feel safe and loved. You. Not Kali, or Mama. You." Mia dragged the heel of her palm across her cheeks, smearing tears. She took a step forward, pointing. "And I wasn't able to come to you because you were the one who caused me pain. I was so lost. Maybe taking those men to bed and drinking myself into oblivion was my only way to soothe that hurt."

Mia's tear-hazed gaze skimmed the vaulted ceiling. Dropping her arm by her side, hand slapping on bare thigh, she barked a laugh, sniffing. "You know what? The whisky and the men did nothing but make me hate myself even more."

Her chest was heaving as she let her voice settle in the air, feeling empty for the first time in an age. She blinked away the last tears she'd cry over it, the salty drops trailing down her face.

Without another word, she turned and stormed up the stairs, Henry's soft calls trailing behind her. She wouldn't stop, not until she was safely back in her bedroom and could force that foul-tasting river water back in. But she couldn't. The truth had flooded the delicate space between them, swelling and warping the tender lines that held them together.

Twenty-Eight

A piece of parchment with Hartwinn's seal lay open on the worn dining table, staring up at Anne. The words were smudged and blurred, a letter written in haste. Mia shifted on her feet, stifling a yawn with the heel of her hand. The night had crept into the morning as she tossed and turned after her fight with Henry, only closing her eyes for what felt like a matter of moments. Her mother sat hunched in the chair, her eyes glassy and a thin shawl wrapped around her shoulders. She had finally left her bed, only to wander the house like a quiet ghost.

Mia decided she was simply not ready for another day of washing paintbrushes and avoiding Luc's leering gaze, so she loitered at the doorway of her family's dining room.

"Mama, what is it?"

Anne's face rose from the parchment to her, and Mia glimpsed a glazed, frightened look for the briefest of moments before her mother schooled it into a calm smile. But it was too tight, almost painful. Her cheeks had a rosy hue, and she had pulled her hair into a loose bun at her nape, but the inevitable sadness still weighed heavily on her.

"Good Morning, my moon. I heard you had a fight with your father."

"And I do not wish to speak about it," Mia quipped, saddling up next to Anne and reaching for the letter. But her mother snatched it up, pressing it to her chest before Mia could grab it, clicking her tongue at her.

"I raised you with more manners than that, Mia. You know you shouldn't be reading letters that are not addressed to you."

"What does Uncle Hartwinn want?"

Anne's hand smoothed out, and she sighed. "He is not well. Something about an illness. Nothing serious. But he was going to retrieve... Kali's belongings from the tower, but he cannot leave the castle. And—"

"I can go today, after work," Mia cut in.

A note from Sorcha was jammed in her pocket, inviting her to come to the tower, as she had found books on the creature.

Anne visibly relaxed, shoulders slumping. "Would you? I don't think your father can face it. Not yet."

"Or you, Mama. I don't think you can either," Mia added softly.

Anne raised her chin slightly, wearing a stoic expression. A mirror of Henry's. "I'm doing absolutely fine, Mia."

Crouching, Mia took Anne's hand. "You're not, Mama. You aren't fine, and you don't have to be anything for me or for Father. You simply can just be whatever you need to be. Sad, joyous or fucking angry. You don't have to pretend to be, because I can be strong enough for the both of us." Mia gave her mother's hand a squeeze and continued, "I can hold up a lantern for you so you can find your way home to us."

She meant every word. She would bear the weight of her family's grief across her shoulders, regardless of how heavy it made each step, thought and heartbeat.

A tear rolled down Anne's face, then another until she was nothing but a puddle of heaving breaths. Mia simply held onto her mother, fighting the hard ball of emotion forming in her throat until her tears dried and she caught her breath. She scrubbed the wetness away with her palm, sniffing.

Anne's gaze met hers, a fiery determination flaring in her bloodshot eyes. "This grief won't drown me, Mia. I will not let it."

Mia didn't have the words. So, she simply gripped Anne's hand tighter, drawing her closer. As if she were the floating wreckage of a ship, bobbing in the ocean, and her mother was clinging to the fragmented piece of wood for dear life.

Anne cupped her own face, resting her elbow on the table. "When did you become so wise, my beautiful daughter?"

She gave her mother a nose-scrunched smirk. "I have been this whole time, Mama. You've just never seen it."

Anne sniffed and shared a small smile with her. "I don't think coming home every day at four in the morning, drunk as a sailor on dry land and waking this entire household—maids included—is very wise."

Mia patted Anne's knee. "Now, that was the old Mia. This is the new, *sober* Mia."

"This is who you were always supposed to be. The woman I hoped to see you grow into. I'm just sorry for what propelled you to being who you are."

Mia pulled from her mother's soft touch, rising on stiff legs. "I think I was becoming her, whether I lost Kali or not."

MIA RAN A HAND OVER KALI'S FORGOTTEN BELONGINGS, deep in the tower. A dog-eared romance novel. A leatherbound notebook with a quill jammed in between the pages. A brightly patterned silk scarf.

Things she would have needed, things that brushed her life.

Mia flipped open the notebook, flicking through. Meaningless words filled the empty parchment in grouped notes, surrounded by her bored drawings of lopsided daisies. Kali may have been the gem in her parents' eye, but she was the better artist. The pages stopped abruptly, ripped from the spine. Mia ran her finger over the jagged scraps of left-over parchment, wondering what Kali tore out. *What did she want no one to see? Or were her scribblings just simply too messy, too hard to decipher?*

"I'm glad I caught you wandering the corridors, Mia. You were about to walk into the birthing suite, and that place is not for the faint of heart," Sorcha said, ending with a small chuckle, slipping onto the table in the sparse room.

Her fiery hair was haphazardly braided over her shoulder, the tail curled as she slipped it between her forefinger and thumb. She nodded to the basket and said, "Lord Hartwinn saved them from Healer Josephine's sticky little mitts. She'd been eyeing off that copy of *Romancing the Rogue* since we heard of Kali's passing."

"Hartwinn?" Mia murmured, thumbing the edge of the stiff leather journal.

"His men came and boxed up her belongings before even the master healer could see them."

Mia paused, eyes rising to Sorcha. An inkling of an unsettling feeling crept over her skin. "His men? Not him?"

"No, one of his guards—"

"Captain Wyn Neverclove?" Mia cut in.

"No, not him," Sorcha answered with an eye roll. "That man would cause such a ruckus that I would never hear of anything else."

"That's...." Mia's gaze lowered to the stack of dark leather books next to the healer. Her eyes roamed over the titles, but took none in. "I don't know, Sorcha. Hartwinn is like an uncle to me, a brother to my mother. He would never simply leave us alone in our grief, not for this long. It's been weeks, and he hasn't come to the manor. This isn't the man I know. Now he is saying he is ill and cannot leave Valliss."

Sorcha cocked her head, confusion flaring in her eyes. "Ill? I wasn't aware of the lord being unwell. I was only there a day or two ago, delivering headache tonics for him."

"Headaches?"

"I just presumed it was because of the stress of the royal wedding."

Mia exhaled the feeling bubbling in her chest and cast Sorcha a tight-lipped smile. Her fingers settled on the soft silk. "He must be too deep in, picking out what colour Reagan's tunic is going to be to worry about a romance novel and a forgotten scarf."

Sorcha nodded and turned to the pile of books. Her hand landed on the top with a thwack. "Now, this was all I could find on...creatures who attack at night, who ingest blood or bodily parts. Which isn't much." She plucked up the first book, flicking through the pages. "Vampyres—

entities of the night—are the only ones who drink blood, outside of strange human cults I found. But vampyres need not kill their victims unless they are starving themselves."

"Like our friend, Idris," Mia confirmed with a nod, slipping onto the table beside her.

"Yes, exactly. But devouring parts—"

Mia's sharp intake of breath cut Sorcha off. Flashes of Kali flared in her mind, making her hand bunch around the soft scarf. Sorcha sighed, the simple action laced with a harsh edge of pity, sending the muscles across her shoulders rigid, and her jaw set. Irritation bubbled in Mia.

"I don't need your pity, Sorcha."

Her orange eyebrows nearly met her hairline, and the flurry of head shakes made Mia want to take her words back immediately.

"I don't pity you, Mia. The furthest from it. I know what it is like to lose someone you love."

She had all but forgotten that Sorcha was fae and would have lost more than a sister. She would have lost her home, her people and her connection to the places she loved. Her own grief suddenly felt smaller, resembling a handful of water above a raging river, bountiful and free-flowing.

"There is nothing in this world like the ache of grief to draw individuals together. It's a singular experience we all someday share, and if you'd like someone to share that load with, I am here. Anytime."

Tears welled in Mia's eyes. "I would very much like to lighten the load."

And with an encouraging nod from Sorcha, Mia did. Her words began softly, then became hurried as if she needed to get them out faster. As if the words would disappear if she didn't speak them.

But not a single tear fell.

It wasn't a moment of sadness and heaved sobs, but one of light and laughter. Of that blessed joy Kali brought to her life. Mia had revived her, filling the cool room with her warm essence. Sorcha nodded, grinned and laughed heartily. Even in death, Kali created delight.

"I had almost forgotten what an amazing sister Kali was. That she wasn't all drenched in blood and death. That she was the sun, as I was the moon; beacons of light."

"What a life she had. I feel truly blessed to know Kali as you do."

Mia leant back. The ache in her chest had lightened, and her cheeks were sore from the unused muscles it took to grin. She reached over and picked up the book, eyes skimming over vampyre lore of royal bloodlines and ancient kings. "So, what were you saying? It's not a vampyre?"

Sorcha slid from the table, shaking her head. With a flurry of hands and the flutter of pages, the healer opened the book atop the stack. She pointed to passages of handwritten letters and the painstakingly printed letter.

Bloodthirsty, monster, night stalker, and *uncontrollable* were the words that caught her eye, causing them to swirl around her mind and add to her current of thoughts.

"Not exactly, Mia. It's vampyre-made—or at least magically made. Here, look at this. A scholar from the *Magicis Academy* wrote about a creature—a vampyrica—that had been stalking women in the outskirts of the vampyres' territory. That was until the villagers banded together and ended its sorry existence. Then, another hunter tracked a creature— wait, what did he call it?" Her finger dragged over the line of words, humming until she slapped the page. "That's right, a dhampyr. He followed it right to the Niveis Mountains, leaving a trail of bodies in its wake, however, he lost it in a snowstorm. No one really knows what they are or who they serve. Many think they are Heylla-made, crawling from the earth to do Diabolus' bidding."

Mia suppressed a shiver, slamming a book closed, wanting to hide away fear. "They are Heylla-made, Sorcha, but I don't think Diabolus had anything to do with it."

Sorcha's attention never left the pages, lips smoothing into a line. "This was all I could find, but they all agreed that whatever this creature is, it's dangerous, bloodthirsty."

"Did they say how they ended it?"

Sorcha's eyes rose to Mia's with such concern flared that she could feel it wrap around her shoulders in an embrace. "None have done so—"

"But the mob of villagers—"

"They did nothing but subdue it," Sorcha cut in, her voice wavering. "Nothing could end it. Not fire, nor steel. Not until a brave mother, who was protecting her remaining children. She tore its head from its shoulders with nothing but her claws and teeth."

Mia blanched, feeling all the warmth drain from her face. She slumped back, hand over her mouth. "I would fear a mother's bite, Sorcha, for they are the most ferocious."

"A mother's love is ferocious, Mia. Their bite is simply a warning."

A snap of boots was making their way towards them. Sorcha slammed the book closed, then glanced at the door. Quickly, she leant in, gripping Mia's arm and pulling her close. "Meet me in one week, after the tenth bell at the eastern entrance of the tower. That's my next night off. I have gained access to books on the witches again. Maybe we can find something—anything—on your shadows. Something to explain what they are."

"You would do that?" she asked, disbelief coating her tone. "Even if it puts you in danger."

"I'm not scared of a little knowledge, Mia. You shouldn't be either," Sorcha joked, smirk edging on her lips.

The footsteps edged closer, making Sorcha step back and speak a fraction louder. "Contraceptives? Have you heard of simply abstaining?"

Mia met Sorcha's burning gaze and allowed a grin to spread on her face as she answered in the lewdest way she could think of on the spot. "Abstaining? Good goddess, you would never suggest such a thing if you had felt the eye-rolling pleasure of Captain Wyn's tongue between your thighs while you rode his face until he pinned you down and fucked the soul from you, leaving you sore and littered with bruises the next day."

Sorcha blushed and let out a stifled giggle from behind her fingers, sending Mia cackling. A glimmer of something sparked in her chest.

Is it hope? No...it's the soft caress of something light in days of only darkness. Mia mulled over it for a moment, then it occurred to her what it was. *It's happiness. I feel happy.*

Twenty-Nine

James commanded the apprentices with sharp orders and poorly veiled threats of violence, causing each snap to attention, poised to draw. His stained hands slid over the whittled rectangles of rainbow colours of his tightly packed charcoal set. He plucked them up in a seemingly random order, sending them scratching over the rough parchment clipped to their easels.

Still life—much better than landscape, in Mia's opinion—was the day's lecture. Not just a lesson in duplicating whatever fruit James had brought from the morning markets, but a study of light; how that bright afternoon warmth caressed the singular red apple with invisible fingers, how the shadows scurry from that light.

Mia paused her sweeping and glanced over her shoulder. Samuel was struggling with the unstructured instructions. Sketching was based on feeling, from the deepest part of your stomach, not from the detailed instruction of dabbing paint on a canvas. His shadows were too dark, too encompassing to capture the radiating light of the sun. The swoops of his hand were sloppy, thoughtless. It annoyed her. She ached to at least trace something on a piece of bloody parchment.

A snap of charcoal and an impatient growl came from him.

"Samuel, you need to lessen your grip. The pastel is too soft to be held like a pencil," Mia whispered to him, leaning closer. "You could fix it by blending it with a—"

"Did I ask for your advice?"

He hadn't forgotten about her slamming the broom into his guts, but he hadn't retaliated. *Yet.*

Mia clenched her jaw, hands tightening. "No, Samuel."

"Then get back to work."

"You've ruined it anyway," she mumbled under her breath.

Twisting away, her hip bumped into Samuel's easel, knocking over his expensive pastels and the half-filled jar holding his leftover paintbrushes. Glass smashed and grey, milky water soaked into the charcoal, creating a rainbow sludge of colours and crystal.

The final straw was the gradual descent of his awful artwork falling over the mess and soaking into the parchment.

Mia spluttered an apology behind her fingers. Her gaze rose from the disarray to Samuel's flushed face. Anger radiated from his narrowed eyes, brushing over her, causing her stomach to tighten and her body to tremble.

"You did that on purpose, you little bitch. You know how much those fucking pastels cost?" he spat, saliva pooling in the corners of his mouth.

Mia knew exactly how much they cost because she had a set sitting in her bedroom cupboard after Henry had seen her lovingly staring at them.

"No, it was an accident. I have a set you can have—"

"As if I'd want your cheap, used supplies."

"No. They are the exact same, I promise. I only used them maybe once or—"

"You're not an artist, girl. Stop behaving as if you are one. You are nothing but Luc's silly little plaything until he gets you fat with his bastard and kicks you out on your arse."

Mia stepped back. His insult cut deep, making irritation bubble up and out of her mouth. "One of you? I'd rather poke my own eyes out than see you paint a bland, colourless landscape again. You know what, Samuel? I have more talent in my little finger than you have in your whole body. You're not an artist, but a glorified, spoilt, rich arsehole whose daddy—"

"At least mine didn't need to bribe Luc."

Silence echoed with the shifting of feet as an uncomfortable tension fell in the studio.

"At least mine isn't seen stumbling out of the whorehouses of the lower city."

"How dare you!" Samuel hissed, raising his arm.

Mia readied herself for a slap, tightening her grasp on the splintery broomstick so she wouldn't throw a punch back. A hand snapped out and gripped Samuel's wrist. Mia followed that arm to a narrow-eyed, tight-lipped James.

"You will never raise your hand at her, or you will be the one out on your arse. Only Master Luc provides punishments, and they do not involve you, apprentice. Mia was correct and saved you the embarrassment of me discovering what a complete fucking imbecile you are. At least she is listening and learning, even with a broomstick in her hand. I cannot say the same for you."

Samuel ripped his arm out of James' grip, a sneer curled on his lip. "You'll regret speaking to me like that, scum."

"I don't think I will, boy," James said, looking bored. "Now, are you going to tattle to your father about me?"

Samuel's hand clenched at his side, knuckles whitened. He muttered a curse and turned on his heel, storming from the room.

James pinched the bridge of his nose, exhaling. "Clean this mess up, Mia. And quickly, because you'll be taking Samuel's easel until he learns who the actual master is around here."

She released the rough wood of the broom, a small smile playing on her lips. "Really?"

He nodded once. "Don't make me regret this, Mia."

"You won't!" she promised, already sweeping the mess away.

MIA'S SWEATY HANDS SMOOTHED OUT HER APRON, HER EYES working over the colours she'd laid out. Her fingers danced over the smooth charcoal pastels, selecting a burgundy red. She could have squealed and clapped with excitement. Instead, she took a steadying breath and let loose the tension in her neck with a crack, determined to show each and every man in the room that she deserved a place there. With just one drawing.

Without an ounce of hesitation, Mia went to work, letting the image flow from her mind to the delicate scratch of the colours blending together. She'd sketched buildings, men and trees. The apple may have been her most difficult yet. Upon Samuel's return, James banished him to the corner to watch and take notes. His bitter gaze burnt into her right between her shoulder blades, creating an uneasy, twisting sensation in her stomach. She shoved the feeling down and focused on the blending of her colours, but a thought lingered in her mind: *He backed down far too quickly.*

Mia sat back, rubbing the dull ache from her neck. It was complete —a perfectly shining red apple. James saddled up beside her, yanking her artwork from the clip. He held the parchment to the fading sunlight, tipping and tilting. He murmured something under his breath, making a rare smile spread across his face.

"This is very good. Very good. Can you all see how Mia captured the simplicity of the light? Colours blended exceptionally well. You used tissue paper?"

Mia beamed a grin at James, chest swelling with pride. With a stained finger, she pointed to the swell of red, mimicking the motion. "Yes, just a small square. But thank you, Master James."

"I'll speak to Luc about getting you your own easel—"

"You will do nothing of the sort, James," Luc said from the doorway. He didn't raise his voice. He didn't need to. That serious, commanding cadence filled the room as much as a shout would have.

Mia found a stain of paint on her apron to look at instead of the grimacing Luc. It felt as if she had been caught doing something wicked, sinful. The warmth of pride turned icy in her chest. That uneasy emotion twisted tighter, forcing her breakfast higher up her throat. It slunk over her skin to form a tightness in the base of her neck.

Her gaze met a smug, smirking Samuel. He mouthed the word *"goodbye"* at her.

"Both of you. In my office. Now."

James exhaled a curse, putting the drawing down. "Let's get this over with."

Mia hesitated in the doorway of Luc's office until a firm push from James sent her stumbling in. She hadn't stepped foot into the room since Luc had held her against the doorway. The soft *click* of the door made her jump. Her sweaty, stained hands wrung in front of her. She couldn't force herself to raise her eyes to Luc. James stood behind her, a firm wall of flesh blocking her exit.

A panicked nervousness had filled her, making her heart thump and her knees twitch under her skirts, and her words came out in spluttered mumbles. "M-Master Lu-Luc..."

He ignored her, treating her as if she were invisible until he decided she was needed.

"Can you please explain, James, why you gave this girl an opportunity to show off after she destroyed an apprentice's property?"

"Because Mia has earnt it, Luc. She knows more than that thick-skulled idiot out there. From just observing, never touching a brush. She is a natural, I swear."

Luc turned and leant his hands on the desk. "I understand you're feeling confident in the girl's abilities. But we discussed that I would be the one to test her—"

James scoffed, cutting him off. "When she finally fucks you?"

Luc straightened. A tension grew over his shoulders, but he didn't turn, nor did he reply.

"Is that when you'll give her what she's probably born to do? Or will you simply humiliate her more until she flees with her reputation ruined and future destroyed?"

Mia's chin hit her chest, her stained hands screwed into fists. Embarrassment heated her cheeks, making tears prickle. She'd had enough of men speaking of reputations and her fate. It was she who agreed to their deal, and by Oryah, she would use her body in whatever way she saw fit. Whether that was making love, or being rutted into in a dark alley. But it was she who chose. No one else, and definitely not a man.

Before she could speak, Luc's belly laugh filled the room. He turned, his face lit up. "James, my friend. Have you developed feelings for my lovely Mia?"

Surprise flashed over his features. "No. She's simply a promising artist, Luc."

"But you want her, James, don't you? She stirs something in you. Deus, here I thought you only lay with men." He cast Mia a slimy smirk, eyes dragging up and down her body. She fought the urge to cover herself. "I have to admit, she definitely stirs something in me. But you can have her when I'm done. I promise I won't wear her out—"

"No," Mia uttered, finally finding her voice.

Luc's smirk faded as a cool malice grew in his onyx pools. Violence threatened in every step towards her. "Did you say something, Mia?"

"I said no," Mia said shakily. "I agreed to *our* bargain. That is all."

"You will shut your fucking mouth and do as you're told."

A surge of courage filled her, melting the icy fear. Mia wouldn't swallow her words. Not anymore. Never again.

She raised her eyes, meeting the hatred beaming at her, allowing it to flow over her. She stepped forward, closing the distance between them. With all the venom she could muster, she finally spoke, "I'm not yours to give, nor am I yours to grope when you desire it. You do not own—"

A *crack* of skin on skin filled the room, making her stumble back. Her cheek stung, sending her skin pebbling. Luc had slapped her into shocked silence.

"You are mine, Mia, and I will hand you over to any man I see fit," Luc spat. "And you will go willingly."

Mia's hand covered the welting skin, her eyes narrowing. Anger fuelled the trembling—hot, sweaty fury. "I'm not yours, and I will *never* be yours."

Luc's hand snapped out, gripping her elbow and yanking her towards the desk. Mia's feet scrambled over the plush rugs. Her fingers snagged on chairs, tables, but not finding any anchor. She cast a frantic look over her shoulder at James. He looked torn, desperately torn.

Luc slammed her chest first against the table, her stomach biting into the corner, making her gasp for breath.

"Mouthy sluts get punished," Luc sneered in her ear.

"Get off me," Mia demanded

James awoke at the sound of her voice rushing forward. His hands reached for her. "Luc, that's enough—"

"Shut the fuck up, James. Another word, and you're out on the street. Or perhaps I'll inform Lord Hartwinn about a particular rat in his streets. It's been an age since I was warmed by a pyre."

Mia turned her head in time to catch the colour drain from James' face.

"You wouldn't..." he whispered, voice trembling.

"Test me and see."

James' arm fell by his side, and he took a stumbling step back, refusing to meet Mia's wide-eyed gaze.

"Get out," Luc snarled, his breath heaving. "I want her for myself."

Luc's stare never left her, gleaming with resentment. Thumping black veins emerged under his eyes, spreading down over his cheeks—veins that weren't there before.

A soft whimper left Mia, pleading for James to stay—to do anything. Instead, he turned and left the room, his eyes glazed.

"It's time for your next lesson: learning to keep that pretty little mouth shut until I command you to open it and use it."

"Fuck you," Mia retorted, her voice rough. "Get your hands off me."

The sound of Luc's belt unbuckling sent her heart slamming in her ears and her knees trembling so hard that her boots kept a losing grip on the smooth stone. Dark acts of pain and bruises around throats engulfed her mind, dragging her deeper into her dread.

A panicked, "No," flew from her, cracked and broken.

She bucked against the hardwood of the table, fighting. Luc's hand shot out, slamming her down, pinning her with strength she didn't realise he had. The other grabbed a handful of her skirts, yanking them up. Exposing her.

The leather of the belt struck Mia's flesh on the back of her legs in a skin-prickling snap. She cried out, hands flying, pushing books and trinkets from the desk to land with a heavy thump. She knocked over an ink pot in her struggle, spilling it across the wood as if it were black, sticky blood.

Another lashing slapped against her.

Tears dripped from her clenched eyes, soaking into the paper below her, smearing ink. Her legs never stopped their futile fight, nor did her torso stop fish flopping against the hardwood. Panted breath entered her lungs, leaving her simultaneously in heaving sobs.

Mia screwed papers into her fist and screamed, "You're going to burn in the fiery pits of Heylla for this. Get off me!"

Her words only angered him further, retaliating with another messy lash, causing the buckle to gouge her flesh. A single viscous drip of blood ran down the back of her thigh, soaking into her stockings. Luc breathed the hot metallic scent deep into his lungs and let out a satisfied sigh—like he inhaled the perfume she dabbed on her skin.

"My, my, Mia, you're bleeding," he crooned with faked concern.

Two jabbing fingers dragged up the soft, tender flesh, making her wince, capturing the line of blood. From the corner of her eye, she watched him consider it, wetting his lips.

"I wonder what you taste like. It would be such a shame to let it go to waste."

He stuck the fingers in his mouth, sucking off the blood, eyes fluttering closed and tongue darting to capture each smear.

"What in Oryah's name are you doing?" Mia breathed, her feet scurrying.

"Now, now, it's just a little blood. He won't be happy with me marking your skin, but you really need to know your place, with the rest of your kind."

His words meant nothing to her. "My kind?"

"Women."

Magic surged awake inside her. Begged, pleaded with her to let it free to put an end to him. Mia desperately yelled for Ozul to stop, to not reveal her secret. Her insides were ablaze, a furious fire boiling under her skin. Even so, she had no fight left. She either fought the magic demanding to be released, or she battled the monster above her.

Mia chose the latter.

She released Ozul, shadows swirling around her outstretched arms.

A dark chuckle came from Luc. "What do we have here, Mia? You have magic, after all."

She said nothing as a singular shadow slithered towards her, slipping over her jaw, right to her ear.

"*Survive.*"

Another lash, then another struck her, directly over her throbbing wound, splattering her blood across Luc's chest.

A scream left her like a rabbit dying in a trap. It bubbled out, then the harrowing sound was all she could hear over Luc's laboured breathing and the strike of leather. The skin across Mia's rear and the backs of her thighs throbbed painfully, sending the raw pain pulsing over her.

Luc's heaved breath warmed her neck as he leant over her. "You know what magic it is, don't you?"

She refused to answer him as she pushed and squirmed, but Luc had such an iron grip on her that all her fighting was futile. Ozul lashed out, sliding misty fingers around his elbows, yanking, but her strength was waning. And that icy feeling was emerging.

Her gaze never left the shadows. Ozul's unseen eyes never left hers. A light in the devouring darkness.

"It's not fae or vampyric, is it, Mia?" he whispered, lips skimming over her skin. "It's *witch* magic."

Mia gasped, and that was answer enough.

His hand slid to the back of her neck, pressing her face against the rough grain of the desk. Her back concaved, pushing with the points of her shoulders. *I should just get enough leverage—*

Luc forced his body weight against her, slamming her back down. A cold ruby pendant struck her on the cheek. A hardness rubbed on her rear with each buck of her hips.

He was aroused.

With two hard thrusts against her, like a dog in heat, he hissed a groan, hips shuddering.

Her stomach turned, making bile rise in her throat, almost spilling from her across his desk. Disgust for the animal panting above her, who thought he owned her, crashed into her, akin to a punch to the guts.

She squeezed her eyes closed, and another set of tears ran over her wet, red cheeks. The last she would cry in that Heylla hole.

"Now, we both have a secret to keep, don't we?" Luc heaved breathlessly in her ear. "Do you understand, girl? You don't tell a single soul about what happened here, and I won't tell the lord about your little shadow magic."

"Yes," she whispered, her voice hoarse.

"Yes, what?"

"Yes, Master Luc."

His body slipped down off her, hand lingering over her rear. "Good girl. You're learning."

Mia ripped herself away from his touch, pulling her skirts down around her. Hiding the throbbing ache away. Blood soaked into her underskirts. Ozul slid up her legs, bracing her trembling muscles, lest she fall to Luc's feet. Her lowered eyes worked in their sockets as her tears dried on her face. Her body commanded her to run, but she remained rooted to the spot, unable to budge a muscle.

"Go, Mia. I'm done with you for today," Luc dismissed her, rearranging himself. A disgusting wet patch had formed on the front of his pants.

Mia dashed from his office, unplanted by his command. She pushed past James, whose eyes were shiny and his skin ashen. Sick was at his feet.

With each step away from that dark Heylla hole, she scrubbed the tears from her face, smoothed her hair and tried in vain to catch her breath. The only sound she heard was the harrowing scream replaying in her ears until a sharp gasp woke her. She stood in the middle of the studio, eyes searing into her. She met each sad, concerned look until she found the smug Samuel.

Mia strode right up to him, her fist as clenched as her face. "You little rat-faced prick."

"I hope you know your place now, down in the dirt with your filth of a father."

Mia's hand shook. Her knuckles ached to crash into his face and wipe that shit-eating smirk right off his lips, but she knew she had no strength in her muscles.

She exhaled and relaxed her hand. With the lingering anger, she spat, "Next time you want to fuck me, buy me a drink first. And I'd watch your back if I were you. Wouldn't want that pretty throat torn out."

Samuel's smile wavered for a moment as fear flickered in his pupils, making Mia sneer. She turned on her heel, storming from him and the other apprentices. Their whispers flooded over her, worming their way into her mind.

"She gets punished differently than us."

"That's too far over a broken glass and some charcoal."

"I could share my easel."

"Did you hear her scream?"

THIRTY

Vomit splashed onto the cobblestones and onto Mia's boots in disgusting green splatters as she threw up in a dank, muddy alleyway of the lower city. Her breath heaved as much as her stomach. Her legs moved with such a ferocity that she barely knew where she was running to. But she knew what she was running from: the ghost of Luc's touch and her terrified, pained screaming.

It isn't the man I wished to hurt.

The thought made Mia slow, wiping her mouth on her sleeve. She had never desired to harm anyone, never had the urge to. *Has something changed in me?* She waited for the malice-filled voice to call her a monster. But he never came.

Mia glanced down, that stray shadow curling around her ankle, slinking like a cat, waiting to be fed. *Have I become the evil witch in all the stories I have heard?*

"*No,*" Ozul uttered.

She pushed off the wall, stepping back into the throng of bodies. The shadow swirled higher up her leg, safely hidden under her skirt. She hadn't demanded them to go. Not yet.

Wandering the street, she found herself under The Cauldron's swinging sign. Her body took her there in search of safety. As strange as it was to feel safe in a rough, seedy pub, she stared at the flecked, faded piece of paint for a long while, letting the breeze pull strands of hair from behind her ear. Her skin was pulsating dully on her thighs and on her rear, crisscross bruises taking form. The smell of parchment and ink lingered in her nose, mixing with the acidity of her vomit. That scared scream played in the distance of her hearing, backing the indistinct murmur of the city, steadily growing louder and louder until she could hear nothing else.

Her name was called, but it sounded far away. The voice resembled Idris, but gentler, almost strained in its softness. It was like those voices on the wind, or the ones late at night under a full moon, desperately trying to cut through the distressed crying. She reached for the sound, only for it to vanish like fog on a chilly morning.

A calloused hand brushed over her elbow, waking her. She jumped back, scrambling. Her bag thumped to the ground, contents spilling across the stones.

"Woah up. It's just me, love," Benny murmured, voice filling her ears, drowning out the screams.

Mia blinked up at him in a daze. He beamed concern down at her. His face clenched into a tight grimace as he took in her tear-stained red cheeks, her trembling body.

"Hello, Benny. You're a sight for sore eyes."

He cast her a soft smile and crouched down, gathering her belongings. "And you're a welcome one. Would you like to come inside?"

Mia sniffed, nodding. "I would love that."

He herded her into the bar with a hovering hand as if her legs would collapse under her at any moment. He led her straight to a stool, ordering her to sit. She slid onto it gingerly, grimacing at the ache radiating up her spine. Her hands spread over the worn, scarred wood, savouring the solid feeling under her palms.

"Is he here?" she asked quietly as Benny rounded the bar.

A glass of whisky and chipped ice was placed in front of her. "Not yet."

Mia gripped the glass around the top, staring directly at the amber liquid, aching for the numb abyss. Instead of gulping it down, she held it to her sore cheek, appreciating the icy sting.

Benny leant on the bar. "What happened, Mia?"

"Pissed off the wrong person," she said bluntly.

"Does this person look as bad as you?"

Luc's face flashed in her mind, flushed and leering. "Quite the opposite, actually.'

The doors of The Cauldron swung open so forcefully that they rattled on their frames. Idris shouldered through. His whole body coiled with tension, eyes dark with anger, deepening the emerald to a forest green. He looked like a man incensed, ready to explode.

A part of her was frightened of him, but another popped and sizzled deep in her lower belly.

Idris' gaze found her slumped on a stool. Surprise unclenched his features. He stalked over to her, and without a word, snatched the full glass from her, draining it in one draw. His hands were bloody, knuckles split open, matching hers.

"What happened to you?" he asked, dumping the empty glass on the bar.

"What happened to you?"

"I asked first."

Mia dunked her fingers into the drink to figure out an answer. *The truth,* she guessed. But she didn't know if she could speak it yet without her voice wobbling. She fished out an ice chip, pressing it to her lips. She savoured the last hint of whisky before crunching down. Idris eyeballed the developing bruise on her cheek.

"I pissed off Luc."

"So he hit you?" Benny gasped, splashing more whisky.

"He punished me," Mia corrected. "As is his right as my master."

Idris took another deep drink and muttered into the empty glass, "That would be the case if you were an apprentice."

Mia shot him a sharp look, her eyes falling to his bloody, bruised hand. *You will heal like a human.* Sorcha's words echoed in her mind. *Well, then, he should treat his body like a human would.*

"Your hand needs some ice, Old Man."

She dug into her pocket for her handkerchief, tugging it free. The fancy lacy edges were stark against the worn bar as she laid it flat to dump the remaining ice into it. She bundled it up and pressed the wet, cold material against Idris' knuckles. He hissed and tried to pull away. But Mia simply grasped his hand tighter, rolling her eyes. "You're fine, you big, bloodsucking baby."

Benny laughed, sending the deep musical sound around the silent bar.

Idris' gaze lingered on their clasped hands, a smirk curled on his lip. "Your bedside manner is lacking."

She scoffed a laugh. "Good thing I'm not a healer, then."

Idris' free hand slipped over hers, holding her tight. "Did he do anything else?"

She trembled, making his eyebrows twitch inwards, creating a deep crease between his brows. A quiet, "No," was all she could muster.

Idris cocked his head like he didn't believe her.

She barely believed it.

Words—even thoughts—about what had happened in that dark office were lost on her. She wanted to forget. Force those memories into a locked box in her mind. But the throbbing was a constant reminder. She pushed off the stool and away from Idris' touch.

"Since we've all shared and cared, can we please track this arsehole for the fifth night, so no more women lose their lives?"

Shadows engulfed the dark side lane where they were huddled. The only light beamed from the wide windows of the white marble building with its distinctive red door. Laughter, lusty moans and soft harp music slipped through, seeping into the night air.

A hooded Mia leant against the cool stone wall, arms crossed, with Idris looming behind her. Reagan and his cronies were easy to follow across Alderdeen's taverns and inns. He drank and laughed his way through the city, spilling gold and curses under the moonlight. Every night.

"Bloody Deus. He really loves this place, doesn't he? He ends up here most nights," Idris murmured.

Mia hummed a response, her eyes locked on the mass of black curls stepping through the throngs of people. "Maybe it simply has the finest entertainment, Old Man?"

"Madame Diamone's has the best whores in all the city, Little Witch. You know this is a brothel, right?"

Mia flashed him a surprised glance over her shoulder. She hadn't ever considered the vast, wealthy building a brothel. Flashes of dirty, dingy buildings with emaciated women lurking around came to mind.

"Of course I knew that," she lied. "He's already moved on and in another's bed."

"You don't have to love a woman to fuck her, Mia."

"I know," she grumbled, crossing her arms tighter around her ribs, refusing to allow the memories of the drunken weeks to inch out. "I thought you might not want to be with someone so soon after losing the love of your life."

Idris went still, and then softly added, "You wouldn't, Mia. Not a single fibre of you would want another. Perhaps he didn't truly love Kali..."

Mia pursed her lips, pulling them to the side of her face. *Did he? Did Reagan truly love Kali? Or did he think she belonged to him, like a piece of property bestowed to him after she gave him what he wanted in that maid's closet?*

She pushed off the wall, wanting to flee from the uncomfortable feeling developing in her chest. "She believed he did. Now, let's get closer."

Mia strode down the lane into a small courtyard, ignoring Idris' harsh whisper of her name. She crouched, edging closer to the warm, clean glass of one of the large bay windows. A rowdy party was going on inside Madame Diamone's. Beautiful women swanned around the room dressed in thin, gauzy material. The seductive curves of their bodies were on show, right down to the pink peaks of their breasts, and the dark hair between their thighs. Men played card games, gold coins flashing on the table.

In her search, she found Reagan, grinning with a moaning fae woman draped in his lap, one hand up her skirt and a drink in the other. Mia's fingernails dug into the paint on the windowsill as bitter disappointment flooded her. "That fucking arsehole..."

Idris slipped behind her, encasing her in his arms. His chin resting on her shoulder, his warm breath swirling in her ear. "Be more careful, Little Witch. Someone might see you."

"So what if I am seen? I would presume they have men peeping in regularly."

"This place is known to be deadly if they find anyone spying on their girls, and I'd prefer not to scoop up your insides from the cobblestone tonight."

Reagan had finished his drink and was whispering in the woman's ear. A sultry grin spread on her face as she pulled from his lap and led him to an entrance masked by thick velvet curtains.

"Let us not lose sight of him," Idris whispered with a nod at the rickety, rusted ladder leading to a roof.

Mia swallowed and nodded, hoping that pile of rust would hold her weight. Ducking under his arm, she crept across the courtyard. She clambered up with only a few squeaks from the metal. Dropping to her belly, she squirmed to the edge of the roof, leaning on her forearms. The chill night air bit at the backs of her legs, causing her skin to pebble. She quickly glanced at each window until she found a Reagan-shaped figure, face-first in the voluptuous breasts of the woman. Idris crouched next to her, pushing his hood back.

"Good goddess, one woman to another."

"Like I said—"

A loud *snap* of his jaw cut off his sentence, resonating loudly in the night's calm. Idris had caught sight of the welts on her legs and the dried blood on her skirts.

"He took a belt to you, Mia. I knew he'd hurt you, but a belt..." he growled, his voice hard. Harder than she had ever heard it.

Embarrassment flushed her cheeks, making her reach down to cover herself. But his hand snapped out, gripping her wrist, stopping her.

Hesitantly, he dragged her skirts up a fraction—enough to see the beginnings of the dark, plum-coloured bruises twisting over her flesh. He delicately pulled her skirt down.

Shame twisted deep in her guts. For what, she didn't know.

"He punished me as he saw fit to," Mia repeated, tears threatening. In the smallest voice, she added, "Maybe I deserved it..."

Idris went so still, she wasn't sure he heard her. Until his body trembled and his eyes bored into her. Indignation burnt in his pupils, bright in the darkness. The thick waves of rage flowed from him, almost lashing at her.

"*Deserved* it?" Idris repeated through a clenched jaw. His head shook with each heavy breath. "No one should ever raise their hand to you, Mia. Ever. Regardless of what you have done."

She turned back to the soft lantern light. A tear escaped down her cheek in a salty stream. She had thought she cried all her tears.

"I've never felt so scared, so weak..." Mia's voice faded as her lips trembled. "He enjoyed that fear. I could feel him enjoying it."

Idris abruptly rose, stalking into the darkness. His shaky exhales filled the silence between them. "You aren't weak, Mia. You burn bright —that's why he wants to extinguish you. Do not allow him to put out your fire."

Mia scrubbed her cheek, raising her chin. "His brutality has done nothing of the sort, Idris. He has simply added fuel to the flame."

"Only a coward strikes a woman. I wonder how he would fare against a man."

Mia spun to Idris' figure in the dark, her lips screwing up into a frown. "You don't need to swoop down and save me, Old Man. I'm no damsel in distress, and you're no charming prince. Your meddling will only make it worse."

"Then quit. If you need coin, you can work at The Cauldron. Benny always grumbles about needing help."

"I'm not quitting," Mia said firmly, turning back to the windows, hugging her knees. "He wins if I quit, and all of it will have been for nothing."

Idris saddled up beside her, shoulders still tense. It was not the revolting scene unfolding in front of them that caught his gaze, but her. The indignation had burnt away. "He beat you, Mia."

"Tell me something I don't know, Idris," she snapped back, tightening her arms around herself. She exhaled in annoyance. "I want to show him that I deserve to be there. That my gender has nothing to do with my ability. I want to show him that a woman can be better than him—surpass him, even."

He scrubbed his jaw. "Until then, how are you going to defend yourself?"

Mia didn't reply, simply watching Reagan lift the woman and take her to bed, moving out of sight. He wasn't going anywhere for a long time. Or a short time. Mia knew it would be the latter.

Idris' question fermented in her mind. *How would I defend myself? I fought when he had me pinned, but could I have truly defended myself?*

"You don't need to be so concerned for me. I'll be fine."

"Convincing, Little Witch," Idris said flatly. "Do you know how to use a blade or throw a punch?"

Mia shook her head.

Idris paused and took a deep breath. Then, he asked in a softer voice, "I can show you, if you like?"

She turned her face and rested her cheek against her knee, casting him a soft expression. "I would like that very much."

"As long as you don't turn the blade on me, Little Witch, we have a deal."

Mia's grin widened, making Idris' lips edge up. "No promises, Old Man. Now, about those creatures..." Her voice faded into the sounds of the city as she explained every detail of Sorcha's research.

THIRTY-ONE

MIA SLAMMED THE BOOK SHUT, SENDING DUST THROUGH THE air. The gush of wind made the candlelight flicker, shadows dancing across the dark room. She said Sorcha's name in a long, frustrated moan. Pushing back from the table, she stretched the tight muscles in her neck. The ticking timepiece on the wall showed that it was three in the morning.

They had been reading for hours, trawling through thick books scrawled in tiny, swirling handwriting until it blurred and her head thumped. Mia couldn't take any more information in. The accounts written by scholars years long before her birth clung to the insides of her mind like sticky molasses.

Evil creatures, hungry for power, summoned their magic from their own blood. Uncontrollable, raw magic. Queens with no kings. Covens of women who had more husbands than sense.

"Just a few more pages..." Sorcha murmured, distracted.

"You realise you could have found me at a more reasonable hour? This is too much reading, and far too serious for this time of night."

Sorcha's eyes rose from the dog-eared, dusty journal she was reading, placing it down, arching her brow at her. "I don't know what you expected, Mia, that we open one book, and bam, the answer will be there?"

Mia shot her a smirk, her fingers flicking another book open. "Deep in the mountains of the north, tales of a coven of witches whose skin burnt hot, with flames surrounding them. They were known as the Ignis—" She snapped it shut, groaning. "I thought maybe you'd have done some pre-reading or something."

A smile curled on Sorcha's lips, her eyes not leaving the words. "No, Mia. I have enough to do, and I have my masters' test in two days—"

"Two days?" Mia cut in, her voice a fraction higher. "What are you doing here with me? You should be studying for that."

The healer waved a hand at her, then resumed flicking the thin pages. "I can pass that test with my eyes closed, and I have all the required experience from my days as a *Slanaigher*. Well, that's if they want to instil"—she paused as a pained look flashed over her face—"a fae healer as a master. Some think it's pandering to the city's current situation. Others think we shouldn't have to beg for scraps, especially a certain Mr Wyn Nightclove. The gall of that man, serving Hartwinn, then being upset at the rest of us for simply attempting to survive. "

"Oh," was Mia's only reply.

She had watched Henry face the same adversity as Sorcha. The same side-eyed looks and whispers, taking it all with a stoicism that Mia herself didn't possess. He was an outsider in a place he had called home for decades. Even with Hartwinn giving him a human title of lord. Their little club still refused to accept him—not that Mia thought he had any interest in mingling with the grey, wrinkled noble class of Alderdeen.

Sorcha bravely faced it on her own, in a place known for eating their young. A strange swell of emotion overcame Mia—close to pride and a light-hearted joy. She'd let her in, and Mia was glad. She needed a friend, and so did Sorcha, it seemed.

Mia grinned and reached over, gripping her hand. "Well, those people can go fuck themselves, because you'd make an excellent master. Pointy ears or not."

Sorcha quickly glanced around and whispered back, "Yes, they can go fuck themselves."

Mia cackled, her shoulders shaking.

A wide grin spread across Sorcha's face, making her eyes crinkle and her cheeks flush. Then, a musical laugh escaped her. She laughed as if she hadn't in a while. She tucked a frizzy curl behind her ear, fingers lingering on the delicate point. "Thank you, Mia. I have found that some people can't see past these."

Mia leant back, straightening out like a cat who had napped in the sun for too long. "There is no need to thank me, Sorcha. And so you know, a great many people are total bloody fools."

Sorcha's gaze dipped back to the tatty old journal in front of her, still giggling. Her eyes skimmed over words, her smile fading a fraction. She breathed Mia's name, eyes flashing up and down. Her voice shook when she read out the line, "A shadow bent at the crook of her forefinger, called forth from nothing. The witch sat upon a throne of solid obsidian, commanding the air as if she were queen of the whole of the land. Her eyes gleamed before she let over to her fae husband and whispered in his ear. And she pointed that same shadowy finger at me—"

"Another account of another woman who men obviously feared or wanted to bed."

Sorcha tapped the page impatiently. "No—well, yes, but 'a shadow bent at her finger,' Mia. A shadow."

Mia's palms moistened as a lick of heat curled around her spine. "I heard you."

Sorcha's eyes worked in their sockets rapidly while her lips moved with muttered words. Her finger dragged over the words, then flicked the page. Her hand froze as her eyes grew wide. She sat back heavily, hand over her mouth, and simply pushed the journal across the table to her.

"What is it?" Mia asked. Her question came out more panicked than she wished it had. She scrambled to pick up the journal, holding the worn leather in her hands. She flicked to the page Sorcha was reading from, eyes scanning the words until she found what had shocked her friend.

The witch was none other than Queen Maeve Magntai, ruler of the smallest but most powerful witch coven of all that I have witnessed for King Ewan: the Umbra Coven. She commanded shadows to do her devilish doing, but her political power came from the treaty that was let slip by a drunken knight. A treaty with the true vampyre king, Mortias...

Mia exhaled sharply as a slither of unease slid down her back. The unnerving feeling of a pair of eyes fell on her, watching her, sending her hairs straight up, but she kept reading, almost compelled to.

The treaty was ancient, secretive. I presume that the guard got punished—or worse, executed—as I never saw him again. No one I asked would tell me what either party did for one another. Another tight-lipped secret. I assume it's a simple trade agreement of goods or services, or maybe even women. Mortias has many sons to marry, but Queen Maeve is either barren or only produces unsuitable bastards for the king. The more I dug, the more the court closed in. Until I was asked to leave. Something's happening here. Something King Ewan will need to know about for his expansion. I may head to Mortias' court...

An ink spill covered the remaining words.

Mia flicked the page over, finding only blank paper. The journal was empty.

She groaned, dumping it on the table. More questions lingered, and none were answered.

"Where is the rest?"

Sorcha shrugged, chewing her lip. "Books on witches are few and far between, and most cannot be read by any old healer. I received permission only after I begged for it. These were diaries of an envoy of King Ewan, Sir Lawrence Oliver. Some of them may exist in the capital, while others may have been lost to time. He could have even died. Plagues and rogue attacks were common in that era."

Maeve.

The name stirred something in Mia's chest, much like the one when she had stood under the painting of her.

"Well, whoever this queen was, she had shadows, Mia. And she is the only witch we have found with the same magic as you."

Her jaw clenched at the word *magic*. Her eyes slid to the corner, where the shadows appeared a fraction darker—they were always waiting, watching.

"But doesn't magic need to be wielded through something?"

Sorcha nodded, her hand waving in the air as she explained. "Yes, but I need a conduit—usually something from nature—to funnel it through. Whereas witches conjure their power from nothing but their own flesh and blood."

Mia resisted the urge to roll her eyes at Sorcha. *She made witch magic sound crude and bizarre. As if it were wrong that they could have that much power just in what pumped through their veins.*

She traced the date stamped into the leather with her forefinger. It was over thirty years ago. Long before Mia even graced the earth, but only a handful of years before the Great Burning. King Ewan had been planning the massacre years before he marched on the witches, gathering information.

"And it's dangerous and unwomanly. I gathered that from the multitude of old, grumpy men who thought it was unnatural that women had all the power. That males were less powerful witches, relegated to the trades and farming and simply being sires for their children," Mia said bitterly.

Sorcha abruptly stood and, without a word, disappeared into the darkness, leaving her confused and gazing in her direction. Her booted footsteps were loud in the room's quietness. Mia wrung her hands together, a bubble of anxiety growing within her. *Maybe I have said too much, been too honest. Perhaps Sorcha doesn't want to listen to me rant.*

Sorcha emerged from the darkness, holding a red rose and wearing a determined expression.

"Oh, Sorcha, you shouldn't have gotten me flowers," Mia gushed dramatically, hand spread across her chest, a grin spreading.

The healer narrowed her eyes playfully, a smile on her lips. "I want to show you my fae magic. Then we can practise whatever your magic is, every night, right here. Until you have a grasp on it. Until you feel in control."

Mia's smile fell, shaking her head. "I cannot ask you to do that, and I don't think that's a good idea—"

"You can and you will," Sorcha cut in, her voice firm but encouraging.

Mia sighed and said, "Fine. But if I blow up the Medicus Tower, I want to let it be known that I warned you. And I'm awfully grumpy when kept up past my bedtime."

Sorcha shushed her with a tight-lipped hiss and held the rose out by the stem with delicate fingers, so as not to crush it.

"Oh, good goddess, you've conjured a rose!" Mia said drily.

"Please hold back your smartarse quips. I'm attempting to concentrate."

She closed her eyes and took a deep breath in, then out. The rose started to shake and tremble in the air.

"*Teine...*" she mumbled. *Fire.* Mia knew enough fae words to know that.

The petals caught flame, blazing hot and heavy. The flames ate away the flower, ash raining down around their boots. Mia gasped, scrambling back. A faded, aged memory exploded in her mind. The warmth of fiery flames against skin, bitter ash on her tongue and a name being called out, painfully and heartbreakingly.

Ophelia.

Hurt flared in her from an ache she couldn't identify. Tears clouded her vision as her hands trembled at her sides.

"Easy, Mia. What is it?" Sorcha asked, her face gleaming with sweat.

Her toes curled in her boots, gripping onto the leather beneath her. "A memory of fire and pain."

Tears rolled down her cheeks as her lips opened and closed. Horrors flashed before her eyes of witches being dragged to pyres, screaming and crying, reaching for one another. Her breath became strangled.

"There is so much hurt, Sorcha. It's suffocating."

That flash of flames had unlocked a box of memories. She expected the pain to be everlasting, forever, but fear froze the heat. That cold sweat, muscle-locking fear. A slip of velvet curled around her fingers, then encircled her arm. The shadows were slipping from the chokehold she held on her magic.

"*You do not fear us. We are you. We are one,*" Ozul whispered.

Sorcha exhaled softly, urging her with a gentle nod. "Emotions, Mia. That's how you tap into your magic."

"Emotions?" she wheezed back. Maybe it wasn't just a hold she had on her magic, but her own feelings.

"Just let yourself feel, Mia. Anger, hurt, happiness. Whatever it is, just feel."

She dragged a lungful of air into her unwilling chest. More tears escaped down her cheeks. "But what if I cannot stop feeling? What if it drowns me?"

Her friend's hands found her elbows, forcing Mia to meet her eyes. "Then I will come down to those depths and drown with you. You are not alone. Not anymore."

She nodded, her own reaching for Sorcha's forearms, gripping on tightly. "Maybe it doesn't always have to be hurt."

"No, Mia. It can be joy or love. Anything."

Love. I want it to be love.

Mia squeezed her eyes closed, picturing Kali as she was before she died: bright and radiant. Her sister danced over the fallen ash, skirts swirling, sweeping it away with each step. She cast her bright light over whatever darkness that memory had unlocked. The love that she had for Kali filled her so much that Mia thought she could sense her standing behind her, urging her to set her magic free and, in turn, free herself from the shackles of grief. She knew shadows were slipping from her; she could hear Sorcha's approving sounds.

"Be free," she whispered to the void. "I will not hold you so tightly anymore. I promise."

"*You need not promise us anything. We are here because you are here,*" her magic replied.

Her eyes snapped open to see shadows spilling from fists. They circled her, creating lashing winds around herself and Sorcha like a misty hurricane. Hair whipped against her face, skirts swirling out. A shadow slipped to each candle, extinguishing the orange flame. Until one was blazing. The darkness lashed out, dousing the last flame, leaving the two in the dark. Then, those deep, booming female voices came from the void, "*We have missed you, witchling. Your sisters are waiting for you...*"

PART THREE:
Desire Can Make a Devil Grow Inside You

Thirty-Two

The dangerously sharp blade weighed heavily in Mia's palm, the ripples of steelwork capturing the midday sun and her soft yawn. Her days were long and her nights late. Between scrubbing paint-brushes, avoiding Luc and Sorcha and her headache-inducing tutoring, Mia almost forgot what her bed felt like.

Out of all things the blade could bring—death and bloody wounds —she savoured the sense of safety more. Something that could protect her from the fear that Luc's hand on her spine gave her, or the wailing cries she still heard.

"Am I boring you?" Idris drawled.

Mia's eyes rose slowly from the dagger to her enthusiastic teacher. He stood across from her, collar open, exposing the scattering of chest hair, with his sleeves rolled up, displaying the ropey muscles of his fore-arm. They had chosen the largest room in her home to train in, pushing aside furniture. Only the soft footsteps and the quiet murmurs of the maids and butlers filled the manor; Henry and Anne were out visiting Wyn in the Westryn District. But when Idris walked the halls, casting Mia that dimpled grin over his shoulder, he breathed life back into the cold, sombre house. Strange for someone who was technically dead—or so Mia knew from the crumbs of vampyre knowledge she had.

"Are you dead?"

Confusion flashed across his features. "What?"

She took a step closer, relaxing her arm to her side. "Like, I know you're alive, but..."

"No, Little Witch. I'm not dead. Our rebirth takes something from our seemingly human bodies as a sacrifice, but leaves us with the wondrous gift of a long life. We are not born bloodthirsty creatures, if that's what you are asking."

Mia shot him an unconvinced look, crossing her arms, careful not to nick herself with the dagger.

"Prove it."

Idris' eyes narrowed, a smirk curled on his lips. He took two slow steps towards her, forcing her to crane her chin to not lose eye contact. His fingers danced over her arm to her hand, pulling it from her own embrace. He drew her palm over the thudding pulse on the column of his neck, making her breath hitch.

"I can assure you, Little Witch, I am very much alive."

The clumsy dancing they had been doing around the feelings growing between them was over. Entwining hands, they gazed at one another. In cascades of emerald and brown, their gazes fell to one another's lips. Mia's cheeks warmed, sending a rush of heat to her core. "Good to know, Old Man. Let's keep it that way, hey?"

"I have no plans of leaving this world yet, Mia," Idris murmured, voice softening.

She searched those limitless pools for a sliver of the feeling that had been in her chest since their first chance meeting, hoping it was growing in him, little by little. Her lips ached for the firm pressure of his, to taste that honeyed sweetness. But words failed her, as did her actions. She didn't want to ruin it by rushing in, forcing the moment.

The world and its constant noise seemed to pause as Idris leant down. Mia's breath came in short and uneven. Instead of kissing her, he leant his forehead on hers, eyes fluttering closed. The simple gesture made her weak at the knees.

She stared up at the spread of black lashes, then over the lines and freckles across his tanned face. She wondered about the life he had led before he sauntered into her own. *What have his eyes seen? Has he felt the specks of sea salt from the distant ocean on his cheeks? Has he had icy snowflakes fall on his lips? Has he known the scorching suns of the faraway deserts?*

All her questions died on her tongue, and she simply allowed herself to enjoy the moment until it was cruelly snatched away from her. Her hand trembled at the bitter grief, taking bites of the gentle joy building in her.

"I'm not going anywhere, Mia," he whispered.

Her eyes betrayed her fear of losing another. "Truth?"

A small smile curled on his lip. "Truth."

She didn't know how long they stood for. Seconds dragged into minutes, then hours. The shadows slid from her to tangle in her fingers. The dull thud of an iron dagger falling from her relaxed hand woke them from their embrace.

"We better make a start on your training before your father returns and finds you in a room, *alone*, with a *man*," he joked, his voice a touch uneven.

Mia cast him a grin and chuckled. But as she began to pull away, he pressed his lips to her forehead, making her heart skip a beat. Her cheeks burnt with such ferocity, she thought steam must be leaving her ears. Before she could think, she wrapped Idris in a tight embrace, that solid thud in her ear.

"I liked that..." he murmured into her hair. "I like just being with you."

"And this is enough. I need nothing more," she replied, pulling away to scoop up the blade.

Was that the truth? Do I need more than a whisper of a promise and a press of lips?

He grinned at her, pointed canine and all. "Now, lesson one: pointy end is the stabby end."

Mia rolled her eyes, raising the dagger. "Obviously. What about this rebirth? I have hazy memories of a scummy vamp weaving me a tale of feeding and...carnal pleasures."

Idris raised both his brows, and a huff of a laugh left him. "Carnal pleasures?"

Mia waved the iron at him to keep talking.

"When vampyres are born, we have a type of malady that slowly eats away at our bodies until we're feverish, delirious. We have to drain most of our blood away to rid ourselves of the sickness over whatever was left of Deus' blessed tree. Praying for him to save our souls, only to have to replace it as soon as we awaken from the delirium. Then, forever onwards, we must consume blood to stop the sickness latching on again."

"So you have just to drink someone else's blood when you awaken?"

"No, Mia, we have to drain another. The rebirth demands and demands until it is sated."

"So you—"

Idris' eyes flashed to hers. An old hurt flared, all joy faded.

"I had no choice, Mia. My father forced my hand. 'Drink or live in a state of permanent hunger, roaming this world until you're put down like a rabid dog,' is what he said. I guess my sense of self-preservation was higher those days." He exhaled. "The woman...was sick. She wouldn't have survived the rebirth, nor would she have lived many more years. I pray it was more of a kindness for her, then a sacrifice."

Mia let the words settle between them for a moment before firing another. "Can someone make a vampyre?"

"I presume you know how babies are made, Little Witch,'" he said, cheeks turning a pretty pink. "But if you need someone to show you—"

She glared at him and continued. "Not birth one, Old Man, but create them. Like those dhampyr in Sorcha's journals."

Idris went wholly still. His eyes hardened, as did his voice. "No. No one alive possesses such power. Now, are we training, or what?"

MIA HAD JABBED FORWARD AND BACK FOR AN AGE. Tiredness had made her sloppy and unfocused. She stumbled, tripping on her boots, and fell into Idris' waiting arms. His hand slid over her soft stomach, gripping around her the swell of her hip and righting her. The blade had clattered to the hardwood at their tangled feet. He breathed her name in her ear with a chuckle, sending a shiver down her spine, the warmth on her face getting hotter.

"You're downright awful at this."

Her heart slammed against her chest, and not because of the exercise she wasn't used to. She squirmed, only making him grip her tighter.

"Perhaps it's the teacher, not the student," she fired back, casting a glare over her shoulder.

Idris leant down, lips brushing on the shell of her ear. "Keep talking shit like that and I'll have you on your back."

"Or maybe I'll have you on your back, Old Man. Have you thought of that?"

"Oh, Little Witch, I've thought about it. Long and hard."

The silence echoed around as their words settled.

The unspoken meaning behind their words was heavy, weighing down the syllables. Reality crashed around her, so she ripped herself from his arms and strode across the room. She had almost forgotten the darkness that had seeped into her life, and the heart-aching reason she greeted his emerald eyes every day.

She caught Idris exhaling and releasing his dark hair from the corner of her eye. "Mia—"

"What is the plan you were sprouting out earlier?" she cut in, turning back to him. A pained smile spread across her face. She didn't want to speak about the moment they'd just shared.

"Like I said, we need to get closer to Reagan before the ball. We need more evidence to determine if he is indeed this master, or if he is involved only in Kali's death. The two could be completely separate."

Mia took a tentative step closer, crossing her arms. "I'm listening."

"We infiltrate the Madame Diamone and get more information."

She arched a brow at him. Her fingers itched to cover her scar. "Reagan and his goons will recognise me. If you haven't noticed, I'm distractingly beautiful."

"Not tomorrow night. Your beauty won't enchant them as you'll be masked, like all the women. It's their annual Night of Sin, a nod to Diabolus."

"How coincidental," Mia muttered under her breath. "But tomorrow? I cannot have a dress made that quickly, and simply have nothing to wear to a place like that."

A mischievous smirk cut across his face, pushing that damn dimple up and sending his eyes gleaming. "Find, borrow or steal something then, Little Witch."

THIRTY-THREE

Dresses of all different colours and materials were strewn across her bed, over the velvet-backed chair, in heaped piles on the ground. Mia stood in front of her nearly empty cupboard, hands on her hips.

A disgruntled curse came from her.

She simply had nothing to wear. Nothing was scandalous enough, nor fit for a night of spying on Reagan in one of the most dangerous places in Alderdeen's underbelly.

The soft tendrils of excitement had begun to eat away at the deeply planted roots in her chest, taking hold. A slip of velvet curled around her wrist. Mia raised her hand, watching the shadows swirl through her fingers like a strip of ribbon. It was curiosity, not fear, that was catapulted into her.

"What shall we wear?" she murmured to Ozul.

"*Green.*"

Mia blinked in surprise and shook Ozul from her hand, forming a soft, black mist in the air. "That is still unnerving, you know. I wouldn't expect whatever you are to be such a chatterbox. Also, it isn't simply green. It's malachite."

She glanced at the only gown she hadn't pulled from the mess of velvets and silks. The swooping neckline of the silk dress stared back at her. With a trembling hand, she picked it up from the bottom of the cupboard. The skirts swirled as she turned, allowing the thick, luxurious material to bellow out. It wasn't hers, but Kali's, given to her after her sister had worn it once.

Her gaze swept over the layers of shimmering fabric, savouring the smooth feeling under her palm. It appeared fresh off the manikin of the dressmakers. The laced back ensured it would fit, however, it would be a tight squeeze.

Tears brewed. Never again would her sister wear a silk gown, or anything else. For the rest of the time, she would don one of golden sunrays. Glorious and beautiful. Mia wondered, as she walked to her bathroom with her sister's dress in her arms, if that was exactly what Kali should have always worn.

Mia's trembling fingers smoothed the soft fabric over her curves, tucking a loose wave behind an ear, cursing herself for cutting her hair so short. The bodice hugged her breasts too snuggly, spilling flesh, leaving little to the imagination. The full skirt billowed out from her waist with a slit that exposed her thigh with every anxious step around her room.

She propped her foot up on her chair, strapping the dagger Idris had given her to her thigh, hoping she wouldn't have to use it. Mia exhaled and checked her reflection once more. Her attention wasn't captured by the pretty pink rouge on her lips, but by the nervous pupil dilation staring at her.

"You will be fine," she said to herself. "Idris is going to be there to prot—"

She could hear Kali's voice in the depths of her mind, chastising her, reminding her who she was, and that she didn't need protection from a man.

She had everything she needed within her.

Mia saw her lips turn up, allowing the nervousness to be edged away from her eyes.

Her gaze dropped to the mess of jars and vials surrounding a black velvet mask. She plucked up an hourglass-shaped amber perfume. The liquid sloshed in the bottle as she dabbed it on the inside of her wrist, and on her thudding pulse. Then, cheekily, on the inside of her ankles. The sweet orange, pine, and musk scent swirled around her.

A memory of Kali rose to the surface. At the Moonshye Market, she sprayed and dramatically smelt each until she had found Mia's perfect scent. Then, in true Kali fashion, she spent thirty minutes bartering until Mia handed over only half of her allowance.

"I'm finally wearing it, Kali," she whispered to the air, eyes searching. "I'm finally living…"

Thirty-Four

The black velvet mask was soft against Mia's face, hiding her from both leering and curious glances. She peered over her shoulder with each step. The streets were packed, and the setting sun deepened the shadows. Whatever monster or man lurked in them was invisible.

She yanked her cloak around her tighter, adding more heat to her already overly warm skin. Nervous sweat coated her, and she hoped it didn't bleed into the expensive material of the dress. She slowed to a stop in front of the red doors of Madame Diamone.

A presence settled behind her, then a soft dance of fingertips trailed over the gathered waist of the dress, spreading out over her rib cage and drawing her back against a hard slab of muscle. She tensed as alarm flooded her already on-edge nerves. She clumsily darted for the hilt of the dagger.

"And here I thought you'd promised not to use that blade on me, Little Witch," Idris crooned. The heat from his breath brushed over that sensitive spot between her ear and the curve of her throat, sending a prickle down her spine.

Mia grumbled a curse, shoving him away with an elbow. Turning, she shot a glare at him. "Don't bloody sneak up on me, Old Man, or you'll be my first victim."

Idris was lit by a burning lantern, that dimpled grin spread on his unshaven face. His surcoat was open, exposing a black-collared shirt tucked into skintight breeches. His amused gaze dipped, sweeping over each curve and dip of her body. He almost groaned. "You look..."

"Beautiful? Amazing? Incredible?" Mia finished with an impish smirk and a swirl of skirts.

He stepped in closer until their bodies were flush. Without a word, he reached up and pulled the gold pin securing the small bun, releasing her blonde curls. He dragged his fingers through her locks, inhaling her.

"Lavender..." Idris murmured. His hand settled at the base of her neck, thumb caressing along her pounding pulse. "That's what it is."

His gaze devoured her, turning that emerald into a sliver of green. He leant closer still, lips brushing over her cheek to the shell of her ear. "You are utterly, absolutely indecent in that dress, Mia. But I think you'd look better out of it."

The plan they had painstakingly gone over vanished from her mind, leaving only honeyed, desire-filled thoughts. That throbbing, sweaty need almost sent her rabid, wanting to tear at his clothing, to press her mouth to salty body parts, then slam into each other as they come undone. Never had she ached for another so painfully before.

Her hands went to each side of his surcoat, dragging him closer. "Idris," she whispered huskily. "Take me home and ruin me fo—"

"I'm going to have that redhead fae screaming tonight. You'll see," Reagan's drunken voice rang down the street.

The tension building between them snapped like a broken bone and left them both aching and breathless. She stepped out of Idris' reach, tucking her hair behind an ear, motioning to the red door with a nod. "Shall we?"

THE NOISES OF THE BROTHEL—THE SOFT LAUGHTER, GLASSES tinking together and throaty female moans—embraced Mia, lulling her in. She swayed into the room, attached to the grim-faced Idris. She shrugged off her cloak to a masked, scantily clad woman, who took it with a sultry curl of her lip and a nod to Idris.

"Welcome back, Master Idris. And I see you brought a guest. Please drink and enjoy each other. Madame Di will be very pleased to know you have returned."

Idris grunted at her and turned, taking Mia with him.

Drinks flowed freely, as did the women who swanned around the party. They donned the same lightweight material, revealing every inch of their alluring physique. But each wore a half-mask of gold, silver and bronze. All their lips were painted an alluring red. Several men acknowledged Idris as they made their way through the crowd. Mia glanced up at him. His face was tight, muscle in his jaw flickered. A darkness mixed with the hard edge of sadness swirled in his eyes.

"Have you been here before?" she whispered.

"A long time ago. A very long time ago."

"Shall we—"

A hand slipped down over Mia's hip to squeeze her rear, forcing another touch to creep over her—one that sent her spine straight and skin crawling. The sharp scent of hard liquor slammed into her, turning her stomach. She turned her head stiffly, a deep frown forming.

A ruddy, elderly patron was openly ogling at her, eyes firmly on her breasts as the amber liquid swirled in his glass. "How much for this one?"

Idris' hand tightened on Mia's waist, dragging her into him and away from the leering man. He leant down, lips curling into a snarl. Growling, he uttered, "You do not touch what is *mine*."

Mia forced the gasp that nearly leaked from her down. The way he growled the word *mine* fluttered right down to the drumming between her legs. She liked Idris claiming her much more than when the slimy Luc had. She wanted to believe that she was his. That their moment under the dimmed lantern light meant more than a lustful glance and wandering hands.

The creep held his palms up and retreated, only to follow another woman.

"Over here," Idris murmured, his voice still husky.

He pulled a tense Mia to a pile of cushions and furs thrown over a velvet circle chaise. Lounging down with the ease of a man who spilt gold and more in that place of bodily worship, he spread his legs and extended an arm across the lounge, scanning the room for Reagan, feigning to inspect the women.

Mia tracked his gaze. But the arsehole wasn't anywhere to be seen.

He came in here, I'm sure of it, she swore to herself.

Idris beckoned her over, with a wink and a smirk. "Come here, beautiful."

Mia stepped closer to him, her fingers swirling over his knee, down his muscular thigh. He caught her wrist, locking her to him. He dragged her into his lap, forcing her to perch awkwardly, hands between her thighs. Iron had fused to the bony points of her spine, causing her to sit uncomfortably straight.

"I can't sit somewhere else? This feels *precarious*, Old Man."

A masked woman carrying a silver tray full of half-filled wine flutes sauntered over, offering a glass to Idris, who shook his head. Mia took one, gulping the sickly sweet bubbles down. The alcohol danced over her tongue and settled heavily in her stomach.

Idris' fingers traced idly over her forearm, gaze dropped away from the milling crowd to count the freckles on her skin. "Play along, Little Witch. Put on a show for those eyes that don't directly fall on us. This place is dangerous, and known to use deadly methods to make sure the pillow talk whispered in these walls stays secret."

Mia exhaled and nodded. She slid an arm around his shoulders, sinking deeper into him. She crossed her legs over his, exposing the milky, freckled skin of her thick thighs. Idris' hand encircled her waist, spreading over the soft swell of her belly, his thumb absent-mindedly tracing circles in the fabric. A wide grin stretched across her face, and she threw her head back, sending a fake, shrill giggle into the air. She leant in, slipping her hand under his surcoat. Savouring the feeling of the hard muscle tensing under her fingertips. She brushed her lips over the sharp edge of his cheekbone, leaving fleeting kisses across his skin.

Capturing his gaze, she allowed the sticky, honeyed desire to seep into her eyes. What beamed at him was the truth—all she craved was him. And, for the briefest of moments, she saw the same need flare in him. She wanted to drown in it. Her lips hovered over his, brushing as she said one word: "Pretend."

"Pretend." Idris exhaled the word, gripping her tighter.

Mia's hand slid downwards, stopping to swirl on each button, right down to his silver belt buckle, slung low on his hips. Her forefinger traced over the warm metal. "If that is what you desire."

Idris' mouth hovered over delicate flesh, whispering hot breath over her prickling skin. A wildfire broke out across her body, when his lips finally met the skin of her bare shoulder. He kissed up the tensed muscle that ran up her neck to the base of her skull, to that bundle of sensitive nerve endings connecting her jaw to her throat.

Teeth scraped over skin, making her breath hitch.

"You have little understanding of what I desire, Mia," he murmured against her.

She ached for the cool night air to quell the heat burning under her skin that had turned her core molten and gooey. That deep throbbing of arousal drummed in time with her heart. His fingers crept closer to the slit of her gown. With a hurried nod from her, he slid his hand under her skirt, dug into her thigh, slowly easing her legs apart.

Mia whimpered when his hand froze only a breath distance from her aching core. She was teetering, almost painfully, on the edge of her release, and he had hardly touched her.

"Idris, by the goddess..." Mia muttered, readying herself to beg him to touch her.

"You know, there was a time"—he paused, his chest expanding rapidly against her spine—"that was all I cared about. Losing myself between the legs of a woman."

"What changed?" She silently added, *Please, you can get between mine and lose yourself.*

"I made a vow, Mia. One that I think about breaking every fucking time I look at you."

She exhaled. The anticipation in his words made a small smile curl on her lips. But Idris refused to meet her eye, nor did his hand move any further. His brows hadn't met in bliss, but in worry—and something else she couldn't put her finger on.

It made the dizzying need for him slip from her, leaving her clammy and throbbing. She needed space for her mind to gain control of her body, for the ache of arousal to fade. She squirmed against him, hoping he would let her loose. Instead, she rocked her hips against him.

Idris shuddered, letting out a hissed curse. He leant up and muttered in her ear, "Would you stop moving like that?"

"I would, if you just let me go—"

Her words fell short as soon as a hardness pressed against the soft flesh of her rear. Every caress of lips and roll of her hips awoke Idris in more ways than one. It took all of Mia's willpower not to grind back on him, to hear him moan and curse.

Instead, she froze, not wanting to further inflame the situation between them. She whispered an apology. *What am I saying sorry for? Have I taken the pretend game too far and made him uncomfortable? Have I forced him to face the hard truth that he wants me?*

No answers came to her questions.

Idris released her fractionally. Space opened up between them, cooling the tension. He exhaled a long breath, his hand slipping from under skirts. Disappointment flickered in her, but she said nothing.

"There is no need to apologise. It's simply a bodily reaction, Little Witch," he said, a strange edge cut through his voice. "I haven't allowed myself to feel anything for anyone in a long time. It's almost like I have been afraid to..."

"What do you mean?"

Idris' eyes lowered shamefully. His jaw ground, so as not to let the truth slip from his lips.

Mia reached for him, but her hand fell short. She wanted him to tell her everything. The strange vow, to who he was, each of the secrets he held deep in that swirling mind. Everything. But he wasn't ready. He couldn't even accept the stirring in his pants for her.

A pair of eyes settled on her, then another, watching them. They looked far too serious.

"Pretend," Mia whispered almost to herself, leaning into his neck, resting her forehead on his collarbone.

Loud, boisterous laughter filled the space as a dishevelled Reagan strode into the room, emerging from upstairs, a grin blasting across his face. That was where he had gone; to have his fill of whichever woman had struck his fancy.

Suddenly, the room came alive with the band picking up pace, playing a bawdy tune. The women who lounged rose and glided towards him, smiles curling, vying for attention. Even she found herself drawn to the pompous lordling's son, not for glittering gold, but something more important—whatever secret was held in that vault of his mind.

Mia pulled away from Idris and teetered on his knee, ready to pounce. He muttered to himself as he reluctantly let her go. Reagan wobbled around the room. He was drunk, messy and loose-lipped. He all but collapsed onto the furs and cushions next to them. Mia's breathing shallowed out, her eyes widening.

"Easy, easy. Not yet," Idris whispered, leaning back.

Another serving of the sweet, bubbly wine was passed around, but Mia barely tasted it. Even the fizz of the alcohol died with the tension in her body. Idris was talking, but Reagan and his conversation held Mia's focus. She heard hardly a word of either man.

"I need to get closer," she muttered, pulling herself from the safety of Idris' lap.

He reached for her, but she moved too quickly for him to pull her back. He hissed her name under his breath, but a wink and a small smirk made him narrow his eyes and lean back. His face was a perfect picture of boredom. Her fingers found a goblet of wine, bringing it to her lips, not letting a single drop through.

Mia dramatically swayed and fell right into Reagan's lap, thankful that her mask stayed in place. But the contents of her glass spilt over one of his cronies, making him stand and curse.

"Oh, my, I'm so sorry," Mia slurred, her lips parted as she breathed the words, "My lord."

Reagan's face spread from outrage into a sleazy grin. "No need to apologise. I was waiting for a beautiful woman to fall into my lap."

Mia pushed up onto an empty seat, jutting her chest out, giving him a full view of her ample, flushed cleavage, and laughed. "And I've been waiting for you."

He reached over and tilted her chin up towards the light. "I haven't seen you here before."

"I came here with him, but he is so boring," she said, pouting. She raised her pointer finger at Idris, who painfully ignored her. "Are you more fun?"

"Well, we definitely can have some fun together," Reagan crooned, his thumb spreading over her lips.

Mia fought the urge to pull away. "You promise?"

"I promise. Now, let's get a lady a drink," he commanded, snapping his fingers.

MIA'S FINGER TRACED AROUND THE EDGE OF THE WINE glass, not daring to take a sip. She needed clarity, and that sweetness only brought the abyss. She leant back, ankles crossed over his lap. His thumb circled the dip in her knee cap. She had to hold in a shudder as her skin crawled. Reagan was quietly talking to one of his brothers, Tobias, whose soft, boyish face looked entirely out of place in the den of sin.

"You cannot drown yourself here. Father wants you at Valliss—and to stay at Valliss. The princess is not happy with you gallivanting around, and she doesn't want her husband dirtied by some...*whore*," Tobias said, nodding to Mia.

She waved her fingers at him, a sly smirk spread on her face. The burden of pureness and wholesomeness was firmly placed on women, never men. *Until a man rips something from you—then you are used, dirty. Goddess forbid if a woman has a lick of desire and wishes to act on it.* The double standard never sat right with Mia. It was as if the fibres of her being were weaved, wrapped and tied differently to those around her.

"Come now, brother. Loosen up. I didn't care before Ewan's daughter came, and I don't care now."

"This is enough, Reagan," Tobias replied matter-of-factly. "You think he will want a drunk, pox-filled man to lead this city? You still haven't gotten an invitation to the council yet because you couldn't keep your cock in your fucking breeches."

Reagan's fingers dug into Mia's flesh, causing her to grimace, and her hand tightened around her glass. "Shut the fuck up, Tobias. Don't speak about things you don't know."

"I don't know? I'm his son too. I would do anything to even be considered, and you just piss it away," Tobias hissed through his teeth, leaning over Mia as if she weren't there. "You don't think the entire court knows you just fucked with Ashmore's daughter on a whim? 'Just to get back at him, to spit it back in his face.' Isn't that what you said? Not to mention the mess of her death. You think the Silver's eyes aren't on you after you bragged about bending her over any chance you got?"

"We are Lord Hartwinn's sons. They have no power over us," Reagan crooned.

"We both know that isn't true. You and I have no power unless we sit on Father's council. I'm so sick of cleaning up your messes, Reagan."

Mia's heart slammed in her chest, but she remained silent. Her knuckles strained against her skin as her grip tightened. Anger made her body tremble and her teeth grind. *On a fucking whim? He played with my sister's heart on a whim?*

Reagan's head lolled back, a smirk on his irritating face. "Isn't that your job?"

Tobias baulked, shaking his head. "No, Reagan. I'm your brother, not your wet nurse."

"Then go. Report back to Father that I will have my fill of each whore in this brothel before I let that snobby bitch of a princess tell me what I can and can't do."

Tobias stood, a bitter expression on his face, and straightened his surcoat. "I don't recognise you anymore, Reagan, nor is this a man Mother would have been proud of."

Tobias strode away as Reagan cursed under his breath.

"You were talking about that lord's daughter who was murdered, weren't you?"

Reagan's head snapped to her. The sharp, haughty look made her shoulders curl inwards to protect herself. His hand left her knee to grip her face, squeezing her cheeks against the mask. "You'll keep your whore mouth shut about that, you hear?"

Mia swallowed the ball of nerves. "Of course."

He pushed her away. "On your knees. I wish to be serviced."

She made no attempt to move. "Here? Not in private?"

"Private? You are new, aren't you?" Reagan asked with a laugh.

Idris appeared above them. His features were schooled into cool indifference, but his shoulders were tense. "Excuse me, sir, this beautiful creature has been reserved."

Reagan sneered up at Idris. "Reserved? By who?"

Idris, ignoring him, reached a hand down to her. She took it quickly, slipping from the warmth of the furs. His gaze never left hers, seeming to whisper, "You're safe."

"Answer—"

"By me," Idris said with a deathly coolness.

Reagan stiffened at his tone, but he continued, "She didn't seem reserved when she gave me those 'fuck me' eyes."

Idris' eyes narrowed fractionally at Reagan's crass words, but that dimpled smirk spread across his face. "Those eyes haven't left mine all night, boy. You think this isn't a part of our game? She gets me jealous, and then I show her who she truly belongs to. Regardless, you will watch how you speak when there are ladies present."

Mia tucked into Idris' side, her hand spread on his chest. Her lips squished together as a panicky nervousness rumbled in her stomach, eating away the anger. Reagan stumbled up, his hand snaking out to grab her by the nape, yanking her from the safety of Idris' body.

"Lady? Ha! That's a fucking joke. She's nothing but a whore," Reagan spat the words, tugging back and forth. "I don't care who you are, vamp. This one is mine for the night."

Mia's heart thundered in her ears, causing the fading bruises on her thighs to throb—a sharp reminder of Luc and that dark, damned office. She refused to let it seep any further than the pit of her stomach. Ripping her body from his grasp, she slammed her elbow into his ribs. Hard.

Reagan wheezed heavily, falling on his rear around the plush rugs and cushions.

Mia leant over him, her finger punctuating each of her words with a firm poke. "Touch me again and you'll regret it, you drunk arsehole."

Eyes fell on her, cautious looks from the women draped over laps, and curious glances from the men they entertained. But Mia continued, unable to stop the words spewing from her mouth. "You're nothing, destined to be a nobody lord in a speck-of-dirt city."

Idris reached out for her, gripping her by the elbow and pulling her away from a snarling Reagan.

"You will see who is nothing, whore!" he called after her.

Idris led her around the reclined bodies, pushing her into the cool night. From the street, she could hear Reagan curse and scream, glasses shattering.

Thirty-Five

Mia dragged herself into an abandoned alleyway, fumbling. The hot lash of courage had burnt away the bindings of fear, liberating her, sending her into a frenzy of trembling muscles and sharp pants. Her skin prickled over and over as the ghost of the belt struck her. Reminding her of the firm hand on her spine, and the hardness against her rear.

Mia backed into a dark corner, curling on herself, eyes shifting in their sockets, but seeing nothing but blurred lantern light. Magic warmed her chest, letting Ozul slip out to wrap around her wrist, attempting to soothe her.

"We are here, witchling."

Idris settled in front of her, arms caging her head. He ignored the dark mists mingling between them. His gaze burnt directly into her, demanding her to return to him. But she couldn't.

The memory held her captive.

Idris spoke, but no words found her ears. She could only hear that harrowing, scared screaming echoing in each corner of her mind. The press of the mask against her skin was unbearable. Her fingers fumbled with the knot, unable to grasp the tight ribbon. Idris murmured her name. With gentle hands, he took over, loosening the knot and removing the mask to reveal a pair of flushed cheeks and a pool of tears.

"You're safe, Mia, here with me. Nothing is going to hurt you here."

"Am I? Am I safe with you, Idris?" she whispered back, her voice cracked. "Truth?"

"Truth," he replied.

Idris' hand found her cheek, wiping the tears away. She leant into him. Her trembling hands gripped his, allowing the firm, warm touch to ground her. She fought to even out her breath, mimicking his ever-steady rhythm.

"You were something else in there, Little Witch. Reagan won't be forgetting that anytime soon."

"Was I? I didn't notice," Mia replied flatly.

Fear remained, sending quakes through her, but the world had stopped rumbling under her feet.

Idris' hand slipped from her face to curl around her hip. He leant down, resting his forehead against hers. Want lingered briefly in his emerald gaze, but he seemed hesitant to take the leap into that drowning pool. Still feeling a tiny spark of courage and a fiery flame of desire, Mia dived in. She pushed up, her lips meeting his. At first, he kissed her softly, gently, but soon, the pressing of lips and sweeping of tongues turned hurried, frenzied. Her hands snapped to the lapels of his coat, dragging him closer. Their kiss was consuming, dredged in their need for each other. She had never wanted someone as much as she did Idris. A small part of her knew she'd never desire another. Not like that.

Idris' lips abruptly left hers, then the security of his body fell away with a sharp hiss. He crumbled to his knees, hand still clenched in her skirts.

"Idris?" she gasped. "What happened—"

"Mia?" a familiar voice called out.

Her eyes darted up, scanning sneering faces to burn into her mind, flicking over scars and moles until she landed on the lumbering man only a foot away. The silver of his blade dulled with inky blood—Idris' blood.

The men parted at the harsh bark of their leader, revealing Reagan standing in the flickering light of a lantern, hands in his pockets. Never the one to truly get his hands dirty.

His hair almost glowing in a soft halo, making him look celestial, heavenly. Deep down, Mia realised he was the opposite, born from Diabolus, crawling out from Heylla. A smug grin morphed into a tight-lipped grimace as soon as his eyes found her face.

"Now, this is a surprise," Reagan crooned, voice a velvet softness. Instead of slipping, it grated against her skin. "What in the Heylla do you think you are doing?"

Mia gripped Idris by the elbow, but his legs failed, making him fall to the hard cobblestone again. A bloom of damp material spread over his side. She swallowed the rise of bile.

"Touch her, and you'll pray to Deus for mercy when I'm done with you," Idris slurred weakly, raising his open hand, still trying to protect her.

"I know what you did, Reagan. I know what you've been doing. Weaving corrupt magic. For what purpose?"

Pulling sharply on Idris, Mia earnt a groan from him. His legs finally found the strength to stand as her arm slid around his middle. His hand clutched to his side, ruby-red blood seeping between his fingers.

"Corrupt magic? I truly don't know what you think I have done. However, this was a mistake," Reagan said, his voice steady. "Coming to this place was a mistake. But your biggest error was you and your lover following me. You thought I was unaware you were trailing me?"

Mia's jaw clenched, her eyes blazed. "Kali would be so disappointed in you. Late nights at the brothels? Have you no shame? Her ashes have only just settled."

Reagan's hand tightened into a fist, lip twitching. He took a step closer, making them fumble back.

"Mia, she would be disappointed in you. Not for whoring yourself out, or even the drinking. But for the scandal in Father's court. There are whispers that you've been seen around the city with him. Scum. You're rubbing dirt on your name. Your family's name. Kali would have hated that."

Idris' warm, sticky blood seeped into her bodice, straight down to her skin. "Don't you ever speak her name.. You lost that right when you put her in a grave."

"Come now, Mia. That is an accusation that has real consequences," Reagan said, his voice beginning to shake as if his anger had boiled to the top, and he was struggling to contain it. "Now, let's depart and leave that scum to bleed out in the alleyway. Let me take you home, away from men like him."

Mia glared at him. "Call him scum again, and you'll regret it."

Reagan ignored her threat of violence and continued on his rambling. "What of your marriage prospects, Mia? No man will want a sullied bride."

Mia scoffed, rolling her eyes. "Gods, really? Do you think that would work, Reagan? I don't give a fuck about any of that."

"Come, Mia, now. I won't ask again," Reagan warned, his hand beckoning her over.

She gripped Idris' middle, pulling him closer. "Or what? You'll beat me up, like you did to Kali?"

Reagan's face tightened as if she had hit him. "Beat her?" he breathed. "I never—"

"Liar!" she hissed through a clenched jaw. "Now, Reagan, you're going to let me and Idris go, or—"

"Or what, Mia?" he asked coolly.

Her hand flashed to the dagger on her thigh, pulling it out. That same dangerous sharp edge gleamed in the lantern light. Reagan held his hands up, making his men scurry back.

"Or Idris won't be the only one bleeding out tonight..."

"When this storm passes, you'll be the one left to clean up the wreckage," he replied softly. His face, a twisted picture of concern, made her stomach flip. "I don't want that for you, Mia. You're not alone in your grief. I'm here for you. Let me be here for you."

"Fuck you, prick," she cursed, backing away.

Reagan flicked a hand, stopping his men, and called out, "Leave her. She has chosen a side, and she has chosen wrong, like her sister."

"What do you mean? Answer me!" she demanded, raising the dagger again.

That skin creeping smirk spread on Reagan's face, and he replied, "You'll see soon enough…"

Frightened, Mia dragged Idris out to the mouth of the dark passage, feet stumbling. His blood gushed with each futile pump of his heart, creating a sticky, bloody mess.

Mia and Idris struggled down the side alley of The Cauldron. Idris groaned less and less, now murmuring in a foreign language as if he'd lost the common tongue. His bloody fingertips brushed along Mia's scar, then down over her lips, smearing red tracks that she could taste with each panicked lick.

Idris' blood was everywhere.

Soaking into the expensive silk, even flicks of it stained the ends of her hair. He struggled to clot, to stop the flow of his life force. For a sick moment, she wondered if she had more blood on her than he did in his entire body.

Mia's boot found the back door, kicking with such ferocity that she was worried she would put a hole through the wood. She darted her eyes to Idris and noticed that his clammy skin was deathly pale, and his gaze was hooded, faraway.

Death was close to him, breathing down his neck. But that cold, ancient being couldn't have him. Death would never have what was hers ever again.

"I will not let him take you from me," Mia whispered. "You're mine, not his."

The back door swung open, a concerned Benny emerging in the doorway. His eyes widened on his friend, then flicked to Mia.

"Help me, please…" she whimpered.

Idris' weight disappeared from her aching body as Benny shouldered him, dragging his limp body through the dimmed store room. Mia strode behind the pair, whispering prayers to any god who was listening.

Benny dumped Idris on the lounge in the back office with a pained groan. "What the Heylla happened, Mia?"

"He's been stabbed..." she answered, her voice trembling.

"Stabbed?"

Mia grabbed Idris by the surcoat, frantically shaking him. "Wake up, you sad sack of old bones. Wake up."

Idris' eyes fluttered open. He moved his lips, but no words came out. Benny pulled his shirt up with a pained scowl. A maroon slit pierced his flesh just below his shuddering rib cage, surrounded by smeared red blood.

"Idris, you fucking fool," he muttered, lowering his shirt.

"Sorcha!" Mia announced, the only thought slamming into her mind. "We need to get Idris to the healers."

Her hands gripping his arms, pulling him. Idris weakly groaned in response. Benny reached out and pressed his over hers, stopping her.

"What are you doin—"

"He doesn't have the time to get to the Tower, Mia. He is dying," Benny said gently.

"No. No!" she cried out, fat tears rolling down her cheeks.

Her heart slammed against her rib cage. Each piece Idris had healed cracked again, scraping painfully in her chest. Ozul slipped from her finger to brush over his face in soft tendrils.

Benny audibly gasped, muttering her name.

"You promised me, you arsehole," Mia yelled at him, shaking him again. "You promised me!"

In a soft voice, Benny explained, "He let himself starve for over thirty years, Mia. There's no way he can survive this. Nothing—"

She shook her head, yanking from his grip. She smeared Idris' blood across her face as she wiped tears away.

"Then he has to feed."

"Mia, he will..."

The screaming echoing in her mind drowned out Benny's voice.

Her trembling hand found the dagger Idris had given her, wrenching it from the sheath. She stared at it for a split second, letting the warped metal capture her attention. Biting down on her lip to stop the inevitable hiss of pain, she slashed herself across her wrist. A dark maroon line bloomed. Blood boiled to the surface and ran down her arm in one visceral drip.

With her other hand, Mia gripped Idris' face, thumbing his lips open. She held her arm aloft over his mouth. Two fat drops of blood fell on his lips and slid in.

It wasn't enough. She had to give him more.

Mia forced her bleeding arm into his mouth. The sharp sting of her wound widening allowed more of her life force to flow from her and into him.

"Drink, Idris," she whispered, thumb stroking his cheek. "I cannot lose you too. I don't know if I can do this without you."

His hand snapped out, gripping her hip with a bruising tension. A soft caress of the tip of his tongue swirled across her skin, capturing the drip of blood, only to have him glide through the gash in one solid lick, sending shivers down her spine. Teeth dug in, but never broke skin. His long fingers spread over her forearm, forcing her deeper into his mouth as hunger overtook him. He held onto her as if he were dangling on the edge of a crumbling cliff side, and the plunge under his feet was deadly. With relief, Mia watched the rhythmic bobbing of his throat as he gulped her down.

The swirling in her head from the rapid blood loss made her sway. He was taking too much, but she would give him her last drop if it meant saving his life. Idris' eyes snapped open, pupils blown out. A golden amber now flecked through the emerald, shining like marble.

"Fuck, fuck, fuck," Benny cursed through a clenched jaw. Grabbing a handful of her skirt, he ripped her from Idris, who barely let her go.

Mia stumbled back, falling into the doorframe, knocking a painting to the ground. The frame landed with a crash, but no one turned to the noise.

"He hasn't had enough," Mia said as she pushed off the wall. "Not enough to heal his wound."

Benny threw an arm out, stopping her. "You really fucked up, Mia. You've not only fed a starved vampyre, but one who hasn't gone through bloodlust for decades."

"I couldn't let him die—"

Idris released a frightened gasp and sat straight up, trembling, hands gripping the edge of the leather lounge, nails digging in. His tongue flicked out, drawing the last of her blood from his lips. His predator's gaze snapped to Mia, boring into her with an intensity that she knew he wasn't seeing flesh and bone, but right down to her very soul. Hungry desire poured from him, lapping at her exposed skin, sending her flushed.

A deep snarl came from him, exposing his lengthening canines. "Leave."

"Idris, I don't think—"

"Leave, Ben," he cut in, his voice rough, gravelly.

Benny glanced back at her, swallowing a curse. He edged around the room, Mia still behind his arm—protection to the snarling beast emerging from the depths of Idris' leather lounge. Benny fumbled with the door handle, opening it a fraction, and the flood of noise came from the bar in rowdy shouts and tankards slamming.

"Close the bar, Ben, and go home," Idris commanded.

"I don't think—"

"Don't think and get the fuck out. I won't kill her. You know that," he groaned, yanking the leather that tied his hair back, letting those inky strands loose to fall around his face.

Benny shook his head, arm tightening around her. "Mia is coming with me, Idris. This is just the blood talking. You don't want to do this, mate. You know what this will mean."

Mia pushed against the barman. "Benny, I kno—"

"No, you don't know, Mia. Bloodlust unlocks a vampyre's basic needs—to fuck and to feed," Benny cut in, voice hard. "It's dangerous at the best of times, and Idris...he has never been good at managing it. He's got too much of his father in him to fight it."

"Benjamin," Idris gritted out, gripping his hair. "I need her."

Those three words landed straight where he meant them to: between her thighs. Mia let loose a small sigh, then swallowed hard. She gripped Benny's elbow, pushing his arm down, and stepped out of his protective shadow.

"He won't hurt me."

Benny scoffed a humourless laugh. "He's not going to hurt you, Mia. He's going to fuck you until you cannot walk straight and leave you littered with bite marks. We shouldn't allow him to submit to it..."

Idris' eyes flashed at him, jaw grinding. He straightened, muscles rippling "Allow? I do not need your permission to bed a woman, Ben. Nor do I wish you to cluck around me like a mother hen. Now, get out. I will not say it again."

A frown spread across Benny's face, but hurt flared in his dark eyes.

Mia needed to put a stop to this before it came to blows. With a smirk, she exhaled softly and taunted, "Come show me how much you need me then, Old Man."

THIRTY-SIX

They were alone with the click of the lock. Utterly and totally alone.

Desire rolled off Idris like wisps of smoke, curling and disappearing into the air. He pushed off the door, body tense. "Are you scared of me, Little Witch? I can hear your heart racing in your chest."

Mia stood her ground, chin still raised. Her brow quirked upwards. "I fear no man or vampyre."

He scrubbed his mouth with the back of his hand, like he was ridding the taste of her. "You really shouldn't have fed me, Mia. You, of all people."

"What does that even mean?" she asked with a sigh. "You needed blood, you old sack of bones. I couldn't just let you die."

"Your blood is stronger. Witch blood is an aged wine, whereas human blood is the sour scraps at the bottom of the barrel."

With hurried movements, Idris swiftly stripped his surcoat. He ripped his shirt from his back as if he was burning up, feverish. He bent over, clutching at his sides. Muscles painfully strained under his skin, making Mia cringe. Groaned curses slipped from his lips. She desperately wanted him to groan those words against her flesh, as she felt the delicious stretch of him pressing inside her. She took a small step towards him, hands bunching whatever was left of the silken material of her ruined dress.

"You needed—"

"You know nothing about what I need. What I ache for, Mia, is *you*," Idris cut in, voice deepening, making each said syllable rough, husky.

"Fuck," she cursed through a sharp exhale.

His head snapped to hers, his dark gaze captured hers, drawing her in, casting her to the deep current of desire. It filled each of her uneven breaths with a lungful of craving. For too long, they had danced around each other with long looks, fleeting kisses and brushes of fingers.

They had reached the crescendo of the song.

The climax.

"Then take what you need, Idris. My body, my blood," Mia whispered.

His gaze dropped to the thudding pulse in her throat, eyebrows meeting. Torn.

A tense moment passed as their heaving breaths filled the room.

"That was a really beautiful dress," he crooned.

Grinning at him, her hands smoothed over the stiffening material. "Someone has to buy me a—"

"Take it off, Mia, and get on that fucking desk."

The roughness of his words slammed her with an unbridled desire, sending her veins singing. She bit down on her lip, a smirk curling around her teeth. "Come take it off, Idris."

Without another word, their bodies collided, lips finding hers. Gone were the gentle kisses. This kiss was all-consuming—furious, hurried, devouring. Raw passion spewed from each of them. Hands roved bodies, gripping handfuls of flesh. The sharp edge of the desk cut into her spine, making her heart skip a beat and break away. She pushed him back a fraction. Memories flash before her eyes of throbbing skin and the distant ringing of her scream.

"You're safe with me, Mia..." Idris muttered, lips brushing hers.

Mia nodded, demanding her mind to be firmly in the room with Idris. Nothing could harm her there. Not with his powerful arms around her. Not with her heart healing with each lingering kiss. Not with the dagger strapped to her thigh.

She was safe.

Idris leant down, brushing his lips against her jaw, right to the curl of her ear. "Mia, I will not tell you again. Get on that desk. *Now*."

She turned, pushing off papers and quills, splashing ink across the plush rugs. Idris settled behind her, his body curving into hers. He dragged his fingers up her spine, tangling in her short locks. With a gentle yank, he pulled her head back. The satisfying sear of her scalp sent her whimpering, building that slickness between her thighs. His other hand dangerously slid down over the swell of her stomach, right to the slit of her skirt, then disappeared under the malachite silk. A tortuous distance from her throbbing core.

"Good Deus, I knew you'd taste...." A soft groan stole the end of Idris' sentence as she rolled her rear against him. His lips pressed against her skin once.

"In a rush, Little Witch?"

Mia smirked and arched against him. This time, she was. She wanted to race to the finish line, to have him heaving and flushed over her as he spilt whatever he could give inside of her.

Her hand slid up over him, gripping him at the nape of his neck. Locked in place. His tongue flicked out, swirling over her, tasting her salty skin. A groan rumbled against her spine. Teeth dug into flesh, over her pounding pulse of her throat. He slid two fingers between the tight squeeze of her thighs, right over her damp undergarments.

"Feed, Idris," she breathed.

"What if I take too much?"

"You won't. I'm safe with you, remember?"

Without a second wasted, Idris' canines pierced the supple, sensitive skin of her neck. Blood gushed into his waiting mouth. An elation flooded her, waking something deep inside of her, shifting, stretching as if it had been asleep for aeons. Her core throbbed in time with each bloody suck. Mia's hips undulated against his touch in untimed thrusts, desperate for relief.

"Idris..." Mia groaned, grinding down. "Don't make me beg."

"You'll never have to beg," he muttered.

He pushed aside her undergarment and plunged between her soaked folds, right over the throbbing bud of nerves. Mia cried out. Her hand snapped out and gripped his forearm—anything to anchor to that world —as undiluted pleasure radiated from her core. His tongue flicked against the bite, drawing a throaty moan from him. Her release rapidly formed within her, but it was wilder, more intense. Idris pressed a finger against her entrance, then, with one jerk, he was inside her. His fingers slipped over her, only to delve into her again and again. Her hips worked, riding his hand in jerky, hurried movements.

"Mia, you feel fucking incredible," he groaned against her neck. "You're so needy for your release, aren't you? Your cunt is dripping for it."

Mia pressed down harder as a reply, forcing his fingers deeper. She uttered only panted groans. She wanted him to let her fall over the edge he had taken her to. And he did. He shoved her over with a final circle of her throbbing core.

Her release slammed through her body as she arched her spine against him, tensing each of her muscles. Her eyes nearly rolled back in her head as the wicked pleasure radiating from the burning warmth of her core tore through each fibre of her being. His name slipped from her lips in a euphoric moan as the sparks flared over her and slowly died.

Idris' hand slid away from her, leaving her trembling, soaked and needy for him to be inside her. He spun her around at a dizzying speed, then helped her clamber up onto the table. With the same two fingers he had pleasured her with, he dragged up her throat, catching the running blood. He dipped them into his mouth, sucking off the mix of her slick and blood.

His eyes fluttered closed, moaning. "Good goddess, Mia. You taste divine."

Her hands moved on their own, feeling solid muscle and rough body hair. She yanked the lacings of his pants apart, then pulled them down his thighs, finding him hot, hard and urgent.

"I need you, Idris," Mia said huskily, clasping a fist around him, giving one firm pump. "Now."

A shuddered breath came from him. "I may come undone in your hand if you keep going."

"Then what are you waiting for, Old Man? A written invitation?" Mia crooned, running her fist slowly along his thick manhood, causing his hips to thrust almost desperately against her.

They locked eyes, and hot, sweaty desire beamed back at her—a mirrored reflection of her own. Idris' hands slipped up her thighs, gripping handfuls of flesh only to drag her closer to the edge, knocking more books to the floor with a heavy *thump*. Looping two fingers in the crotch of her damp undergarment, he roughly shoved them aside to press against her entrance. The relief for her ache was only moments away.

Idris leant in, his forehead against hers. "Tell me what you want. Tell me how you like it. I want to please you."

"I want you to take me right here on this desk. By the goddess, I want you so deep inside me, I don't know where I end and you begin."

"As you wish, Little Witch."

With a single, hard thrust, he seated himself fully inside her. Their bodies flush against each other, neither looked away, nor closed their eyes. They searched each other's gaze as his hips worked slower, drawing out the aching pleasure. He was so close, she could almost taste his whisky and ash scent oozing from him on every gasp and groan.

Words escaped her—ones she'd suppressed when held against alley walls or in threadbare sheets. "You, Idris, I just need you. All of you. I care not how you take me. I just need you."

Idris leant in and pressed his lips to hers, then up over her cheekbone, right to her forehead. "Then you'll have all of me."

With that, he shifted on the balls of his feet, then slammed his hips into her, sending their mixed moans through the air. He forced her back onto the desk, splaying her out with a firm grip behind her knee. His lips captured hers again, tongue swirling. His pace was hard, brutal. With each plunge into her body, he moved the heavy wooden desk under her. The scraping mixed with their grunts and soft moans.

Mia's fingers gripped his back, holding on as she sank deeper down into the abyss of pleasure. Her cries became louder and louder with each thrust. Another release was building, sending her wild. She could not form a single thought, only need. The hot, toe-curling need for Idris, and the ecstasy he was radiating through her.

Her release crashed into her in panicked grips and screamed names, setting her already oversensitive nerves alight. She couldn't look away from his satisfied gaze as her body contorted. She had never felt such pleasure before, not from a single man she had taken to bed. None had set her aflame like that.

Mia was feverish, her magic boiling inside of her. Shadows slipped from her fingertips, spilling into the room, surrounding them with misty tendrils and curling around sweaty limbs, caressing skin.

Idris repeated something in that foreign tongue, over and over. His eyebrows met, eyelids tightly shut. Mia gripping his chin between her finger and thumb. "Eyes on me, Old Man. I want to watch you come undone..."

His golden-hued pools snapped open, pinning her with that primal gaze. A reverberating moan came from him, from somewhere deep in his chest. He dived into her at a furious speed, making his face contort and lips fly open to spill a guttural groan. His bruising grip on her thigh spread her wider still, forcing himself deeper to spill that sticky heat inside of her.

Mia flopped back onto the desk with a wide grin, breathless. Sweat and blood covered her body, and she ached in places she didn't know existed. Each nerve in her tingled, right down to the soles of her feet.

With a stray finger, she traced his jaw, the sharp edge of his cheekbone to the half point of his ear. He froze above her, heaving from the exertion. Each sweep of his eyes over her caused his brows to furrow in the middle. Gone was that lusty, desired-filled look. Another flared in those emerald pools to the brim.

It was shame.

Mia knew it anywhere. She'd seen it in the mirror, from those weeks of nothingness.

Idris hurried off her and collected his clothing with strange, tense movements. He didn't relax his eyebrows until he was fully clothed. Mia tried to capture his attention, but he refused to meet her confused gaze.

She slipped to the edge of the table, yanking her skirt over bare thighs. Her smile faltered with each step he took away from her. Her mind slowly woke up, and the beginnings of that soft, cruel voice whispered. It stamped on the joy, desire, coating it with an oily film of bleakness.

"Idris, what's wrong?"

He cast that gut-wrenching, shameful look over his shoulder, unlocking the door. He refused to meet her gaze. "We shouldn't have done that, Mia. We should have *never* done that."

With that, he simply strode into the bar, leaving her alone, cold and confused.

THIRTY-SEVEN

Mia allowed the leather lounge to engulf her further into its soft cushions. That was, until the sun cut through Idris' office, beaming the hot warmth directly into her eyes.

She'd slept deeper than she had in weeks.

Sitting up too fast sent the room turning at a dizzying speed, almost making Mia fall straight back down. She squeezed her eyelids closed, demanding for the world to slow, to return to its axis. Her blood-encrusted fingers encased the scabs at the swell of her throat, right where Idris drank from. An emotion bloomed in her. Something that was light, delicate, entwined with chest-swelling pride. She had saved Idris, even at the risk of losing her own life.

She had finally saved someone.

Mia shifted to the edge of the couch, readying herself for the dizziness, but the sharp sting between her legs snagged the breath in her.

Idris hadn't been exactly gentle with her.

Raised voices came from the bar, a mix of the smokey-accented and a surly, low rumble. Mia stood, gripping onto the furniture, and crept closer to the ajar door.

"You need to stop leading her on. She looks at you with those big brown eyes more than she should, Idris. You look at her more than you should—"

"She fucked like she was made for me, Ben," Idris said with a groan. "It's taking all my goddamn willpower not to storm back in there and take her again. And it isn't bloodlust."

Mia smiled to herself, biting down on her lip. But her excitement was short-lived when Idris banged his hand on the wooden bar.

"I broke my fucking vow. One I kept for thirty years. 'I will drink no blood from a witch. I will father no children, take no wife—'"

"I will have absolutely no fun until I last a measly handful of moments with the only woman who has turned my head in a fucking age. You used to have better stamina," Benny pointed out, voice laced with humour.

Even from the doorway, she could feel the annoyance radiating off Idris.

Benny sighed as his footsteps neared Mia's hiding place. "I saw them, mate. Don't think I didn't."

Mia tensed, her gaze dropping to her shadow entwined hands. Benny had witnessed her magic. Panic lurched inside of her, almost making her spring from the door, but a rumbled curse kept her in the shadows.

"We both know what they mean. That you're royally *fucked*, mate. That's what you are. Vow or no vow. You need to stop this before it goes any further than it has. She isn't meant for you."

"But she cannot be for that monster either," Idris grumbled. "It's something more now...for the both of us. This is more than it should ever have been. More than I dreamt and wished for her."

Mia screwed her face into a pout. Words spoken truthfully could be the worst to overhear.

"End it, Idris. It will only lead to heartbreak for both of you."
Silence settled.

Idris broke the quietness with soft, hesitant words. "She tasted like nothing I have ever had, Ben. Like starlight, sweet and...right. I don't know how to explain it."

"You were so starved that any blood would taste like honey."

"Her blood is not like honey, but tangy, like firebud smoke—addictive, intoxicating."

The pub's doors swung open, and the clanging of armour strode in. A knight from the Silver.

Mia pressed herself against the door, determined to hear what they had to say.

"Idris, ya told me to come to ya if there were any more murders."

"So, there's been another one, Mylo?" Idris asked, sighing.

Mia tensed. *Lieutenant Mylo? What is he doing here?*

"More than one. Three. Humans this time. Bloody awful stuff. More than anythin' before."

Benny mumbled a curse under his breath.

Mia's stomach dropped. The warm elation vanished, only to be replaced by the cool iciness of reality. She had lost sight of what mattered, and surrendered herself to those green eyes of the vampyre who spoke half-truths, and whose touch awoke a fire in her. Women were being hurt, and Reagan was getting away with it.

"Has that girl been around again?"

"The Ashmore girl?" Idris questioned, feigning puzzlement. "No, she came sniffing about, but I haven't seen her since. Maybe she's given up on finding her sister's killer."

Mylo barked a laugh. "I doubt it. She is like a dog to a bone. Let her know I am lookin' for her. She's hard to catch."

"I'll be sure to pass on the message, Mylo."

Mia heard the clinking of coins being scattered on a countertop.

"Is this enough?"

Mylo grunted in response.

"Have you found out anything else? Aside from whatever manner of creature it is."

"It's a dhampyr, that's for sure. How was it made? No clue. The healers have been scourin' the tomes. It's only pointin' to him. Nothin' else, I'm afraid."

"Then your investigation is failing, much like ours..." Idris paused, letting out a hiss of air. "I mean mine."

"*Ours?* Please, for love of all that is holy, tell me ya haven't teamed up with her, Idris," Mylo bemoaned with a heavy groan. He sounded exhausted.

"I..." Idris hesitated. He couldn't lie.

"Listen, Idris, we've been friends for a long time, so don't start bull-shitin' me now."

Mia exhaled a sharp breath, her hand trembling against the scratchy blanket. She had some information, but did Mylo know more? Desperation made her slip from the shadows of Idris' office and into the empty pub, not caring for the dishevelled, blood-soaked state she was in.

Mylo's eyes slid from Idris, his brow cocking. A huff of a laugh left him, stretching his tired face into a grin. "Well, hello, Miss Ashmore, and a good morning to ya."

She dropped into a short, mocking curtsy, pulling her blanket out. "Sir Mylo. I hope you're well, because you look like shit."

Mylo laughed again, leaning on the bar. "So do you."

Mia rolled her eyes and slid onto a barstool.

"Good Morning, Mia," Idris said softly, not looking her way.

"Hello, Idris."

She fiddled with the edge of her blanket, hiding most of the blood. "So, I was obviously eavesdropping on your conversation, and I want us to discuss what we know."

Mylo considered it with a purse of his lips and nodded. "You first, Mia."

"Of course. Me first, as I have much more information than you, sir. As always."

Benny scoffed, but Idris still didn't glance at her. He just rolled his tongue around his mouth. Mia ignored the sharp stab of pain in her heart and began, "I know the creature is a dhampyr, but who is creating them? A vampyre? No, from what I've been told, it cannot be a vampyre. They are already hunted and outcast in the human lands. What is the purpose of creating a being to only breed more hatred and fear?"

"Mia..." Idris started.

"It's magically made, I'm sure of it," she said, kicking her bare feet. "What if someone had that power? What if someone absolutely full of fae magic could do this?"

She cast Idris a wide-eyed stare, trying to hint at the only suspect they had ever considered. Reagan. However, he simply shook his head.

"What if this person created these creatures to silence the women he hurt? Like Kali, or that barmaid?"

Mylo and Idris exchanged a glance, neither responding to her. She knew she was right.

Benny sighed, running a hand over his jaw. "They're vampyre-made, Mia."

She shook her head, glancing around at the men. "Why are you all so sure?"

Idris finally found her gaze. An emotion flashed over his eyes in a split moment. It was fear. Absolute, unbridled fear.

"Who are you talkin' about?"

"Mia, don't—"

"Reagan Novak."

Silence engulfed the pub. Only Alderdeen's quiet rumblings were heard outside The Cauldron. Mia looked at each man, her ire burning hotter with each diverted eye.

Mylo cursed, shaking his head. "You better be sure to make sure ya aim is true if ya making accusations like that."

"Tell him, Idris," Mia urged with a wave of her hand, not looking away from Mylo. "Tell him what we found out."

"We found nothing, Mylo. Nothing of importance."

Mia's gaze snapped to the vampyre, her brows clenched in confusion. That was the truth.

"Mia, I've been lookin' to speak to ya—"

She raised her hand, pulling the blanket tighter around her with her other, composing herself. "And I have nothing to tell you."

Mylo's face dropped a fraction. "I'm not ya enemy, Mia. We want the same thing."

"And what is that?" she replied flatly.

"For whatever this creature is to face the king's justice."

"Or should he face a different justice?"

Mylo arched a brow at her, displeasure flattened his lips. "Ya want to be the judge, jury and executioner then, Mia? Is that how ya wish to respect ya sister's memory?"

"How I honour Kali's memory is none of your business, and what happened to Miss Ashmore?"

"I decided I like ya far too much to keep being so formal," he said, cracking another smile. "I would love to stay and chat with ya all day, but I have a murderer to catch."

"How is that going, anyway, Mylo? Especially when you're lurking around here for scraps."

"And how's yours goin'? From how ya look, it seems you've been investigating *thoroughly*," Mylo retorted.

Benny and Idris shared a look, making Benny press his lips together until his deep chuckle broke the tension in the air. A flush stained the high points of her cheeks.

Mia raised her chin a fraction, a smile playing on her lips. "Good luck, lieutenant. You'll need it."

Mylo's laugh echoed as he strode from the bar. He waved a hand over his shoulder. "See ya soon, Mia."

"Not if I can help it," she muttered to herself.

Benny had finally composed himself when she turned back, but Idris couldn't meet her gaze. Her fingers found the gore-soaked fabric of her dress, only to run them through her bed hair.

She felt dirty.

And it was not just the blood that caked around her fingernails or the lingering of their mingled sweat on her skin, but the feeling that she and Idris had done something beyond a simple kiss. Her hand covered the bite on her collarbone. A strange tension swept the room, simmering between Idris and Mia.

Benny's gaze flicked between them, then exhaled. "You do look godsdamn awful."

She rolled her eyes and tucked a frazzled lock behind an ear. "I guess you know my little secret."

Benny grinned at her, dragging a pinched finger across his lips and locking it, making her huff a laugh.

Safe. My secret is safe with him.

Idris' eyes rose to hers tentatively, slowly. Another shot of shame stabbed at her right in the guts, twisting the blade deeper.

"Stop looking at me like that, Idris. We did nothing wrong."

His gaze sank to the floor, frowning, and muttered, "At least for one of us..."

"Good Oryah, you're truly insufferable, do you know that?" Mia snapped back. Sighing, she crossed her arms across her chest. "Do you think we really found nothing? Or was that a show for our friend in silver?"

"We needed to consider it, Mia, or at least discuss it before you spill everything we know to the Silver. We are missing something—"

A low chime of a timepiece swallowed his words. Mia's eyes flicked to the ill-timed clock on the wall, the bronze hands reading eleven o'clock. She had little time to consider what she had overheard or what had transpired between them before she had to be stretching canvas and avoiding Luc.

"*Shit*," Mia cursed. "I have to go. I'm late."

Idris and Benny exchanged a puzzled look. Idris pushed off the bar, shaking his head. "We have bodies—"

"No, Old Man. You have bodies to inspect. I have to get to work, or Luc is going to have my arse again."

Idris tensed, a grimace emerging on his face. "If he lays a single finger on you, Mia—"

She exhaled sharply, striding across the room, grabbing Idris' cloak and slipping it over the worst of the blood, encasing her in his scent.

"Or what, Idris? Now we are doing the protective 'she is mine' dance again? Or is this your 'safe with me' act? I can't work out what you want from me." The words stung to say, but his actions had left her hurt. More than she'd realised. "First, you're begging to worship my body, then you leave me, alone and confused. Look, I know I didn't want to be treated sweetly, but..."

He was right. Because it meant more than either of them were ready to accept. Or need. Mia didn't need yet another complication in her life.

Idris' jaw ground down as if his words were ready to spill from his lips. He whispered, "It was all real, Mia."

She paused at the door and shot over her shoulder, "I'll come find you tonight, Idris. You better tell me everything then. No more secrets."

Their gazes locked, and in that brief moment, she glimpsed her future in those sparkling emerald eyes adorned with specks of gold.

A life together.

And in the look Idris returned, Mia swore he saw the same thing.

Thirty-Eight

Anne's voice rang through Rosda Manor just as Mia was making the arduous climb up the stairs to her bedroom. She quietly cursed herself, dragging Idris' cloak around her tighter, knowing she was still covered in dry, flaking blood.

"And where in Heylla have you been?"

"Out," she replied shortly.

"You will look at me when you lie to me, Mia."

She turned on the step and glanced down at Anne, who stood with her hands on her hips and a rare frown pulling her lips down. She felt raw, ripped open, and a festering had taken to the wound. It seeped out, poisoning her thoughts and her words.

"I was out, now I'm not. I don't have time for you to yell at me. I've got to get to the studio."

Anne's face tensed a fraction as her eyes skimmed over the smudged kohl and her mass of curls. Mia hoped, prayed that whatever remained of Idris' blood on her face had stayed behind on the leather cushion of his lounge. A strange emotion made her stomach flip—they hadn't even spoken about how close to death he was.

"Mia, has something happened?" her mother asked, voice a fraction softer.

"Nothing," she lied. She hated withholding the truth from her. "Nothing happened."

Anne sighed and crossed her arms. "Your father was up all night, worried sick. I don't think he even came to bed. He was waiting for the Silver to turn up at our doorstep and tell him you were gone too. That we had lost you too."

Mia blinked, willing the tears that brewed to dry. Her gaze dropped to the step below her feet , and that nauseating feeling of disappointment bubbled and spat at her like a pot of boiling oil, sticking to her skin and burning through.

I should have known better, she cursed herself.

A single tear slid down her cheek. Mia's arm darted out to wipe it away, but flashed a sliver of ruined material from under Idris' cloak.

Anne gasped her name and climbed the stairs.

"Mama, no—"

It was too late.

Anne ripped the cloak open, exposing the blood-stained material of her dress to the harsh morning sun. Her face burnt as warm as those rays when her mother's gaze landed on her neck. Right to the bruised, scabbing wound on her throat. Mia scrambled back up the last few stairs, her eyes anywhere but on her mother.

"What in the goddess' name has happened, Mia?"

"It's not my blood."

"I bloody hope not. You would have hardly any left. Is this what you've been doing...allowing others to feed from you?" she asked, no hint of disgust or shame, only that gentle genuineness that only her mother possessed.

Mia's eyes flashed to Anne. Worry clenched her mother's brows. "And so what if I am?"

"I will never question what you want to do, my moon. I simply hope we have taught you enough to be out in that wicked world alone without us holding your hand."

Mia blinked, those damn tears still brewing, and within a heartbeat, she rushing her wrapping her arms around her mother. Anne hesitated briefly before surrendering to the embrace. Before Mia knew it, her shoulders shook with each sob, and her eyes burnt with salty tears.

I have been alone, so wretchedly alone, for such a long time. And I almost was cast back to that cold, dark loneliness with a blade to the ribs. I don't want to be alone again, walking this world with only my shadow. Not with the terror lurking around each corner, and my own scream in my ears.

Her mother rubbed her back in soothing circles until Mia pulled away, cheeks wet and red. She had emptied out on her mother's shoulder in a damp patch surrounded by smudged kohl.

Anne's hand instinctively went towards her cheek, rubbing the wetness away, right over her scar. "You're a wonderful, beautiful woman, Mia, and I will always love you. Always."

Mia's chin sank to her chest, brows bunching. "You will?"

"Of course I will. Now, you dry your tears, and let me do something about that scab. I know my way around a love bite."

She cast her mother a suspicious glance, but allowed her to lead her up to her bedroom.With each step, Anne weaved a tale full of giggles from her and disgusted groans from Mia. It was about a young woman in love with a fae emissary who was particularly interested in marking her with his teeth, and how she had to hide them from a certain lord.

MIA SPRINTED THROUGH THE PACKED STREETS, HER shoulder bumping into the masses of people. Her damp blonde hair was flying free, drying in the midday sun. The dull toll of the morning bell harmonised with her footfalls, rattling through her sore head. She skidded to a stop at the back door of the studio, her sweat sticking her loose blouse to her skin. She pushed through, door chime jiggling, struggling to even out her breath.

Each apprentice cast her a small, welcoming smile. Less had whispered salacious things, and even less had given her that judgemental stare. She hadn't crossed paths with Luc. Not a single lusty look had fallen on her, nor had a stray touch brushed over her, much to her relief.

James, with a paintbrush in hand, stood in his regular spot in front of the class, wearing a sour expression. His eyes rose to her, then lowered back to his work. An uncomfortable look flashed across his features, making his lips tighten further.

"Good of you to join us, Mia. We have pallets and brushes piling up, and the floor! Great Deus, sweep, then take to your easel. Lord Hartwinn is requesting to see more pieces from Luc's apprentices for a wedding present for the princess."

"My own easel?" she repeated slowly, confused. Her hand clenched around the strap of her bag.

A tiny bud of hope blossomed in her.

"Master Luc has decided you've worked hard enough for your own," James explained, voice strained.

A stray chuckle, then a whisper—no doubt from Samuel—was followed by muttered denials.

Mia cocked her head, confusion still working its way through her. There was something off about him. Something tight, laced with... shame. There was shame in his voice.

"What did he make you do?" Mia asked, not thinking about the words leaving her mouth.

The whispers died out, and all gazes fell on her, then slid to James. His eyes narrowed, his chin raising a fraction. "He simply decided you have proven yourself. But you can only join the others after you've done all your chores."

Mia stared at him a moment longer, then nodded, dumping her stuff and grabbing the broom. Her mind was a tangle of thoughts and questions, ravelled and knotted, only growing tighter with each sweep.

The day crept by.

Minutes turned into hours and hours into days with each tick of the whirling brass hand.

Mia was impatient to leave, making her sloppy, unfocused. She knew she should have been trying her best to prove she belonged. That whatever she created was up to Luc's standards, even if she couldn't find a sliver of respect for him. But those swirling thoughts distracted her, dampening the excitement of creating in his studio.

The sun had set hours before, and the streets had dangerously darkened, lantern lights beaming through the windows, leaving only James and Mia in the building.

She leant away from the easel, her shoulder aching. She had chosen —surprising even to her—the landscape of that misty morning with Idris. The deep green of his cloak and the hint of his face from behind the hood. He drew the eye in his broad, masculine glory. But the browns and yellows were muddy, and the entire scene lacked light. Colours smudged when she wanted them sharp and crisp. Her strokes were sloppy, messy, not like the deliberate brushstrokes of her portraiture work. But it wasn't awful. Unlike the drab, dull field of poppies Samuel had been fiddling with all day.

James clicked his tongue. "Good. Very good, Mia, but it's lacking the emotion you are obviously trying to convey."

Mia glanced at him from the corner of her eye, pursing her lips. "Whatever you did for me, with Luc, thank you."

James cocked his head, staring deep into the painting. A tension had grown across his shoulders. "I..." He paused, sighing. "You're welcome."

Mia unbuttoned her stained collar. The studio was unseasonably warm, stuffy, causing a bead of sweat to form on her spine. The powder that Anne had painstakingly placed had rubbed off, exposing the scabbing wound. James slumped heavily on a stool next to her, arms crossed. Mia knew a stern talking to was about to happen—Henry used to corner Kali the same way at home.

"I covered for you. That's all I did. And I will keep doing it. However, now that he has given you an easel, you need to treat this more seriously," James cautioned. His eyes dipped to the wound on her neck, making her hand slap over it. "Luc won't ever regard you as a serious artist. And that's a damn shame. You're tenfold more talented than half of these idiots. But coming late, day after day, breaking things, fighting with the others...It's not showing me or Luc that you want to be more than the maid here. You must show more commitment."

Mia exhaled a long, strained breath. Irritation rose in her, not at James' hard words, but at the hidden meaning behind them: *You aren't enough. You haven't done enough.*

That malice-filled voice slithered around the base of her spine, awakening at her dark thoughts.

"How have I not shown my commitment?" Mia asked, voice laced with a deadly venom.

"Mia..."

She couldn't stop. The words needed to come out, to be spewed forth into the air.

Damn the consequences.

"I walked in the next day, bruised and terrified, knowing full well that all these men heard me scream and didn't do a single thing. Did I not show dedication when I swallowed the anger and faced that pompous prick who ratted me out? Instead, I apologised for breaking his things. And what did I get? A hissed reminder from a rich brat of where I supposedly belong—either under a man, or being bossed around by one. What else can I do to show my commitment, James? Do I truly need to get on my knees for Luc and let him take whatever scrap of myself I have left?"

James sat quietly for a long moment, staring at his paint-stained hands.

Mia almost regretted her words—almost. She wasn't angry at him, not at all, but at the situation she'd wound up in, from her own foolish, naïve dreams. It was a mistake for her to agree to the bargain. A bigger mistake was to set foot in that place to begin with. But she was in too deep to back out.

"You come in, grin and bear whatever Luc wishes for you to do, and you create fucking masterpieces, Mia. That's what you do. You sacrifice. You swallow your words and you keep your head down. You're an exceptional artist, with skill and talent to produce more than anyone here, but you seem not to understand the disadvantage you were born into. This is a man's world—"

"And what if that's wrong? What if this world is wrong? Should I merely be relegated to some warm body for Luc to rut into, to be barely able to paint here?" Mia scoffed and shook her head. "If that is the price I have to pay, damn it all to Heylla, then. Nothing is worth the sticky shame he leaves me with."

James sighed and stood. He ran a hand through his hair, gaze fixed firmly on the billowing cloak of Idris. "Then only pain and disappointment await you here. Luc will never see you for more than what's between your legs. And these men here, though sympathetic, would push you down to get ahead—or worse, consider you a threat."

Mia dumped the paintbrush into the jar, creating a flurry of milky grey streams.

"Maybe they should," she said harshly, swirling the brush around, splashing water on her apron. "Maybe they should see every woman they encounter as a threat. We have claws and teeth, James. Sharp claws and teeth."

He crossed the room to shoulder on his coat. "You should show those claws then, Mia. Then Luc would think twice about taking a belt to you."

"Luc should think twice before laying a hand on me ever again," she whispered, tightening her grip on the brush until her knuckles whitened.

"Good night, Mia. We both have things to reflect on. Now, I want this place to shine before you leave."

With that, he left, leaving Mia seething and irritated. The sharp scratch of broken wood cut into her palm. In her anger, she'd snapped a paintbrush clean in half. The shards fell to her feet, clattering on the stone, just adding to the morning's worth of cleaning to do, and she had little time to do it. She needed to find Idris and demand he answer her questions.

Thirty-Nine

Mia's name was being sung in a soft, crooned singsong way that made each of the hairs on her neck stand straight up. Hours had passed since James had left her in the studio, and she thought she was alone.

Luc.

An alarm bell was ringing in her ears, twisting her stomach in knots. Visions of bruising, groping hands and ripped clothing flared before her widening eyes.

I need to get out of there. Now.

Mia scurried off the stool, knocking it to the ground. The cluttering *ring* of wood on stone gave her franticness away. Cursing under her breath, she rushed across the room, closer to the back door.

Footsteps stopped at the entrance to the studio, and the song of her name faded off.

"Hello, beautiful. You're here late."

Mia froze and cast a quick look over her shoulder. Luc stood in the doorway, head cocked. An unsettling smirk had spread on his face—one that was strained at the edges, that didn't meet his eyes. He sported a purple, bruised cheekbone, as well as a sore-looking split lip.

A cold sweat covered each inch of her skin, and her hands trembled against her sides. A ball of emotions choked her, not allowing a single deep breath to enter her demanding lungs. She took a wobbly step back, towards the door.

"Did you tell anyone our little secret, Mia?"

She stiffly shook her head.

"*Liar,*" he hissed.

He stepped into the studio, sending a skin-prickling chill over her. He muttered to himself, smoothing his hair out. Each movement towards her was calculated, slow, to marinate more fear in her body.

Mia fumbled backwards away from him, her side hitting the brass handle. "My father is waiting for me at home. You see, we have a family dinner each week, so I better be off now or else I will be late. If you will excuse—"

"You did, Mia. You told someone."

"I didn't—"

"Then please explain why I got dragged into an alley and warned to leave you alone?" Luc straightened his tunic and a smoothed ruby necklace to his chest. The stone gleamed and glistened, pulling her in—like Hartwinn's had. He lurked closer still, enough for his putrid stench to slither into her nostrils, coating her lips. "Can you not keep a secret? Do you wish to join your sister?"

Mia spluttered the word, "Sister," back at him, brows bunching in confusion.

"Yes, your screaming, begging sister," he crooned, eyes widening. His tongue slid over the sharp edge of his teeth. "How delicious her sounds were. Almost as delicious as yours."

"You don't get to speak of her like that," Mia gritted out.

"I will do as I wish! And you, you filthy scum, will shut your whore mouth until I tell you to open it," Luc snapped back. "Your sister should have learnt that lesson before opening hers."

"What?"

Luc reached out, causing Mia to grimace, and tucked a stray strand of hair behind her ear.

He was too close, far too close.

In the dark lantern light, Mia swore she could see those pulsating black veins under his onyx pools. His icy fingers trailed over her jaw as a soft, caring but conceited look spread across his face, making his lips pout.

A mask for the rage that brewed, that hid the monster under his skin.

Mia's sweaty hand gripped the handle, opening the door a fraction. "You have lost your mind, Luc. I'm leaving."

"Mia, my beautiful—"

Luc's leer had dropped to her bare throat, right to the wound left by Idris—the man who helped her, cared for her. His conceited smile morphed into a lip-curling snarl. Spit pooled in the corners of his mouth. His hand snapped to her jaw, forcefully twisting her head, further exposing scabbed wounds. Venom poured from his thin lips, spitting directly in her face. "You fucking slut. That filth has had his fill of you, hasn't he?"

Mia struggled against the tightening grip, her simmered anger flashing to a boil again. No one would ever shame her for her desires or wants again. She'd bare her teeth—each pointed one at Luc—and show him how razor-sharp her claws were.

A hollow laugh filled the room, right from Mia. Her eyes skimmed over his dishevelled appearance, over the lank, greasy hair and the sunken cheeks, disgust curling her lip. She had thought him handsome. Now, all she saw was a panting beast.

"You are vile, Luc, and I wish—no, I pray—that when you meet Diabolus, he is not kind to your soul."

His stained fingers dug deeper into her, yanking her closer. He dragged the tip of his tongue over her cheek in one slimy streak. His lips brushed her ear as he sighed. "You seem to not have learnt from our last lesson. You are mine—"

"I'm not yours, Luc, and I will never be yours." Mia spat the words right into his face.

"Like your sister was his to do whatever he pleased with until she looked into things that did not concern her."

"What are you saying?"

"Your sister had to be silenced."

Mia's breaths came sharp and fast. "And you silenced her?"

"No, daft girl," he answered, but that unsettling, toothy smirk spread across his face. "But I made sure she went to that pub, that she was waiting in that alleyway for her dearest sister. Your handwriting is easy to forge, you know..."

"What did you do?"

"What? What? What?" he mocked in a high-pitched tone. "You think your idiot sister even blinked when she stumbled into his trap? No, she didn't. She just waited for you..."

"You bastard! I'm going to end you," Mia growled.

Luc threw his head back and laughed a mirthless laugh. "You? You're weak and worthless, with an inflated ego. Women always seem to perceive themselves as something greater than their gender is supposed to be. You're not meant for this life. You were solely born to be his bride and bear his children. And I'd learn to shut your mouth, because he is going to do much more than take a belt to your rear, girl."

"What are you—"

"*Enough!*" he yelled in her direction, close enough to spray her with flecks of spittle.

As Mia's body jerked backwards, that surge of courage faded. She found herself thrown back into that dark office, with her face pressed into the wood, Luc's body on top of hers.

"Enough with this incessant questioning. Now, come to my office. It is time for your next lesson."

Mia's eyes widened. She knew what lay in wait for her there: nothing but pain and more nightmares. Her hands shot up, gripping his wrist, pulling and yanking, but there was no way to loosen his grip on her face. "Let me go, now."

"You're being ridiculous, Mia. Stop acting like you don't want me."

"I'm not that good of an actress. I don't fucking want you. Let me go, or—"

"Or what? You'll scream. And where did that get you last time?" he crooned, voice flecked with anger. "Where did that get your dead sister? Hmm? She screamed so loudly that I thought my eardrums would burst."

"Fucking let me go!" Mia snapped, squirming.

She lashed out, striking anywhere she could find flesh. A stray hit clipped him across the jaw. Rage overflowed from him, making his movements sloppy and frantic as he battled to capture her. The soft licks of warmth emerged in Mia's chest, rushing to aid her. Shadows leaked from her fingers, but not enough to drag him from her.

Luc slammed her against the door, causing the glass planes to tremble, her only exit snapping shut. His hand slipped from her jaw to her throat, squeezing hard. Her breath turned strangled as her lungs lost precious air. Her fingernails found the skin on his ugly face, gauging into his cheek. Black dots marred her vision, and her limbs grew heavy.

The tight band around her neck loosened for a moment. Mia gasped in chest-heaving breaths. Luc leant down, dragging the tip of his nose along her exposed collarbone, right to her throbbing pulse. His lips spread out, sucking painfully on her skin, drawing it into his mouth.

Without warning, he sank his teeth into her, tearing through her delicate flesh.

Blood pooled and dripped into Luc's waiting mouth. He guzzled her down in a sickening gulp. That same harrowing scream left Mia, her limbs thrashing, kicking out. Her shadows grew as her magic poured from her. He pulled back with a wild, bloody grin on his face.

The prick looked satisfied, like a cat who got into the cream.

Luc's free hand rushed up Mia's leg, pausing on the dagger. He yanked it from its sheath, the wickedly sharp iron glimmering in the light. "Planning on using this, were you?"

"Yes, to damn you to Heylla."

He dragged the iron between her breasts, up over her throat until the tip pressed into her cheek, dimpling the skin.

"Maybe I should scar you more. Make something more truly hideous than that little blemish. But I don't think he will like that." He turned the blade against her cheek. "You should have seen what he did to the man who gave you it. Horrific."

"Do it, Luc. Cut my face. Create something absolutely stomach-turning." She leant forward, pushing the tip a fraction deeper. "I fear not for my reflection, but for what my father will do to you when he finds out you hurt both his daughters. He will tear you apart and throw whatever is left of you into the pits for Diabolus to devour. You know the Dark One detests men who harm women, right? Your immortal punishment is bound to be especially cruel. And I welcome it. So cut me. Do your worst."

His upper lip twitched, and that satisfied smirk faded away. That's when Mia released what he truly wanted.

He wanted a fight.

He wanted her to scream.

He wanted her to fear him.

He needed it as much as she needed air.

She refused to give it to him. She refused to satisfy his sick needs. Not anymore. Never again.

Mia stopped, her shadow-enchanted arms falling by her sides. A deep frown cut over his face as pure rage boiled in his eyes. Violence lurked there, devastating violence. But she wouldn't cower from it. She refused to let that harrowing scream haunt her anymore. She glared up at him with all the fury she had been suppressing. Anger rolled out of her, covering her in a protective shield.

"You think you're tough, then?" Luc asked, pushing harder, piercing the soft flesh of her cheek.

A sharp sting radiated across Mia's face. But she'd faced worse and come out stronger.

She made no move to whimper or to cry, squeezing her lips into a thin line, dousing whatever pleasure he got from pain out like a bucket of water on a blaze. He pulled back, yanking the iron out of her skin. A sharp exhale left her—the only sign that he had hurt her.

Luc discarded the dagger on a table, the metal falling with a clang. His eyes bulged at the single drop of blood running down her cheek, and his jaw worked in uneven twitches as hissed. Intelligible words came from him. His shoulders rolled in awkward jerks, yanking her back and forth.

"Just a little more, Mia. He won't mind me taking a tiny bit more," Luc muttered to himself, dragging her closer to his snapping jaws. "I need you—"

"You've lost your godsdamned mind, Luc. Stop. Drinking my blood will make you sick..."

"No, girl, you're mistaken. My mind has opened—cracked open— and the truth has poured in. Blood is a life force. One for my genuine nature to emerge. The true king has told me tha..." His words faded off as his speech slurred and came in mumbles. His wide eyes darted about as his body twitched.

Mia's knee shot up and slammed into his thigh, missing his groin by mere inches. Hissing, Luc's hand tangled in her hair, yanking her from the door and throwing her against the table. The sickening *crack* of bone snapping echoed within her chest. A sharp cry of pain slipped from her. Water pots and clean palettes hit the stone with loud smashes, sending shards of gleaming crystal around her feet.

Luc scurried to her, boots crunching on the glass. The clicking of his belt unclasping sent her flesh prickling, and the fading bruises pulsating on the backs of her thighs. Her magic exploded to a blazing fire, spreading down her clenched fingertips and toes. It filled her with such heat, she thought her skin would be searing to the touch.

"I need to taste you. I crave it..." He groaned, sounding pained. "I cannot hold back, Mia, not when you taste so fucking good. I don't care what you mean to him. I want you all for myself."

She glanced up in time to see his hand disappear into the front of his pants, sending a sickening, gagging feeling around her body. His tongue circled his lips as he hunched over his twitching wrist. His skin was dripping with sweat and had an awful grey pallor. Those black veins throbbed and spread down over his jawline. His eyes, already filled with molten rage, darkened further until none of the whites were seen.

Mia gasped—Luc was turning into a dhampyr.

He crooned her name again, but his voice was breathless, angry. "Don't you want to know what happened to your sister? Don't you want to know who killed her? Give yourself to me, and I will tell you everything."

She straightened, a hand grasping around her cracked ribs. The creature knew nothing about Kali's death. Even if he did, he would kill her before he spilt the secrets locked away.

Mia knew what she had to do—survive. One way or another. She knew, without a single ounce of doubt, only one of them would walk away from that terrifying exchange. And it would be her. She had promised Kali she'd live, and she would do anything to have a breath of fresh air free from the dark, rumbling storm cloud haunting her.

Her magic was calling out to her, demanding to protect her. By Oryah herself, she was going to allow it to be free.

"No, you sick, depraved worm," Mia snapped back, her words wavering with pain. "I would allow every vampyre in this city to feed from me before I let another drop of my blood enter your disgusting lips."

Luc's hand paused, his black eyes flashing to hers. Contempt radiated from them, not just for her, but her whole kind—women.

The warmth of her magic pooled at her fingertips, spilling shadows in the folds of her skirts. She needed something to protect herself. Anything.

"*We help,*" Ozul whispered. "*Let us free, witchling.*"

Mia exhaled, allowing the fluttering of bravery to fill her. A single shadow flowed between her fingers, morphing into the familiar weight and the cool metal of a dagger.

A blade carved from shadows.

Mia held it behind her back, gripping it so tightly that her knuckles strained against the thin skin. Luc patted the table, his snarl turning into a sly smirk. She stepped towards him, now close enough to see the sweat beading on his upper lip, the wild look in his eye, and the twitch of the corner of his lip. His body strained under the weight of the transformation.

"You're going to moan for me, Mia. Scream my name."

She let a sweet smile spread on her face. "No, Luc. That's where you're wrong. You are going to scream for me."

She slammed the shadow blade down, piercing his hand to the table. He bellowed out, eyes bulging. He scrambled for the discarded dagger, but Mia got to it first. She held it out, right over his cold, black heart, words beyond her.

Something else took hold, not laced with simple anger, but a furious storm brewing in her since she'd realised her sex, her gender, would disadvantage her in the world. Not anymore. She refused to be used, nor would she be commanded to bend to a man's will, to be a trophy, a jewel. She was powerful, wise, and that fire in her belly would never be extinguished. Especially not by a snivelling, pompous speck of scum.

He spat insults at her, but none found the soft flesh of her heart. He intertwined the expectations of men, and only men, with those words of disgust and uncleanliness. And Mia was sick to death of the expectations of men.

Luc lashed out one last time. His jaw snapped, but her shadows launched from the corners, binding his wrists. He fought against the misty shackles, spewing more hateful words at her, about her burning. But if she were to see a pyre, he wouldn't be there to witness it.

Mia raised the blade high over her head and slammed it down into his chest. She found more resistance than Idris had warned her about, making her forearm strain. Black blood bloomed through his shirt, like a sick ink blotch, with each pump of his useless heart, and split right down his front, pooling with the piss in his half-undone pants.

Mia stabbed him again and again, unable to stop.

The fear he had instilled in her in that dark office was being freed with each slice of his worthless flesh. Blood splattered her, soaking every inch of her. He gargled, bubbling ooze seeping from his slack mouth, drowning him.

Mia drew her shadows back, slipping the chains from him. His knees gave way, flesh ripping away from the blade that secured him to the table, pulling her with him. Her hand was still on the blade buried deep in his chest. Mia pulled it from its fleshy scabbard in a sickening *squelch*, rising to her feet. She spat on Luc's dying body, then scrubbed the stray tear that fell.

Her shadows surrounded her, flaring out like misty swirls of black smoke, wholly freed from their bindings within her. Each lashed at the flickering lanterns, devouring the light. The back door swung open, and the bell rang in the silence. Then, a voice exhaled her name.

FORTY

The sound of thumping leather hitting the stone floor, intertwined with the hiss of her name, filled the deathly quiet room.

"What in Oryah's name have you done?"

Mia slowly turned from the cooling, expired body of Luc to find a slack-jawed James standing in the doorway. His eyes hurried over her, taking in her trembling, blood-soaked frame.

Mia's blouse stuck to her skin, pulling from her with each heaving breath. The throbbing bite mark lingered, and the sharpshooting pains on each shaky inhale were reminders of a brush with darkness—one she couldn't name. Tears spilt from the floods welling in her eyes, creating rivers of salt down her cheeks. And she was cold. Bone-achingly cold.

The bravery had worn off, leaving her in the throes of the aftershocks.

Still white-knuckling the blade, Mia's trembling hands rose to her eyeline. The cooling, black blood covered them, settling into the wrinkles of her knuckles and the webbing of her fingers. The metallic stench slammed into her nostrils, filling each breath with flecks of copper. She could even taste him on her lips with panicked swipes of her tongue.

Mia's stomach flipped, sending the acidic bile racing up her throat. She spun away and vomited. Gagging and retching until nothing remained in her, she straightened, rubbing her face on her forearm. Much like her belly, her mind was empty, spilt over the bloody floor.

Ozul lingered in the air, not disappearing to dark corners, their unseen eyes taking James in, deciding if he was friend or foe.

James' gaze slid from the gruesome massacre back to her, widening even further when her shadows simmering around her. "Good goddess..." he mumbled under his breath, words fading off.

Mia swore she heard the name *Ophelia*.

"He tried...to force himself on me. He was raving mad, talking about Kali and needing blood," she said, her voice hoarse.

His eyes darted to hers, then dropped away. As soon as their eyes met, she saw surprise, disbelief. His jaw clenched closed, but through it, he hissed, "I didn't think he'd..."

"He'd what, James? Rape me? What do you think he did in that office while you just stood outside the door?"

He refused to meet her gaze. That was answer enough.

The bitter taste of betrayal coated her tongue and made her shadows lash out. A tendril snapped under his chin, forcing him to face her disappointed glare. "You will look at me when you tell me you knew what that monster had planned."

He swallowed hard, shaking his head. "I didn't know he'd do that, Mia. I knew he was rough, heavy-handed. That's—"

"You left me here!" she shouted. "Commanded me to stay, unbeknownst to the monster lurking, like I was a rabbit caught in a snare. And I was oblivious to the fact that the hunter was looming over me. Getting ready to snap my neck."

"Mia—"

"Was this payment for my easel or for whatever he made you do? Was all this a game? Or was it a hollow promise, knowing that I would be shamed and unable to return to this place of pain?" she asked, the questions falling from her uncontrollably.

James shook his head, his face pleading. "No, Mia, I came back to stop whatever he had planned. Luc had this mad gleam in his eye. He has been ranting and raving about you, your sister. I had never seen him like that before. It unsettled me. I would have never agreed to that, I swear."

"Swear to Oryah. Swear to Deus. Swear to Diabolus."

"I vow it to any gods casting their eyes on us," he said desperately. "I never knew he had anything to do with Kali, Mia. I promise."

She eyed him. Mistrust swirled in her. She wondered if he'd fall to his knees, with how pleading his words were. James had only ever warned her, kept her from Luc's lessons, but promises could be broken.

"I vow it, Mia."

"Let him go," she commanded, waving her hand.

Ozul slipped from his face and slithered back to her, curling around her wrists. A drumming pulse radiated off them, echoing in time with the beat of her own heart.

James approached her slowly, hands up as if she'd spook and cut him. "But it's all okay, Mia. He's burning in the pits of Heylla now. He cannot hurt you. Now, pass me the blade."

Mia realised she still gripped the black, gleaming dagger. She raised it slightly. "I've stabbed one arsehole today. I'm not above stabbing another."

"Give it to me," he repeated, a fraction firmer.

She shook her head, stepping back. "I don't think so, James."

"I shall return it to you after I wipe all the evidence from it," he explained, eyes roaming over the broken glass, spilt paint and blood. Then, his gaze landed on the expired Luc. "And clean this mess up."

Mia faltered for a moment, resolve wavering. "You're not going to call for the Silver? I murdered him."

James shook his head, his face softening. "No, Mia, I won't be bringing the Silver into this. He deserved this. He finally got what was coming to him. Many women have suffered because of him, and you were the only one who had the strength to put a stop to it."

Mia shook, her lips pursing. "No, it didn't take strength to wipe his scum from the earth. A sharp blade and will to live. That's all that was needed. Any of the women he hurt could have ended him. But now I wear his death across my shoulders, simply another burden to carry." Her eyes fell on the swirling mists at her wrists. "And my shadows? You won't tell Lord Hartwinn what they are, will you?"

"You won't be feeling a single lick of those flames, Mia. I promise you that."

Mia breathed the word, "Flames." Falling ash and burning wood crept into her mind. Her hand slid over the back of her neck, tangling in her hair as she fought another wave of crashing panic. Her gaze rose from the pooling blood to James. His gaze hardened, his lips thin as if those same sparks played in his eyes.

"You're a witch," Mia whispered.

James' body awoke at the word as he launched himself across the close space. His hands gripped her biceps, eyes wild, fearful. "Hush, girl. Do you want us both to face the flames? We cannot speak of it here. Ears listen and mouths whisper, even if we believe we are alone."

Mia pushed. She needed him to answer her question, if only to hear she wasn't the only one. "Please, James, are you a—"

He exhaled, letting her go. "I'm something that doesn't exist anymore. Do you understand? The place I lived doesn't exist either. Maybe you were from there, too."

Mia shook her head, holding the blade out, handle first. He took it with a pinched face and dropped it in the sink. The *clatter* made her jump, startling her. An uncomfortable tension had grown between her shoulder blades. She could have lied, denying what the shadows were. Instead, she spoke the truth. The hard, honest truth. "I don't know what I am—who I am. Not anymore. It frightens me."

James focused his gaze on her, face softening. "You need not decide who you are. Not here, bathed in blood, or even in a stained, mustard-coloured dress in a lord's ballroom. You'll know, deep down in your guts, who you are. Who you are supposed to be. Now, I've coddled you enough, Mia. Let us clean up your mess."

THE CHILLED NIGHT AIR WHIRLING AROUND THE DENSE pines deep in the Sliva Forest made the soil solid and terribly hard to dig in. The moon was full, sending stretching rays of silver over the patch of grass of Luc's last resting place before the maggots and scavengers would pick at his bones.

Neither Mia nor James spoke.

The sharp scrape of shovels striking the dirt mingled with their huffing breaths. Curling steam slipped from their lips with each exhale. Mia was afraid to talk, fearing she wouldn't stop. It was clear in the sweat across James' face and the muffled curses into his elbow when he mopped his brow that he didn't want to answer her questions.

Mia peeked over her shoulder at the drop sheet they had unceremoniously wrapped Luc in before dumping him into the studio's cart. The last of his blood leaked out, creating black splotches in the white material. "We cannot tell anyone what I did. This must remain a secret. One we will take to our graves."

James didn't speak for a long moment, solely focused on digging until he broke the silence. "To our graves, Mia. I will never talk of this again, nor should you linger on what he said. He was mad, Mia. Something had switched in him. Push this away. Bury it deep. Let Luc and his memory die here."

She bit down on her lip. The ache in each breath and the thumping twinge at the base of her throat would fade, much like the sting of memory. But she knew, as the dark voice slithered from the recesses of her mind, that Luc's ghost would haunt her until she met the goddess.

"Why did you even work for him? He was awful."

James slammed the shovel into the dirt, stomping his boot down on it. "He wasn't always so full of hate. And besides, he was unfortunately a fantastic artist...when he actually painted."

"What do you mean, 'when he actually painted'?"

He sighed, scooping dirt and dumping it in the pile. "You think our lovely tyrant ever put a brush to canvas? He'd take his students' finest pieces, including mine, and say they were his. Stealing our work for him to claim fame, so he could spend his days at court and abroad, rubbing shoulders with the rich and powerful."

"Which one is yours, then?"

James flashed her a look, then leant a foot on the shovel. Mia waved a hand in the air for him to start, expecting him to gloat, boast. Instead, he began softly, almost shamefully, listing off the names of the art.

Luc only ever painted his signature on many of the artworks Mia loved.

James would never have his name carved into brass under his artwork —Luc took that from him. Just like King Ewan ripped everything else from his grasp when he took James' home, his people, and his magic.

"And The Burning of the Witch Queen."

"You painted her?"

The image of the serene, calm queen burning flashed before her open eyes. Then the stench of melting hair filled her nose as a disgusting, oily flavour coated her tongue. The echo of a scream beat against her eardrums. Only a sharp shake from James brought her back to the quiet of the Sliva Forest.

"Where did you just go?"

Mia shook the stray curls of smoke from her mind, then spat the nauseating flavour from her mouth. "Somewhere on the edge of a memory, or maybe a dream. I can never tell."

"What do you see, Mia?"

"Nothing clearly, James, just flashes of images. It completely overwhelms my senses, like breathing in smoke, the spitting of the oil-soaked wood in my ears, the heat of the flames on my skin."

"Have you tried painting it?"

Mia narrowed her eyes at him, irritated by his suggestion. The bone-deep tiredness of the past few hours took its toll on her, thinning her patience.

"All right, just paint what I cannot see."

"Your art isn't a series of images, Mia, it's emotion. Feelings. Capture the emotion, and it will come to you. There is magic in artmaking. Yours especially."

She exhaled the irritation, kicking the clumps of dirt with her boot. "You'd be a great master, James. You know that, right? Even if your blending is awfully rushed and messy."

He drove the blade of the shovel down. "The guild knows exactly what I am, Mia. Who I am. They'd not want to see me burn, but they don't want to be rubbing shoulders with me either."

"That's a damn shame."

He cast her a small smile, returning to the task at hand: burying the only master both of them would know. In that moment, something bonded them, bringing them closer. Mia was aware that it wasn't the expired body behind her, but the secrets they shared. Because secrets were tangled and knotty, entwining people together.

"To answer your question, Mia, yes. I painted her. Then Luc made me paint her with her breast out, debasing her, like how he saw all women. Nothing but objects for him to..."

Mia exhaled, slamming the shovel into the red dirt and splitting it like wood.

"You painted her like you saw her. For the woman she was, not the wicked, cruel queen history makes her out to be."

He leant back, a wistful look cut across his face. But the shine in his eyes told a story of loss, grief. It caught the breath in her chest.

"Because I knew her, Mia. She was my ruler, my friend—"

"If you say lover, I might spew again," she joked, a sad attempt at humour.

James huffed a laugh, casting her a rueful smile. "No, Luc was right about one thing. I much prefer men."

"Can you tell me about how it was before..."

A part of Mia ached to dive in, to ask him a million and one questions. Yet, another part wished to escape from any information, any knowledge of who she could be. To hide away and not accept the truth that she was a witch.

"For each shovel of dirt, I will answer one question. Now, get digging."

Mia nodded rapidly, diving into the dirt with a strange vigour for someone burying the body of a man they'd just murdered. She cast the earth over her shoulder, the soft pattering hitting the sheet covering Luc. "Were you a part of the Umbra Coven?"

"Yes, born and bred. My mother was an elder at Maeve's table—which, before you ask, was a council made up of six women from noble families, all deemed trustworthy to help Maeve rule."

"No men?"

James scoffed, scraping around a twisting root. "No men served on a council, in any coven, in any witch territory, Mia. They could advise, but never would they be offered a seat at that table."

"How strange," Mia muttered, slowing her digging. Her mind drifted to a world governed by women, not controlled by a single man. She wondered if hurt would still run deep in the land's soil, from wars raging to lands conquered.

"What was your home called?"

"Vespera, and it was glorious. There was a looming castle surrounded by a bustling village nestled in a towering blood oak forest. You could see the spires from miles away. That's how you knew you were coming home."

"Vespera…" Mia repeated, her tongue rolling around the word as she leant on the shove.

"In our ancient language, it means, 'Dusk, where the shadows are the longest'."

"Do you have magic?"

James arched a brow and nodded to the dirt not being shovelled out. They dug in silence until he broke the muted dim with a soft sigh. "No, Mia. Male witches do not possess magic. But those shadows…" His hands tightened on the rough wooden shaft. "They are not typical witch magic. Not a conjuring of flame, or the spine-tingling sensation of foresight."

"Then what are they?"

"Rare. Exceptionally rare. Only one person—well, one family— possessed them, bent them to their will."

"Who?" Mia asked, already knowing the answer.

Deep down, she had known since she stood under James' artwork of a burning queen to when she cracked open that journal, and those words spilt into her lap, only magnified by the tendril of shadow that soothed her in the darkest part of the night.

"Queen Maeve Magntai."

Those three words resounded in Mia's chest as they backfilled the dirt over Luc's body, and continued on the silent cart ride back into Alderdeen, and as she walked the hushed streets of the lower city. Right to a door with carved swirls, to a home well lived by one soul behind it.

She knocked three times.

The wait for the door to crack was excruciating, not because the soft sirens call for sleep, but because of the need, the demand for her to curl up in a sanctuary. She felt safe. She knew she should have gone home, but the cool, lonely sheets of her bed were the last place she wanted to be.

The door finally opened and let a current of warm air flood over Mia to seep into her chilled bones. The soft glow of the lantern light lit the bloody, dirty mess she was. Idris wore an open-collared shirt, with loose pants and dishevelled hair from sleep, confusion tightening his face.

"Idris..." she breathed.

His broad frame tilted as the dark embrace of unconsciousness swallowed her. She clawed and fought, but it was too strong, dragging her deeper. It swirled around her while he called her name, but then it morphed, crackling until she heard nothing but that malice-filled voice. The one she'd thought she had beaten. Only this time, it wasn't whispered words of self-hatred, but the long, crooned sigh of a word that chilled her to her bones.

Murderer.

An unsettling cackle rattled through her before her vision went black.

Forty-One

The midmorning sun had begun its slow crawl across the room, caressing Mia awake with warm, long fingers. Her gummy eyes took in the half-lit furniture, the scatter of clothing and the meticulously placed trinkets in Idris' bedroom. Like the rest of his house, it felt lived in and cosy. Hints of who he was had been shoved onto shelves and hung on walls.

A rich scent of whisky, ash and leather mingled with clean linen. She breathed it in, allowing it to permeate each shallow breath she dragged into her lungs. Even just breathing hurt, sending a sharp slash across her rib cage and shooting up her spine, making her bite down on her lip.

Idris' hand rested barely above her head as if he'd fallen asleep stroking her hair. Mia pushed up on an elbow, rubbing the sleep from her eyes. Dirt and black blood encrusted her nail beds, drying in the lines and webbing of her fingers, even flecking over her arms. Dried sweat and lingering tears coated her skin.

Mia felt dirty, disgusting.

She rose, careful not to wake Idris. He slumped against the headboard, still wearing the clothes from the evening before. His face was slack from sleep, making him appear younger, like only in the depths of slumber was he truly relaxed. That in his waking life, he held such tension in the muscles of his face that it aged him.

She ached to trace over his sharp cheekbone, down over the soft pout of his lips, then to tangle in his hair and drag him to her. Instead, she curled her hand into a fist, lest it betray her and travel over the rumpled sheets to him. She couldn't stomach that look he'd cast at her after he had her on that table. Not then.

Mia reached down for her boots, determined to creep out. She needed time and space to think, to pace, but the downward momentum shifted the cracks of her broken rib together, causing her gasp and tears to flood her eyes. She rose stiffly, hugging her boots and her rib cage. As she padded around the bed, her strained muscles burnt with the movement.

"Now, Little Witch," Idris' deep voice spooked her, making her fumble with her boots. "I didn't think you were the type to come and faint at a man's doorstep, then sneak out when he finally falls asleep."

Mia's feet took her backwards, trying to find an exit for the sudden panic in her chest. Her hip struck the curled arm of a well-worn armchair, sending her flailing, dropping her boots with a dull *thud*. Her rear hit the creaking leather and expelled the air from her lungs in a huff.

"Good goddess," Mia muttered, gripping her side a fraction tighter. The abrupt movement strained her rib bones apart, shooting another searing through her. "You've never heard of saying good morning, Old Man, or even just clearing your throat so you don't scare me to death?"

"I wasn't the one sneaking out like a lover at midnight."

"I wasn't—"

"Enough. What happened to you?" Idris cut in. No hint of humour laced his tone.

Mia clenched her jaw at the ghost of Luc's hands across her body, of his last expiring breath cascading over her. Her fingernail caught her nail bed, scratching dirt from her skin. How comfortable she had become with blood staining her; from queasy fainting to a complete numbness. It scared her. *Who am I becoming?*

"Nothing."

Idris arched a brow at her, then tilted his head. "You stink of grave dirt and blood, and by the looks of how you're holding your side, you have a broken rib. Let's not start lying to each other now."

"You've lied to me."

"I'm incapable of lying, Mia. You know this."

Her lips pressed together. *Truth or deception? Truth.* She'd speak her truth from then on. She'd never swallow what she wanted to say. Never again.

"You lied when you said I was safe with you. One part of me has never been safe with you."

That worried line formed between his brows. "Which part?"

"My heart, Idris."

Mia's eyes fell on a wooden chest, hidden in a shadow of the tall cupboard. Carved into the wood were images of a towering spire and crude oaks. At that moment, she wanted to take a piece of tracing paper and pencil and shade right to the top of the castle. But she knew she was trying to escape the uncomfortable emotion inside her.

Idris didn't reply. His eyes lowered to her tangled fingers, covered in dried blood and smeared dirt. It made her worry she'd given too much, said too much.

When he spoke, his voice was hesitant, soft. "To hold a heart like yours is a pleasure and honour, Mia, and I'm not worthy of that honour. But maybe, one day, I'll be able to hold it and cherish the pouring of love that comes from it."

Mia's eyes rose to his. A tender emotion beamed from him. It was the beginnings of more—something real and everlasting—but carried an edge of sadness, like an old wound that stretched but never ripped open.

"Truth?"

"Truth."

Tears welled. Her fingers tightened as she squeezed her lips together, shifting them from side to side, demanding not one to fall. She'd shed enough tears.

"Please, Mia, no hurt can harm you here. No ghosts of pain can haunt you here. Not in this room. Not in this bed."

She raised her glassy gaze to Idris and whispered, "You promise?"

He sat forward, an earnest look making the line between his brows deepen. "Yes, Little Witch, I promise."

Mia began talking with waving words and strangled breaths. Like a cracked dam, a tear escaped, trickling down her cheek and falling onto her tangled fingers. Then another, and another, until rivers of salt blasted through, creating deep canyons of clean skin down her face.

Idris slipped from the bed and knelt at her feet, hands gripping the leather arms of the chair. He never cut in, nor did he add anything but his grounding presence. He just let her spill the horror she'd experienced across his floor, like the vomit she'd spewed when they first met. Her words faded off with a final sniff.

Idris breathed her name, softly, reverently. She awoke with that whisper, flinging her arms around his neck. Bodies colliding, he encapsulated her. One large hand slipping to her nape, the other to her lower spine, dragging her closer still. She could feel her heart beat in time with his. That solid, rhythmic thumping.

His embrace felt safe, protective, and she never wanted to leave it.

Mia lost track of how long she had been wrapped in him, her tears drenching his shirt. But when Idris eventually pulled back from her, she felt unexpectedly hollow without his warm touch. He rose, stretching like a cat who had slept in the sun far too long. Between the flashes of material, a sliver of tanned skin with a flurry of dark hair became exposed.

"I have ruined it. For you. For Kali."

Idris glanced down at her. "Ruined it?"

"I killed him, and now all his secrets have gone to the grave with him. He knew more, but I got nothing from him. I have failed her, and myself, and you."

"You have failed no one, Mia. He was turning. You couldn't have stopped it, nor could you have gotten more information than you had."

"We are no closer now—"

"We are much closer. We know that someone wanted Kali in that alley and went to great lengths to get her there, and maybe that's what drew the other women in. Letters and notes. You remember the first fae woman? She had a letter for employment on a farm crumpled in her hand. Was that forgery as well?"

"Maybe we should break into the Pali and take a peek at their evidence ourselves."

Idris cracked a small smile and offered his hand to her. She stared at it. The dark voice slithered, curling around her ear, and whispered that one stomach-clenching word. *Murderer.*

Disgust coated her in venom, and she worried that if he touched her, he would be poisoned.

"How can you stand to touch me, after all I told you?"

"Because you wouldn't hurt someone without cause."

She shook her head, biting down on her lip. "I wanted to hurt him, Idris. I wanted to drown him in every drop of fear he'd instilled in me. But in the end, all it felt like was putting down a rabid dog, foaming at the mouth."

Idris said nothing when he took her hand and pulled her from the chair. His silence continued as he walked her across the expanse of his bedroom, around the strewn clothing to a closed door. Mia fought the urge to fill the air between them with her rambling, tangled thoughts. He rested his hand on the door handle and then cast over his shoulder, "You should have wanted to hurt him, Little Witch. You should have ripped his throat out with your bare teeth and cast his putrid soul right to Diabolus. Let him burn in those Heylla pits not only for what he did to you, but for the part he played in Kali's death."

"But does that not make me the same monster as him? Wishing for pain and hurt."

"No. You are no monster." He paused, voice wavering a fraction. "I've known my fair share of monsters."

With that, Idris pushed open the door, and whirls of golden marble shone back at her. Mia exhaled and pulled from him, drawn into the warmth of the bathroom, even though the tile underfoot was cool. She turned, seeing flashes of a spouted shower head and a long vanity, a small mirror above it. The most wondrous thing was the expanse of glass opening over the bath. The haphazard, tilted roofs skimmed the bottom half, but she could see right to the beginnings of the Sliva Forest. Beyond that wide stretch of soaring pines sat a dark castle, nestled in a mountainous valley. The Death Court.

Idris brushed past, leaning over to turn the bronze handle. Water spluttered to life, splashing through the empty tub. He passed her again, eyes lowered, heading towards the door. He was going to leave her alone with her thoughts, with that unsettling voice. And she didn't want to be alone.

Her hand snapped out and gripped his wrist. "Stay."

"Mia, you don't need to—"

"I want you to stay, Idris." Her words fell between them, heavy like gold coins scattering to stone. "I've never wanted to simply be with someone. I want..."

"What do you want?"

Her heart quickened, and she spoke before her courage left her. "*You*, Idris."

He drew in one long breath, then exhaled it. "Then you shall have me."

The same words he had said when he was deep inside of her on that table, but this time, it wasn't lusty, desire-filled. They were soft, tender, and most of all, the truth.

"May I undress you?"

"Yes."

She felt every trail of warmth Idris left on her bare skin as he pulled the ruined silk and cotton from her bruised and battered body. Fingers slipped over the empty sheath attached to her thigh, unbuckling it with a tug. His gaze danced over each of her curves and dips in wide-eyed appreciation. As if she were a masterpiece of colour stretched over a canvas, and each of those silver scars that spread jaggedly over the curve of her hip was a vein of bright gold cutting through the colour.

Mia had never had someone look at her with such regard.

Her bruise-speckled arm crossed her over her breasts—not to cover her nakedness, but to hold herself from erupting again from that one look. She reached out, allowing herself to smooth the creases in his shirt, savouring the hard muscle under the linen. Her hand bunching around the material. "I want this off."

"Then take it off, Little Witch."

With bated breath, she pulled the fabric from his torso, dropping it at her bare feet. Her eyes traced over the hair-speckled, honed muscle, over the scars and freckles that marked his skin. His fingers yanked apart the lacings of his pants. Slowly.

"And these?"

Mia nodded.

Idris released himself from the last of his clothing, dumping them with her bloody clothing. Mia's gaze never lowered. It was more than a tryst in a back alley, or even on a desk in a dingy pub. Her trembling hands gripped her underwear, pulling them down and kicking them into the pile of bloody clothing. She was completely bare to him, both heart and body. Yet, she didn't want to run from it; she relished in it. She was safe, and nothing could harm her there.

Mia stepped forward, climbing the steps that lead to the bath, ignoring the concerned glance from Idris.

"Mia, wait. The water is too warm"

She plunged her leg into the filling bath. The water was hot, scalding. She savoured the stinging hotness that stripped the dirty feeling away. With another step, Mia forced herself deeper into the water, sinking to her knees. She submerged herself, right down into the serene dim. She could only hear the dull *thud* of her heart and Idris' heavy steps, allowing the feverish water to wash the disgust and shame off her skin—and almost off her soul. But Mia knew she could never wash that from her. No amount of scrubbing would remove that stain.

The swirl of water showed another body joining her. Mia broke the surface to see Idris sinking into the steaming bath. Their gazes met. Both knew that it was even more than bodies meeting; it was hearts tentatively reaching out for the first time.

"I can wash you, if you desire it," Idris whispered so softly, she wasn't sure if he had even spoken.

She blinked the water from her lashes. "I would like that very much."

He reached out under the water for her, fingertips slipping over the dip of her waist. Mia let him pull her closer until her legs draped over his, and her back met the cool side of the bath.

"This seems extravagant, Old Man."

With a small curl of his lip, Idris grabbed an amber bottle of oily soap and poured it into his palm. "What can I say? I love a bath."

He began right at her fingertips, scrubbing away the muck left around her nail beds, slipping his fingers between hers to work the sudsy bubbles over the webbing. He held her hand a little longer with each scrub, savouring it.

Idris dragged the soft slippery soap over her arms in long, soothing strokes, making sure none of the horrors remained on her skin. His hand skimmed the curve of her breasts, only to drag his soapy hands over the soft swell of her stomach, but not an inch lower.

All his touches carried a gentle affection, not a heavy lust. As if she would slip away in a mist of shadows if he held her too tight. Mia wasn't sure if she wouldn't.

Idris reached for her face, spreading the leftover suds across her cheek. A soft, masculine scent wafted into her nose. A soft smile spread across her face. It was his soap that hypnotised her. Had she known what it was, she would have drowned in it.

Idris' gaze caught hers, his emerald pools lightening to a sea bottle green. The look was not one coated in sad shame, or an exhaling look of joy, but something deeper, more permanent. But the sting of the cut on her cheek brought reality splashing into the surrounding water. The voice slithered around the bony points of her spine like a treacherous snake until she could feel his hot breath on the shell of her ear, and the beginnings of the words he would mutter to her.

"May I wash your hair?" Idris muttered into the space they shared.

"I would love that, Idris," she answered, reluctantly pulling from his grip.

Mia turned, nestling between his legs, bringing her chin to her knee. Gentle fingers dragged the wet strands from her face, then a heady lavender scent filled the silence between them. Hands worked in soft, swirling movements around her crown, dragging down to her nape, sending her skin prickling.

"It smells like mine."

"I guessed correctly then," Idris replied, his thumbs working those tense muscles at the base of her skull. "I wanted something that smelt of you close to me when I couldn't be."

Her breath caught in her chest as her eyes searched the whirling marble in front of her. "You did?"

"You sound surprised."

Mia raised a dripping hand out of the water. The droplets falling from each of her fingers made the surface ripple and break, much like the river in her dreams, and the man who looked like Idris. Warmth radiated from her extended pointer finger, and a ribbon of shadow swirled from nothing, snaking through her damp fingers, spinning into the air.

"I didn't think—I know about the vow, Idris. I overheard you and Benny talking about it. What we did in your office broke that vow, and I know"—she paused—"you hurt because of it."

His fingers paused. "Mia, we can talk about that later—"

"No. I want to talk about it now."

"Out of all the things you wish to talk about, you want to talk about that?"

"Yes."

He let out a deep exhale, chest brushing her shoulder blades. "What do you want to know?"

"Who would make you take a vow like that?'

"A long-forgotten queen," Idris replied, that soft sadness edged into his tone.

"Can you tell me about her, or is it too painful?"

"Can I tell you a story instead?"

Mia leant back into Idris, his arms encapsulating her. Through her fingers, Ozul threaded and darted into the air filled with steam. "Weave me a tale, then, Old Man."

"Long, long ago lived a prince, whose only wish was to be free from a golden crown, from the suffocating grip of his father. Then..." He hesitated, his thumb circling the soft skin of her stomach. "His entire court was slain, leaving him alone in the world. Seemingly, he had his wish granted. Yet, he lost his way as he wandered lands, trying to find a place to call home, finding nowhere he truly fit."

Mia exhaled, leaning deeper into Idris' arms, her eyelids growing heavy.

"That was until he stumbled into a court full of laughter, love and life—so much you could have bottled it, Mia—in every person he passed, in each noble, right to the fair queen herself. This place was so far gone from the cold, grey place he grew up in. But this court was secretive and trusted no one. The queen had this prince—in ragged clothing, drunk and bloody hopeless—brought to her. She cast her wise gaze over him and saw a spark of something inside of him."

"Go on," Mia murmured, her hand finding his.

He sighed and continued. "Then, she gave the prince an offer—serve her as her royal guard, but vow to her to take no wife, father no children and drink no witch's blood. Give up everything for her and her court. Or she threatened to cast him to the wild, where he would roam like a ghost in the mist. But..."

"But?"

"The prince never knew what he was truly giving up. He never knew what joy and happiness he was forgoing to stand at her side, to protect her and her family."

"That seems an impossible choice, Idris."

"It's a tough one, Mia, not impossible. When you have nothing, you care not for the things that may come in the future. You only care for the distant dream of a safe place to rest your head."

His words settled in her chest, sadness weighing them down. Mia turned, brows raised. "I bet he fell madly in love with her, vowing to her only to love her?"

With a chuckle, Idris' eyes crinkled, dissolving the sadness. "No. The fair queen had more husbands than she knew what to do with. But it was more than love or lust. It was friendship, Mia. One they both needed."

"Then yo—I mean, this prince served her for many years, faithfully. Loyal to only her."

"That he did, right until the night of the Great Witch Burning. With every plume of smoke, he lost it all. The only family he had ever known, his home and his purpose. Then, he became lost again in a world that only saw him as a coward. His heart in pieces, he began that worrisome wandering again, hoping to be found."

The silence was heavy.

Idris' eyebrows met, and his hooded eyes became glassy. His lips smoothed into a thin line, pressing firmly together as if he was trying to stop himself from crying. Mia reached out, dragging her fingers over the furrow of his brow, smoothing it under gentle pressure. Her hand skimmed over a day's worth of stubble until she could feel the sharp prick on her palms. She drew him closer until his forehead touched hers.

"Until now, Idris. You've been *found*."

Forty-Two

Idris tasted like the bitter koffee they had choked down between bites of breakfast shared in his sheets. Their kisses were peppered with quiet chatter and long, searching stares. Her fingers danced over each part she had always ached to touch. She dragged her thumb over the line of hard muscle across his shoulders, swirling through rough body hair, to grip onto his ropey forearms. A small, wondrous smile had stretched on Idris' face, lighting a twinkle in his eye that she had never seen. It made her heart swell.

Mia reached for his hand, guiding it over the expanse of her thigh, up over the edge of the borrowed shirt she'd pulled on, right over her bruised ribs to her breast. His thumb circled her nipple over the rough linen, hardening under his attention. She rolled her body against him in undulating waves. Every slow touch was gentle, savoured. He allowed her to control each part, waiting for her to nod or a, "Yes," to fall from her.

Pleasure left her in low moans and gripped sheets as Idris slipped fingers between her thighs. Her own slid down over his body, disappearing lower to fist around velvet-wrapped hardness, drawing pants and furrowed grunts. Both found the release they sought, but found more between those sheets than either knew. Emotion had pulled taut between them, dragging them together.

The day had shifted into night. And the last of the sun's rays pushed heat into Idris' bedroom. His hand settled around her throat, his thumb applying the slightest of pressure on her slowed pulse. A flash of cold, angry eyes and strangled breath made her tense, and her hands went to his chest, readying to push him away. His grip instantly dropped away. He pulled himself from her, giving her space to sit up. The heart-racing spike of fear dampened the overwhelming feeling of desire singing in her veins.

Mia groaned in frustration. Luc still ruined things from his shallow grave.

Idris reached for her, capturing her chin. "We need not rush to the end, Little Witch. I can wait for you to be ready."

Her hand slid over his, feeling those crisscrossed scars across his knuckles. "But I can't, Idris. I can't have his touch haunt my skin for a moment longer. I need you to scare away his ghost."

"It will be my pleasure, and my absolute privilege," he whispered, and she believed him. Each word he uttered was the truth. That was their agreement. Nothing in that bed could hurt them. Not the outside world, not the ghouls in their past. Nothing.

"Perhaps we go slow," Mia added quickly. She wished that, when their bodies melded together again, it would be perfect. Not a table in a dingy bar, with her blood singing in his veins, or with a spike of fear in her. Maybe Idris was right; they needed not rush to the sticky conclusion.

"Slow," he repeated, smirking. "I can go slow."

Crawling closer to her, Idris knelt between her legs, his broad body looming over her. The yellow sun's rays caught each edge of him, lighting him with an ethereal glow, much like the golden veined paintings that hung in the dusty churches of Deus, depicting ancient gods battling evil. Mia's fingers ached to draw, to sketch him bathed in light, to relive the moment in sharp clarity, not in a faded, hazy memory.

Idris' eyes roamed her splayed body, taking in the deep dip of her waist, right over the softness of her stomach peeking out from her bunched shirt, tracing the lines of silver that erupted over her hip, and the scattering of freckles that made constellations across her skin. Discovering every part of her with a wide-eyed marvel that she'd expect of a man seeing Oryah for the first time. Her cheeks warmed, and a hint of shyness emerged in her. Her hand rose to cover the scar that cut over her cheek, but it fell behind her head.

"You know it's rude to stare, Old Man."

"It's rude to look that good in a borrowed shirt, Little Witch."

Idris parted her legs with a push. He kissed on the dip of her knee, then dragged his lips along the soft skin of her inner thigh. He peppered kisses over her stomach, over the curve of her hips, leaving her skin tingling with each gentle bite. Mia groaned, her hips rolling, desperate for any friction. Each time his teeth had barely dug into her skin sent her core throbbing, clenching around nothing.

"Oh, so desperate for another release, are you? Have I not pleased you enough?" Idris murmured against her skin, his voice gravelly.

Mia mumbled under her breath, her words little more than exhaled sighs. His finger glided over her core, sending waves of pleasure through her. She arched against him, back bowing off the mattress.

"It appears not with how needy you are—and gods, so wet. We have to rectify this at once."

Her breathy pleas ended with a throaty moan as his tongue caressed her core, lapping at her arousal.

"Use your words, Little Witch," Idris said, fanning his warm breath over her, almost sending her undone. He swirled his tongue over her most sensitive nerve endings, stealing the words from her. His voice dropped an octave, and a demand slipped from him. "Speak, Mia."

"Please do that over and over," she breathed, words punctuated with moans. "I want you to make me release with just your tongue."

"I haven't stopped dreaming of how fucking incredible you taste..." he muttered before he dived back between her legs with a ferocity of a man starved, tongue circling, curling around her, demanding more pleasure. More than she knew she could give. Her hand threaded through his hair, only to anchor herself to him. She shattered into a million pieces, coming undone when Idris drew her into his mouth, tongue lapping.

Heat burst inside of her. Her magic was seeping out of the cracks.

Ozul slipped from her, swirling in the air in misty tendrils, skimming over sweaty skin and crumpled sheets.

Mia knew she could get lost there, in that bed, with Idris. Whatever was growing between them was laying roots in her chest. Pleasure and that tender feeling of love were mixing. Something she had never experienced, and she didn't shy from it. Not anymore.

Far away, a door slammed shut, and Benny's bellowing voice popped their serene bubble. Idris cursed under his breath. Mia's fingers reached for him, but he had slipped away from her, out of the bed. Whatever had grown between them snapped, like a frail twig.

"I should get dressed," Idris murmured, turning his back on her. A stark white, knobbed scar wove over the column of his spine. Someone had taken a whip to him. He swiftly pulled on a shirt and hid the scars away. He cast a look at her over his shoulder, that torn expression emerging on his face. "This is—"

Mia raised her hand, preventing him from spoiling the moment they had just enjoyed. She didn't want to hear the words. Especially not the ones he muttered after they had shared that space for the first time.

"I understand, Idris. We can only exist here, in this bed. Not outside these walls."

"I wish things could be different, Mia."

Each word pulled at the stitches in the weeping edges of her heart, snapping the delicate thread that held those wounds together. She slid from the tangled sheets without speaking another word. Gripping the edge of the borrowed shirt, she pulled it down to cover herself. Neither knew what to say, or even what to do.

Mia felt awkward—a cheek-heating awkwardness.

She glanced at the door—the only exit—and not at Idris, whose gaze burnt into her. She knew he wanted to say more, let the truth unwind in front of them like an unravelling ribbon. Even so, Mia couldn't hear it. She escaped across the room, leaving him and his burning truth behind.

Benny was leaning against the wall next to the front door with a bundle of dark blue material in his arms. Mia could hardly meet his gaze, that twisting, awkward feeling consuming her. Could she tell a man she'd called a friend what had occurred between her and Idris? She didn't want to keep what was growing inside her a secret. "We—"

"Are sleeping together? I presumed as much," Benny finished. He ran a hand over his short, coiled hair, eyes squinting at the spiral staircase. "Pleasure is not something to be ashamed of. You're the first woman he has brought here. The first to share his bed for—gods, an age. But I fear you're seeking something that Idris cannot give you. That you shouldn't give him."

Mia's eyes rose to his. Only concern beamed from them. "I'm here to find my sister's killer. Nothing else. This is all..." She waved a hand to the stairs, searching for a lie—anything—but she let the truth slip free. "This is—this cannot be more than us rolling in his sheets. As much as I want it to be."

Benny cocked his head, lips pursing. "You're going to get hurt, Mia."

She sighed softly, eyes dipping to the dress he held. It was hers. She reached out, brushing over the golden stitching and soft cotton. She smelt the delicate, clean scent of the soap flakes Abigail used to wash her clothing. "I've already been hurt. What's a few more scars on my heart?"

Benny dumped the fabric in her arms, his eyes flashing to hers. A silent look—one mixed with concern and sadness. It weighed his lips down and made his shoulder sag.

"You're too young to be so hurt, Mia. Don't let whatever this is with Idris add more."

She took an unsteady step back and turned on her heel, desiring to evade the tidal wave of feelings that slammed into her. But she couldn't fight it, nor could she escape that malice-filled voice whispering to her, *My sweet creature, did you think that boy wanted you for more than what is wet between your legs?*

You're disgusting, and don't call me sweet creature, Mia replied, words curling in her mind.

But I wish to give you a pet name, something to call you outside of what your mother named you.

Her hands trembled against the fabric. She had never had a conversation with the voice before, only whispering demands for it to leave. *What are you?*

I am you, but I am not. I was once adored, and in the same breath, feared. However, they have banished me to the darkness. And, my sweet creature, you are mine.

The word *mine* slid around her throat, soft as a lover's touch, but laced with the threat of violence.

I am most certainly not yours.

That dark cackling followed her into the cooled lounge room, skimming over her as she pulled the borrowed shirt off to yank the dark blue cotton dress over her bruised and sore body.

We shall see, sweet creature, we shall see.

Mia ignored the ominous threat and the hairs rising on her neck. She glanced over her shoulder to find Idris in the doorway. His eyes skimmed over her, only to fall away. "Tell me what you found out, Ben."

"As you command, Idris," the barman replied, striding into the lounge room.

FORTY-THREE

MIA LEANT A HIP ON THE WINDOW FRAME, ARMS CROSSED over her chest. She watched a glossy, plump raven hop down the quiet street, then launch into the sky, black wings cutting through the late afternoon sun. Benny was relaying information she already knew—more bodies, more deaths.

"And Reagan was with the whores of the velvet road all night. I swear to Oryah, I'd rather watch paint dry than witness him bury himself in yet another woman," he finished as he ran a hand over his face and shivered.

"Does that mean Reagan is out?" she asked, glancing at Idris. "He couldn't have committed these murders, nor could he be this master. A vampyre has to be involved. You all said so."

Idris grunted a response. His eyes were on the flickering flame of the fireplace, expression hard. Mia fought the urge to smooth the line between his brows, to take his hand, to wake him from the memory he was trapped in. Instead, she gripped her arm and turned back to the window.

Benny groaned, reclining. "Maybe it's not a dhampyr. Maybe it was Luc. You said he was raving mad."

Mia frowned. Her fingers slipped over the purple splotched skin, feeling the already scabbing wounds.

"No, Ben. It's a dhampyr. Luc was turning when Mia ended his sorry existence," Idris replied in a soft voice. "The bodies were...mutilated, and not by blade, but by teeth and claws."

"And no human could do that? They are devious, mate. We know this."

He shook his head once as if to shake an image from his memory. "This thing isn't just drinking blood and eating their flesh. It's devouring them, Ben. Only his creatures—only dhampyrs could do that."

Mia paled. Kali's lifeless body, covered in gore, burst into her vision in blinding flashes. A living nightmare—one she couldn't escape with the sun's day break. Her hands clenched her biceps so tightly that she had added to the flurry of purple dotting her skin.

"His creatures? Reagan's?"

The men exchanged a look, but didn't reply. Idris shook his head slightly.

"All these women must have something in common," Benny muttered, his hand slowly rubbing his clipped scalp.

Mia sighed, then spoke. "They do, Benny. They were vulnerable, from faraway lands, brought here to work, to live, with no ties. No one to miss them, no one to search for them. They have been selected, or known to whoever is controlling the monsters. Are we sure they didn't know each other?"

"Not to my knowledge," Idris answered.

"What about to Mylo's knowledge?"

He shook his head. "Even he is stumped. There is no connection."

Mia pushed off the window, shaking her head. "Mylo knows more than he is letting on. They must know something. We need to see their files."

Idris' eyes flicked to her. "He wouldn't let us simply stroll in and ask them."

"Line his pocket with more gold, then."

"That is more than I think it's worth, Mia. There is nothing in those files Mylo hasn't told us about."

She shook her head. "I don't trust him—"

"I do," Idris cut in, his voice hard. "Now, we need to work on what information we actually have, and not these fantastical ideas you sprout."

Mia gritted her jaw, ready to argue. "Why? Don't you want to see—"

"Because there is nothing good there, Mia. *Nothing.*"

"There is nothing good here either, Idris."

Silence settled in the room as their gazes locked, and a battle began. Whatever step they had taken when they were wrapped in each other's embrace was dragged back into those murky waters. They didn't know how not to hurt each other—with words or looks.

"Kali just doesn't fit, Old Man. Not a single bit." Mia's gaze dropped, and her brows knotted. "She is the loose end I cannot work out. Her death is too noticeable, turning an eye on the murders. If you chose these women because they would never be missed, why would you—"

"Kill a lord's daughter. One beloved by Hartwin and his court?" Idris finished. "We are missing something. It's just out of reach."

Mia flashed him another annoyed expression, rolling her eyes. *Perhaps that's why we need to uncover what the Silver has on her, Old Man,* she added silently. *I cannot believe Mylo knows nothing, and I'm going to see those files, whether Idris likes it or not.*

Idris paced. His long legs took him across the room, repeating the information over and over. Mia stepped closer, her mind working to fit pieces of the confusing puzzle until one slotted in, clicking into place.

"Reagan mentioned the night he had you stabbed that I had chosen the wrong side, like Kali. I presumed at court, but maybe he was talking about something more sinister. Kali found something she shouldn't have and had to be silenced, according to Luc. My sister knew a secret that was worth her killing over."

Idris' eyes flashed to hers. "Have you searched her room for letters, notes?"

"I haven't been able to go in since..." *She went to the eternal gardens.*

Once, days after Kali was reduced to ashes, Mia found herself standing in front of her sister's door, unable to open it, only to be reminded of what she had lost in each corner of the room, in each object. She had never returned.

"Have your parents? Have the maids?"

Benny flashed him a wide-eyed look, but Idris was too deep, yanking at threads that should have stayed sown in. Mia watched his eyes work in his sockets with a strange, chest-tightening feeling of apprehension.

"No one has been in her room. My mother won't allow it."

"Then we need to go look. *Now.*"

Benny muttered Idris' name like a curse, shaking his head at him.

Mia's hands dropped to her sides. She strayed close to that old familiar ache. "I don't know if I can," she whispered.

"What if the key to solve all of this is in there?" he asked, continuing to press her for a decision. "What if the answer to Kali's death has been in the room one over from yours all this time?"

Mia exhaled sharply as the reminder of her grief slammed into her like a punch to the gut. She had locked it in a box, away in her mind. Suddenly, the lid had lifted a fraction, letting the feeling seep out. That creeping voice whispered again in her ear. *Sweet creature, what if? So many questions from the boy. But he won't be pleased with the answers.*

"Idris, enough," Benny snapped. "You cannot force her into this. That is cruel, even for you."

Swallowing, Mia returned her gaze to the window. Her fading reflection showed wide, glassy eyes. She blinked, a tear rolling down her cheek. Sadness embraced her like a long-forgotten friend, squeezing out any joy she had felt rolling in Idris' bed, leaving her hollow, empty. A hand hovered on her back. Her gaze rose to Idris' in the glass. He tracked the single teardrop. Regret lingered on his features.

"Let's go rifle through my dead sister's belongings, then, Old Man."

MIA AND IDRIS WALKED THROUGH THE LOWER CITY IN silence. Neither wanted to speak about what had grown between them in his bed, nor did they want to talk any further about the murders. But with each swing of her arm, Mia's fingers brushed over his scarred knuckles. Until he slipped his hand into hers—a reminder he was there.

A cart clunked going over cobblestones, and the soft bays of a mule rose over the indistinct murmuring of the people.

"Move. Official Silver business! Stand aside!" a deep voice called out, but the crowd didn't budge, instead pressing in further.

More demands to shift, to move, filled the air.

The sea of warm bodies swept Mia from Idris. She was spat out, hitting the hard wooden edge of a cart. Her eyes came across a hessian sheet covering a body, then a hand flopped out. The grey, sickly flesh had puckered and split from the centre of the palm to between the middle finger and pointer.

Luc.

They had found his body.

The memories of pain and blood gathered at the base of her skull, surrounded by the word *murderer*.

Mia's world spun. She backed away, bumping shoulders and chests.

"Move, this isn't for ladies' eyes."

"Who..." She paused, gathering herself. "Who is it?"

The knight glanced back, then at her. "Some noble artist. Liam? Larry? Nah, that's not it—"

"Luc."

"Yeah, that's it. You all right, miss?"

Mia didn't answer the knight, but spun on her heel and forced her way out of the crowd. She needed air before she collapsed on the cobblestone. She erupted out of the masses, right into Idris. His hands gripped her biceps, steadying her. She curled into him, holding onto him for fear her legs would give away.

"They found him..." she whispered into his chest. "How?"

He wrapped his arms around her, pressing his lips to her crown. "I don't know, Mia."

She pulled from him, her eyes searching the air, but not falling on anything. "James is in danger. We have to warn him."

Mia grabbed Idris' hand and yanked him down the street towards the art studio for the last time.

Mia peered into the darkness of the storefront. A closed sign hung on the door.

"It's locked up—"

"But James may be here."

Mia had to defend the secret they shared, but she had to protect James more. She pushed past Idris and rounded the building to the alleyway, pausing at the back door, inhaling slowly. Her hand brushed the brass handle, making the memories surge in stomach-turning waves. His lips squeezed on her throat, clanging his belt buckle, his fingers on her thigh. Her bruised body throbbed in response.

Mia shook her head, casting the visions away. He was dead. He couldn't harm her anymore. Her hand trembled as she wiggled the handle. Locked. She pressed her face to the window. Her eyes worked around the dim room.

Nothing had changed.

No corpse, no blood, no broken glass.

Nothing.

"It's as if it never happened..."

"It's closed, Mia," a voice rang out. Samuel pushed off the wall. In her haste, she hadn't even seen him. "No one knows when the place will open again. Haven't you heard? Master Luc is dead."

Mia turned, all her muscles tensed. "James—"

"Is no Master Luc. He was brilliant, a true visionary. Like nothing we will ever see again."

"A visionary? That's a fucking joke. He barely put paint on a canvas. He stole art from those who have actual talent and passed it off as his own, let alone what he did in the dark of the night. Preying on women, hurting them," Mia snapped back. Her arms crossed over herself as if to contain her rage. Or was it to stop Ozul from erupting from her? She couldn't tell.

Samuel sneered, his gaze dragging over her. "Some women are asking for it, aren't they?"

"Excuse me?" she gritted, narrowing her eyes at him.

"Women seek powerful men just to be abused by them. They like it."

"That's *disgusting*, Samuel. No one seeks to be hurt by others. I've had quite enough of this conversation." She turned on her heel, striding past Idris to the alley mouth.

"Look at you, Mia, throwing yourself at both men. We all knew the bargain you struck with Luc. And you must be good on your knees, if they let you play artist," Samuel said, a smug smile on his face. As if he had her all worked out. "But I see you've moved on to the next rich man, like a common whore."

His eyes found Idris, who was glowering at him. "Tell me, what does she do with that pretty mouth that gets all these men all hot and—"

Idris moved so swiftly that Mia struggled to track him. His fist flew, cracking against Samuel's jaw and sending him stumbling back. His hand threaded through Samuel's curls, yanking him back. "The next words will be an apology, do you understand? Or do I have to beat it into you?"

"Fuck you, bloodsucker."

"I hoped you would say that," Idris crooned through a clenched jaw. He slammed his fist into Samuel's stomach, sending a tight wheeze through the air. "Apologise."

"Do you know who my father is?" Samuel wheezed, gripping his middle. "He will fucking end you."

Idris leant in close as a snarl came from his mouth. "Do you know who my father is, blood bag? Perhaps your wet nurse whispered the warnings of his bloody reign to you late at night, in the low candlelight. Maybe he haunts your dreams, stalking you in the shadows. Blood is all he seeks, and you are fucking full of it."

Samuel's eyes widened at each of Idris' words. Fear crept into his eyes, making his skin pale a fraction.

"Mortias Blackwood," he whispered. "That blood-crazy vamp who massacred his entire court?"

Mia shuddered at the name, stepping back.

"Yes," Idris hissed into his ear. "If you even look her way, or speak to her in a tone that does not befit her station, I will find you and show you some of the horrific things my father showed me."

Forty-Four

"Truth?"

Idris flashed her a look and let out a long breath. "Truth."

It was the first word he had spoken since they had begun the laborious trudge up the steep hill that led to Mia's home. She chewed her lip, sneaking glances at the vampyre, whose face was downcast, pulled into a tight grimace. Mia stopped. Her eyes searched the dirt, over each rock and abandoned footprint, as her mind worked to place the pieces of the limited knowledge she had together. She raised her confused expression at him. "I thought the entire court was mass—"

"Yes. Every man, woman and child."

"All but you."

Idris paused, not looking back. She could see the strain across his shoulders under his shirt, running to the slight tremor in his hand. *Is it from fear or anger?*

"Why? Why did he keep you alive?"

He didn't answer, but continued up the hill, leaving Mia in his dust. She rushed after him, reaching out and grasping him by the elbow. Before she could speak, he yanked his arm from her grip. "He just couldn't find me because I was locked in a fucking maid's closet for what felt like days. He meant to end every single one of his court, myself included."

Mia's hand found her mouth to quieten the gasp that came from her.

He turned from her with a sharp exhale. "I do not want nor need your pity. Stop looking at me like that."

Her chin dropped to her chest, her cheeks warming. "I don't pity you, Idris. I'm just trying to understand."

When he faced her again, a wild, desolate sadness forced his face to tighten to the point of pain. He pointed a finger at her and began. "Then, stop, Mia. You won't ever understand the pain, the helplessness of listening to your whole family being slaughtered by the man who was supposed to protect you. Then, only a handful of years later, watching the people who took you in, cared for you, being burnt at a stake. All because you made one stupid fucking mistake."

Mia backed up a step, holding her palms out. "Idris, I didn't mean to make you upset. I'm just fumbling in the dark."

He stepped with her, leaning closer. "If you think this constant questioning will help me feel anything but lust for what is between your legs and what pumps in your veins, you are wrong. This, between us"—his hand pointed backwards and forwards between them—"will not be allowed to grow into love, no matter how much as we want it to, Mia."

Her mouth snapped closed, her eyes searching his face. Speechless. A crack formed in her heart, and a hot, fiery rage seeped from it, filling her every word with the lashings of anger. "You think I'm falling in *love* with you?" Mia asked, scoffing. "That's laughable. I'm not, I can assure you that."

"You appearing on my doorstep bruised and bloodied, asking me to bathe you and then rolling in my bed, speaks of a girl—"

"A *girl*?" She stepped forward, her chin raised to keep the burning eye contact. "I'm a woman, Idris. Not some brainless simpleton ready to fall at your feet, in love, because you took me to bed. Remember, you wanted me to help you, and all I wanted was for you to help me find the monster that fucking slaughtered my sister in the street. Not for you to complicate my life even more."

Idris winced at her words but didn't break eye contact. "No more,

Mia. No more showing up at my door, rolling in my bed, begging me to take you. No more. We focus on the case."

"Agreed. It seems we have both become distracted."

Mia strode past him, her jaw clenching and unclenching as tears sprang in her eyes. She wouldn't let him see her cry.

MIA AND IDRIS STOOD IN FRONT OF KALI'S DOOR IN complete silence. She reached out, hand sliding over the cool metal handle. Choking on the ball of emotion, she swung open the door. Kali's swee, cinnamon smell slammed into her, making her back up a step, trying to elude it. Right into Idris.

"Steady, Little Witch. I'm here."

Gone were the hot lashes of anger. Slow, creeping sadness filled each of her muscles, locking her in place. He simply guided her through the doorway, forcing Mia to face her grief.

Kali had decorated her room with scattered throws, rugs and pillows, creating a plush, comfortable warmth that made her want to sink in. A desk under the window was stacked with medical books. A blue ribbon was tied to the back of the chair. The bed was left unmade.

Without a single thought, Mia walked over to it and reached out for the blanket, straightening it. "She never tidied her sheets. 'Why make it, just to sleep in it again?' she would say. It made Mama and the maids so infuriated, they refused to clean both our rooms..."

"That doesn't seem fair," Idris replied, his eyes scanning the room. "Let me guess, you make your bed?"

"Every day."

Mia lifted the pillow. A dried flower was tenderly placed under it. A swirling feeling grew in her—not the sharp cut of jealousy, but something softer. However, she was so full of sadness that she couldn't name a single other emotion. She replaced it with a gentle toss, sitting heavily on the bed. "Now, if I were a secret letter, where would I be?"

Idris lifted each book on her desk, flicking through it.

Mia rolled her eyes and stood. "You've obviously hidden nothing from your parents..."

She regretted the words as soon as they left her.

He pulled a drawer open and pawed through the contents without looking at her. "He wasn't always cruel, you know. But, the happy memories seem overshadowed by what he did."

Mia strode over to Kali's closet, pulling the doors wide. An array of colours shone. She ran her fingers over the fabrics, feeling soft velvets, rough cottons and the slip of silk. She pushed the gowns aside, pressed the cupboards back and slipped over each seam, searching the panels for hidden compartments. "At least you have memories. The good and the bad. I have none of my birth parents, not even a sliver of a memory."

Idris' hands paused for a fraction too long. He stared at her with that line forming between his brows. Another stab of shame sliced against her already tender flesh. She crossed her arms, protecting herself from the look. "Have you found something, Old Man?"

He shook his head as his gaze dropped away.

Mia pouted and moved around the room. Her eyes travelled over each of Kali's trinkets. She paused, head cocked. A black box obscured by a brightly patterned scarf hid in shadows at the back of a shelf in her cramped bookcase. She stepped closer, pulling books away and dumping them at her feet. Her fingers gripped the material and yanked, exposing the strange runes carved into the wood.

"What are you?" she murmured, bringing the box down.

A warmth radiated from her chest; her magic was responding to it. It felt right. Her thumb dragged over the meticulous etchings, feeling each swirl and bump. "What does it say?"

Idris' gaze fell on the black wood, causing him to breathe out a hushed exhale. His forefinger tracked the same runes she had.

"By the shadows," he murmured. "It's an Umbra Box."

A woman whispering those words in a shaky voice played in her ears. But it was gone as soon as she reached for it.

She flicked her eyes to him. "A what box?"

"A Umbra Box. It's a witch relic, Mia. Good goddess, I thought they had destroyed all the enchanted objects. This must have survived the purging." He reached out and fingered the worn brass keyhole. "This was used to transport secret missives and letters of war to each coven. Only the witch queens possessed the skeleton keys to open them."

Mia sat on the bed, resisting the urge to hug the box to her chest. Her thumb traced the runes, over and over. *This is the closest I have ever been to my coven.* The simple thought made her hand tremble. *My coven? Have I accepted what I am? Who I am?*

A shadow slipped from her, skimming over the polished wood. *"Open."*

Mia shoved the box further down her lap. "There must be a key somewhere in here—"

"Just conjure one, Mia, just like that shadow blade you crafted," Idris interrupted with a frustrated groan.

All her muscles tensed, and her gaze snapped to him. "What do you mean?"

"Mia—"

She scrambled from the bed, backing up a step, then another towards the door, holding the box to her chest. "How do you know about the blade? I didn't tell you."

Idris opened his mouth to answer, then closed it. He reached out for it, and she slapped his hand away.

"How. Did. You. Know?" she asked, emphasising each word.

"I cannot tell you, Mia. Now, conjure a key, and let us see what Kali was hiding. My patience is wearing thin, and women are dying while we continue to waste time on this."

Her grip tightened, shaking her head. "Not until you answer me."

"No."

"Tell me how you knew."

"I cannot. Not yet. Not until I know for sure it is safe."

"For who?"

"Who do you think, Mia? *You.*"

"That is not an answer, Idris," she snapped. "And I don't need you to protect me."

"That is my answer, Mia, and you'd be stupid to think you don't need protection."

She turned on her heel, sick of the conversation, and strode to the door. She yanked it open. Idris' hand snapped out, slamming it shut and stopping her exit. Abruptly, she was back in that Heylla hole, with Luc's mouth on her throat, draining the life from her. She didn't turn, but curled around the smooth wooden box. Quick breaths entered her unwilling lungs as a hot, clammy sweat broke over her skin.

Panic drowned her, rushing through each and every nerve.

Ozul responded, spewing ribbons of black mists to unspool around her boots. Her eyes fearfully searched for something to anchor her as she felt herself losing control. But she saw nothing but the cold onyx gaze of Luc, filled with contempt. The sound of his belt clicking, snapping against her skin, morphed into the animal-like pants, then a scream— her pained, terrified scream.

"Let me out now," Mia demanded through heaved breaths.

Ozul—moving without command—slammed into Idris, making him stumble back.

She whirled around, finding him chained in her shadows. "Don't you ever do that again."

Idris fought the misty shackles. His face was contrasting—soft, pleading—to the strained muscles of his body. "I never meant to scare you, Mia. We need to see inside that box, and I don't want to wear any more deaths on my shoulders while we fight and hurt each other."

She met his gaze as a fat tear rolled down her cheek, then another, splashing onto the black box.

"You think I do? These aren't faceless women to me, Idris. Every one of these women wears Kali's face, suffers the same wound she did. I'm in a living nightmare. Everywhere I turn, every time I close my eyes, I see her—and not in the way I wish to. I see her bloody and dead." Her breath caught in her chest as sobs escaped. "You think your patience is wearing thin? I'm barely a person, Idris. I'm broken bits, held together by thin strings. Everything I do is for my sister, and it is still not enough."

A glassy-eyed Idris whispered her name softly.

"And I'm here, wading through all of this with you, dragging all my broken parts behind me. I made a promise that I would live, and I'm not sure I have been living. Not until I met you. You've shown me I can be enough for someone, even if it's hidden away in the sheets of your bed, even if we keep hurting each other. By the goddess, I just want to live, Idris, without this hurt following me."

"Then live, Mia. Not for me, not for Kali. For yourself."

"I don't know how to," she whispered, the final truth slipping free. "I don't know how to do any of this."

"Neither do I, Mia. Shall we learn together?"

She scrubbed the tears from her face with the heel of her palm and nodded. Worried her words would slip more than the fact that her feelings that she'd grown for him, she waved her fingers, releasing him. "No more half-truths. Promise me. No more."

"I promise, my Mia, I promise," he said, taking a hesitant step forward.

Her breath caught again—not from the sobs. She loosened her grip on the box, glancing down to the runes carved into the wood. "And I will hold you to it, Idris. Now, shall we make a—"

Henry's voice rang through the manor, calling her name.

"Shit, shit," Mia cursed. "No men in the house, remember?"

"We aren't rolling in bed, Little Witch. Calm down."

"Might as well be."

Grumbling under her breath, her hand snapped out, grabbing him by the front of his shirt. She yanked him from Kali's bedroom, shoving him into the hall. With one glance back to the cheerfully coloured room, she could see Kali twirling and singing, a grin spread across her face.

I miss you, Kali. Every single day. Every single hour. There is not a moment I don't wish you were here.

Her vision of Kali paused, sharing that radiant smile with her. *I miss you, too, but you have to live, Mia. Not be stuck in the past with me.*

The vision faded away when she pulled the door to her sister's bedroom closed.

Mia stomped down the hallway, still yanking Idris along. She pushed him into her room, striding past him. She dumped the Umbra Box on her paint-covered desk and took a steadying breath, then crossed her room. He turned in slow circles, eyes searching each paint-splattered, messy corner.

Before she closed the door, she glared up at him to find him smoothing his fingers over the pattern of her quilt. "Don't you dare try opening that without me, Old Man, or there will be Heylla to pay."

Forty-Five

Mia bounded down the stairs, her boots heavy on the wood. She paused three steps from the bottom to a frowning Henry. He said her name—more like growled it. Each shift of fabric to remove his coat was strained, irritated. He wasn't just angry, he was furious. At her.

"And which bar am I expecting a bill from this time, Mia? You've been gone for two bloody days—again—without a word or even a note. And you've been drinking, haven't you?"

Mia scoffed, shaking her head. "Really, Father? That is your first thought, that I was lost in the bottom of a bottle?"

"You did it for weeks. Why would this instance be any different?"

"Because I'm different," she snapped. "If you haven't noticed."

"How am I to notice this sudden shift in you if you're out doing gods know what with gods know who? I have ordered Abi not to get your contraceptives from the apothecary anymore. If you wish to gallivant about the lower city, you will be responsible for the consequences."

Mia rolled her tongue around her mouth, brushing on each of her molars, then trained her best glare on Henry, who returned one tenfold. They battled, challenging the other to drop their gaze. She stepped down the remaining stairs into the fading daylight. His eyes dipped to the scabbed wound on her face, then to the purple, yellowed bruises on her throat.

He inhaled sharply, stepping forward. "Who did that to you?"

"You don't care who did this to me," Mia said, anger flickering in her tone. "All you care about is what my *gallivanting* means to those fuckers in Valliss Castle. Rubbing our name in the dirt. Isn't that right?"

"Whatever are you talking about? Who left those bruises on you?" he asked, concern lacing his voice, a sharp contrast to his serious face.

"Do you even care—"

"I care, Mia. All I do is care for you!" Henry thundered, throwing his arms out. The boom echoed around their home.

She startled, stepping back. Her anger fled from the rumblings of her father.

Henry continued, his features clenching with emotion. "My world is you and your mother. You own my heart, Mia, even if you don't wish to hold it anymore."

Her eyes dropped away as that stomach-tightening feeling of disappointing her father forced bile up her throat. She descended the stairs, and then to him. With a tentative hand, she reached out and took his. She flipped it, allowing the scars of his past to stare back at her. A hand that took life, but pulled her sister into the world from her mother's body.

"I..." her father started, voice thick with emotion. "I'm not coping."

His words bounced in her mind. Her stoic father—who she thought could handle anything, who fought battles, and lost, who faced a court that didn't accept him—wasn't coping. The same man who would tell her everything was going to be okay when her nightmares would shake her awake. And on those dreadful nights, when the terrors in her dreams became too much, he'd curl beside her and whisper tales of his homeland. Promises that, one day, she'd see the great forest castle of the fae.

"I'm not coping either," Mia replied softly, and slipped her fingers through his, her hand looking tiny in his. "I haven't found myself at the bottom of a bottle, just so you know, but the temptation is there."

"I feel like we have drifted away from each other, and now we are yelling in the night mists, searching for one another. And I don't know how to get back to you, Mia. You had me so worried that I had even the

Silver looking for you. I even went to that fucking pub—The Casserole Dish?"

"The Cauldron," Mia corrected with a smile. "I think we will find our way back to each other, Father. We always will."

"Can it not be today, now?" Henry asked, so softly she felt her heart skip a beat. "I miss you."

A tear ran down her face. "And how I have missed you."

"Can I hug yo—"

She didn't let him finish his sentence. She launched herself at him, wrapping her arms around him, squeezing tightly. *We will never be lost in that mist again,* she promised to him silently. *I won't just hold his heart, I will protect it. Like a dragon protecting her gold.*

"My moon, who hurt you?" he asked into her hair.

Sweet creature, are you going to tell Daddy Dearest where you buried Luc?

Mia pulled from her father, her fingers spreading over her throat. Her eyes lowered, right to their boots. Those haunting images flashed again. She couldn't elude them. Not while she was so raw, so torn open.

Henry's hand found her elbow, waking her. "Mia."

"Luc—"

She slapped her palm over her mouth, muffling the sob that left her.

"Then he is a dead man."

Henry launched himself from the stairwell, straight across the entranceway, yanking the front door wide with such force that Mia worried he'd pull it off the hinges. His whole being trembled, shaking the ground under her feet. A chill filled the air as Henry's magic fought under his skin. Pure, deathly rage flowed off him, snapping teeth at her.

"That *fucking* bastard," he growled, voice deep and biting. "He's going to regret ever raising a finger to you. I'll make him beg to see those fiery Heylla pits after I'm done with him. No one lays a hand on my daughter and gets away with it."

Mia reached out and gripped him by the back of his shirt, stopping him. Henry stilled, harsh breaths leaving him.

"He's dead," she murmured.

"And I presume you had nothing to do with it?"

"No, Father. I had everything to do with it."

Her words fell to the floor, crashing to the cool stone like shards of lead. Mia wondered for a moment if Henry would push her away, cast disgust at her and throw her from his home, his heart. Instead, he just sighed and muttered her name.

"To take a life is a heavy burden to bear, my moon. It is a weight I am all too familiar with. One I had hoped you would never experience."

"I only hope the goddess shows kindness to me when—"

A throat cleared, and both of them turned. Mia's eyes widened, then narrowed. At the top of the stairs, Idris stood with hands in his pockets and a sheepish grin on his face.

Forty-Six

Anne fluttered around their kitchen with whispered requests to the maids, who loaded a silver platter with teapots, cups and a plate of crumbly ginger biscuits.

Mia leant on the bench, arms crossed. "I don't think he will want tea and biscuits, Mama."

Anne raised her chin.. "If they are discussing your marri—"

"Idris isn't here to ask permission to marry me, Mama."

"Maybe it's better for your father to have something in his hand when he finds out why there was a male in your room unsupervised."

"Don't you think I'm a bit too old for that rule now? I'm nearly twenty-two."

Anne ignored her, still fiddling with the teacups and pot. Mia stole a biscuit from the fine porcelain plate, biting into it. The sweet ginger crumbs filled her mouth, making her stomach grumble.

"Idris and I aren't like that." She paused, taking another bite, considering their conversation. "Well, I don't know what we are..."

Anne rested the tray on her hip, her free hand tucking that stray lock of hair behind Mia's ear. Her mother searched her face, over the scattering of freckles and along that shiny white scar. "That's a pity for him, as your love is the strongest."

She shared a soft smile with Anne. Her mother returned one of her own—one that crinkled her eyes and lit a fire in her that Mia hadn't seen for weeks. "Now, shall we go join them before your father interrogates the only man you've brought home?"

Mia groaned and followed her mother.

The fading afternoon light filtered in, illuminating the soft dust particles floating in the air, grazing over the furniture, right to the worn, lived-in dining table. Idris sat across from Henry, and they faced off against each other. Her father sat with his chin in his hand, assessing Idris like he was sizing him up for battle. The straight-backed Idris met him with a strained, tight-lipped grin that looked more akin to a pained grimace.

"So, boy, what do you do, aside from creeping around my property?"

Mia couldn't look away from Idris' fingers drumming on the table. The rise and fall cut through the cast of the afternoon sun, making shadows dance across the worn wood. His hands were long and elegant, resembling those of a master pianist, but the thin skin on his knuckles bore the scars of a life of fighting. A strange beauty was in the mix of violence and grace. She worked hard to sear the image to her mind, determined to sketch it, even though she was the worst at drawing hands. Fingers turned to sausages, and graceful movements to rigid stumps. Her eyes rose, meeting Idris' gaze from across the table. Mia leant over, snatched another biscuit from her mother and shoved it in her mouth, chewing obnoxiously.

Idris arched a brow, the muscles in his jaw relaxed a fraction. "I own a bar."

"The Cauldron, I presume. My daughter seems to spend more gold there than Hartwinn does on balls."

Idris' hand flattened on the table, and he cast Henry a dimpled grin. "Yes, that's it. We appreciate the patronage, my lord."

"Just Henry," her father corrected. "Before that?"

"I was in service to a royal family."

"Oh, a royal family," Anne gushed, depositing the tray between the two men. She had formed the battle line. One dared not cross.

Steaming tea splashed into the delicately painted cups, then, with a soft *clink*, her mother placed one in front of each man, as if they'd not come to blows if they had something in their hands.

Anne slid into the seat at the head of the table, her own tea steaming in front of her. "You must tell us who. King Ewan? Or further abroad across the ocean to Queen Ratha?"

Mia smothered a sigh, slipping into the only chair left—beside Idris.

"One that does not exist anymore," he replied softly, blowing into the cup.

Mia fought to not watch his every move. Henry hummed a response and took a sip. She could see the cogs turning in her father's mind, putting pieces together. A nervous energy filled her, making her fidget. She slid a hand under her thigh to stop herself from reaching for Idris.

"Beautiful brew, *mo chridhe*." Henry glanced at Anne with a smirk, giving Idris a reprieve from the intense staring match.

Mia mouthed, "Sorry," to him, brows rising.

Idris huffed a laugh and shook his head. He shifted in his chair and pressed a hand to her knee. Whether it was to stop the constant shifting of wood underneath them, or to help ground her, she couldn't tell. Her own fingers slid over those scarred knuckles, savouring the warm comfort of his skin on hers.

Mia swore she heard Idris sigh.

"Who is your clan?" Henry asked, turning back to Idris. He exchanged his soft smile for a cool glare.

Mia stifled a groan. It was intolerable. A constant battle of men deciding what she needed, who she needed. A conversation that didn't involve anyone but who she decided. Especially not her father. She cast Anne a reproachful look, willing her to stop the volleying of sensitive questions at Idris. But her mother found the floral pattern on her teacup much more interesting.

"Father, I think that's eno—"

"They also do not exist anymore," Idris answered softly. His gaze lingered on the worn wood, full of nicks and grooves. His forefinger traced a deep scar left by Kali after an especially vegetable-filled meal.

A lifetime had been lived on that table.

Henry's question hung in the air, heavy as if lead weighed it down, as he asked, "You're *his* son, aren't you?"

Mia's heart clenched, squeezing hurt into her bones. She snuck a glance at Idris, whose shoulders twisted as if he was uncomfortable in the chair.

His eyes rose, a warning in his gaze. "I haven't been *his* son for a very long time."

Her hand slid from under his to fall on his wrist, thumb swirling around the divot, causing him to lean a fraction towards her. They were drawn together, even if they clawed and fought each drag.

Henry's stare glazed as if replaying a memory. "I knew your mother, Idris. Ella. A beautiful, intelligent woman. A spitfire, if I remember correctly. I was very sorry to hear of her passing, along with the rest of your family."

"Thank you, Henry. She was a bright star in the endless night," Idris said, a soft sadness flecking his voice.

Henry agreed with a heavy nod of his head. "You have been through much hurt, young man."

"What is life without pain and suffering?"

Her father laughed—his favourite humour was dark and dry—and a smile spread across his face. Mia relaxed a fraction in her chair, her knee bumping into Idris' leg. He glanced at her, and she returned a half-smirk.

Idris had won the battle, but not yet the war.

"As was your daughter, Kali, sir. May she shine the brightest."

Anne's narrow shoulders tensed, her grip around the teacup tightening. But she raised her chin. "My daughter is not a speck of light in the sky. She is the burning sun. One that heats the day and warms your bones. She is the one that leads you home. A true north."

Idris reached out to Anne, but his hand stopped short before falling to the table. "I don't speak of Kali to bring you pain, Lady Ashmore, but happiness. Mia has told me many things about her. A great many things. She loves her very much."

Anne's hands relaxed on the teacup. "Our beautiful Mia is truly a gift to us, as was her sister. But her love is the true blessing. As I am sure you are experiencing, being in love with her."

Anne took a sip of her tea as a mischievous smirk curled around the white porcelain. Idris coughed and spluttered. His cheeks turned a flushed pink, to Mia's surprise. His mouth opened and closed, like a fish gasping for air. It made her snicker and squeeze his wrist.

Anne leant in and patted his arm. "We can discuss a dowry later—"

"Mama, *enough*!" Mia demanded, splotches of red forming on her chest as her embarrassment flared to the surface.

Anne's eyes twinkled as her smirk transformed into a toothy grin. A lightness was in the air, lifting the solemnness that had lowered in their home.

Idris leant back, wearing that dimpled grin. "What are you offering? I think she is worth at least two cows and three chickens."

Anne snorted, waving a hand at the artwork that surrounded them. "I can throw in a few pieces of her art. She's quite the painter."

"I'm more interested in the handsome, green-eyed man she has on her easel, but these would do."

Mia grumbled a curse, rolling her eyes, causing Anne to inhale sharply and burst out into a cackle with her head thrown back. Mia cracked a smile at Idris, who smirked back at her. Her heart fluttered, coming to life at the sight. His gaze dipped to her chest as if he could hear her heartbeat. A softness grew on the edges of the smirk.

Henry hadn't spoken, or even laughed. Only his sharp gaze took in each of the people around his dining table. Always assessing, searching for danger. "What are your intentions with my daughter?"

Idris' eyes met her father's across the table. "Do I have to have intentions with your daughter to enjoy her company? Mia is her own woman. She will decide on her own well enough."

"Father, Idris and I are just friends," she said sharply—too sharply— dampening the joy that had spread over the table.

"I may be old, Mia, but I'm not blind. You don't look at each other like friends."

Her gaze returned to Idris shyly. She hadn't realised she looked at him with such emotion that her father could see it from across the room. The same stare echoed back at her, as if Idris hadn't realised either.

Henry leant over to Anne and grasped her jaw, thumb circling her cheek. Her mother encapsulated his hand with hers. A tenderness had softened the muscles in their faces. His eyes searched hers. "Life is too short, even for those blessed with long lives, to deny yourselves the pleasure of being in love."

IDRIS ROSE FROM HER VELVET-BACKED CHAIR, STRETCHING with a groan. It had been hours since Mia and the smirking vampyre slinked off to her bedroom, with Henry's grumblings and Anne's musical laughter following them up the stairs. She had been attempting to make a key—with Idris' poor description of a skeleton key—with no success.

Keys of all shapes and sizes were discarded on the desk, surrounding the Umbra box.

Idris stepped around her room, his fingers brushing over the tubes, brushes and glass jars full of murky water, over the base of her easel. The handsome stranger sat on the wood, emerald eyes burning from the darkness. The splash of red across the tans and emeralds. Tracing a finger over the dabbed paint, Idris tilted his head, searching the painting. "This looks like me, Little Witch."

"Does it? I've been working on that since before I met you, Old Man," Mia replied flatly, pushing the box away from her. "Does my power extend to me seeing the future?"

"No. That is a different coven of witches," he murmured.

A throbbing headache had worked its way behind her eyes as she glared at the misting shadows surrounding her hands. They simply stared back at her. "A skeleton key, Ozul. Make the damn key. I know you know what it looks like."

They said nothing, sliding from her fingers, forming yet another rudimentary key. It fell with a *clang* on the desk. She groaned and waved them away, vanishing into nothing. There had to be a reason they weren't creating what she demanded. *What is in this box?*

"You never told me you were this good..."

"And you still haven't told me how you knew I made a shadow blade?"

He shot her a sharp look, but didn't reply.

"And when would we've time to discuss my prowess as an artist between the desk and your bed?"

His eyes remained on her artwork, narrowing and leaning forward, seeing something Mia couldn't.

She shouldered him playfully. "You know, you're supposed to laugh when someone makes a joke."

"We hardly know each other, don't we?" Idris replied softly, casting his emerald gaze on her.

Mia sighed and turned to her desk. She flipped open tins of charcoal, then swirled pencils in the mugs she'd stolen from the kitchen, wood clattering against the porcelain. She selected a worn, thin pencil and picked up her sketchbook, ignoring the shining black box sitting amongst the rainbow colours of her paints.

"We don't know each other at all. Now sit down."

"Mia, the box—"

"Can wait. Death can wait. He isn't going anywhere."

Mia nodded to either her bed or the high-backed velvet chair. Idris arched a brow at her and chose the bed. He slid his long body along the sheets to rest against the headboard. Mia kicked off her boots and clambered onto the foot of the bed, crossing her legs, the mattress sagging under their weight. She balanced her sketchbook on her knee and cocked her head at Idris, already deciding where her shading would sit on his face, where the light would curve to create those cutting cheekbones.

"Maybe we can start here...a proper introduction," Idris suggested, his voice soft.

"Are you saying you hovering over Kali's body wasn't a good place to start? Now, stay still," Mia ordered, eyes lowered, the graphite scratching across the paper.

"Nor you vomiting across my entire house. What are you doing?"

"What does it look like? Drawing you. And it wasn't your entire house."

In a rumbling whisper, he asked, "How do you want me, Mia?"

Her eyes flicked up to him to find him smirking at her. She pointed her pencil to the left. Idris turned his heated stare right to her wall of sketches. His gaze danced over the long, nude bodies and shaded apples.

Mia cocked her head and searched his profile. She traced down his straight, strong nose, to his parted, full lips, all the way down to the flash of chest hair, lit by burning lanterns. He was more than handsome; he was beautiful, as if crafted by Oryah herself.

Circles and lines formed on her page as her hand slid over to form his features. "Fine, fine. Real introductions, then. You go first."

Idris relaxed a fraction, hands linking on his stomach. His chest rose and sank with each breath. "I'm Prince Idris Blackwood, the first son of King Mortias, heir to the Death Court, then the captain of Queen's Maeve's guard." He turned to look at her. "Your turn…"

Mia raised both brows and nodded to the wall again. "A pleasure to meet you, Prince Idris, previously Queen's Maeve's guard. I'm Lady Mia Ashmore, adopted daughter of Sir Henry, Emissary of the Westryn Fae. Oh, and I may be an evil, cunning shadow witch, but I can paint a mean bowl of fruit. I do hope that is all right?"

Idris laughed, shaking the bed a fraction. "Lovely to meet you, Lady Mia. I fear no witch or fruit bowl. Now, ask me another question."

"What is your favourite colour?"

"You know when the sun has almost set, hiding for the night, and the sky is that deep purple, not yet black?"

"Indigo," Mia murmured, working on the sharp edge of his nose.

"Yes, Little Witch, indigo. Now—"

"What do you dream about?"

His brow furrowed, but he didn't move. "A river, rushing around me, washing away the sins of my past. I sink below the surface. Not to drown, but for a blessed moment of silence."

Mia's pencil froze. She hadn't expected him to answer, at least not so honestly. She returned with her own truth. "In my dreams, I see a face below the surface of a river. It's blurred at the edges and slips through my fingers when I wake. I remember only flashes."

"Do you see me?"

Mia exhaled, brushing a fleck of graphite away. His visage was emerging with each scratchy swipe of her hand. "A face like yours, Idris."

"*Like* mine?"

Mia hummed a response, flicking to create his thick eyelashes. "It's hard to explain. Sometimes, there are flashes of you, but flashes of another. Like two sides of a coin."

Silence settled between them, only the scribbling on paper heard. In the periphery of her vision, she noticed Idris leaning forward, hand creeping across the blanket. Until she could see those scarred knuckles beneath her sketchpad. When her eyes rose from the sketch, he was only an inch away from her, lips parted. His hypnotic scent swirling in the tight space they shared.

"Tell me who you are, Mia. Who you truly are."

Her gaze dropped, eyebrows lowering. "I don't know who I am, Idris."

"Who do you want to be?"

She let the words swirl in her mind until he hooked a finger under her chin, raising her gaze to him. It was dangerous. Emotions stretched out, allowing each to capture the wind.

"Tell me, Mia."

"I want to be the woman you see. Who my parents see. Who Kali saw."

"No, Mia. Who do you want to be?"

She didn't know.

She once wished to be an apprentice to a famous artist, to be lost in paint and canvas. When her world had tilted, all she desired was to cease to exist. Then, she simply needed to survive the darkness that wanted to smother her. She desired to be all those things—and more—more than she could even comprehend.

You are nothing, sweet creature. Only what I wish you to be...

Mia ignored the voice, fighting the urge to snap back at it, knowing her ire only fed it.

"I want to be free to be whoever I choose to be. Witch, artist, lover. I just want to be *free*."

"You're already free, Mia. You simply cage yourself."

She decided at that moment that she would make one final reckless decision; cast herself from the cliff, to free-fall right into the ocean of feelings she had for Idris. Not fearing the crash of the rocks or the swirling current that could drag her to the depths.

Pushing her sketchpad off her lap, the half-finished illustration of the smirking vampyre fluttered to the rug. Her black-stained fingers gripped each side of his face, slipping into his hair. She closed the distance between their lips, hoping, with each press of lips, that the tender feeling would seep between his teeth and plant in his chest, growing in him as it grew in her. But could love bloom where grief had taken root?

Idris kissed her back. A soft hunger was all she could taste.

She broke away, resting her forehead on his. "I want you, Idris. Every piece of you. Do you think you could hold whatever pieces are left of my heart?"

He said nothing, instead pulling her into another embrace and dragging her body to his. His lips encapsulated hers, stealing away her words. Soon, pleasure was all she knew, lost in it with him. Even so, her mind whispered thoughts she tried to ignore, slipping through the cracks. That he never replied, that he never said yes. He never promised not to crush those shards of her heart into nothing. Because he couldn't. He couldn't lie.

Forty-Seven

The bed was empty, cold where Idris should have lain. He hadn't lingered, slipping out of the tangled sheets before the sun rose. Before the morning light could illuminate any truths they had bared, or any lies that were mumbled when pleasure was drawn from them. She had poured herself out, and he simply let her slip through his fingers.

Mia blinked the tears away. His letter shook in her hand, the words smeared and written hurriedly. She read them over and over as the sting of each stitch that Idris had sown in her heart was cut by his words, allowing oozing rotten pus to leak out, poisoning her thoughts.

Once again, her eyes scanned the page.

Mia,

I could not stay and whisper those words to you, I ache to say, because I cannot be with you, Mia. Not with this secret hanging over my head, over my heart. You deserve someone who can offer themselves completely to you.

I know this will break your heart.

Come to the corner of Oak and Starseeker tomorrow night at eight o'clock. There is something I must show you.
Idris

Mia screwed the letter into a ball and threw it against the canvas, curses bursting from her. She reached down and gripped the forgotten sketchbook, determined to tear the drawing of him out. But she couldn't, let alone rip the feelings for him from her. They had laid roots, and were entwined deeply around her rib cage.

A shadow slipped from her, swirling around the half-completed drawing. "You'd never leave me, right?"

"*Never.*"

That one word settled in her chest, combating the hurt building there.

Scrubbing the tears away with the heel of her hand, she spat at the painting, "You bloody coward."

Mia slipped into the bathroom, pulling the clothing from her body and cleansing Idris' lingering touch from her skin. She yanked on a fresh dress, the soft cotton slipping over her torso and covering the worst of the yellowing bruises. A strange feeling encapsulated the very guilt she had felt; a peculiar sense of justice that maybe wiping Luc from the world was the right decision.

She sighed and looked over her shoulder at the Umbra Box and the pile of useless keys. Approaching it, her fingers trailed over the edge of the table until she found herself right in front of the glossy black wood. She reached out, tracing the runes.

By the shadows.

Mia pulled at the lid, but it didn't budge. She cursed under her breath. It was locked. Glancing at her bedroom door, she didn't dare to set foot in Kali's room again. Not while she was torn open, seeping emotions.

Snatching up the box, she whirled around and threw it to the ground, determined to smash her way through the smooth wood. The box struck the hard stone floor and bounced, only denting the side. She groaned in frustration, scooping it up, raising it above her head and slamming on the stone again. This time, the wood cracked, but still kept Kali's secrets locked inside.

Mia disgruntledly eyed the box, crossing her arms. She would have to search the gardener's shed for a hammer. Before she could stomp through her house, a stray shadow left her, swirling.

"*We open.*"

Ozul glided over the stone, over the cracked corner and slithered into the chamber of the lock. With a *click*, the lid popped open, spilling the contents across the floor.

Mia scoffed and side-eyed her shadows. "You could have told me you could do that before I brutalised a priceless relic, or spent hours making useless keys."

Ozul turned, observing her with unseen eyes, and said, "*More fun watching you try, witchling. Good to practise magic.*"

Mia grumbled under her breath and squatted, pawing through the contents of the Umbra Box. Piles of letters, trinkets and a gleaming diamond ring sitting snugly encased in black, shiny velvet, staring back at her. It looked concerningly like one given with the promise of forever love.

She pulled out the letters, flicking through each. Her eyes recognised Kali's messy handwriting, and the elegant, sloped script of Reagan. She skimmed over the words—words of love and love in return—only to glare at the ball of parchment in the darkened corner. She clenched her jaw and continued on. The bottom of the stack held a sealed letter with *HN* written on it. Mia turned it over. Her thumb brushed over the wax glob—her family's crest. A mighty oak with long, deep roots.

"I'm sorry, sister. I have to know."

Mia cracked the seal and hurriedly pulled the parchment from the envelope. She flicked it open, eyes taking every word until a sharp gasp left her. Kali had stumbled onto something—a secret worth dying for.

Uncle Hartwinn,

This letter is written in haste, and honestly, I'm scared. I shouldn't have been digging, but this illness isn't just affecting you. But others in the court's inner circle, all infected. They are monstrous, bloodthirsty. Even the grand healer is worried, even if she says nothing. She writes off their deaths as a sweating sickness.

What connects them?

Nothing.

Outside of being noble. Some of them had rallied behind Reagan, breeding contempt for you.

But I have found other things, Hartwinn. I'm worried about putting the evidence in a letter. I think I am being watched, followed. I can feel eyes on me. Worse, I can feel his eyes on me.

He has something to do with it.

How?

I don't know. I believe the tales, the stories, but I think there's more to all of this than what I know, what we know. He is the cause of this. I'm sure of it, Hartwinn. He is the only one who can create this sickness—or these creatures.

I fear for her, Hartwinn. I'm so scared for her.

I will be at Valliss tomorrow. I shall show you what I have.

Kali

Mia shot up, leaving the mess of letters and trinkets scattered across her floor. The letter was dated the day before Kali's death.

Her last words.

She launched herself across her room, bounding down the stairs two at a time. She had to find Wyn, Idris—anyone. Then she needed to see what the Silver had in the Pali.

Anne strode out from the sitting room, hand to chest, with her eyebrows meeting, lips pursed. "Mia, by the goddess, what is the matter?" she asked, a fraction breathless. "I heard crashing in your bedroom."

"I knocked over my easel. Nothing to worry about, Mama."

Anne's eyes took her in—teary-eyed and frazzled—then her gaze trailed up the staircase, and she clenched her jaw. "And where is Idris?"

"He won't be around again."

Anne's face softened. "*Oh.*"

Mia's hand slipped into her pocket, hiding the letter. "It seems Idris doesn't want me, nor whatever I thought was happening between us."

"And he decided this after he spent the night?"

Mia frowned at her mother's words. He had allowed himself one more night of aching pleasure to be close with her without the harsh reality of what it meant. It wasn't a clean break, but a forced snapping, bone puncturing skin. Messy and painful. Her legs demanded she flee, to get away from the pain erupting in her chest.

"I have to go," she murmured, pressing her lips together to stop the flow of tears.

Anne advanced on her, her hand catching Mia's wrist. "You're needed in the sitting room. A lieutenant from the Silver is here."

A cold sweat spread on her skin as she numbly let her mother lead her into the overly warm room. Anne pulled her to a stop in front of Mylo. He looked bedraggled, unshaven and tired. She knew more deaths had happened.

Death simply took and took, greedy for souls.

Henry's face was pinched as he leant forward, motioning to Mylo. "Mia, this is—"

"Lieutenant Mylo," she said stiffly.

"It's a pleasure to see ya again," he replied, a soft smile on his lips. The same one he wore after she had found that other body—the one made for ease and comfortability.

"What do you want?"

The lieutenant leant an elbow on the arm of the lounge he sat on. "Your employer was found dead, Mia."

Henry's eyes flashed to hers. His face remained neutral. *This is dangerous.* She needed to sprinkle enough truth so she could throw Mylo off her scent.

"What a *shame*," she sneered, unable to keep the venom dripping from her words.

"Mia!" Anne scolded. She dipped her head at Mylo. "How very sad for his family."

"Ya were"—he paused, clearing his throat—"entwined with him, weren't ya?"

"Here I thought you were above court gossip, Mylo. I was his apprentice. That is all."

"Then why did at least three of his apprentices hear ya screaming for help in his office only a handful of weeks ago?"

Henry stiffened as that tiny muscle knotted in his jaw. "What do you mean, sir?"

"I think ya know what I am talkin' about, Lord Henry. We need not go into graphic details, for ya wife's sake."

Mia's palms were slick, and her heart thundered at the dark reminder of what horrors Luc had forced upon her. Her eyes dropped to the plush rug under her boots, eyebrows lowering. "I don't know what you're talki—"

"Mia, please. Whatever ya agreed to didn't give him the right to just take anythin' he thought he could."

Her tear-filled vision rose from the floor to Mylo. She would not cower, be afraid of him anymore. Even if she ended up in shackles, with a hangman's noose around her neck.

"He thought he owned me, Mylo. That I was his to do whatever he wished to me, to my body. He was wrong. Deathly wrong. And he paid the price for that lapse in judgement."

The creak of the lounge filled the tense air as Mylo pushed from the couch. Mia's bottom lip was trembling by the time he made his way to her.

"He was hurting ya, wasn't he?"

"Yes, and I ended his life."

Henry launched himself from the chair, already shouting in her defence.

Anne strode over and gripped Mia's elbow, yanking her behind her.

"If you dare try to take my daughter, sir, you'll be burying more than one body."

Henry flanked Mia, snarling at Mylo. "Mia is above your king's law. She is under the protection of King Sundryl, as his granddaughter. If you even attempt to arrest her, it will be a declaration of war."

"I will not be forced to keep what he did to me a secret any longer," Mia declared, raising her chin and glaring at the assessing lieutenant. "He whipped me with a belt, forced himself onto me, then decided he wished to do it again. But this time, I fought back, putting him in the ground."

"Ya were actin' in self-defence, weren't ya?"

"Yes. He would have done unimaginable things to me, and I would have been the one in a shallow grave."

Mylo sighed, scrubbing his jaw. "Ya willin' to make a statement, detailin' what he did to ya, and that ya life was in danger?"

"Yes. I will swear on it, even."

"Then I believe no crime has been committed. May Diabolus rot his soul. I'll take my leave. Good day, Mia. I will be expectin' ya down at the Pali in the next few days to make ya statement, but I don't think ya'll see the Silver on your doorstep again about this."

"I'll pray to Oryah that you don't darken my doorstep again, lieutenant," Henry gritted out.

Mylo nodded and turned on his heel, heading towards the door. Mia slipped out from behind her parents and rushed after him. She found him shouldering on his coat, casting her a confused look.

"More crimes to confess to?"

"No." Mia stepped in, lowering her voice. She reached up and yanked down her collar. Revealing the deep purple, yellowed wound on her throat. "He did this."

"Then ya need to tell Idris to be a bit more gentle with his love bites."

"No, this was Luc. He was...transforming into a dhampyr, Mylo. He needed my blood."

"What are you saying?"

Mia hid the scabbing wound away, a frown cutting across her face.

"You must look into what's lurking in Valliss Castle, rubbing shoulders with Hartwinn. You will find answers then."

Mylo cast her a quick glance, eyes narrowing. "What do—"

"How did you find him?"

Mylo stilled. "We were tipped off."

"By who?"

"One of my informants passed a note," he said with a shrug. "He said some rich wanker gave it to him to deliver to me. Someone wanted ya locked up, Mia. Ya've been pokin' the wasp nest. They wanted ya in a place they could control ya. Silence ya."

Her mind spun, her eyes flickered around. "No. There is more to this. I'm just not seeing it."

His hand grazed her elbow, making her gaze snap to him. "You could've come to me, Mia. I could have done something about it. About him. You aren't alone in this."

"And have him belittle me in court? Twist the truth to make me look like the temptress, the whore who sold her body? No, thank you." *Let alone exposing Ozul to the world, and me to a pyre,* Mia added silently.

Mylo sighed. "That's not how it would have—"

"That's exactly how it would have gone. Now, you better go, before Father kicks you off his property. You've been thoroughly embarrassed by one fae male. Let's not make it two."

He stared at her with a mix of concern and confliction, lips opening to say more. Instead, he exhaled and left.

Mia sighed, then spotted Anne in the doorway with a determined expression. With two quick steps, she had her arms around Mia, drawing her into the warmth of her embrace.

"You've always had a fire in your belly, my moon," she said into her hair. "And I hoped you would never let another try to extinguish it. We Ashmore women are made of stronger stuff."

"Am I? I feel broken in ways I don't even understand. I spent weeks lost. Maybe I'm still lost."

Anne pulled back and searched her face. "You're not lost. You're simply on a forest path and your way is overgrown, that is all."

"How can you see so much good in me when I've done such a terrible thing?"

"Because I love you, Mia, and that love surpasses whatever deed you may have committed. You may not have been born of my blood, but you are my daughter. Bound by love. Now, go. I know you've been searching for what took Kali, and I hope you find it."

With a gentle shove from her mother, Mia slipped from the manor and thundered down the dirt road. She knew exactly where she was going.

Forty-Eight

Valliss Castle was bustling. The lush green grass was scattered with nobles, soaking up the last rays of the sun. Soft chatter and gentle music filled the air as women waved fans and exchanged sly smiles and lingering, lustful glances at the men.

Hartwinn always seemed to entertain guests, filling the marble castle with noise. Mia wondered if he had been lonely after Lady Seanna died, and was determined not to allow that slow, creeping silence to settle in the dark corners, like a haunting spiderweb.

Gravel crunched under her toe as she veered off to the guard's barracks. Right to Wyn. The man who knew the Pali inside and out.

It was time to seek favours and call in promises made.

The hand-carved doors, depicting solemn knights standing guard, seemed to grow as she approached, and that lick of courage fizzled into nothing. Rambunctious laughter echoed from beyond the wood. With a sigh, she slammed on the wood. Chairs scraping and muffled whispers was her answer until the door swung open and a broad-shouldered, bearded guard glanced down at her. His eyes crinkled with a grin. Dilon —Wyn's second-in-command. Henry and Wyn may have drifted apart, but his men were almost as loyal to her father as they were to Wyn.

"Miss Mia! It has been ages since I saw you last. Now, what do we owe the pleasure of your company?"

"Hello, Dilon. The pleasure is all mine. I need to see Wyn. Is he around?"

He stepped to the side, waving her in. "Finally letting him teach you a thing or two about fighting?"

Mia laughed, echoing down the corridor. She smiled and waved at the men at the small wooden table, cards in hand, in the rudimentary mess hall. Ale and silver coins adorned the table. She saddled up next to one of the newer recruits, who studied his cards even more intensely. He seemed scared to even glance at her. His hand was dreadful—all threes, no queens or kings. The pile of coins in front of him were slim compared to the older men's.

He was losing.

"I'd fold if I were you," she whispered. "Dilon is far too good for him not to be a cheat."

He threw an eye roll at her and then pushed all his coins into the centre of the table. Smirking at the other guards, Mia shoved off the table with a chuckle as cards flashed into their suits, and the young man groaned.

Turning, she found a pair of steel-blue eyes watching her from the doorway. Wyn stood, his arm resting on the doorframe above his head, his lithe body stretched against the soft material he wore. A smile played on his lips. The table thumping with laughter, and the rumbling of arguments seemed to quieten for a moment as she lost herself in the shining blueness. A plucked string of tension sent a shivering wave through her. Her feet took her right to him until she had to crane her chin up to keep eye contact.

"Hello, Wyn," she said, a fraction breathless.

His eyes dipped to her lips, then back up. "Hello, Mia."

With that splash of courage—that she had believed had fizzled—she reached out, slipping her fingers over scars and rough skin until she broke through, slipping her hand into his.

"Do you want to come make some terrible choices with me?" she asked, repeating the same words that had them tangled in bed.

Wyn searched her face. That look of concern was muddled with the heat of desire.

With a gentle squeeze, he led her from the mess hall, right to his bedroom. She turned, finding a neat desk, a worn cupboard and an inviting, comfortable-looking bed, with gauzy, soft material canopied around the straightened bed linen.

It looked out of place in his soldierly room.

Anticipation popped inside of her. Not for the heat that grew in her lower belly from how Wyn rubbed circles over the bump of her knuckle, but from that single look. She knew he'd agree to anything she proposed.

THE QUIET CREAK OF THE MATTRESS SAGGING UNDER MIA'S weight as she slumped onto his bed, legs aching from pacing. She revealed everything in a rush of spluttered words, leaving Wyn shocked into silence. He sat next to her, hand scraping against the sharp prickles of his unshaven face. Kali's letter, folded and crumbled, sat between them, blazing.

"So a sickness is spreading?"

"No, Wyn, not an illness. Someone is turning nobles and rich men into dhampyrs," she explained. "And I think I know who, but I need evidence before I can level any accusation."

He sided-eyed her. "Go on."

"I have to see what the Silver has on this case, and they aren't going to let me waltz in there and demand it."

"Mia..."

"And you said you'd always be here for me."

"I did say that—"

"I need your help to break into the Pali," Mia cut in before she could lose nerve and not ask.

Wyn turned his whole body towards her, a frown pulling down his lips. "Have you gone mad? Say we break in, then what?"

"Then I can get justice for Kali."

"And will this justice have you digging another grave out in the Sliva forest?"

Mia raised her chin, determination singing in her veins. "If I have to, Wyn. There isn't much I wouldn't do for my sister."

He sighed softly. His hand crept across the linen, over Kali's letter, until the tips of their fingers touched, entwining with each other. They both stared at their hands, allowing their shallow breaths to mingle in the air. In the serene moment, Mia wondered why she felt inextricably drawn to him. *Is this heady need to be in contact with him simply desire, something left over from our night together, or is it more?*

Wyn's fingers caught her chin, raising her face to his half-hooded eyes. He breathed in as if dragging her scent into his lungs. "And here I thought you had come to—"

"See stars?" she finished.

"You saw stars?" he whispered, lips brushing hers.

"I saw *constellations*, Wyn."

He exhaled, eyes widening at the confession. He didn't push himself into her space to press his lips against hers. Instead, he waited, wanting her to take the plunge. However, Mia had fallen enough, plummeting through the air, only to crash into the shallows, breaking bones and rattling her own heart. Maybe the fall would land her on a feather-stuffed mattress and not in shallow water.

"What about Henry?"

His brows twitched together, and that desire dimmed a fraction in his eyes. "He would understand."

Her hand slid over his cheek, to his nape, drawing him even closer still. His thumb dragged over her jaw, awakening the aching throb of arousal at her core. She leant forward and brushed her lips over his. A low whimper came from Wyn, and the hand that held her trembled.

"*M'eudail Mia,*" he whispered against her. My darling Mia. "You will ruin me."

She grinned and allowed the soft pressing of a kiss to be her reply. Their knees bumped as the embrace deepened, tongues swirling.

He tasted of hops and sweetness.

He tasted right.

You had a man in your sheets last night. Now, you're about to let another between those thighs. Sweet creature, do you have no shame? The dark voice crooned, his tone hinted with barely disguised disgust. *You are nothing but the whore those men wanted you to be.*

That snapped whatever desire was forming in her.

She yanked her body back with such force that she all but tore herself from the bed, leaving Wyn blinking and confused, his hand still raised in the air.

"Mia—"

"Maybe you were right. We shouldn't be alone," she spluttered, smoothing her hair behind her ear. "I don't want to ruin whatever hurt you and Henry have mended."

Wyn's hand dropped in his lap, and he lowered his eyes. She had expected spitting anger, not the gentle sadness that found its way into the lines on his face. "If that is what you wish."

"I don't know what I want. I desire you, Wyn, I do, but my heart and mind are too entangled with Idris. I'm so lost, not just in my wants and desires, but in every way I turn. It's like I'm stuck in a sick hedge maze, and I keep hitting dead ends."

When Wyn's eyes finally rose to hers, something lingered in his gaze, like a mix of disappointment and disbelief. "Then let me help you find your way out. Let's break into the Pali."

They had waited until the sun had set, and the slow creep of people returned to their homes. The streets were nearly empty, with only those lurking for a warm fire in a loud inn or the cool sheets of a woman. Wyn had dashed any of Mia's plans, poking holes in them until they were worn and threadbare.

The Pali's centre dome stood sharp against the twinkling night sky, with the near-naked figure of Deus, muscular and broad, holding the scales of justice and law. Mia's eyes trailed down the impressive columns and brickwork that held the blood and sweat of those who toiled inside. The wide wooden door was closed shut.

She swallowed the ball of nerves and yanked on the hood of the borrowed cloak. "This isn't going to work. I'm pretty recognisable, you know."

Wyn grasped her elbow and dragged her closer to him. His lips were flush against the material, exactly over her ear. "You keep that hood up and your mouth shut, then."

Mia's cheeks heated, and she bit down on her lip to stifle her grin. "Yes, sir," she crooned, dragging out her syllables.

Wyn muttered under his breath, as he grasped the circular handle. With a creak, he dragged it open, pulling her through.

Knights strode around, some dressed in soft leathers, others in their gleaming silver armour. If Mia dared to crane her head, she could trace over the gold marble until her eyes could devour the painstakingly painted frescoes of Deus in his heavenly realm, ruling over the afterlife.

Towing her along, Wyn approached the empty desk. She glanced down at a worn brass bell and struck it, sending the ring chiming through the muted hall.

"Stop it—"

"Or what?" she cut in, meekly struggling against Wyn's grip.

He glared at her, but a playfulness had lightened the blue. "Do you really want to make whatever punishment you'll face for trying to nick the lord's silver worse?"

A flash of teeth from her grin came from under the hood. "I was merely shining it, captain."

"Before shoving some in your pocket, thief?"

A shuffle of boots, and a bored-looking silver approached the pair. "What do we have here, captain?"

"Just caught this one with her hand in the honeypot, and Hartwin has commanded me to take her personally to the cells."

"I can take her. I presume you have got more—"

"Are you questioning Lord Hartwin's orders?" Wyn cut in, unimpressed.

The knight paled and spluttered, "No, no. Of course not, Captain Wyn. But this lowly criminal is not worth your time."

Mia scoffed. Those men really saw Wyn as more than a captain.

"What is your name?"

"Braydon, sir."

"Well, Braydon, between you and me, this one has been sniffing around Hartwinn's son, Tobias—"

"He wouldn't know what to do with me, captain," Mia murmured, earning a sharp, silencing shake from Wyn. She pressed on to her toes, careful to not let the lantern light capture her face. And she added on quietly, "I don't think you do either."

Wyn's grip tightened, but he ignored her. "As I was saying, the lord found her with silver spoons in her pocket, as well as batting eyes at his favourite son. So he wants her to spend the night in the cells. Learn a lesson about where she belongs."

"That is...*unusual,*" Braydon said, glancing over his shoulder. He wasn't convinced.

Wyn leant on the counter and cast him a grin. "I presume Commander Dayvis has retired to his rooms for the evening. Is he still a grumpy old prick when woken?"

Braydon barked a laugh. "By Deus, yes. He's bloody worse now that he is in his eightieth year."

Wyn huffed and shook his head. "Good gods, he never changes. Shall we not wake the grumpy bastard, aye? Let me take this one to the cells, chuck her in somewhere for the night, and I'll come back and get her in the morning after she's pissed herself. No paperwork. No one needs to know."

Braydon pushed off the counter and sighed, rubbing his eyes. "You'd think that we'd be less busy with the curfew, but every man, mother and their dog has been reporting crimes, and we've been running around the city. You'll have her out in the morning, right?"

Wyn straightened and nodded solemnly. "I promise. Cross my heart."

Braydon waved them away, disappearing down the hallway. Mia exhaled a shaky breath. A sudden nervousness filled her, but she had been brave before, faked and half-hearted, and as well as had molten gold in her veins.

I can do this—for Kali, for those who have lost their lives.

Wyn kept her close as he led her down corridors and through doors, eyes flicking over his shoulder as if someone was following them.

"Do you miss the Pali?" Mia asked. "You were here for years."

"Not particularly."

"Weren't you supposed to be the next commander?"

Wyn flashed her an annoyed look. "Yes."

"Then why aren't you?"

"Because they didn't mean it," he replied tersely.

Mia pulled to a stop, brows bunching. "What do you mean?"

Wyn's sigh was soft, almost inaudible, like a hiss of pain. His eyes lingered on the gloomy end of the corridor.

"Do you think they were selecting me because of my skill, my promise as a commander? No, they choose me because my ears are pointed, Mia, and those bastards wanted to see me fail. You should have seen what they tried to do to Henry..." He exhaled his annoyance. "Then, Hartwinn offered me the captaincy, a place to prove myself, not because I'm fae, but because I'm a godsdamn good fighter and an even better leader. I have men's respect, and not from scraping and bowing like your father, but from busted knuckles and bloody grins. He is what they wanted, alas, I'm not. I'm far too wild, too reckless to be yanked to heel."

"Wyn—"

The sharp snap of boots cut into her words and made him scramble backwards, forcing her into a tight, dark alcove. Their bodies firmly pressed together, legs tangled. Mia and Wyn's breaths mingled in the space between them. His fingers slid from her elbow, over the curve of her hip, right to the small of her back, holding her as the footsteps approached. Her gaze found his—not that she had anywhere to look but up at him. Over the sharp stumble that surrounded his lips, to the lines that age had etched into face, to beyond that, right to the thick spread of lashes that rimmed his cool blue eyes. Flecked and simmered like a blade caught in the sun. Warm and safe.

Neither spoke, but their bodies seemed to slide into place, fitting together as she leant into him. Her face pressed to his chest, and his heart was racing, thundering in her ear.

Wyn was nervous.

A stray press of lips brushed her crown before he tucked her under his chin, holding her steady. The tired knight strode past the darkened alcove without a single glance in their direction. A door creaked open and slammed closed. But neither moved.

"You are...truly something else, Mia," Wyn murmured into her hair.

A soft smile played on her face. Her hand slid up his chest, fingering the soft material. "I am?"

"You're an extraordinary person, Mia," he answered. And with a shove, he pushed her out into the corridor. "But that doesn't mean I'll be willing to share a cell with you. Now get moving."

Mia grumbled, but the lantern lights captured the white flash of her teeth as she grinned at him. "Lead the way, Wyn."

He slinked out from the alcove and reached for her. Mia froze, breath held in her chest. With two fingers, he caught the edge of her hood and yanked it down. "When I told you to keep that hood down and that mouth shut, I meant it," he crooned, returning the grin.

Mia deadpanned Wyn, eyes nearly rolling to the back of her skull. "You think me a fool, Wyn Neverclove. I don't believe for a moment that the Pali allows its most secret information to be held behind a door without a lock."

Wyn shrugged, crossing his arms. "I don't know what to tell you, Mia. They rarely have people breaking in. It's usually the other way around."

Mia eyed the plain wooden door with its simple iron bolt. There was no elaborate padlock or fizzling magic—not even a growling guard dog. "This is unbelievable," she muttered.

She yanked on the bolt and dragged the surprisingly heavy door open. An alarming creak came from the hinges, making Wyn glance over his shoulder. He cursed and gripped the wood, yanking it wide enough for them both to slip through. It was dark, but a single lantern burnt, casting the flickering flame over the rows of waist-height shelves.

Wyn leant in and whispered, "Welcome to the vault."

Files, ranging from thick ones her hands wouldn't meet each side of, to those holding only one sheet of paper, were neatly stacked on the shelves. Mia's hands clasped behind her back, stopping her from dragging her fingers along the yellowed parchment. Her eyes flicked over files, desperately seeking her sister's name.

"It's a surprisingly complex ordering system," Wyn explained, flicking through the records. "Its based on a numbering system with correlation—"

"Found it," Mia cut in, yanking a file from the shelf. A concerningly thin file.

Wyn popped up from behind a shelf, surprise on his face. "How?"

She shrugged. "It has 'Ashmore' on it."

"Wait, let me find the others. Tell me what the dates and victims are again?"

Mia absent-mindedly listed as Wyn darted shelf to shelf, pulling files. Her eyes never left her last name, swirled in black ink. Her hand smoothed over the rough parchment. She was so close to answers, almost tasting them on her tongue, breathing them in with every shallow breath.

"I'm here, Kali," she whispered. "I'm finally here."

Wyn dumped files—much thicker than the one she held—in front of her, spreading them out with a sweep of his hand. She pressed Kali's protectively to her chest as he began the arduous task of sifting through the horrors transcribed onto the pages. His lips pressed into a thinner and thinner line with each passing moment.

"It's bad, isn't it?"

Wyn exhaled, leaning his elbows on the shelf, holding his head. "It's very bad, Mia."

She turned the papers around, took a steadying breath and dived in. Body parts and cold, emotionless words for their wounds assaulted her vision, sucking the air from her chest. Observations and questioning considerations lined the pages.

Was she waiting for someone? Did she hear a sound? Did she know something?

Mia's trembling finger traced over the question, holding it in her mind.

She found the blood splattered, jotted notes and letters for employment that had been scrunched in their hands—most likely forgeries by Luc.

Someone was luring these women here. Why?

The Silver had the same query, written with obvious frustration. Perhaps it was Mylo, hunched over a desk, cursing whatever—or whoever—was doing it. She kept going, flicking pages over, discarding them. One victim—a barmaid—had complained of a handsy noble, but someone quietly swept it away. Mia's mind flashed to the night in the brothel, and how rough and angry Reagan was.

"Mia, you look like you had a thought..." Wyn said from beside her. She hadn't even realised he had moved. She still clutched Kali's file tightly to her chest. "What is it?"

"What if these women were too loud, too furious to be silenced?"

"Why would they be furious?"

"Because someone hurt them, Wyn. Took something that wasn't given freely."

The realisation hit him, his face turning dark. "I would never think Hartwinn would ever be on board with silencing *rape* victims, Mia."

"But what if he isn't aware? Think about it, Wyn. These women were refugees, or a part of the lower city too poor for anyone to care about. And a man—who is seen in more brothels than council rooms—thought he could merely silence them from spreading the truth or upsetting the apple cart. But I don't think it's just about silencing women. I think it's hungry, searching for more blood. Out of control."

"Reagan?" he whispered, eyes narrowing. "Mia, that—"

"It's got to be him."

"No. I watched him grow into a man. He's not capable of this."

"He hurt my sister, Wyn. Even if he didn't rip her throat out, he held the chain to whatever did. I'm sure of it."

Wyn said nothing. His glazed eyes shifted around the pages, not taking any of the words in.

Mia, annoyed, opened yet another file. Someone had scrawled and rushed this one. But she could make out the words *dhampyr* and *vampyre*. More circles and more question marks were written.

They had even interviewed vampyres—even Idris. His name blazed on the page. Her heart clenched, and a strange spit of betrayal popped in her. She glanced at Wyn from the corner of her eye. *Would things truly have broken between me and Idris if I had gone to bed with Wyn? Would my betrayal come out in the spits and splatters of rage, only driving us further apart?* Mia sighed and shook her head. It was definitely not the time to be thinking about men and the complications they had brought to her life.

Mia pushed back the files, mind overloaded with gory images and more information she'd need days to sort through. If it had shown anything, it was that the Silver was at a loss. However, she hadn't opened Kali's file yet. Not yet. She placed it down, her hands encircling it.

It was time.

"Mia, I can read it…"

"No," she said softly. "I have to do it."

That sharp scratch of grief awoke inside her chest, scraping against her tender rib cage with jagged claws. Even her thudding heart felt delicate. A thin band of velvet curled around her ankle, hidden by her skirts—Ozul, holding her legs steady. Wyn's hand slid over to hers, settling beside it. He was there with her, for whatever she found on the pages.

Mia exhaled and flicked open the file. A sharp gasp came from her, then a muffled curse slipped from Wyn.

A single slip of paper with two lines swirled handwriting stared back at her.

In the possession of Lord Hartwinn Novak.
CONFIDENTIAL.

The loud creak of the door made her slam Kali's file shut and yank Wyn behind her. A beam of lantern light cut through the air like a sharp blade slicing through flesh to expose the soft, squishy insides.

Mia and Wyn were flayed open, caught red-handed by Mylo.

The lieutenant's eyes narrowed, mouth forming an unimpressed frown. But what was more frightening was the man who stood behind him. In the lantern's glow was a pale, gaunt Lord Hartwinn, with a skin-prickling gleam in his eye. Mia's hand gripped Wyn tighter.

"And what do we have here?" Hartwinn asked, cocking his head. "You better start explaining, and now."

The glare that Mia cast at Wyn when he stepped out of her shadow was hot and furious. He thought he could speak for her. Hartwinn lifted one finger—that gleaming ruby capturing the light—silencing him.

"I'd rather hear it from the girl, Wyn."

"Yes, sir," he murmured, dropping his gaze.

He played a part in it. Now, he is playing another for Hartwinn, she realised. Criss-crossing over an invisible line, unable to decide what side he wanted to be on.

"What do you think I was doing, uncle?" Mia asked flatly.

"I think you were in here tampering with evidence, or sticking your nose where it doesn't belong."

"Tampering?"

"I know about Luc."

Mia's jaw snapped closed, but that boiling didn't cease in her eyes. "And what do you think?"

"I think you should have come to me, Mia, and asked for my help to force Luc's hand to take you on. Not"—his eyes dropped over her—"sell yourself."

"What I do with my body is my business."

"From what I've heard, you've been making it everybody's business."

Wyn and Mylo shared a look and shifted on their feet. Neither glanced her way.

"And is this how you speak to your oldest friend's daughter? Shaming me for what your son does on a nightly occasion. Reagan spends more time in between a whore—"

"Do *not* bring him into this, Mia!" Hartwinn snapped, his eyes hardening.

A deep, rattling cough came from him, quelling her anger. Then, another echoed in the dust filled room, and then another, until she worried he'd never stop. Mia glanced at Wyn. Concern radiated from his features. *Did he know Hartwinn was sick, and didn't tell me?*

Burying the thought, she withdrew her handkerchief from her pocket. She held it out for him. He took it, wiping it across his mouth. A brief glimpse of black ink stained the crisp white fabric.

"You're sick, and she knew who was making you sick, didn't she?"

Hartwinn's gaze rose to hers, a flash of fear and then worry making the fine muscles around his eyes twitch. "I..."

"Please, Hartwinn. I just want the truth."

"Reagan has nothing to do with this. That is the truth."

"I don't believe that for one second—"

"Stay out of it, Mia. I will not warn you again," Hartwinn gritted out.

Crossing her arms, she replied, "Or what? Will I be silenced too?"

"You think what they did to your sister was silencing her? No, Mia, it was a threat."

"A threat? From who?" she asked in one breath.

"Someone I thought was so deep in the pits, he couldn't crawl out," Hartwinn uttered, staring at the bloodied handkerchief. "Someone who once said he needed not to set foot in Alderdeen to reach into it and rip me from my seat of power after I denied him."

"What did you do, Hartwinn?" Wyn asked, finally speaking.

"Sold myself to one ruler, only to condemn my soul to the fiery pits. And I fear Diabolus has come to collect. Now, go, both of you. And Mia, stay out of it. I would prefer Henry not to have to stare into yet another pyre. "

PART THREE:

~~Fate's Strings Have~~

~~Tangled Us Together~~

Fuck Fate.

FORTY-NINE

MIA PACED OVER THE GRIME-FILLED PUDDLES FOR WHAT seemed like an eternity, her mind tangled and knotted. But she had no time to unravel it. She had gone to Idris' call, meeting him where he had demanded in his letter, dragging Sorcha with her. She had given a poorly executed lie about safety in numbers. Selfishly, she didn't want to face him alone. Her pinched expression splashed away with each stamp of her foot. Huddled in a cloak, she sighed out each irritated breath, casting a mist into the moonlit sky.

Winter was rolling in, with cool breezes and frigid nights.

"...then after all that was said and done, he just fled in the middle of the night. Leaving a just note, Sorcha. A *note*!" she groaned, tucking her hand back into the warmth of her cloak. "The audacity of this man, I swear to Oryah."

"He must have a good reason why he left, Mia. I dare say that man does anything without thought," Sorcha replied. She yanked her dark blue shawl tighter around her, hiding away the deep burgundy gown. "You've been missing our lessons, you know. I don't have time to waste on a woman who came for help, only to leave me waiting up."

Mia exhaled, casting her friend an exasperated look. "I've been busy, Sorcha."

"And so have I. Now that I'm a master healer—"

"You passed?"

Sorcha ducked her chin, hiding away her smile. "Yes, with the highest possible score in recent years, if I may add. I have my swearing-in ceremony in two weeks. I would love for you to come."

Mia rushed towards the master healer and threw her arms around her in a tight embrace. "The highest score? You're absolutely brilliant! By Oryah, what an achievement. You should have told me."

Sorcha froze and then melted into the hug. "I...am not used to being so boastful."

Mia leant back. "I want you to boast. Yell your accomplishments to me, so I can tell everyone that I'm in the company of the future grand-master of the Alderdeen healers. That's what friends do."

She nodded, and her true grin spread on her face, crinkling her eyes. "I showed those fuckers, didn't I?"

Tears rushed into Mia's vision. "You showed them, pointy ears or not, that you belong there."

Sorcha's gaze sank to her battered throat, illuminated by the crack-ling lantern. The worst of the bruising had risen to the surface. "Did something happen?"

Mia nodded her head once, her fingers spreading over her collar. His touch remained like a ghost on her skin.

"Luc?"

Another nod.

Sorcha's hand reached for hers, pulling it away from the dark marks left by a monster. "You're not alone, remember? I'm down in the depths with you, Mia."

"I'm drowning, Sorcha," she croaked out, a tear rolling down her face. "Drowning in all of this. I try to keep swimming to the surface, but a firm hand snaps out, keeping me just under the water's edge."

"Then we drown together."

Her eyes softened as she reached for Mia's throat, thumb brushing over the bruises.

"*Leighis...*" Sorcha murmured—the fae word for heal.

Mia gasped as a warm, tingling ring emerged around her neck, and the ache of bruised skin disappeared. Her hand snapped out and gripped Sorcha's wrist, eyes locking with the healer. "You aren't supposed to use fae healing magic. It's against the law."

"To heal is as natural to me as breathing. I will not hide away the gifts that Oryah blessed me with. That is the most absurd thing that bastard Ewan has ever decreed. You will teach a person how to fight, but not to heal? Bloody ridiculous."

"You know why, Sorcha. He collared all the fae healers he could get his grubby little mitts on, only to keep them all in the capital," Mia said, shivering—and not against the cold. "Healing is the most powerful of all the fae magic, isn't it? One you don't need a natural conduit for. Think about how the tide of this senseless war could change if he allowed healers to be free. His armies wouldn't survive."

"Magic is balance. You cannot take and take, and not expect to have any consequences. This land remembers, Mia, even if he does not."

Mia nodded solemnly, glancing up the road. He still wasn't there. "This has all been a waste of time, Sorcha. Let's go. "

Whirling on her toe, she ran headfirst into a warm, broad chest, driving that whisky-and-clean-leather scent right into her lungs. Idris' deep, smokey voice glided over her skin as he replied, "What is a waste of time, Mia?"

She stepped back. Her gaze snapped to him. "There have been a great many things that have been a waste of my time, Idris."

A fresh flare of pain flickered in his pupils.

Good, she thought, then instantly wanted to take it back. She wished to hide away behind that spite and anger, but she knew it would only expose the truth.

He winced at her words. "Mia—"

Her hand shot up, voice hard when she said, "Don't, Idris. I don't have the patience for your excuses. Not tonight."

"And I have little patience for your pouting tantrums, Mia. I specifically told you I had something to show *you,* not a healer of the tower."

"Where I go, she goes."

With each strangled breath, her heart seared with the ripping of the barely healed wounds. Their gazes met, battling not for dominance, but to see who hurt the most. A sick competition. The pain that lurked was hidden by simmering irritation.

Mia knew she had won.

Idris had hurt her more than she had ever hurt him. In that moment, she wished she had never let whatever grew between them take root in her chest. She had so much growth tangling around her rib cage, she couldn't tell which gnarled limb to snip.

Sorcha cleared her throat, motioning down the road with a nod. "Shall we, or do you both need a moment?"

Idris muttered a curse under his breath and pivoted on his heel, striding down the street. The women scurried after him, struggling to keep pace. With each step, Mia's eyes burnt a hole between his shoulder blades as her irritation simmered over.

"You could start a fire with that glare," Sorcha whispered.

Mia grunted, narrowing her eyes, hoping he would catch aflame.

The master healer arched her brow at Mia. "When you told me about him, I didn't think you were...*together*."

Idris turned his chin slightly, but kept up his brutal pace.

Mia shook her head, her fingers sliding over the pink, flat scars on her collarbone.

"Not in the way it matters, Sorcha. I guess none of it mattered, in the end," she replied, voice sadder than she intended.

Idris' shoulders tensed into a solid line as he stopped. He turned to face Mia. "What we did mattered to me."

"I guess it would when you make a vow of celibacy. What was it again? 'Take no wife, father no children—'"

"Enough. I get it, you're angry at me. You need not rub dirt on it."

A smirk spread across Sorcha's face. "A vow of celibacy, hey?"

His shoulders raised and lowered as he let out a deep, annoyed sigh.

"How long?" Sorcha asked, amusement edging up her tone. "You know that's not good for your health—"

"Thirty," he cast over his shoulder. "Thirty years."

Mia's jaw hit her chest, and shocked, choked noises came from her. "No, Idris, you didn't break a thirty-year vow with me."

He said nothing.

She shook her head, repeating her words with a fraction more shrillness.

Idris paused for a moment, then whirled, his cloak billowing the wind. His eyes blazed with the same desire-filled heat he had poured over her when she was tangled in his sheets. He took a step towards her. Mia didn't retreat. His trembling hand reached out, gripping her around the chin. Not tightly, but enough for her to pull away if she wanted to. But Mia didn't. She didn't want to. She wanted Idris to drag her into his arms and beg for her forgiveness.

Reaching up, she gripped his wrist, locking him in place. At that tense moment, the world vanished, leaving only their burning gazes, rapid breaths and the pain they have cursed on to each other.

"It's the truth, Mia. I broke it on a desk with you, your glorious body hidden from me. Now, what we did clouds my mind, lingering on every thought and in the mists of every dream. And I would do it again. The only thing I regret is how I left last night. How cowardly it was, and how I didn't mean a fucking word in that letter, and that you turned to Wyn Neverclove for help when it should have been me."

A flicker of hope awoke in her chest, taking the edge off the pain. "Then why?"

His face clenched as if the words he needed to speak caused him discomfort. "Because I cannot feel anything for you, Mia, as much as I ache to. Fate has us tangled, but not in love."

She uttered his name, a silent prayer.

"Don't beg, Mia. It is below you, of all people, to beg me to love you."

Sounds of the world flooded back. Faraway laughing voices of the streets of whisky and abyss. The dull tome of the evening bell, and the spattering of rain on the tile roofs. The sharp sting of pain as the shards of her heart cut into her soft flesh, filling her chest cavity with a thick, viscous coating of self-loathing.

Mia took a step back, her gaze lowering. Her hand found Sorcha's, gripping tightly, only to stop her from running. "Then we have nothing else to discuss."

"Oh, Little Witch, that's where you are wrong. We will have plenty to discuss," Idris crooned bitterly. "We're here."

MIA STARED AT THE NONDESCRIPT HOUSE WITH PLAIN sandstone walls and a thatched roof. They stood deep in the bowels of the lower city. Triple-storey homes surrounded them, housing up to three families on each of the wobbly stories, with muck at their feet, stray cats slinking around. The hairs on Mia's neck rose as she splashed through the muddy puddles towards the home. Her hand rose to smooth them, a strange anticipation growing in her stomach, like the flapping wings of a butterfly taking flight in the midday sun.

Something was about to happen—something that would change her life forever.

Idris strode to a plain wooden door. His eyes glanced up and down the alley, searching for unseen foe. Then, he slammed his fist against the wood.

The door cracked. "Password?"

Idris grumbled a curse, then answered, "The day grows long as the moon meets the sun. There we are, joined by the shadows."

"By the shadows," the voice replied—the same words carved into the Umbra Box.

The door swung open, letting the beam of light catch Mia in the face, making her squint. She exhaled as her adjusting eyes met the grey, stony gaze of James. A slow grin spread across his face. "About time you found us, witchling."

Idris bent at the hip, motioning for Mia and Sorcha to enter with a swing of his arm. Mia stepped through the threshold, allowing the warmth of the room to encase her, stripping the chill from her bones. She discovered a handful of mostly women, whispering to each other at a small table.

No, not simply women, Mia quickly thought. *This is a room of witches.*

She found Benny at the end of the table, a smirk on his lips. He winked at her and leant back. A hushed silence fell around the plain room as she found herself caught in the suspicious gaze of the witches. Mia struggled not to fidget as she met each hard stare.

"Is this her, James?" a female voice called out.

"She is only a witchling. Not even entered the Ritus yet," a gravelly voice croaked from the left side of the table.

A tall, broad-shouldered man pushed off the wall. Her own eyes, deep brown with specks of green, shone back at her. His face felt familiar. Not as if she had seen him before, but like she was staring into a mirror. A burn-scarred hand went to his mouth to cover the small cry that left him.

"Ophelia?" he uttered from between his fingers.

A thick intensity filled the warm room after the man uttered that name.

"By Oryah, it is you," he shuttered out, dropping his hand to his side. "You survived."

Voices called out and began arguing. Words she had little understanding of were thrown around the room.

The man stepped closer, still holding out a hand, whispering that name again. *Ophelia.* There was a strange desperation in his eyes, making them glassy and wide.

Mia backed up a step. "I'm sorry, sir. I don't know who that is."

"Sir?" he repeated, his brows furrowed. "You don't remember me?"

She blinked at him, her mind unable to grasp the memory that tried to surface. "I don't think I do."

For a split moment, Mia thought she stood in front of her birth father. They looked too similar to not share blood.

A soft sadness relaxed the muscles between his brows, but a small smile edged his lips. "I'm your uncle, Alaric. Your mother's twin brother."

"My...*uncle?*"

The rushing of feet dragged her from the man's sad gaze to a wizened old lady whose grey hair flared haphazardly around her wrinkled face as she strode towards her. "We need to strip her to see if she has a queen's mark!"

Mia's head snapped to Idris, eyes wide. Her hands darted to her bodice, gripping the material tightly. Hurried footsteps backwards landed her in Idris' arms, hand finding her elbow, steadying her.

His arm shot out, blocking the elderly woman's approach. "Take another step and you will regret it."

Alaric's eyes hardened. "Unhand her, scum. You're lucky I allow you to be that close to her."

Benny's deep voice rumbled through the room as he strode past Alaric, flanking Mia. "Now, now, love, Idris is bound to whoever sits on that obsidian throne. If anyone should have their hands on her, it is him."

Mia's hand snapped out and gripped his wrist, dragging him closer. "What are you doing here?"

"I'm backup if this goes pear-shaped," Benny whispered back, a tight smile spreading on his face.

Alaric's jaw tensed at their whispering. "Considering the ruinous events of the past, I hope she has more sense than her mother. Has the vow been made?"

Idris tensed behind her but said nothing.

Mia leant back into him, her hand gripping his wrist. Voices rose, spewing words of queens, of witches, of a Divine Bride.

The slamming of a blade entering the wood cut the tension in the room.

Mia jumped. Her fingers dug into Benny, causing him to wince. The echoing sounds of leather against flesh and her scream made her heart race, her palms sweaty.

"Mia conjured this without training or guidance. She made a shadow blade from nothing," James announced. "Just as Maeve did. Just as her bloodline has always done."

The elderly woman yanked the blade from the table, brandishing it at all those in the room. Stray hands reached out, brushing over the dull black metal as if it were a holy relic.

"I have seen the full force of her shadows," Idris called out, adding to the chorus of murmurs and whispers. Many turned to him, their eyes narrowed. Disgust cut across their faces.

A snarling need to protect him almost overcame her.

A woman pushed from the table, her narrow face screwed into a pursed, bitter grimace. Tears wet her cheeks, shining in the lantern light. Her thin shoulders hunched, her hands in trembling fists. "No one asked you for your testimony, coward. What are you even doing here? You're not welcome here. Not after what you did."

Mia glanced up at Idris, finding nothing in those emerald pools—hard and devoid of emotion.

"Idris, what does she mean?"

The woman scoffed. "You haven't told her, have you?"

Alaric stepped forward, shaking his head. "We need not talk of that night, Vivan. This should be a joyous—"

Vivan held a hand up, silencing him. "He was supposed to be on guard the night the witch hunters came. He was supposed to be guarding Queen Maeve."

"Viv, not here. Not like this," Benny urged, stepping closer to Mia.

Idris' gaze shifted, turning into that same shame-filled look. This time, it didn't stab Mia, but struck her like an arrow to the guts. A burst of pain, then a searing ache.

"He was too busy feeding and fucking. Weren't you, bloodsucker? With Maeve's sister, no less," she sneered, her tone dripping with vitriol.

"That's not what happened—"

"Half-truths, Idris. That's all you can give me," Vivan interrupted. Her voice shook with emotion. "You were supposed to protect her and her family, but all you did was let them massacre us and destroy her name. For what? To get your cock wet? I hope it was fucking worth it."

Vivan trembled so hard that the stray tear flung from her cheek. Mia believed for a moment that she was furious, but it wasn't that intense anger that erupted from her.

It was grief. That lonely ache.

Mia released Benny and pulled from Idris, stepping towards her. Her own grief was twinned in the woman. Vivan had lost her people, her land, her queen. Perhaps, deep down, Mia understood a fraction of the feeling that shook Vivan's voice.

Vivan watched cautiously as Mia reached out and took her hand. She exchanged a small smile with the crying woman, whose eyebrows knotted more. A small sob left Vivan.

"My heart breaks for you, for all of you. I couldn't ever imagine fleeing from your home with a devil on your heels. But what does this have to do with me? Why are you telling me this?"

Idris exhaled softly. She almost knew the words he was going to speak before they even left his mouth. The reason he had taken her there, the secret he had kept from her.

"Queen Maeve was your mother, Mia," Idris replied, gaze dropping to the wooden floor they stood on. "And that night, I was..." He cleared his throat, eyebrows furrowing deeper. "I was..."

The words bubbling from his mouth looked painful.

"Idris, mate," Benny muttered, his hand finding his friend's arm. "If you're not ready..."

"I was with Rowena, yes. Breaking my vow, I was not. I had no choice in that."

"What are you saying?" Alaric hissed.

"She was deep in the Ritus, and I...couldn't stop her from taking what she demanded from me."

Idris' confession shocked the room into an awkward silence. Eyes that once held contempt suddenly held strange pity.

Mia's guts twisted, and her heart ached. She wanted to reach for him, to draw him close, to tell him it wasn't his fault. None of it was his fault. His name fell from her lips. The emerald pools rose to hers. And in that moment, nothing else mattered but him. Not the hurt one another had caused, or what had happened in the past. Nothing.

"Liar! You accuse someone who cannot defend themselves," Alaric snapped. "My sister would have never. It would have been more likely that you put yourself in her way, didn't you? Knowing she'd be vulnerable."

"You fucking take that back, Alaric. Right now, or so Oryah help me, I'll make you," Benny warned, stepping forward, lip snarled. Idris' hand found his chest, stopping him.

Mia frowned at Alaric, indignation tightening her features. "How dare you—"

"He's telling the truth," Vivan muttered, distracted. Her eyes had a glazed and glassy look. "Rowena was...forceful with Idris, ignoring his requests to stop. But she took what she wanted, without his consent."

Mia exhaled. Her jaw trembling, holding in the welling tears. She made her way to him, her hand sliding in his. Alaric spun to Vivan, denial falling from his lips.

"By the goddess, Idris. All these years?" Vivan whispered, her eyes snapping into focus, stumbling back onto the table.

"All these years," Idris repeated. He closed his eyes as a stray tear rolled down his cheek. Mia, without thinking, reached up and wiped it away with her sleeve.

With a deep breath, Idris spoke. "Vivan is right. Regardless of what was happening to me, I wasn't doing my sworn duty to protect Maeve, and I certainly didn't protect any of you. I'm so terribly sorry. It's a shame I will wear for the rest of my days."

The soft, comforting warmth of her magic built in her chest as her shadows fought the grip she held on them. A singular shadow slipped free, curling between her fingers.

"*Free us, Mia,*" asked Ozul. "*Let us be those we missed.*"

Vivan's eyes rose to hers, nodding as if she had heard the voices "Let Ozul free, witchling."

"Do they not scare you?" Mia asked, letting the shadow spill around Vivan's feet.

Vivan's eyes widened at the sight of her misting shadows. She shook her head with such force, her curls sprang around her face. "I will never be afraid of you. None of us are afraid of the magic in your veins, Mia. You're with your people."

A tear rolled down Mia's face—one she didn't understand why she was shedding. "I am?"

"You don't have to hide who you are. Not anymore."

Have I been hiding?

Have I lived a lonely life, locking a part of myself away? A part of me like the freckles on my skin or the scar that cuts across my face?

Am I a witch, blessed with shadows?

Have I finally found who I am?

The questions swirled, twisting and knotting in her mind until they were nothing but a tangled mess of thread.

"Won't I enter the Ritus—or whatever that is?"

"No, sweet girl," Vivan said with a soft smile. "You're far too young, and it's not yet a full moon."

Mia nodded, closing her eyes. She exhaled a shaky breath, allowing herself to feel right down past the hurt Idris had planted in her chest.

She dug deeper, to the love Kali had filled her with, like the bright sun beating down on her limbs on a hot summer's day. She uncurled her fist on her magic, allowing it to flow freely from her.

Curses and prayers surrounded her.

Mia opened her eyes to see the shadows spilling from her outstretched hands and filling the dark corners, flickering the lanterns. Then, the icy void in her chest emerged, and the room spun. She hadn't used that much magic. Not since she had found Kali's body.

The shocked faces of the witches stared back at her. People began lowering to their knees, mumbling the word *queen*.

"Please, get up," Mia begged as she whirled around with her hands out. "I am no queen."

Benny and James shared a sly grin and lowered themselves down. Sorcha, wide-eyed and shocked, sank next to Vivan, who cast the healer a long sideways glance.

Mia's heart was beating so fast, she was worried it would break through her tender rib cage and flop to the floor like a fish out of water.

Idris was the last standing, his gaze captured hers. He still cast her the same sad expression, but something else lurked within those green eyes—adoration. A true warmth she dared not read too much into.

"My queen," he said, dropping to a knee. With an even softer voice, he whispered just to her, "My Mia."

Panic fought its way up her throat, making the walls of the already tight room feel smaller, closing in on her and making every breath laboured. Her lungs were unwilling to take in the precious air, and her mouth was dry, gummy. Her mind was spiralling as flares of ashes, harrowing screams and the sickly scent of burning flesh consumed her senses.

Mia needed to get out—now—before her own scream returned.

She pushed past the kneeling people. Like reeds in the river, their hands held onto her tightly, pulling her into the depths of pure panic. Mia's body felt heavy, slow, caught in the current. Her fingers fought to reach for the door handle, but a hand snapped out, gripping her elbow, stopping her.

"You can't just go," Alaric murmured, eyes pleading with her. "I just found you, after all these years."

Mia knew the relief she would feel if Kali skipped back into her life, but she couldn't be their queen. She was barely a witch, barely anything. Just a bundle of emotions, pain, and hurt, lost to the events that had been thrust onto her. She didn't know who she was. Not truly.

Yanking from his grip, Mia fled into the night.

FIFTY

Mia sprinted as fast as her legs could take her
down the cobblestone streets, past the dark, closed stores and soft
lantern lights of homes readying themselves for bed. She ran
through the pebbling of rain, splattering on her skin in chilled
drops, sliding around corners, and pushing through people,
erupting from the masses. She didn't know where she was going,
but she knew she sought an escape from the truth spilt at her
feet.

Mia ducked under an archway at the edge of the city and darted
right into the Sliva Forest. The rain, a pouring deluge, stuck stray
strands of hair to her face. Her skirts tore on bushes, cutting her legs on
the barbed limbs. Her boots slipped on the slick leaf matter as she
dashed under the haunting trees.

Mia skidded to a stop, her hands on her knees, demanding air to
enter her lungs.

A sad, wailing sound circled her as while ghostly fingertips slid up
the curve of her spine. She straightened, her eyes taking in the time-
forgotten buildings of the necropolis, lit by the silver moonlight.

Mia had run to Kali.

Her legs gave way, collapsing to the hard stone. Angling her face up to the crescent moon, Mia wept, cool drops of rain mingling with the warm rivers of salt on her cheeks.

"Kali, I need you. I need you to tell me what to do." Her voice cracked and wavered. "I need you to be strong, to be brave."

Mia's shoulders heaved as the tears she'd held back for her sister finally left her. Her wails filled the deathly silence. She released the shame, grief, anger and sadness in her body with each heave, soaking into the ancient stone beneath her—just as it would have for all those who begged and pleaded at the foot of Death to return those they loved. But he never answered their pleas.

Mia curled in on herself. She let each tear drag the longing for Kali down her face. She would miss her sister every day, every minute, every second that her heart was beating. A ghostly presence settled behind her, smoothing her hair and curling into the curve of her back.

She knew it was Kali—or maybe she just wished it was.

With a soft sigh, Mia began talking, recounting all that had happened since Kali had left the earth. Her voice softened as she explained she had taken someone else's life, and how the guilt was intertwined with a strange sense of justice. In a whisper barely louder than the pattering rain, she told Kali's ghost she was a witch, and those shadows meant more than she could have ever known.

"I can't do this without you," Mia sniffed, her finger still tracing. "Without you, sister, I feel completely lost. I never thought that I'd be this lonely when I was surrounded by people—"

A twig snapped, making her sit up. She rubbed her stinging eyes and glanced around. She couldn't see anything, but the dark forest edged closer to her. The creeping, spine-tingling feeling of being watched inched over her exposed skin. Then, another snap in the opposite direction made her heart pick up pace. She pushed to her knees, her legs weak. A cold sweat leeched over her as her breath came shallow and fast.

"Hello?" Mia called out. "Idris?"

"Hello? Idris?" her own voice echoed back. But it was warped, garbled. Something was mimicking her—or trying to.

She could hear the rush of boots crunching across the forest floor behind her.

"Run, Mia! Now!" Kali's voice slammed against the stone.

Mia scrambled to her feet just as the brush of fingertips slid through her hair. She launched into the tree line, not sparing a glance behind her. Slamming footsteps followed in her wake as she bolted around trees, ripping through bushes.

She knew what creature was chasing her, and it was almost on her.

A dhampyr.

Manic giggles surrounded her as it crashed through the forest. Mia's foot caught the edge of the jutting rock, sending her sprawling with a cry. She clawed her way through the mud and dirt towards the shadow of a tree. Slipping on the mossy, wet ground, she found safety in the deep groove of a root. She pressed her body against the bark, her hand clasped over her mouth.

"I will find you, witch," a male voice hissed. "I can smell the fear on you. It only makes you more delicious."

Mia curled further into the darkness, her shadows slipping free, surrounding her like misty armour, readying to defend her against the snapping teeth and sharp claws.

"Where have you gone?" the dhampyr crooned. "You cannot hide from me forever."

She bit into her hand to muffle the scream that almost spilt from her.

The monster was closing in. His hunched searching of the air was only a few feet from her. His face screwed up into a snarl, onyx eyes rolling in their sockets, looking for her. Black, thin veins ran from purple bags, running down over his gaunt cheekbones. She recognised him—a noble's son from Hartwinn's court. She couldn't even remember his name.

He licked his lips with a film-covered tongue as a stomach-dropping, snarled grin cut across his face. "I cannot wait to taste you. You know, I've never had a witch. Human, fae, but not a witch. But, my first...oh, Deus, my first was the most delicious. Your half-blooded bitch of a sister tasted the sweetest."

Mia gasped against her palm, tears filling her eyes. She had found Kali's murderer, only to be lost in the forest with him with no way to defend herself.

He leant closer, causing Mia to shrivel back into the tree. Her nostrils were flooded with a dead scent, like an animal left to rot in the scorching summer sun. She could taste it on each of her laboured breaths, making her force her gag down.

"*We are losing strength. Please forgive...*" Ozul had faded to nothing as her magic sputtered out, leaving her exposed.

His black eyes roamed down the thick trunk until his gaze locked with her wide, terror-filled gaze. "Found you."

Mia screamed, launching herself from the depths of the roots. Her body slammed into the dhampyr, causing him to stumble and trip. She darted past, but not fast enough. Jagged fingernails caught her, digging into her sensitive scalp, yanking her off her feet, slamming her to the ground and knocking the air from her lungs. Her ribs had barely healed from the last attack she endured, burnt with each pant. Her shoes scrambled on the dirt and moss, but his boot pinned her to the damp forest floor.

Screams erupted from her—pleading cries for help.

"Yes, scream. I want to hear it," the dhampyr rejoiced sickly. "Scream like she did. No one is coming to save you."

Mia needed a weapon.

Anything.

Her hand slipped over rocks, fingers wrapping around a smooth stone. He squatted over her, his warm, disgusting breath fanning over her face. He licked the corners of his blood-stained mouth. "Master said we cannot eat your squishy bits or drink your blood, like I did with her. Yet, I don't think he would mind if I had a little taste. Witches are supposed to be the best, you know."

"Fuck you!" Mia cursed at him, squirming.

The bloodthirsty monster actually cringed at her. "Such a vulgar mouth. Master will not like that..."

"I don't think he'll like this either."

Mia swung with all her might, cracking him in the skull. A sickening *crunch* came from the impact. He bellowed, his hands flying to the dark, inky black blood pouring from his temple. She shoved him off, raising her arm again, then she slammed the rock down with a bellow, striking the dhampyr across his cheek. Blood splattered up her chest and over her chin. She scrambled to her feet to stand over the dying dhampyr. Her eyes took him in—his gaunt face, emaciated body, his once-fine clothing, hole-ridden and threadbare. He was almost unrecognisable as the fresh-faced teenager she had seen only weeks earlier.

"What have you become?"

"I am his creature, his soldier," he gurgled. "I am what he desires, just as you are."

"You're a monster. I'm no monster."

"I am what my master created, as you are what Deus created for him."

Mia's fingers released the stone, letting it drop next to his caved in face. His breaths gargled, then stopped. Her name was called. She turned to see a sweaty, flushed Idris standing at the edge of the small clearing, his skull-headed sword drawn.

"You can put that away. It's done—"

Mia suddenly flew through the air. A body had slammed into her, forcing her to the ground. Those same haggard nails cut through fabric, piercing her skin, then slicing right to the bone as if she were nothing but soft butter. The dhampyr smashed her face against the cold ground, muffling her desperate cries against the dirt. Her cheekbone took the brunt of the impact, leaving her dazed. All the while, crazed, gargled curses screamed in her ear. Even that sounded hollow, edged with a sharp ringing.

Mia fought, but it was useless.

Blood gushed down her body, pooling in the disrupted earth. She convulsed, distressed at the sudden lack of blood in her veins. Her vision marred with black dots, each breath a pained struggle. Death lingered on the periphery, poking his shadowy head around trees, waiting for her.

"Get off her!" Idris bellowed, his boots slamming on the ground.

"Master is going to love this. I can scent her all over you. You've sullied his bride."

"Well, you will soon burn in the pits with him—"

"The pits? My master is living and free, you fool!"

Idris grunted as a whoosh of his sword filled the air. The slack-jawed creature's head thudded against the earth and rolled across the leaf litter. Mia groaned, struggling to lift her now too heavy body, but her arms failed, making her slump back into the dirt.

She couldn't clot those wounds.

Idris scrambled down next to her, sword discarded. His frantically searching eyes found hers. His fear brushed over her oozing gashes, right down to each dripping pool of ruby-red blood. His hands hovered over her as if unsure where to place them.

"You're losing too much blood, Mia."

"Am I?" she asked weakly.

She knew that. The moment the monster's claws found her skin, she knew she wouldn't see the sunrise again. She rested her aching cheek against the dirt. The pain was almost all gone now, leaving only a tired, bone-deep wariness. The forever type of tiredness that death brought on. A soft smile spread on her face as tears leaked down over her swelling cheeks.

"Why are you smiling, Mia? This is not a time to be smiling," Idris said, an edge of panic cutting through his voice.

"Out of anybody, I wanted you here. You," she confessed, coughing. Blood splattered on the knees of Idris' pants. "I will always want you. All of you, each broken piece. I don't care what happened in the past."

"Keep talking. Just keep talking to me, Mia, please," he demanded, ripping strips from his shirt and pressing them to the gashes. But her blood just soaked through, covering his hands.

Her eyelids fluttered, heavy like lead. All she wanted to do was sleep. Death's skeletal fingers were close, reaching for her.

"No, Mia, you keep your damn eyes open."

"I think...you saved me, Idris...My salvation," she said, her voice fading in and out. "I love..."

"If you're going to tell me you love me, then you have to get up and look me right in the eye and say it. Get up, Mia, and tell me."

Her arms tensed, weak. Her fingers twitched, digging into the dirt. The constant flow had stopped. Her breaths were laboured but steady. Her body was fighting the pull of Death.

"Get up, Mia, and tell me you want me. Tell me you want this," Idris pleaded desperately. "I will not let him take you from me. You are mine, not his. He cannot ever have what is mine."

Her own words returned to her—the same ones she had whispered in that alley as Idris was dying. That's when she realised Death would have to pry them apart, finger by finger, or take them both.

"You heard..." she breathed.

"Of course I heard you calling for me in the darkness. I will always hear your call. Now, tell Death to fuck off, and live, Mia. *Live*."

She grunted and pushed up. Her body screamed in pain, but she only allowed sharp hisses to slip between her clenched teeth. She wavered, falling right into Idris' waiting arms. The sudden movement stretched the gashes down her back, causing whatever blood was left in her to gush over his pants and arm. Everywhere. The Medicus Tower was too far. They were too deep in the forest for help.

Mia was dying, and neither could stop it.

Idris smoothed the hair from her face, pressing his lips to hers. A gentle, lingering kiss. He pressed his forehead to hers, tears dripping from his eyelashes on to her face.

Time was slipping away.

She was going to go to her funeral pyre without him hearing her say those she desperately wanted to say.

"Let me say it, Idris..."

"No—"

"I love you, Idris. I always have."

He stopped breathing, then emitted a soft, heartbreaking cry. His jaw trembled as he pulled her tighter to him. The stray drops of rain struck his forehead, streaming down his cheekbones as if the sky were also wallowing in their shared anguish.

He shook his head, eyes finding her again. A desperation flared in his pupils. "No, Mia. You don't get to tell me you love me and then depart this world. I will not allow it. I only know one way to save you, by binding us together. Bound in life, and in death. Sharing one pool of life for the rest of our days. I cannot think of any other way."

Mia groaned, lips unable to form words. But she would have screamed her answer: *yes, yes, yes.* She wasn't clinging to life, desperate just to survive; she yearned to be tied to him forever, to wherever that may lead.

Idris tore into his wrist, teeth slicing through skin. His blood bloomed and dripped down his arm. He gripped her, turning her arm out, the scar shining in the low moonlight from where she had saved him. He brought it up to his mouth, his breath cascading over her. He was whispering against her skin in rushed, mumbled words. Mia realised he was praying.

She groaned, legs meekly moving. Death was now standing over the top of them, his ghostly presence cooling her skin.

Hastily, Idris bit down on her wrist, but she hardly felt the sting. He drew a mouthful of her precious life force into himself, then he pulled away, lips stained with her.

"A heart for a heart, soul for soul, binding in blood shared. I, Idris Blackwood, give my life freely to share with Mia Ashmore. One pool to drink from, one life to share, until the great goddess calls us home. I call on the watchful gods to bless this union, to bind us." He pressed his bleeding wrist against her lips. "Drink, Mia."

A trickle of a herbaceous, bitter liquid coated her tongue. She swallowed it down, letting a sickly feeling settle in her stomach. She pushed his arm away weakly, but Idris persisted, forcing his arm deeper into her mouth.

"More. You need *more*."

His blood smeared over her face as she choked down the hot liquid in hurried swallows. Her hand clasped his arm, digging in.

"Bind us! I demand you, Oryah. I demand you, Deus. I demand you, Diabolus!" Idris bellowed into the forest. "Bind us!"

A brush of unseen fingers slid over her, then dived into her chest. A gentle grip encapsulated her slowing heart, her back arching against him as an invisible hand yanked her upward.

"Beware, lovers, fate has a funny way of correcting itself," a soft female voice whispered over them.

"Bind. Us," Idris gritted out, gaze searching the air above them.

"As you command, son of Mortias. I will allow you to snip fate's strings just this once. But never again."

Heat. Burning heat flooded her, setting her whole being aflame.

Mia's body convulsed in erratic fits. Her eyes rolled as her teeth chattered together. Even so, Idris held her tightly, even though her skin must have been boiling. "Come back to me, my Mia."

No, no! I will not let you go, Sweet Creature. You are mine. This isn't what was supposed to happe—

A high-pitched, pained scream cut off the malice-filled voice.

The heat seared her gaping wounds back together, leaving her flesh scarred but healed. Death had taken a swipe at her and missed, only to hiss and slink away. She had cheated him once again.

Mia rolled off Idris' lap, falling to her hands and knees. Her fingers dug into the dirt, right down to the cool soil. Rain poured down, hitting her skin in sizzling splashes. She threw her head back, resting back on her heels, letting the fat raindrops spill down her face.

She was alive.

Mia turned her face to Idris, wiping his blood from her lips. "Now, what the fuck was that? Who the fuck was that?"

"That was Oryah meddling, Little Witch."

Mia swayed, tears filling her eyes. She couldn't drag her gaze away from the pools of glittering emeralds that shone back at her. A sob leaked from her as the realisation slammed into her like a punch to the guts. They'd finally found the monster who had murdered Kali. But Mia was still so far away from understanding why her life had been ripped away.

FIFTY-ONE

"A *THANK YOU* WOULD SUFFICE, LITTLE WITCH, AND I WOULD actually appreciate it," Idris grumbled, leaning back and tilting his chin to the dark canopy. He looked exhausted, as if saving her drained something from him. Yet, the sagging relief relaxed the stiff line of his shoulders. "Especially when your valiant rescuer binds themselves to you."

"With iron chains or silk, Old Man?"

"Iron," he answered flatly.

Mia's eyes dropped to her dirty, blood-stained hands. A faint thudding played on the edge of her hearing. She would recognise that steady rhythm anywhere.

"I can hear your heartbeat," she whispered.

"As I have always heard yours."

Mia crawled, dragging her heavy body across the same earth she had nearly died on, right to Idris, kneeling in front of him. His chin lowered, capturing her gaze. He steeled his face, preparing for the clumsy dance of hurtful words and bruised hearts they had been exchanging for weeks. He didn't speak, either, seeming to wait for her to drag back those words she spoke as Death caressed her.

But Mia wouldn't.

She meant every single one, and now they were floating between them like wisps of campfire smoke on the breeze, stinging eyes and irritating lungs. But you know what they say about smoke; it follows beauty. In the drizzling rain, with only shards of silver light beaming down over them, both blood-stained and muddy, clothing ripped and ruined, Mia hadn't ever seen such glorious beauty.

Her heart squeezed, letting out an emotion she had long forgotten —one that wasn't dredged in sadness or grief. Joy—elated joy—filled her chest on the fluttering of butterflies' wings. She wanted to breathe it in, sinking that seed of light right down to her guts. To let it grow, feeding it with the feeling Idris gave her. And not only that, but the love that overflowed from her parents, to the rare smiles from Sorcha, from her art, and even from Kali from beyond the grave. Allowing the darkness to wither and die.

Mia wet her lips, tasting the drying copper. She reached for him, gathering the front of his shirt in her fist, drawing him closer. "What are you waiting for, Old Man?"

"I'm waiting for you to realise that those words you spoke—"

Her hand slid over his mouth, silencing him. "Don't, Idris. Don't push me out of your heart again."

His eyebrows furrowed over his eyes, but he wasn't angry or irritated. He was beaming such emotion at her that she could feel it slip around her racing heart, settling in, finding a home.

Idris' gripped her hand, placing it over his steady rhythm. "This heart, Mia, has always been yours. Each beat plays a song for only your ears, and here I was, wishing and praying that maybe our melodies match. Now I know they do. I hope it plays in my ears until Oryah takes me from this earth, then, in every lifetime she casts me as well. I will always find you by that thundering beat of your heart."

He closed the gap between their lips, stealing her reply with a kiss. Not just any kiss, but one that dragged the air from her lungs, leaving her dizzy and aching for more. Idris pulled Mia into his lap, one hand tangled in her hair, the other pressed in the small of her back. Her arms slid round his neck, drawing him closer still.

"What have we done?" she murmured between kisses.

"We have cut and retied those strings of fate, Little Witch. Ones that were divinely made. Ones the gods will not be very pleased about us snipping. Now, let us get rid of this body before the sun rises."

"Divide fate? That is horse shit, Old Man," Mia scoffed, rolling her eyes.

She slumped against the solid stone of a long forgotten building, deep in the Sliva Forest. Sunrise peeked through the trees in a pink orangey hue. She glanced towards the small clearing, where they had left the dhampyr's body for the beasts and maggots of the wood to take their fill of the rancid flesh. To rot. Much like what destiny had in store for Luc.

She stretched her aching legs out. Their bond may have healed her wounds, but she felt battered, bruised. Wisps of shadows had returned to swirl around her fingers. The unnatural feeling of the remaining blood churned in her stomach, sitting heavily inside of her.

Idris' gaze slid to her, eyes narrowing her words. "Denying your own fate is a dangerous game, Little Witch."

"What is my fate, then?" she urged him on with a wave of her hand.

"To unite these warring lands under one ruler."

Mia shot him a wide-eyed, incredulous look as a laugh spilt from her. She gripped her sides, muscles straining with each chuckle. "Good joke. You're finally catching on."

"I'm not joking, Mia," he said blandly.

"Then you've completely lost your mind, Idris." She picked a drying clump of mud off her skirts, flicking it away. "I have only just found out I'm a witch, but I'm not destined for anything. Especially not to rule."

His lips pressed into a thin line, eyebrows furrowing in thought. He was hiding something.

She sighed, crossing her arms. "Back to keeping secrets again, are we?"

"No, I'm thinking. We're missing something. Something important."

"We killed the creature that was hunting women, and its master was obviously Luc. Done and dusted."

Idris shook his head, his eyebrows edging closer and closer as his mind ticked over the information. "Luc? He was no master, but a pawn. We've been distracted with Reagan, who has only led us to dead ends. There must be more."

Mia groaned, fingers yanking on tufts of grass, and told him about Kali's letter, Hartwinn's sickness. All what she had learnt.

"It could be Hartwinn," Mia whispered, scared to even say it. "Whatever dark magic is used to create these creatures could be eating away at him. Making him sick."

She groaned before Idris could reply, kicking her legs out. "I want this all to be over. I just...'

"Just?"

"I just want things to go back to when my biggest worry was being chosen by stuffy old guild masters."

He reached over, taking her hand. His thumb ran over the valleys of her knuckles, soothing her. Each dragged movement entranced him. "You were born for more than that life."

Mia let loose another groan, suppressing the urge to throw her hands in the air in frustration. "Please, Idris, we may have only just tied ourselves together, but I'm very close to strangling you."

Idris was silent for a moment, then he sighed. "Only one person can create dhampyrs, Mia. And it's not some human lord or his children."

"What do you mean?"

"The only man who has this power is in the pits, and cannot...be doing this."

Mia's hands trembled, but not from the brisk morning stealing her warmth. "It was Mortias, wasn't it?"

Idris glanced away and said nothing. His silence was answer enough.

"How long have you known about this?"

"All my life, Mia. He would threaten to turn those who couldn't survive our rebirth. Even in the Death Court, they are frowned upon. We vampyres aren't bloodthirsty monsters, ripping out throats, and the dhampyr are shells of who they used to be." He paused, exhaling.

"That's why I have been investigating, searching for answers. I wanted to stop his ghostly hand from hurting more people."

Mia didn't want darkness to tarnish the tender moment they were sharing. Instead of delving deep into Mortias, and the hand he was playing from the grave, she narrowed her eyes at him, a smirk curling. "Now, you'll have to pay the price for not telling me."

A ghost of a smile played on his lips. "What punishment do you deem worthy, Little Witch?"

"One dance at the royal ball."

Idris groaned, throwing his head back in fake disbelief. "That is a punishment not befitting the crime."

Mia batted his chest, rolling her eyes. "Regardless, you know we have to break into Hartwinn's office to see Kali's file, and the ball is the perfect guise."

That lopsided, dimpled smile emerged, lighting his eyes. Idris leant closer, lips hovering over the sensitive skin, where her throat met her collarbone. He glanced up at her. "And who do you wish to accompany you? Your queen's guard?' he breathed out, fanning his warm breath over her skin, prickling. "Or your blood bond, my Mia?"

Mia giggled, baring her neck a fraction more, hands digging into the ruined material of her skirt. "Well, you haven't fallen to your knees, vowing to me, Old Man."

"Oh, Little Witch, if you desire to see me on my knees, all you need to do is ask," he crooned, smirk turning into a mischievous grin.

Mia shifted, pulling her skirts up a fraction. "Do you need to vow to me to be my guard?"

"I'm honour-bound to your mother, Mia. You need not say any vow until you're ready."

She sat back, the mention of her birth mother snapping the building tension.

"Anne will be delighted to hear that," Mia muttered, frowning. "No—"

"I understand what you meant. But Maeve isn't my mother, Idris. I don't even remember her, or anything before Alderdeen."

He reached up, tucking a stray strand behind her ear. "Perhaps that's for the best."

Mia caught his hand, turning to press a kiss to his palm. She feared Idris would pull away, leaving her alone again if they got too close to his festering wounds. "Will you tell me about her one day? When it doesn't hurt so much?"

"It would be my honour."

She longed to stay lost in the woods with Idris, his hands on her body. All she actually wanted was protection from the harsh truths of the world. But she wasn't wandering down an overgrown path, lost anymore. Maybe, instead of a path, she had stepped onto the busy King's Road, being pushed in confusing directions, narrowly avoiding being hit by a carriage. She exhaled, dragging herself to her feet. As she heaved Idris to his, Mia realised that she hadn't stepped onto King's Road, but one of a queen's. It was paved with ash, smoke and shadows, skirted by a forest of bloodred oaks, leading her to a place she'd never been so hopeful to see. Her home—her *true* home.

Fifty-Two

Valliss Castle would be in full swing, readying for a night of music, swirling across dance floors and spilt drinks. However, deep in Rosda Manor, Mia was preparing herself for battle. The ball was upon them, and she would finally find Kali's missing file—and the evidence she needed to demand justice for her sister.

The black corset clung tightly to Mia's curves, cinching her waist to an almost impossible size. Her hands gripped the wrought iron of her bed as her breath was snatched from her. Her body was made to be adorned with floating tulles, allowed to curve where it naturally did, not being forced into a corseted prison, meeting only the expectations of men who knew nothing about the uncomfortable truth of being a woman.

Yet, Anne, her loving mother, demanded it, raised in the cages of court to be proper and right—well, until she'd met Henry.

Anne had spread a nervous, frantic energy throughout the manor, creating a sparking tension between herself and her daughter, arguing over each last detail, even down to the way to curl her hair. Mia had eventually relented. She needed entry into the castle. And if they had forced her into Alderdeen's most hideous gown, she would have worn it.

She wasn't wearing a dress shaped like a dessert, nor a slip of cotton. Black tulle and glittering silvery black gemstones adorned the tight corset that cupped her breasts. One could see glimpses of her pale skin through the sheer panels. Beads ran in glimmering rivers down her skirts, capturing the afternoon light. She shifted the off the shoulder sleeve, ensuring that the lace detailing spread smoothly across her arm.

"I'm sorry, sweetheart," Abigail murmured from behind her. "Is it too tight?"

Mia straightened, hand bracing against the sharp poke of the gemstones. She shook her head, testing how deeply she could breathe—it was not much.

Turning to the mirror, Mia found her eyes twinkling. More often than not, she lowered her gaze from her reflection, not wanting that self-loathing to bubble inside of her. But she stared directly at her reflection, unafraid. Appreciating the sharp edge of her jaw, the spattering of freckles across her nose and the soft shine of blonde curls. She found beauty in every inch of herself. But more than her flesh and bones, she discovered power.

Abigail gathered her hair, preparing for the painful pins.

Mia reached up and stopped her. "Leave it loose," she directed, before adding on with a small smile, "He likes it down."

The carriage lurched forward, rolling under the archway that led through the dark gardens. The castle loomed in the darkness, the shining marble tall and foreboding. Mia's leg bounced. Henry sighed, straightening his coat, and Anne chewed the corner of her nail. The ball meant more than anyone was letting on. Her family had the court's eye, and they needed to gleam and shimmer like prized jewels. But one of their gems was missing, fallen from the gold that fused them together.

"Goddess, I hate these things," her mother breathed, smoothing her hand over her skirts.

"As do I," Mia replied, distracted, her eyes searching the masses of bodies leaving carriages for the broad shoulders of Idris. She twisted the opal ring, the smooth stone warm under her fingers.

"My moon," Henry said, his voice soft from his corner of the carriage. "All you need is yourself. You don't need a man or anyone to make you whole. You are enough."

Mia's leg paused its shifting, and she cast her father a half-hearted grin. "I'm just nervous, Father. I wish to make a good impression, and Kali isn't here to charm the princess."

"Is that why you are nervous? Mia, these people are family, and you know this castle like the back of your hand. You deserve to be here as much as some faraway princess," Anne quipped, raising her chin.

Her mother belonged to the court, but Mia wasn't sure if she herself ever had.

"What do you think she'll be like?"

"What did you think she would be like?" Henry asked, raising a brow.

"Pompous, stuck-up and boring."

"Ewan keeps a tight leash on those he sees as beneath him. I would think he would include his daughters in that."

"Praise be to our kind and benevolent king," Anne muttered under her breath.

"She's tasting freedom for the first time in her life, so maybe do not judge her so quickly," her father said, hand squeezing Anne's knee.

"Have either of you ever met royalty?"

"Aside from your grandfather, Sundryl?" Henry asked, cocking his head.

"I wouldn't call that monster that," Anne added drily.

Henry was bastard-born, and his kingly father never let him forget.

"Like, princesses? I heard they may crown a Diabolus priestess across the sea as queen in Moonmire."

"How marvellous, Mia," Anne murmured, eyes shifting to Henry.

Mia knew neither of her parents had paid attention to a single word. They were locked in a long, strained, staring match, relying on only the slightest movements to communicate with each other. And Henry was losing.

"Mia—"

A morose-faced butler pulled the door open, letting the night chill seep in and cutting off her father. Anne clambered out, muttering about the new fashion of the skirts and their impracticalities. She shuffled to follow behind. Henry's hand flashed out, blocking her path. His gaze explored her face, seeking something that Mia didn't know if she had in her.

"I've never known princesses," Henry said in a hushed whisper. "Only queens of lost lands. Do you understand?"

Mia searched his face, then realisation slotted into place. Without waiting for her reply, her father leapt from the carriage and pushed into the masses.

Night had fallen, and so had Mia's hope that Idris would come.

They had planned to meet at the sixth bell, and it had already rang, leaving the droning noise in her ears. And he hadn't appeared, wearing that dimpled smile and casting those emerald eyes at her.

What is keeping him? Mia thought, her thumb dragging over the scar on her forearm. *Would I know if he was hurt, bleeding out again?*

She had longed to hear the deep rumble of whispered compliments on her skin as he pressed his lips to hers. Instead, her heart kept leaping at the sight of a male, only to feel heavy disappointment when they would politely smile at her and disappear into the castle. Maids and butlers shared confused looks, waiting for her to enter the party so they, too, could enjoy the steady flow of alcohol. Music and laughter had already spilt out into the night-cloaked garden. She waited for one moment, then another, until a butler cleared his throat and gestured to the door.

Mia cursed, swinging through the doorway. Her fingers wrapping over the scar, hoping that whatever bonded them would call through the night and draw him to her. She stepped into the over-warmed entrance to the castle, lips screwed into a pout. A nagging, annoying thought stuck to her mind. *Have we truly ended the creature's bloody hunt?*

With each snapping step on the marble floor, she kept glancing over her shoulder, searching for him. Until the court herald squeaked, yanking his foot out from under hers. Mia cringed and sputtered an apology.

Grumbling under his breath, he turned and bellowed into the crowd of muttering voices and clinking glasses. "Presenting Lady Mia Ashmore, the adopted daughter of Lord Henry and Lady Anne Ashmore, Emissary to the Westryn Fae."

Many glanced her away, and Mia simply held her chin higher. Hushed whispers behind fans and intrigued looks surrounded her. No one was looking at her, but beyond her.

"And her escort, Prince Idris Blackwood, first of his name, son of the true ruler of vampyres, King Mortias."

Mia whirled around, expelling the air in her lungs with a relieved sigh. Idris was standing in the doorway, clad in crushed black velvet, fitted tightly to his muscular body. His hair was loose about his broad cheekbones, free of the stubble. An ethereal glow cascaded encircled him, much like the one that lit him when she was in his bed.

Idris stepped into the room, commanding the air as if he were still a prince, destined to sit on a bloody throne, meeting each curious gaze with a cool, indifferent glare until his glinting gaze met hers. He winked as that smug smirk spread across his face.

He'd arrived just in time.

The world quietened for a moment as their gazes locked, and a spark flared. An urge surged within her to keep anyone from laying eyes on what was hers.

Mine. He is mine.

Idris stalked over to her, bowing low, then offered her his arm. "Lady Mia. You look breathtaking this evening."

She reached out and slipped her hand over the soft velvet, feeling the hard muscle under her fingertips. "You honour me with your presence, my prince," she said, her voice flat.

"The pleasure is all mine," he shot back.

She pulled him closer, stepping around people, ignoring the side-eyed looks. "I thought you were..."

Idris' hand caught hers, running a soothing thumb over her knuckles. "I was only late, my Mia. I made a promise to stay alive."

Mia pushed up onto her toes and pressed a kiss to his cheek. "And I will hold you to that, Old Man."

An outraged noise came from an over-powdered woman, dressed in outdated fashion, who looked both of them up and down in disgust as if they had stripped down and he'd taken her right there on the marble.

Idris sighed and clenched his jaw. "They hate my father, and by extension, me. To be honest, I was avoiding this. But now, your reputation is tarnished, and people are dragging your name through the mud with mine."

Mia barked a laugh. "My reputation? That has been ruined since the Delectu Processum, let alone the poison Luc whispered through the court about me. Being seen on your arm is the least of my worries tonight. Do you recall the plan?"

A thoughtful look flashed over his face, melting into that smug smile. "The one you made me recite in your bed? I vaguely remember, but truth be told, my mind was elsewhere. I wanted to make you moan my name again with just—"

"Idris, please. We're in company," she cut in, giggling. If she wasn't already hot, that would have sent her boiling. "I was surprised you felt comfortable coming to my bed after..."

Idris stiffened, and that smirk faded a fraction. "I feel safe with you. I always have."

An emotion swelled in her chest. "And that makes me glad, Idris."

A well-dressed blond man stepped into their path, his pointed teeth bared. Mia recognised him—the scummy vampyre from The Cauldron. His eyes flicked over him, then at her, revulsion curling his lip.

Mia had little patience for any shame-laced words he'd spit at her. Not then.

"It seems like you have finally found a man to feed from and fuck you," he spat at her.

Mia scoffed. "Please, as if you weren't begging to touch me only a few months ago."

He ignored her, turning his venom on Idris. "And you, scum. You're bold to show your face here. Go back to whatever feeding den you've crawled out of. You're no prince. Not after what that monster did."

Idris' eyes hooded as the muscle in his jaw fluttered, but he said nothing. The blond vampyre snapped a hand out, shoving him. Idris stumbled backwards.

"You're not welcome here. Go."

Mia stepped close to the raging vampyre, demanding his gaze with a raised chin. He turned the snarl to her, but she wouldn't baulk or show a drop of fear.

She had faced scarier men and won.

"And who in the Heylla do you think you are? Prince Idris is my invited guest, and you will treat him with the respect he deserves, or Lord Hartwinn will be the one you answer to."

His snarl transformed into a sneer. "*Respect?* Did his father have respect when he killed my sister, her children? When he massacred innocents? This man—if you can call him that—knows nothing of respect."

Idris stiffened beside her, but again, he remained silent. He cast his eyes across the room, unfocused.

"Not scared of Henry Ashmore, now, are you?" Mia snapped, stepping a fraction closer. "Not going to run at the mention of his name? Should I beckon him over and tell him some things you said to me?"

The vampyre rolled his tongue over his teeth, shaking his head. "Do you have your blood whore speaking for you now? Not man enough to defend yourself or the monster you were shot from?"

A low growl came from Idris. "Say that again."

"Blood whore."

A punch was thrown, knocking the smirking vampyre to the ground. Sharp gasps and whispered words surrounded them. Guards pushed off walls, stepping towards them with hands falling to pommels.

Idris loomed over him, chest heaving. "Speak about her like that again, and you'll be begging to meet the rest of your family in the afterlife after I'm through with you."

Mia flicked her hair over her shoulder and smoothed her skirts, then leant over. "You're a snivelling nobody. You pray on drunk women at bars and pubs. It makes me wonder who the actual man is here. Now, I wish you a good evening, sir. May Oryah shine on you."

Mia gripped Idris by the tunic, pulling him away. The vampyre whispered, "Slut," as she passed him, making Idris pause, fist clenching.

"Come, now, we have to present ourselves to Princess Constance. She is expecting us."

Mia dragged Idris into the line of those waiting to scrape before Hartwinn and his future daughter-in-law. Anger radiated off Idris, bristling him. Mia could hear the sharp, skin-prickling sound of him grinding his teeth.

"You won't have anything to chew with by the end of the night, if you keep going," she joked, attempting to cut the tension.

He exhaled, relaxing his jaw a fraction. "You let that worthless vamp talk to you like you were nothing."

She scoffed, rolling her eyes. "I don't particularly care what a random vampyre says about me. Especially one who is afraid of my father."

The line shifted forward, and Mia slipped her arm through his, pulling her to him. "He spoke to you much worse than he spoke to me."

Idris lowered his gaze, his eyebrows knotting. "I have been called far worse."

She nodded, pressing her lips into a pout. "I'm very sorry to hear that, Idris."

He raised his eyes to hers. Words threatened in her chest—ones Mia wanted to say—but instead, she swallowed them. She peered around the man in front of them to Princess Constance, who looked dreadfully bored. Her narrow face was in her gloved hand, lips pouted. Her dress was a pale blue, her skirts spilling over the arms of the chair. However, it wasn't the princess who had her heart racing.

It was Wyn.

He was clean-shaven, wearing gleaming armour and had a sword on his hip—a striking image of a dashing knight.

A rush of traitorous heat flooded Mia's lower belly as their eyes met. Something battled between them, fighting for dominance, making her breaths speed up. Wyn's gaze dragged over her, pulling the tension taut. He exhaled, causing his lips to pop open. He took a small step forward as if transfixed by her. A sharp shake of his head had him settling back into his place, hand tightening around the pommel of his sword until his knuckles whitened.

"*Beautiful,*" he mouthed at her.

Mia cast a grin at him, dipping her chin and casting a glance through her eyelashes. Softening, his face betrayed the hurt he felt upon seeing her arms encircled around Idris.

"Why is your heart rac—"

"No reason," she cut in, her voice an octave higher

She dropped Idris' arm, eyes falling away from Wyn, only to grasp herself around her rib cage. Her skin was blazing. *Is it from Idris' words or Wyn's gaze? Or are the fires burning, heating the room to a stifle point?*

A drop of sweat ran down her spine as she fanned her face.

She was hot.

"Are you well?"

Mia puffed. "Just warm. Is it too warm for you?"

"No—"

The sharp movements of Wyn cut Idris off, indicating for them to step forward. Mia did so, smoothing her skirts. Hartwinn came into view, sitting on his own throne, dressed in thick green velvet lined with threads of bronze. A solid ring of gold sat on his sodden brow. But his face was pale, gaunt. He looked sicker than when she had seen him only a handful of days earlier.

"Uncle Hartwinn," Mia called out, racing up the stairs, skirts in hand.

He pushed off his chair with a slight sway, grinning. "God Deus, Mia, you look absolutely awe-inspiring."

"And you look—"

"Well, Mia," he cut in, grin fading. "I am well."

Those hawk-like eyes flashed to her, making her slow her steps.

"As you say, my lord. Hopefully, we can find each other and discuss the events of the other night. I have many questions."

Hartwinn sighed and slumped back in his chair. A slight sheen of sweat coated his brow. "As you always have, Mia. But I'm afraid I'm far too busy to answer them tonight. How about tomorrow? Tea?"

"Tomorrow, then. Not too early. I fear I may have a sore head in the morning."

From the corner of her vision, she could see Idris' eyes narrow and eyebrows pull together. Confusion flashed across his features. Mia turned to him, hand waving, reminding him to bow. He bent at the hip, low and slow. When he rose, his gaze captured Mia's. That mischievous twinkle had returned.

Their plan had begun.

Hartwinn's stare slid over Idris—slowly, calculated. "You're a surprising guest tonight, Prince Idris."

Mia gripped him around the arm, her hand patting the tensed muscle of his bicep. "But he is welcome here?"

He chuckled. "Yes, Mia, always. Any friend of yours is a friend of my court. But I fear he will not find fast friends here. There is too much hurt from the past, I believe."

"Thank you, Hartwinn. Now, where are your sons? I have to make my rounds."

Hartwinn waved his hand to the bustling crowd. "Somewhere in here, I think."

"Not getting up to any mischief, I hope," she said, still smiling.

"So do I," he mumbled. "Now, Mia, this is—"

"And what is this we are discussing?" Princess Constance interrupted, her accent indicating a life of governesses and ladies' maids. Her pouting lips smoothed as she took Mia's gown in. "That is quite a dress."

Mia gave her skirts a rustle, letting the light capture the beading. "Thank you, Your Highness."

"We appear to not have met yet, and here I thought I'd bet all the eligible ladies in Alderdeen."

"I'm far from being an eligible lady. I'm Lady Mia Ashmore."

Princess Constance scoffed a laugh, her blue eyes twinkling. "You are *the* Mia?"

"The one and only," she replied drily.

"You're all this court can speak of. I have heard a great many things about you."

"Wicked things, I hope."

"Downright sinful, and this is..."

"Idris Blackwood, Your Highness," he answered, bowing his head.

Mia waited for the pupil-dilating expression of desire to emerge on the princess' face, but found only the cool calculation of a shopkeeper inspecting goods. And she wasn't too pleased with the offerings.

"At least he is, well, something to look at."

Idris tensed, but his mouth curled into a grin, his pointed canine brushing over his plump bottom lip. Mia could barely keep it together at the sight.

"I presume both of you are attached. What a shame. I could have had fun with you." She paused, smirking. Her eyes lingered on Mia's heaving chest, then returned to her face. "Actually, I could have fun with you both."

"Constance, stop this leering and discussion of topics that are below you. You're marrying Reagan, and that is final," Hartwinn snapped, his voice cutting, sharp, thick with threat. A ruby flashed on his finger as he reached over for the arm of her chair, snapping a hand around her elbow. "If you continue to proposition men and women, you will be confined to your chambers until the wedding,"

Mia's stare widened, eyebrows knotting. She had never heard her uncle speak so sharply, or so roughly. Her gaze flashed to Constance, who pursed her lips, sitting back, her eyes shiny with tears.

"Princess—"

"Is none of your concern, Mia, and your presence is becoming arduous. Now, take your leave," Hartwinn said, turning his hard gaze on her.

Idris tapped twice between her shoulder blades—the signal. Mia swayed, clawing at her dress. Breaths came in short, panicked pants. Idris turned, whispering her name, voice laced with faked concern.

Constance straightened a fraction, arms relaxing. "Lady Mia, are you well?"

"I feel so faint," she panted, swaying. "My bodice is too tight...Can't breathe."

Mia's eyes fluttered closed as her knees gave way, throwing a hand out.

Idris caught her before she hit the cold stone floor. He heaved her into his arms, embracing her snugly against his chest. "I will take care of her, Lord Hartwinn. Let me see to this pesky bodice."

Mia heard footsteps, then a stray, clammy finger pushed a strand of her hair back. "See that you do, boy. She is precious to this court."

With that, Idris carried her from the ballroom, past whispering women and the clinking of glasses into the cold, quiet corridor. It was time to find Kali's file.

Fifty-Three

The cool air of the corridor brushed against Mia's overheated skin, swirling Idris' abhorrent male scent into her nostrils. She dragged him deeper into her lungs as if she had been pulled from a crashing current, and he was the precious air she desperately needed.

Suddenly, she was aware of Idris' firm grip on the outside of her thigh, the warm fan of his breath on the bare skin of her décolletage, and how it sent a shivering sensation down her body, right to her tingling core.

"You're a piss-poor actress, Little Witch," he whispered in her ear.

Mia grinned into his chest, allowing her hand to slip over the soft crush of velvet to the nape of his neck. She pulled him down closer, only inches away from her lips. She wanted to press her lips to him over and over, to taste his salty skin with swirls of her tongue.

"Now, you may play a damsel in distress, but there is no need to kiss this prince charming."

"But what if I want to?"

"Then you must show some restraint."

"Can you put me down, Old Man?"

Idris set her on her feet, but his hands lingered on her biceps, burning his touch into her skin. She pulled from his gentle hold, rubbing the feeling away. Something was boiling inside her—a deep, swirling desire, a feverish need, a devilish want.

She couldn't shake it.

Mia whirled around without mentioning for him to follow her. She needed distance, as her mind was foggy, clouded with Idris, when she should have been sharp, focused. His footsteps hurried behind her. She could sense his presence lingering with every step she took.

"Mia, are you sure you're well? Your scent has changed," Idris whispered, words sliding down her spine, adding to the popping boiling at her molten core.

She arched into him like a cat in heat.

He could smell her.

She wondered what she smelt like to him. Was it the sharp stink of turps from her art, or the delicate lavender of her shampoo? Or was it a wild, untamed scent of fresh rain, mixed with the heady fragrance of roses, encased in the woodsy scent of moss? Like a long-forgotten garden, with overgrown shrubs.

Mia shot him a grin over her shoulder. "I'm well, Old Man. I was simply worried I would have to employ Wyn again, but you finally showed up."

He didn't share her grin. "No, I'm serious, Mia. Are you—"

"I'm fine, Idris. We should hurry, before our absence is noted."

Her head snapped each way, searching for oncoming guards. She was familiar with all the nooks and crannies of Valliss, like the deep lines on her palm. But the path to Hartwinn's office was one she knew the best. As a child, she would race Kali through the hallways and court-yards, right to Hartwinn's bronze doors.

They soon found themselves in front of a metal-encrusted wooden door. Mia gripped the worn handle and yanked it down.

Unlocked.

An unsettling feeling skittered up her spine, putting her on edge. There weren't many locked doors in Vallis, but that one should have been.

With a soft *creak*, Mia swung the door open and dragged Idris inside. In a shuffle of limbs and gripped material, she shoved him against the wood. Sticky sweat had pooled under her breasts and in the deepness of her armpits, making her skin slick. Her body was hot—not sitting-in-the-sun warm, but like a feverish sickness had taken hold.

Idris peeled her hand from him. "Concentrate, Little Witch."

"I'm trying to..." she breathed. "But you've made me very distracted."

Idris smirked but gently pushed past her, striding over to the large, impressive desk made of the same wood that surrounded Alderdeen.

She took a steadying breath and shoved off the wall.

"Do you wish to discuss Wyn?"

"Wyn?" Mia asked, circling the desk. She pulled open drawers, shifting papers and forgotten trinkets. She hoped her voice would remain even. She hadn't told Idris how she had almost fallen into his bed again. "Why do you wish to speak about him?"

"You don't think I saw the way he was looking at you?"

"And you don't think I see the way people look at you?"

"Don't change the subject." Idris paused his searching with a sigh. "Mia, he looks at you as if the heavens have opened, and he has had a glimpse at Oryah's great gardens. Was he one of the me—"

She shot him an unimpressed glare, stopping him mid-sentence. "First of all, he does not. Maybe he simply had something in his eye. And I would prefer to keep whatever happened between me and Wyn in the past, where it belongs."

"He is transfixed by you, Mia. You can't tell me you cannot see it," Idris muttered with a scoff.

"I care not for how Wyn Neverclove looks at me, and neither should you. I am yours, Idris. All yours."

He stepped in closer, tucking a strand of hair behind her ear. "I guess if I'd face death—even the gods themselves—for you, Mia, another man's gaze is nothing."

She reached for him, finding his muscular forearm. "And you will never have to face them alone again, Idris."

"Bound by iron, if I recall correctly."

Mia frowned at him, eyebrows furrowing. "Can't it be something soft?"

"I can bind you in velvet, if you wish," he murmured, voice rumbling like a summer storm, eyes alight with a hungry look.

Mia swallowed hard, mopping the sweat off her brow. Her mind wandered to an erotic vision of her hands pinned above her and the weight of his body on top of hers as she squirmed, begging for that wicked release.

"Concentrate, Old Man."

Idris chuckled, and it skidded over her skin. She quietly cursed, yanking on a locked drawer and almost pulling her shoulder from its joint. "Of course."

Mia crouched, pursing her lips, inspecting the lock—simple, made of brass. She swirled her finger over the round edge. She hadn't seen a key in her scrambling through Hartwinn's drawers, nor did she have time to conjure keys until her head spun.

She concentrated on the fluttering emotion Idris gave her. Warmth fell from her fingers, as a slip of a shadow swirled from her, right the lock. She commanded them to work the teeth and the gears. To unlock the secrets held in that drawer.

"Mia, you need to be careful—"

The *click* of a lock opening stopped him mid-sentence.

Mia captured the soft mists in her hands and whispered, "Clever Ozul."

She shot Idris a shit-eating grin, making him groan and roll his eyes.

Pulling the drawer open, she picked through papers with names, locations and figures, caring for the only file with Kali's name embossed on it. It was at the bottom, under maps of proposed city extensions. A soft sigh fell from Mia as her fingers traced over the neat script of her sister's name.

"I have finally found you, Kali," she whispered.

She straightened, leaving the drawer open. She could see Idris crouch down and pluck up the worn, thinned golden ruby-encrusted ring Hartwinn used to wear—replaced by the shining one he wore that evening. He brought it to his face, his eyebrows narrowing with each sweep of his eyes.

Mia was too engrossed with the file in her hands to notice the soft curse Idris emitted, nor the soft tremble in his fingers. She finally had found the evidence—the bloody dagger.

Apprehension filled her. Even so, she didn't let the shake in her hands stop her from finding answers. With an exhale, Mia flicked open the file. Her eyes scanned the words, describing her sister and her wounds in cold, unfeeling details. She turned pages to find the Silver's reports of how Reagan's rage left bruises on her body, of her fear for him.

Kali was crying out for help from those who were supposed to protect her.

And they did nothing.

Her jaw ground, and her anger ignited inside of her as the words, "Close file. Lord Hartwinn to pursue," burnt into her mind.

"Bastards," Mia muttered, slamming the documents to the desk, her hand digging and searching in the drawer. Paper scattering across the floor. "There has to be more."

Her fingers slid over a ripped envelope. Kali's handwriting curled over the front. She snatched it up, yanking the letters free. The date on the first was over two years earlier. Only days after discovering Kali and Reagan in the maid closet.

> Hartwinn,
>
> I am writing to implore you to reconsider our marriage proposal. We are in love, so deeply and totally in love.
>
> We could bind our families in love, like you attempted all those years ago.
>
> I will be the best wife and daughter you could ever ask for. This will be a happy marriage, and bring forth an heir you would be proud of.
>
> I'm not below begging.
>
> Kindly Yours,
> Kali Ashmore

Mia flicked the worn, yellowed pages over to find Hartwinn's swirled reply, a day after.

Kali,

My decision is final. Please come to Valliss for tea, and we can discuss further. There is nothing I would like more than to have our families join. However, there are many reasons I cannot approve of this marriage.

Hartwinn

Mia's eyes darted across the words. There was years of correspondence between them. All with the same story of Kali's pleas to marry, slowly morphing into replies that screamed fear and confusion about what their love had transformed into. What Reagan had turned into.

Kali's last letter was dated six months before her death, and was written hurriedly. Mia smoothed it out, almost feeling her sister's emotions lingering in the words.

Uncle,

I have just heard about Reagan's engagement to King Ewan's daughter, and it broke my heart.

Not for me, but for her.

I implore you to reconsider casting her to him. Marry her to Tobias, to Brimm. But not to Reagan.

He is a monster.

I have no other words for it.

I see flashes of the man I once loved, and I tried holding on, like you suggested.

But I cannot believe the man who went to his knees to tell me he loves me would do such wicked things. He scares me, Hartwinn, and I worry I cannot stop this heart from loving him, even if he is Diabolus himself...

Is there a cure for true love?

Any way to rip him from my very being before he tears me apart?

I feel so alone, Uncle.

No one knows but you, and I'm scared I will lose you too, as I have lost Mia in her paints. She cannot see what is happening, and I don't know if I can go to her. She holds such anger for Reagan. This would only fuel the fire....

Tears blurred the last of Kali's letters. In two stray teardrops, the unspoken words she wanted to whisper to her sister slid down her cheeks, falling on the page, smearing the ink.

"We have found it, Idris—the bloody dagger—and I'm going to see Kali get the justice she deserved. The one that was withheld from her."

Enthralled by the gem, he made no attempt to answer her.

"Are you even listening? I said I found proof," Mia snapped as she stomped over to him.

She snatched the ring from him.

"Mia, no—"

An iciness emerged from her palm and extinguished the flames under her skin. Something slithered over her wrist, coated in sticky darkness.

Sweet creature, that malice-filled voice whispered. *What have you found?*

Mia dropped the jewel, scrubbing her forearm with tight fingers. It bounced across the plush rug, finding home against the whirling marble. With an unseen eye, it stared up at the pair.

"What the fuck—"

"You shouldn't have touched that, Mia," Idris murmured, voice wavering. Fear had gripped him. "He knows about you now."

"He? Who are you talking about?"

"Mortias."

"Mortias is dead, Idris, and that is simply a ruby."

His unwavering gaze never left the ring. "That is not a normal gem. That is a sanguis ruby, seeped in Mortias' blood. They were a conduit for his magic, and if fallen into the wrong hands, they could create havoc."

"Not havoc, Old Man, dhampyr. They are vampyre-made. This is how they are being made," Mia stated, realisation making her breathless. "But if he is dead, then shouldn't his magic have died with him?"

A flicker of emotion triggered the muscles in Idris' face to tense. "He shouldn't be able to use any magic where he is. These stones disappeared during the massacre. No one knew where they had gone."

"Then how are they here? How does Hartwinn have them?" she asked, her questions firing hard and fast.

Idris' gaze snapped to her. "Them? What do you mean by *them*?"

"He is wearing one tonight. But so has Reagan. Even Luc wore a ruby necklace the night he tried to...hurt me."

Idris ran a hand over his jaw, eyes working in their sockets. "Good goddess, Mia, this is bad. Unquestionably bad."

Booted footsteps came from outside the office.

With a curse, Mia launched herself across the room, dragging Idris with her. She slammed Kali's file back into the drawer and scooped up the scattered letters, jamming them into her pocket. After kicking the drawer shut, a wisp of a shadow flew into the lock, securing it.

Mia pushed papers and trinkets from the desk, letting them fall off the table in graceful descents and hard thuds. She worked fast, sloppily, pulling Idris' shirt from his pants, unlacing them. Sharp protests came from him, but he didn't stop her furious movement. She slid herself onto the solid wood, yanking her skirts up. She grabbed him by the waistband and wrenched him between her legs. His hands, almost instinctively, went to her thighs.

"Come here, Old Man, and kiss me."

"As you command, my Mia," Idris breathed over her.

As soon as her mouth met his, a dam broke, flooding her with desire. She pulled him closer, leaning back on an elbow. His hands slid up, dragging her skirts up. Nothing mattered—not Kali, not the witches, or the creatures lurking. She only cared for the soft press of his lips on hers and the tight grip he held on her thighs.

The wooden door swung open, then a sharp gasp came from behind her. But she couldn't stop. Only when Idris pulled away was the spell broken. She blinked, confused, lost in the magic of their embrace. Mia glanced over her shoulder. Hartwinn stood in the doorway, flanked by Wyn and Dilon. His face pulled into a sour grimace, arms crossed.

"Mia Ashmore! What do you think you are doing?"

She pushed Idris back, a dramatic sigh coming from her. "You said you locked the door!"

"You told me you didn't want it locked, Mia. What did you say? It was more thrilling if we almost got caught."

She narrowed her eyes at him, lips pursing. His mischievous smirk curled again, dimpling his cheek. She wiggled off the desk, righting her skirt. "I just thought we could share a private moment, Uncle. I didn't think we'd be interrupted."

"Mia, you shouldn't be alone here with him."

Idris slipped his arm around her, pulling her closer. "It was my idea. We barely get a moment of privacy. I thought we wouldn't be missed."

"You didn't think, Idris. That's the problem. You will sully Mia's good name by acting untoward her. Especially you."

Wyn refused to meet her gaze. An icy, neutral look had spread across his features, making her heart clench, allowing that slither of shame to unfurl in her guts.

A strained smile spread on her face. "Uncle Hartwinn is right. I believe we got swept up with each other. We should get back. Mother would be looking for me."

"Yes, you should," Hartwinn said, his voice cutting. "Next time you want to ruin yourself, go to a room that won't be used. Maybe a maid's closet. Your sister was fond of those, wasn't she?"

Mia locked eyes with her uncle, a frown forming. "So was Reagan, if I recall correctly, or do his tastes only extend to those who wish to see how deep his coffers are?"

"What my son does is his business, Mia, and you best remember that. Or has the drink you seem to enjoy muddled your mind?"

Her gaze dropped to the floor, cheeks burning, capturing a glimpse of the gold and ruby glint on the marble. She silently cursed. With a wobbly step, she fell to her knees. Her hand captured the ring, swallowing the uncomfortable feeling creeping across her skin.

"My mind works just fine. What about yours, Uncle?"

Hartwinn's eyes narrowed a fraction more. "Get up, Mia."

Idris pulled her to her feet, tugging her behind him. Her fingers slid the ruby into his back pocket.

"May we have a moment alone?" Hartwinn asked, waving a hand. "If you please, leave us."

Leaning down, Idris pressed a kiss to her crown and whispered, "I'll be right outside."

She nodded, squeezing his arm. She watched the men slip out, closing the door with a soft click.

Hartwinn's shoulders sagged, fingers pinching the bridge of his nose. "Does your father know about him?"

"Of course he does."

"And he approves of him?"

Mia shrugged, linking her hands together. "Henry has little say in the men I pursue, Uncle, as it should be."

Hartwinn leant against the wall, crossing his arms. "You're something we don't see in this court often. Someone who cares not for the rules and ways of proper society. Your mother was the very same."

"Anne always speaks fondly of her time in your home. I wouldn't think that this life chafed her as much as it does me."

"Well, considering who you are, I presume it goes against your nature."

Mia froze, her hands clenching tighter. "I'm not sure I follow…"

Hartwinn pushed off the wall, gaze hardening. "Don't play coy with me, Mia."

She took a step back, shaking her head. "I don't know—"

"I know what you are," he said evenly. "Exactly what you are."

Her world tilted, breath constricted in her lungs. If she weren't already damp with sweat, she'd have been pouring it.

"And that is?" she asked, through a stiff giggle and an unconvincing smile.

"Do you really wish for me to say it out loud? You should be more concerned about who will hear it."

Mia could feel the rough rope on her wrists, and the heat flickering at her bare feet. She needed to get out—now. But, if she fled like a scared cat, she would give herself away. Instead, she slowly edged around the rug, towards the door.

"I don't know what you're talking about, Uncle Hartwinn. You aren't well. Maybe you should sit down and rest. I'll call for a maid—"

"No. You know exactly what I am speaking about, girl!" he cut in harshly. His eyes blazed with something that verged on madness.

Mia cowered back from his tone. She couldn't help it. The ghost of Luc's fingers brushed over her throat, and that stomach-clenching fear spiked in her.

"I don't, Uncle," she spluttered. "And I would like to leave now because you're scaring me."

"No. Not until you say it."

"I..." Mia started, blinking. "I don't know what you want from me."

"I want you to confess to me what manner of monster I've let grow up in my court and be around my family."

"I want to go, Uncle, and enjoy the party."

"No! Not until you tell me who you are," Hartwinn demanded, pointing at her. "What you are."

"I'm Mia Ashmore, the woman you watched grow from a little girl. The same one who you gave that paint set for Starmorn. Do you remember? You even let me hang that god-awful portrait that I did with those paints right in this castle. I'm your family."

"It was truly awful," he muttered, scrubbing his face.

Mia shared a calming smile. "It was. Now, I think that ring is making you sick, Hartwinn. That's no regular ruby."

"Reagan gave it to me. He wears a matching one."

"That is what I am worried about. Let me help you. This isn't you—"

"Help me?" Hartwinn leant forward, his hand flat against his chest. "You existing here has put us all at risk. How do you think King Ewan will take it? He will not be kind after we have hid you from him for all these years, especially after he has been searching for you. No, I will burn. Alderdeen will burn."

"He doesn't have to know. No one has to know, Hartwinn. This can be our secret."

"A secret?" He scoffed at the words. "You cannot fathom what I had to sacrifice, Mia, only for you to ruin it all."

"I don't understand, Hartwinn."

"I want you gone, Mia. Out of my city. And if you refuse, I will cast you to those flames myself."

She took a stumbling step back, blinking. "I have nowhere—"

"You have until the end of the week to go, or so Deus help me, I will not hesitate."

"You're exiling me?" Mia asked breathlessly.

"I'm giving you a running start. That is the only kindness I can give you."

"A kindness? Casting me from my home is not a kindness."

"What I am doing is nothing compared to what Ewan will do once he gets his hands on you. The end of the week, Mia. Not a day later."

"King Ewan's coming, isn't he?"

"No. Something much worse," Hartwinn said softly, his eyes becoming misty. And that boiling rage dissipated, making his shoulders concave. It was as if his rage had exhausted him, draining him for all that he had. "Something I have spent years hiding from and praying it wouldn't come. Death, Mia. My end. And the beginning of something much more monstrous, terrifying."

"Please, let me help you. I've fought death and won."

"There is nothing you can do, Mia, but leave Alderdeen. I'm an old man with regrets of decisions made by a young man, desperate to prove himself."

Mia set her jaw, shaking her head. "There is something—"

Hartwinn's hand snaked out, gripping her by the elbow and dragging her to her tiptoes. In his bloodshot eyes, she could see her own fearful expression reflected at her.

"Run, Mia. I mean it, unless you wish to light your own pyre," he commanded through clenched teeth. He dragged her closer until she could feel his warm breath on her ear. He smelt wrong. Not the warm spice she recognised, but the same rotting flowers Reagan smelt of. "And stay out of that tree, witch."

FIFTY-FOUR

Mia ran past a confused Idris and Wyn. Her legs couldn't take her fast enough away from Hartwinn.

Witch. Witch. Witch. Witch.

The word grew in her mind until it was a roaring scream.

Her breath came in pants, her lungs rejecting anything deeper. She launched herself into the crowd, searching for her father, but the bodies were so tightly packed that she could hardly see past the ruffles of fabric and the sheen of velvet. She needed to find Henry, tell him she loved him with all her heart, and that they would find each other again. Then she had to escape Alderdeen and run into the woods before she felt the lick of flames on her skin. Yet, Idris dragged her back, his hands gripping her thighs, and his firm and sure kisses snatching her breath away.

Jumbled thoughts filled her mind as the need to flee tangled with irrational feelings of desire. Even her body was torn, mixing the panic with a throbbing need.

A hand locked her around the wrist, dragging her on the swirling dance floor. Her other found hard muscle, trying to shove them away. Instead, a tangle of arms dragged her in closer as fingers slid dangerously close to her rear.

Her eyes flashed to those twinkling blue orbs.

Reagan.

He crooned her name in one long sigh, fanning his too-hot breath down her neck.

Her stomach turned, allowing a creeping prickle to sweep over her clammy skin.

"You look obscene in that dress. I can almost see the pretty brown swell of your nipples. Not that I'm complaining."

Mia clenched her jaw, squeezing her eyes closed. A concerning dizziness overtook her senses, making her feel intoxicated, but not a sip of alcohol had passed through her lips.

She was at a melting point, right when a fever was at its worst.

"I know what you're doing, and why you did it," she whispered back.

Reagan led her into another dance, the strumming lute music picking up around her. "And what is that, Mia?"

"You've been making the dhampyr, and you sent one after Kali."

He flashed that sickly sweet smile at her. He leant closer, lips skimming over her cheek. "Do you know what is sad? You're right, Mia. The dhampyr are of my creation, but Kali was digging into things that didn't concern her. But all she was digging was her own grave."

Her eyes widened as his words sank in. She broke free from his iron cage of his arms and shoved him so roughly that she stumbled forward.

"You did it!" Mia yelled, voice cracking with emotion. "You killed her!"

As the music screeched to a halt, people turned, and those dancing milled around them. Curious and judgemental eyes fell on her, but she ignored them.

Idris pushed his way through the crowd, standing behind her, ready to defend her or fight with her.

Reagan's mouth curled into a sly smirk. But something was wrong with it—too tight, too twisted. "By Deus, how much have you had to drink tonight? See, everyone? Mia is exactly what Luc said. A *drunk*."

She wiped her forehead on the back of her hand, smearing strands of hair across her face. "I have drunk nothing."

"Then do you have no shame anymore, Mia? I just heard that you were caught in my father's office. Can't resist a bit of blood, vamp? Much like your father."

Her gaze flashed over her shoulder to a tense Idris, his hands bunched into fists. A frosty, deathly glare skimmed her skin, only to burn into Reagan.

"Don't you dare speak about him like that," Mia warned, stepping forward, her boot catching on the hem of her dress and tripping her. She fell hard on her hip, right at Reagan's feet. Her body was sloppy, with movements untimed, uncoordinated.

Something is truly wrong.

"Kali really kept you in check, didn't she? Now you're nothing but a belligerent drunk." Reagan leant over to a lady, dressed head to toe in gold, and said, "I swear, I saw Mia at Madame Diamone, throwing herself at men for a handful of coin—"

"I'd watch your tongue, boy, if you ever wish to use it again," Idris interrupted, his voice bone-chillingly terrifying.

Princess Constance forced her way through the crowd, her small hands pushing people past. Concern tightened her narrow face, her gaze flicking to Reagan. "I demand to know—"

"Shush now, betrothed. You're in no position to demand anything," Reagan interrupted, silencing her.

Mia's heart raced, thumping in her ears. She shifted to her knees, readying herself for more venom to be spat on her. He was tarnishing her in the eyes of the court, portraying her as a fool so no one would believe a word she spoke.

"And I guess we all know how you got your apprenticeship."

His final barb cut deep, right down to the bone, spewing images of Luc's expired body over her open eyes. Her hands clenched so hard that her nails dug crescent-shaped marks into her skin. Whispered gasps surrounded her as more judgement-filled gazes fell on her.

"Fuck you," she spat, the curse full of vitriol.

"What is the meaning of this?" Henry thundered, pushing through the crowd.

Wyn followed close behind, snarling at any he deemed a threat. Henry's eyes found Mia on the floor, then flicked to a smirking Reagan. His face hardened, lips smoothing into a thin line. Mia struggled to her feet, her body swaying. The room spun out of control, making her eyes lose focus on Reagan. Idris stepped in closer, hand on her lower back, steadying her.

"How much, Mia? How much have you had to drink?" Henry asked, gripping her elbow, jostling her.

"I'm not drunk!" she yelled at him. Tears welled, leaking one at a time down her red cheeks. "He killed her, Papa, and he's going to get away with it."

Reagan stepped forward, a hand over his heart. A condescending expression crossed his features—one Mia wanted to claw off. "I loved Kali. I would have never hurt her. We're family, and it's clear you're hurting, so I will forgive you for this."

Mia spat right in Reagan's face. The sticky glob dripped down his cheek, then onto the lapel of his jacket.

"Shove your apology up your arse, prick."

The silence was deafening.

Henry roughly pulled Mia behind him, his broad body protecting her. "You'll pardon her, Reagan. She is still in the throes of grief and acting without thought. As we are all aware, she loved her sister more than anyone."

Reagan pulled a handkerchief out of his pocket, flapping it out and wiping the spit from his face. "Of course, Lord Henry. However, I will expect an apology when she's sober for ruining mine and my betrothed's ball."

"You have ruined it yourself, Reagan," Constance muttered, lip curling in disgust.

Mia shot him a glare that was sharp, cutting, hoping it would find whatever was left of his cold, dead heart. She fought the hands that held her. "I'd rather claw out my own—"

"Stop," Idris whispered in her ear. "Don't let him keep baiting you. It's what he wants."

Mia slumped back into him as Reagan gripped Princess Constance by the elbow and dragged her off. Henry refused to meet her gaze, but the frown and the ire burning in his eyes made a sob leave her. Then another, and another.

As the crowd dissipated, gossiping amongst themselves, she found herself encircled by the three men who cared about her most in the world.

Mia stomped into the night-cooled gardens, cursing herself as she scrubbed the tears from her cheeks. She had lashed out and poisoned her own claims against Reagan.

No one will believe me now.

The chilly air swirled against her clammy skin, taking the edge off her anger. But it still burnt deep in her belly. Heavy-footed strides followed her, boots crunching on the gravel. Henry's hand snapped around her elbow, turning her to face him. She had seen him angry, seen him rage, but this was worse. The emotion flowed off him like thick vines, lashing at her. His magic seeped out, making even the manicured hedges lean away.

He was furious, blood boiling and all.

"What in Oryah's name was that, Mia? Have you lost your damn mind?"

"He did it," she pleaded, tears welling. "I know he did, Papa. You have to believe me."

"Save it, Mia. You're not a child anymore, thinking you'll get your way with a few stray tears and a wobbly lip. You not only embarrassed myself and your mother, but you accused Hartwinn's son of *murder*. That is serious, and if unfounded, damaging to not just you, but our family's reputation."

"Is that all you care about? My *reputation*? I couldn't give a fuck about what a single fucking pompous arsehole thought of me. Don't you care about finding who did that horrible thing to Kali? Do you care at all?"

Henry's eyes narrowed, but the tremble in his jaw made Mia wonder if she had gone too far. "Of course I fucking *care*. She was my daughter, Mia. My daughter," he hissed, slapping his hand on his chest. "You don't get to say that to me, Mia, after you...disappeared for weeks on end, making me worried I'd have to identify your body at the Medicus Tower as well."

She raised her chin, determination filling her. She hadn't sunk into the abyss, even with its sweet siren's call of nothingness. What she had done was not let herself feel, pushing it away. All so she could be strong for her family. That was a different numbness. A concentrated separation of what she was screaming inside, and what actually left her mouth.

"I disappeared? I've been picking up the pieces of whatever remained after Kali died. I have. I have worn our family's grief across my shoulders like an ox in a field, dragging my sadness behind me, unable ever to look back. Pushing it aside so I can be strong for you and Mama." Mia flung her arm out, pointing at the beaming light from the rambunctious ball. "That, in there, was my last straw. I won't stand for it one moment longer. I will not allow myself to swallow words when I should be heard."

Henry's face crumpled, hiding away that fury, leaving only chest-tightening sadness. "Have you been hurting on your own all this time?"

Mia shook her head. "No, not on my own."

"But you needed us, and we weren't there?" he asked, voice wavering. His jaw shifted from side to side as if he was willing himself not to cry.

"I needed you when I went through Heylla, Papa. But I found that all I needed was in here," Mia explained, pointing to her chest, right over her heart. "I have a fire burning in my belly, and that is all thanks to you and Mama. You're the reason I survived."

A sob left him, and he crumpled into her arms. Her stoic father was heaving, crying against her.

It crushed whatever shards were left of her heart.

Mia didn't want to hurt him, not in the slightest. She realised that hurt and love were on a scale, and it was a delicate harmony to get it right. All her attempts had swung the scale, forcing it to teeter, never truly balancing. She enveloped him up as tightly as she could as he apologised over and over. All she did was squeeze him tighter.

"He did it, Father. You have to believe me."

Henry pulled from her, turning away, scrubbing the tears from his face. Mia slumped on the closest bench, her joints aching as if she had spent the whole evening dancing.

"What is your proof?" he asked with a sniff.

Mia hesitated for a moment, then, her hand slid into her pocket. Her fingers dragged out the letters she had taken from Hartwinn's office. She smoothed them on her lap and traced Kali's words.

"Reagan was hurting Kali, and she was afraid of him. Terrified. But she had stumbled onto something relating to Hartwinn and this court."

Henry's shoulders coiled tightly. "What does Hartwinn have to do with this?"

"He is acting bizarrely, Father. He just cornered me in his office and was ranting about his death."

Henry turned, surprised. The emotion worked its way through the sadness on his face. "No, you are mistak—"

"Why does he have Kali's files? Why are they corresponding about a sickness affecting the court, about Reagan hurting her? Kali had found something, and Reagan silenced her by sending a bloodthirsty creature after her. It was him, and Hartwinn is hiding it for his son."

Idris stepped into the garden, Wyn hot on his heels, their looming presence cutting through the long shadows cast by the torches. Her eyes immediately locked onto them, grappling with the incessant need for both men.

Mia dragged her gaze back to her father, who was smoothing a hand over his shaved scalp, gaze hooded, lost to the knowledge she had given to him. "I don't know, Mia. That is pretty flimsy evidence."

"Flimsy? He just confessed—"

A sudden slice of pain from her womb cut her words from her mouth, making her arch, and a soft hiss slid from between her teeth.

Henry reached out and held the back of his hand to her sweaty forehead. "Mia, you are burning up."

"Something is off, Papa," she gritted out as agony erupted again, forcing each of her muscles to snap tight.

"It's the *Ritus*, Henry," Idris said quickly. "She is entering it—"

"She isn't old enough for that," Henry cut in, words sharp.

"Witches are supposed to go through the Ritus at twenty-five. Mia is only twenty-one. Do you know anything about my daughter, aside from what her bed feels like?"

Idris' lips smoothed, but Mia spoke first. "You know what I am?"

"Of course I do," Henry stated matter-of-factly. "You are my daughter."

"Hartwinn. He knows. I have to..." A deep groan ended her words as another wave of pain crashed into her. "He exiled me, Papa."

"He did what?" Wyn asked, the strain clear in his voice.

"More importantly, how does he know what you are?" Henry asked, shooting a dark look at Wyn.

He held his hands up, shaking his head.

Mia had no clue how he knew, but it frightened her. She rubbed her lower belly with the heel of her palm. *Is this fever and this pain a seed that hasn't taken root inside of me, demanding to be shed from my body?* She shook that thought away. She'd been careful, even with Idris.

"He said something is coming," Mia answered. "Something evil, dark. That it was a kindness to exile me."

The mens' gazes met, and a hardness emerged on Idris' face. "I have nothing to do with it, Henry. I promise."

"He is—"

"I would never let him near her, and I dislike what you're implying, sir."

"Near who?"

No one answered her. The men closed the distance between them.

"You were his favourite son, weren't you? Is this all a trick?" Wyn asked, gripping Idris by his shirt.

"How dare you! I love Mia. I would never let that monster—"

"You love me?" Mia cut in, softly. "Truth?"

Idris' gaze fell on her, and she saw nothing but that sweet, warm beam of comfort he'd often look at her with. "Truth."

As fast as that fluttering feeling grew, pain's sharp claws slashed it. "Something is really wrong with me."

Wyn cursed, shoving Idris back. "We should get her to Rosda Manor."

"And have her exposed to Henry's help and put her in more danger?" Idris asked, shaking his head. "No, she is coming with me."

"How dare you! My staff would never," Henry gritted.

"I'm going with Idris," Mia mumbled.

"What?" Wyn and Henry asked simultaneously.

She pushed off the bench, her legs weak. Idris reached out, taking her elbow. As soon as his fingers brushed her sweaty skin, a switch flipped inside of her. She threw herself at him, slamming herself into his torso. Her lips found his, forcing them apart with a roving tongue.

"Mia, stop," he muttered against her. "Not here."

Her hands frantically roamed his body, slipping down his abdomen, right over his soft manhood. She dragged her hand over it, hard and fast, aching for it to stiffen.

He pushed her back, just to an arm's distance, but it felt like miles. His face was serious, yet something akin to fear lurked in his gaze. "Mia, you're in the throes of the *Ritus*. You need to control yourself."

"Am I?" she murmured. She traced her spilling cleavage with both her hands until she skimmed over the heavy roundness of her own breast, biting down on her lip.

Wyn hissed under his breath, eyes diverting away. He looked pained, as if her desire hurt him.

"When did this start?" Henry asked.

"She has been in the beginnings since she stepped into the castle. The feverish skin, that wild look. Even her scent has changed. Her magic is free-flowing off her. It's only a matter of time before her companions appear, exposing her to the entire court, and I doubt they will be as accommodating as Hartwinn," Idris explained.

Mia was hardly listening, more focused on getting the silver buttons of his tunic undone. She couldn't think of anything else aside from that delicious stretch as Idris pushed inside of her. He slapped her hands away and cast a hard look at Henry. "You know I'm the only man she is safe with, right? She's vulnerable, and I can resist the pull of her lust."

"'The Ritus takes what it wants'. I remember Maeve saying that," Henry said absent-mindedly, as if lost to a forgotten memory. "They become...overwhelmed by it."

"Their magic is cruel and raw. Therefore, we cannot know how she will react."

Wyn settled behind her, his hands skimming over her biceps. He leant in, pressing his lips to her crown, and whispered a solemn fae prayer into her hair.

"Be safe, *m'eudail Mia*."

Henry's eyes narrowed. "You step away from my daughter right now, Wyn Neverclove, or you'll lose your favourite appendage."

Her hand snapped out, yanking him closer to her by his sword belt. Pushing onto her toes, her lips grazed his.

"Wyn," she breathed. "I *need* you."

He gently pulled her fingers from the leather and placed it over Idris' thundering heart. "Go with the vampyre, Mia. You belong with the man you love over one you simply spent a night with."

Mia shook her head, biting down on her lip to quell her disappointment.

"Go, Mia," he repeated, a fraction harder.

"You're wrong, Wyn," Mia said, her voice growing soft. "I am drawn to you, as I am to Idris."

His gaze flashed, and in the split moment that their eyes met, she saw hope. The emotion sent a jolt through her as a whisper of something old and something fated electrified her, sending her skin prickling. Both Henry and Wyn's gazes rose to the darkened heavens.

Wyn stumbled back, his face aghast. That lightness dying in his eyes, he murmured, "This cannot be..."

Without finishing his sentence, he fled into the night, his shining armour catching in the flickering lanterns, leaving her almost choking on her need for him.

Mia had found herself ensnared with both men. Idris and Wyn had tangled like prickly vines around her thundering heart, squeezing. What flooded out was pure desire. She needed someone to dive into the current and save her. Idris had stormed into the water, pulling her to safety, whereas Wyn had allowed her to splash and sink.

Idris hoisted her into his arms, pulling her close to his warmth. "Come, my Mia. Let me take you home."

"Please, Idris," she whispered, before nuzzling her face into his chest, arms looping around his neck. A calmness filled her as soon as his grip tightened around her hip. Idris turned, walking from her father.

Henry called out, "You keep her safe, boy. If not, I fear for you and what I will do to you."

Then, all Mia heard was the soft *thud* of Idris' heart, and a harsh curse from her father as the man she loved carried her from Valliss Castle.

Fifty-Five

Mia groaned, loudly and frustratingly, as Idris deposited her down on a leather-backed armchair in the cosy lounge room of his home. With slow bated fingers, she drew small circles over the fine stitching, her head lolling to the side. "Good goddess, I think I'm going to die if you don't touch me."

Idris grumbled something under his breath that sounded awfully like, "Stop being dramatic." He strode around, yanking curtains shut and dumping more logs onto the fire. The flames flared, sending sparks through the fireplace, radiating heat in the air. Mia writhed in the chair, attempting to flee from the warmth with her hands clenched in her dress.

He rose, turning to her. "You have to sweat it out, Little Witch. Your magic is building in your body, preparing you for the Ritus. But it is clouding your mind, taking away your better judgement. Making you—"

"Ablaze for you, Idris."

Mia dragged her skirts over her calves. The soft tulle glided over her knees until the heat of the fire licked at her thick thighs. She drew the toe of her boot across the floor, spreading herself before him. His eyes dipped once between her legs, and the tip of his tongue skimmed over his bottom lip.

She knew he could almost taste her. Both her blood and *her*.

"The lust has something to do with your connection with the magic building in your womb. Only female witches have true power. Males only have a flicker, whereas you have a bonfire."

"Fascinating," Mia muttered, letting her other thigh splay out.

He breathed out an uneven breath. "Witches conjure their magic from just their own blood, so their ritual is the most dangerous. The most destructive for both themselves and for those around them. Your heart will beat until it stops. But only for a moment, for your magic will restart it. One is the most vulnerable during the early stages of the Ritus. Usually only women care for them, or they hand-select males for breeding."

"How intriguing." Mia drew her forefinger over her knee, trailing up her thigh, right to the ribbon of her stocking, circling around the knot.

Idris took a step towards her, then another until he stood over her, chest rising and falling. His eyes devoured her, each flushed, sweaty part of her.

"Kneel," she commanded.

Idris bit down on his lip as he did as she instructed, making her swallow hard. Her fingers reached for him, feeling the sharp prickle of his stubble. He captured her hand, pressing a kiss to her palm, then to her wrist. A ghost of teeth dug into her flesh. "Shall I make my vow, Little Witch?"

"I think you've vowed enough to me, Old Man."

"I cannot believe..." he half-muttered to himself, shaking his head.

Mia hummed a response, cocking her head. Her finger traced his hairline, skimming over the point of his ear.

Idris didn't answer her. Instead, he let his hands spread over her thighs, fingers digging in, dimpling her delicate flesh. Then, a hand ran over her hip, gripping her. In a seamless movement, he yanked her closer until she sat precariously right on the edge of the chair.

She released a soft yelp, a smile curling her lip.

His hands slid from her, leaving a trail of warmth over her knee, down over her skin. He pulled on her boot laces, tugging them off and tossing them over his shoulder.

"By Oryah, I want to take you and your smart mouth to bed, but I cannot."

Mia's body tensed at his words, cutting into her like dulled razor blades. "You cannot?" she repeated, panicked.

She was going to drown in her desire for him, taking lungfuls of both sweetness and roughness until she sank to the bottom.

He shook his head, eyes fixed on the emerald green ribbons that held her stockings up. She had chosen the colour just for him, to match his eyes, hoping he'd drag his lips across her skin and yank them off with his teeth.

"You're not in your right mind, and I wouldn't want to take advantage of you."

"Please, for what is good and holy, take advantage of me."

Idris laughed, eyes crinkling. A smirk curled at his lip, but he simply slid the ribbons apart, peeling her stockings from her, fingertips dragging over her flesh. Then, with a gentle push, he closed her thighs.

Her hand went to his jaw, tilting his chin up. "I want to, Idris. I want you to touch me everywhere."

A line formed between his brows while his eyes became hooded. His shoulders caved in a fraction as he exhaled. "But I cannot have you touch me, not when you're like this. It brings up too many...memories."

"Memories?"

He yanked his face away from her as if he couldn't stand her touching him. Her name slipped from his lips as a warning, cautioning her. He searched the rug until his mouth formed a thin line. "Dark memories, Mia. Ones buried within the depths of hurt and shame."

"I don't under—"

"Rowena was deep in the Ritus when she took what she wanted."

Her hand dropped to her lap, eyes on him. That darkness dented the lust she experienced, striking against it with a powerful swing.

"Idris, I..." She lost her words for a moment. "I understand."

With a soft exhale, she spread her hands over her thighs, easing her legs apart again. "Do you want to watch me instead?"

His gaze snapped from the floor, right to her. "Watch you?"

"If you cannot touch me, then watch me touch…myself."

"Good goddess," he uttered, biting down on his plump bottom lip.

"Use your words, Idris."

"Yes," he murmured breathlessly.

"Sit back."

Mia pushed up on her toes, shimmying her undergarment off. He all but fell on his rear in haste to do as she commanded. She hitched her leg over the armchair, allowing the orange flame of the fire to capture the glistening between her thighs.

Her eyes never left his as she slipped her fingers down her centre, meeting her slick arousal. She circled and curled against herself in undulating rolls of her hips.

Breathy gasps and brief moans filled the warm air, swirling with Idris' soft pants.

She couldn't tear her vision from him, roaming over his face, over whatever exposed skin she could see. Her body contorted with that tight coil of pleasure that only a release could soothe.

"Touch yourself, Idris," Mia breathed amid her erotic noises. "If you wish to."

"*Fuck,*" he cursed.

She let the rough word slip over her, adding to the molten at her core. She wanted him to mutter like that against her flesh as he was diving into her. But if this was all they could do, then it was enough.

Idris tore into his pants with such speed, she worried he'd rip the fabric from the seam. His fist disappeared and she watched, salivating, as the muscles in his forearm flexed with each rhythmic stroke. She ached to drag her tongue over him, to savour that sticky saltiness, and to have his fist threaded in her hair as she choked him down.

"Good goddess, Mia. I've taken myself in my hand more times than I can count, just thinking of you."

"Tell me what you fantasised about. I want to know each dirty, filthy thought."

Idris whimpered her name, his hand working faster. *He must already be close.*

"Tell me."

"How divine it feels when your pretty little cunt flutters around me when I'm pleasuring you."

Mia's fingers worked hastily, dipping inside of her, only to encircle her swollen nub. Her nails dug into the soft leather as her eyebrows met in the middle. Her release was building in crashing waves.

"What else?"

His chest heaved as his breath came out as a shudder. He closed his eyes for a moment, as if to centre himself. "That you tasted unholy, something conjured by the gods to only send a man mad. And by Diabolus, I want to sin."

"Sin? What we did is not sinning, Idris, it's making love," Mia breathed.

Idris rolled on to his knees, hand gripping the arm of the chair. His whole body strained under the material of his shirt, so as not to crash too quickly. As if he didn't wish the moment to be lost, gone in the seconds it took for the pleasure to peak and subside.

He moaned her name with each stroke.

Panting and writhing against the leather, Mia teetered on the edge of her own release. Her toes curled as her back bowed off the leather. She uttered his name.

"Not yet, my Mia," Idris commanded, voice gravelly. "Not yet."

She glanced at him, her face pleading. "Please."

Something snapped in him.

Idris was suddenly all over her—lips on hers, fingers skimming over her curves. He pulled her from the armchair, right to the floor. Yanking her underneath him, his broad chest caged her.

"Are you attached to this dress?"

"No—"

"Good."

Idris' hands flew to her on her bodice, ripping the delicate fabric away, sending the glittering gemstones scattering. He cupped her breast, sucking at her brown nipple, making her moan and shift her thighs together, desperate for any friction.

He peppered open mouth kisses up the large swell of her breast. Teeth dug into sensitive skin. He glanced up at her, tongue swirling over her, waiting for her to say the words.

"Feed, Idris."

He smirked at her, showing those damned dimples. His teeth sank in, blood gushing into his mouth. Her hand grasped around the back of his head, threading her fingers through his hair. Elation and desire entwined as he drank deeply, making her core throb with each gory suck. His lips popped off her, pressing bloody kisses up over her collarbone, up over her throat. "I want to give you everything I have—my heart, my body, my soul—right here. Until we cannot think of a single thing outside of this room. Until nothing can touch us."

"Nothing can touch us here, Idris. Nothing."

A lie—a dirty, rotten lie.

They both knew it.

The real world always fought its way back into their lives, hurting each of them, scarring each of their hearts.

Mia brushed her fingers over his lips, making his tongue dart out, tasting her. "These are mine." Her hand dropped to his chest, spreading over his thundering heart. Over the scar that maimed him. She raised her gaze to him. "And this is mine."

"It's yours. For as long as you'll have it."

"Until the great goddess calls us home, Idris, and in every lifetime after that. I am yours."

Those three words had been growing in her chest with each fleeting kiss, each soft smile fusing with that fluttering, light feeling.

Idris exhaled, his eyes searching hers. "Truth?"

"Truth."

Mia pulled him down, right to her lips, tasting the sharp copper on his tongue. The frantic need was gone, as was the roughness he had taken her with before. A careful softness had replaced it. As if it was now more than the demand for each other, more than the ache of a release. It was a yearning to be closer than she had been with anyone, to allow their bodies to melt into each other.

Becoming one.

Mia revelled in it, not shying away, yet Idris hesitated, as if he stood at the cliff, knees locked.

"We can stop..."

He pressed a kiss to the sharp edge of her jaw, then over her cheek. "No, Little Witch. I don't want to stop."

Mia reached over, pulling his face to hers. That darkness lurked just beyond his gaze. "You never have to do anything you don't want to, Idris."

"There will be things I cannot do, Mia. You're going to do things to me that will evoke those memories."

She stroked his cheek with her thumb. "I only need you, and by Oryah, I have you. That is enough."

He remained silent, solemn. Until he broke it. "What if I do, Mia? What if I desire more than those sweaty nightmares that haunt me? More than that, what if I want them gone? It's been so long, I almost forgot what feeling safe meant. But, Mia—my Mia—in your arms, I feel safe."

She could have wept. Instead, she pulled him closer until their foreheads touched. "Then let's fill the spaces between where our hearts are cracked with love and joy. What do you say?"

Idris kissed her softly, but she could taste the wanting, the need in each sweep of this tongue. And she had her answer.

A passionate, unwavering *yes*.

Soon, clothing was stripped from bodies, casting the luxurious, heavy fabric to the floor. Corset lacings were yanked, freeing her as his fingers smoothing over the redden marks left by the cage of steel and fabric. He leant down, pressing kisses to each of her freckled shoulders, right to the sensitive spot near her jaw.

"Mia. My Mia," he breathed in her ear as his hand slid between her legs, fingers finding her at last.

Mia gasped, pressing her forehead into Idris' shoulder, reading herself to plummet into her release. "Idris, my love."

His hand tangled in her hair, pulling back. "I want to see you."

Mia's hand went to his bare chest, pushing him back right to the floor until he lay flat on his back. If he desired to see her unravel, he would, and she would give him her all.

Idris cursed under his breath as she straddled him, hands splayed on his muscular chest. With one quick thrust, she slid down onto his manhood, groaning with each aching stretch.

Through hooded lids, she watched as pleasure pooled in his eyes, spilling across the muscles in his face as she rolled her hips, allowing him deeper inside her. A slip of his thumb over her core built that radiating pleasure.

"You look glorious," Idris muttered.

Their eyes never left each other. No more filthy words were whispered, only the sounds of their bodies meeting as pleasure was pulled from them in languid thrusts. Breathy moans and sharp pants filled the air as they fought to the precipice of their desperate releases.

An intense release shattered her over and over until she was nothing but a moaning, panting mess of pleasure. Ozul exploded from her, filling the warm room with misting shadows, spreading from her in black tendrils.

Idris hissed under his breath, eyebrows meeting. He drove his hips up, forcing himself even deeper until he was flush against her. Mia watched with satisfaction as his face contorted with ecstasy, as a foreign phase slipped from his lips in hurried murmurs. With one final thrust and a rough mutter of her name, Idris spilt a warm heat inside of her.

Mia collapsed onto his heaving chest, sticky and sweaty. A coolness brushed over her bare skin. For the first time that evening, her body was not on fire. That fever had broken when she moaned his name into the air.

Idris held her closely as if she would slip away and disappear, like the morning fog. He pressed a kiss against her temple and murmured that phrase again.

"What are you saying?"

"A prayer, Mia. Pleading with whatever god is listening to let this last," he mumbled against her forehead. He continued with a soft voice, so soft she wasn't sure he had even spoken. "Begging all the gods to let me have you. To let me love you for the rest of my days."

Mia curled deeper into his arms. She wanted that moment of serene peacefulness to last. But like all things, it would only fracture and break if she held it too tightly.

Fifty-Six

Mɪᴀ's sʜᴀʀᴘ sᴄʀᴇᴀᴍ sʜᴏᴏᴋ ᴛʜᴇ ɢʟᴀss ɪɴ ᴛʜᴇ ᴡɪɴᴅᴏᴡ frames in Idris' bedroom. Her pain echoed around the too-small space. Bodies of those she loved crammed into the room, hovering over her, pensive and afraid.

Time had drawn thin as the Ritus built and built for three days to the final demanding stage. Each tick of the clock reminded Mia that the agony would drag on until her heart stopped, only for her magic to surge, awakening the beating once more. Until then, agonising pain awaited her at every turn.

With each jerk, her sweaty body slapped against the hard stone. Lost was the pleasure that filled those nerves. Her magic was painfully pulling each muscle apart, stitching them back together to rip apart again and again.

Her magic could not be contained inside her, crawling under her skin, desperate to break free. Shadows flowed from her overextended fingertips, lashing out at any which they deemed a threat, who was anyone who strayed too close.

"Quickly, Ben. Hold her down. She needs the tonic," Idris bellowed.

Strong hands grasped her shoulders, forcing her down. Panic slammed into her chest, only reminding her of Luc and the horrors she had faced. Her arms lashed out, her nails catching skin. A cry escaped her, followed by a wet sob. "Let me go. Please. I want to go home."

Hands released her with a painful *hiss*.

Mia's eyes snapped open, her body arching off the stone floor. Her jaw burst apart, spewing shadows through the air from her agape mouth in thick black smoke. Ozul swirled around her extended arms to soothe her. But nothing could calm her—not even Oryah coming down and laying her healing hands on her. Nothing.

"Come on, Mia," Benny encouraged, kneeling beside her. "You're stronger than the pain. Fight it. Sorcha will be back soon, with your father and more potions."

A sobbing howl fell from Mia as she curled in again. Tears hadn't stopped flowing, leaving salty trails over her reddened cheeks and soaking into the collar of her shirt, and in the painful cracks in the corners of her lips. What was worse was that her body rejected any food or water, making her sick across the stone, and over anyone who stood too close.

Pain dragged its long bony finger over her soft flesh, only to dig ragged fingernails in, splitting skin over her back, opening scars which should have stayed fused shut. Blood bloomed on the oversized white shirt, staining it a maroon red. Her delirious, panicked gaze caught Idris —who looked utterly terrified. She wanted to reach out to him, but her limbs were numb, too heavy to lift.

James' tense face appeared over hers, his lips in a tight line. "This is women's business, Idris. It always has been," he explained, unstopping yet another vial of poppy milk. "We shouldn't even be here. We need to call Vivan. She needs a witch to share the pain."

"Aren't you a witch?" Idris snapped.

"Do I look like a fucking *woman*, vamp?"

"Fucking Heylla. Just give her the potion, James, then get the damn witch," Idris said, his voice harder than she had ever heard it. "She's in agony. Can you not see that?"

James' gaze flashed to him, eyebrows knotting over his eyes, but his hand stilled.

"Give her the potion, witch," Idris repeated with a growl, stalking over to them.

"You've blood-bonded, haven't you? You're feeling her pain—"

Idris snatched the vial from him. "I have done none of the sort. That would be stupid and reckless."

Mia whimpered, her body trembling against the stone.

Benny's hand found hers, squeezing tight. "This is not the time to discuss this, nor is it any of your business what Mia and Idris have done, James."

Idris grunted in agreement. His face was relaxed, but terror still lingered in his eyes. He slipped a hand under her head, lifting it up. "Open up for me, Little Witch."

She parted her dry lips just a fraction. A bitter liquid splashed over her tongue, but her body seized again, spitting the potion down the front of his shirt.

Magic was demanding she feel every single ache. No potion would stop that.

Another gash bloomed down her chest, right between her breasts. Pain had taken a fresh swipe at her for trying to ruin its fun. Mia bellowed, rolling to her side, curling tighter and tighter. If only she could have retreated further inside herself, she might have evaded the pain. But it found her every time she hid away.

"Go! Now," Idris commanded roughly, causing James to scurry away.

Idris' hands hovered over her, but his eyes wholly focused on the pooling patches of blood. His eyebrows met in the middle, deepening the crease between them as he bit down on his bottom lip. Benny's calming hand on Idris' forearm caused him to jump and scramble back from her. He shook his head, trying to shake away a thought—one she knew was coated in the same warm stickiness that ran down her skin.

Mia lifted her aching arm, whispering his name.

"I cannot..." he spluttered, shaking his head vigorously. "I cannot be here. Please forgive me, Mia."

Idris backed towards the door frame, bumping his shoulder on it, and fled down the stairs.

She cried out, her hand still reaching for him.

She *needed* him.

Her voice echoed with a soft, wallowing cry as she called his name again and again, all while spasms of pain shuddered through her body. A loud banging and crashing came from downstairs as Idris rampaged. Even so, Benny never left her. His concerned gaze skimmed over the seeping patches of blood until the wounds clotted and the blood dried.

"He cannot be around you. Not like this. It'll be awfully hard for him to listen to yet another witch scream," Benny explained gently. "I think it brings up too many painful memories."

"But I need him," Mia cried, sniffing. "I cannot do this without him."

Footsteps slammed up the stairs to fall heavily beside her. Mia's eyes could only make out their boots. She rolled onto her back, more tears leaking down her cheeks.

"How long?" a woman demanded an answer. A soft cotton of a skirt brushed over her arm, as someone knelt next to her. "How has she been at this stage?"

"Three days," Benny answered, sounding far away.

"Three days? Fucking Heylla, and you only just now called for me?"

"I thought I could—"

"You thought wrong. And James, I expected better of you. She needs a sister witch."

"Sorry, Vivan..." James grumbled.

"Three days ago was the new moon? Strange. Did she become—"

"Yes," Idris cut in sharply. He had returned. "Like all the others."

The woman with the wildly curly hair leant over Mia, searching her face. A soft hand rested on her arm, making her jump.

"You."

"Hello, witchling." Vivan softly smiled down at her, then her eyes dropped to the wounds peeking from Idris' shirt. Cringing, she continued, "I'm here to help take some of your pain away. All witches grapple with the Ritus at twenty-five—"

"Twenty-one," Mia whispered hoarsely. "I'm twenty-one."

Vivan frowned, cursing. "You're far too young for the Ritus to be sparked, and it is much too dangerous for it to proceed. But I don't have the right ingredients to make a potion to stop it, let alone the time. You've come too far." The witch shot a glare at each man in the room.

"One of you should have really called for me, for this may actually kill her. Her magic may be too immature to restart her heart."

Mia's eyes slid over to a glassy-eyed, red-cheeked Idris. He shifted on the balls of his feet, refusing to look at her.

"Well, you're here now, Vivan. Please help her, save her. Do whatever you need to do." He paused, his voice getting softer, gentler. "She hasn't stopped screaming."

A pensive smile clenched the fine muscles of Vivan's face. "You're at the pinnacle of the Ritus, witchling. The suffering you've endured until now will only worsen."

"Get...worse?" Mia spluttered. *How can it get worse than this?* It was torture, pure agony.

"Yes, but I'm going to take your hands and share your pain. This is the way of the witches. No one goes through this alone."

"I haven't been alone," Mia said, nodding to the men. "They haven't left me."

"I'm glad to hear that. Now, let's get you onto your knees."

A door opened and slammed. Her name was being bellowed in the expanse of Idris' house, hurried and breathless, but it wasn't the softly accented tones of Sorcha.

It was the deep rumbling of her father.

"Papa!" Her voice cracked as she called for him.

She could hear boots racing up the spiral staircase, still calling out her name. He emerged, wide-eyed and sweaty, in the doorway, with Sorcha following close behind him, her healer's bag in her arms.

"I found him, Mia."

"Papa!" she exclaimed again.

"My moon," Henry breathed through a relieved sigh. He shouldered himself right between Benny and James. "You're alive. Praise Oryah."

"You're truly here?" she cried. *Am I so lost in the pain that I have become delirious, hallucinating him?*

"I would search high and low across this cursed land to find you, Mia. I will always come when you call."

Fresh tears fell down her face, her heart swelling at the sight of the dishevelled healer. "And you came back."

"Of course I came back, Mia. A bit of screaming wouldn't scare me away. "

"Hello, healer. It's lovely to see you," Vivan purred at Sorcha, making the flush deepen on her face. "Now that everyone is here, shall we begin?"

* * *

Vivan's grip had tightened on Mia's forearms, dimpling the tender flesh. She commanded all to be quiet, and closed her eyes.

That was ten minutes earlier.

Mia kept letting soft groans slip through her clenched lips. The witch's eyes flickered under her lids, searching in her mind's darkness.

"This is no normal Ritus," Vivan finally said, breaking the silence.

"No shit," Benny whispered with a scoff.

Mia's gaze snapped to Idris, who watched from the corner, his muscles coiled so rigidly that she worried they would snap under the strain. But with each muffled groan, his face twitched, as if he could feel her distress.

Sweat poured from her body. Pain was brushing against her skeleton, deciding which bone to break first. She swayed, her consciousness was slipping. Idris' name fell from her lips—a quiet plea for him to be closer.

"You're not helping, witch," Idris growled.

Sorcha whirled around, dropping to the floor, hands digging through her healer's bag, glass clinking with each hurried dig. "I could try some more poppy seed and banes root—"

"No, healer. No more," Vivan commanded, her voice filling the room.

Her eyes snapped open, an iridescent glow circling her pupil. Vivan's magic swept over Mia's skin, sending her hairs straight up. Her own responded to the call by pulling and reaching. A single shadow slipped from Mia to swirl around Vivan's narrow wrist.

"Let go, witchling," Vivan said, her pupils still glowing. "You need to let go of the hold on your magic, on yourself. It's demanding to be set free."

"*No fear,*" Ozul murmured. "*We keep you safe. We force you back into the land of the living.*"

Mia shook her head. Her cracked lips moved, however, no sound came out. Terror kept her grip on her shadows at a stranglehold. She dared not loosen a finger. Not while she was so out of control.

"You must, or it will kill you."

Mia's fingers trembled. In the silence before Vivan spoke, a serene voice whispered right into the shell of her ear, "*Let go, my heart.*"

Then, another called out, and then another, until it was a choir of womens' voices. All chanting, singing to her, filling her with such choking emotion, Mia wept.

They were no ordinary women, calling to her from beyond. They were witches.

A soft smile spread across Vivan's face, her eyes glistening. "Hello, sisters. How I have missed you."

"You can hear them too?"

"Yes, Mia. I hear them on the summer breeze, late at night under the full moon and in the last whisper of dreams. It's our fallen sisters, guiding us, protecting us. You need to heed their call."

Mia needed more than ghosts of witches' past. She needed him—Idris. She captured his gaze from across the room, and love sparked between them like thunderous cracks of lighting, shaking the ground.

"Come here," she whispered, her voice more hoarse with emotion than the wailing she had endured. "I need you here with me, holding me to this plane of existence."

Idris launched himself at her in hurried steps, slamming onto the stone next to her. His hand cupped her cheek, his eyes searching her face. A desperation glowed in his emerald pools. "I can't lose you too."

She shook her head, a worn smile edging on her lips. "You will not lose me, Old Man. We are bonded now. Me and you. Tied together."

A tear rolled down his cheek as he smiled. "Chained together, Little Witch."

Mia pressed a soft kiss to his trembling palm. "With iron, until Oryah calls us home."

She cast her teary gaze around the room, meeting eyes with each of those she loved. Lost after Kali's death, she had thought she was alone wandering the world, but that was never true. She found a blazing light amidst the darkness, burning in the people surrounding her. In those who loved her for who she truly was.

The voices were building again.

Sorcha and Henry glanced above them, as if their fae ears picked the rumbling vibrations, concern bunching their brows. But Benny cracked a wide grin, his eyes glassy. "Hello, sisters."

Her father lowered himself next to her, pulling something from his pocket—the glittering gold and emerald bracelet. His eyes lingered on the gems and rose to hers. "Kali is here, too, watching over you."

Mia reached out for her father, gripping his hand, squeezing the gold between their palms. "I need not for Kali when I have you, Papa."

Henry exhaled, a smile spreading. "Then you must listen to those who came before you."

Vivan hissed in pain, her face clenching. A gleam of sweat coated her forehead. "Hurry, Mia."

Sorcha's touch landed on her forearm, then Benny's on her shoulder. James enclosed his fingers around her wrist. And the man she loved tenderly slid behind her, dragging her to his chest—a solid presence when her world was slipping away.

A blaze of heat burnt in her belly, her magic roaring against the pain.

"Let go, my heart, and let that wondrous magic flow from you," that soft, serene voice said, floating over her and settling on her aching shoulders like a cosy blanket. "Your sisters and I will keep you safe. Free yourself from the chains that have shackled you."

She knew the voice. It was Maeve Magntai. Her birth mother.

Hazy golden memories burst over her open eyes. Ones of children playing in sunny fields, warm tight hugs, of squeaked laughter erupting from tickling fingers and a solid hand on her back soothing her. A blissful time before the ash and smoke. It made Mia weep, her shoulders shaking. The flare of magic uncovered memories that had been hidden from her. She was loved, so wholly, so fully, by someone she could hardly remember. But her heart remembered, and that was enough.

With a sniff and a shaky breath, she simply let her magic go, like a soft exhale from a lover's touch.

It felt as natural as breathing.

Mia's body snapped back, her spine straining under the unnatural angle. Shadows blasted around her, escaping from every crevice and orifice. Words spilt from her—not her own, but those of witches who came before her. The words swirled in many voices, but Mia was the loudest.

"I give myself freely to the magic inside of me, passed down from my blessed mother, from her mother, from the great goddess Oryah herself. I do not fear the power that dwells within me, as it is mine and mine only to command. I fear no shadow, be they of men, fae or witch, as I live and die by the shadows. The day grows long as the moon meets the sun. There, we are joined by the shadows."

"By the shadows," Vivan, Benny, James and Idris murmured, their voices harmonised.

Mia's hands slipped from those who held her to raise to her sides, calling to Ozul, beckoning them to her. Her constant companions.

"I am Mia Ashmore, I am shadow-blessed, and I will be free."

Shadows swirled in the room, creating a black, shadowy hurricane. Her hair slashed across her face in blonde tendrils. Her eyes snapped open as that warmth flared inside of her. It burnt her from the inside out, but Mia would withstand it, as she had withstood the pain. A ring of pulsing golden orange surrounded her pupil, reflected in Vivan's widening stare.

"*Divina Sponsa,*" Vivan murmured in a language Mia didn't recognise. "The Divine Bride."

Mia's thundering heart slowed, then stopped.

FIFTY-SEVEN

MIA SLAMMED INTO THE GROUND, HER HIP TAKING THE brunt of the fall. Towering, maroon-barked trees surrounded her, with grey storm clouds threatening a deluge rolling overhead. She pushed to her knees, dragging a lungful of smoke-peppered air in, making her cough and splutter. Black specks of cooling embers fell on her hands.

It was raining ash.

A male begged. His voice cracked with the desperation of a father trying to save his child.

Mia recognised the voice from a distant memory—one she could never touch until then. The man would sing to her, grumble at her, whisper soothing words to her late at night. Her real father.

She hadn't fallen into a nightmare of her mind's making, but a memory of ash and smoke. Before crashing carriages and dying horses. Before she had even stumbled into that courtyard in Rosda Manor.

"Burn, witch lover," a cruel voice spat. "Along with your bitch queen and your half-blood scum of a child."

The crackling sound of fire sparked to life, then the whoosh of flame licked up Mia's back.

"Cidran!" a woman shrieked. "*No!*"

That's when the screaming began.

Mia dared not turn, not shifting a single muscle to witness the horror behind her. Ash fell around her, covering the grass. But the screams persisted for a long, bloated moment until a soft groan and then silence. Complete silence. She didn't know which was worse.

A rough hand shot out and gripped her by the elbow, yanking her to her feet. "You're next, scum."

Her head snapped to the voice. A human loomed over her, his broad frame enveloping any stray light peeking through the storm clouds. He clenched his features, and pure hatred radiated from his pupils.

Mia froze.

She couldn't fight back, push against the roughness of the man. She dared to glance over her shoulder at a smouldering pile of ash and half wood. A blackness seen in the centre. They had burnt him. Alive.

"No! No!" she screeched as her broken heart throbbed in her chest.

A forceful yank pulled Mia roughly away from the embers. Her slippered feet dragged over the grass, his thick fingers tightening around her with each rough pull.

Her eyes never left ashes where her father's soul lingered.

"I'm going to end you," Mia spat at the man.

He grinned a mouthful of rotten teeth at her and crooned, "And how do you plan on doing that, princess? You're next."

A stifled sob made Mia look up. Tied to a wooden stake, with kindling surrounding her, was Maeve Magntai, Queen of the Umbra Coven—more importantly, her mother.

Her narrow chin held high, blonde strands loose around her face. Her brown eyes burnt with a fury that would force an army to falter. No tears marked her cheeks—her rage had burnt them away.

"Unhand my daughter," she commanded, with all the quiet authority of a queen.

"I think not, witch. I want to make you watch this creature you spawned burn first."

A shove brought closer to Mia's mother, and the stench of kerosene filled her nose.

Maeve's gaze dropped to her, her face softening. "Close your eyes, my heart, and think of the giant oaks that surround your home. Think of the warmth of Vespera's grand hearth. Think of the love Mama and Papa have for you, and how we will love you always."

Mia screamed out, thrashing against the grip. "Let me go! Let her go!"

"Do you reckon she'll scream like the rest of your precious sisters?"

"Ophelia is just an innocent child. Nothing more. She has nothing to do with any of this."

The man dragged her from her mother to her own pyre. Mia fought, screaming. Maeve's voice entwined with hers, pleading, begging. Her legs thrashed as he locked an arm around her waist, lifting her over the kindling.

Mia's fingernails caught him on the cheek, gouging into his flesh. He threw her down, slamming her into the dirt. Out of nowhere, a large hand swept out, slapping her. She pushed to her knees, wavering, and spat a fat glob of bloody spit right on his boots.

"You little—"

"Fuck you," Mia cursed.

He raised his fist again, but dropped to his side. The same sneer spread across his face, unnerving her. He ripped her from the forest floor, slamming her against the pole, bounding her hands. "Now, now, princess, I was about to put an end to your sorry existence before you burnt. Instead, I'm going to cut you a little, and see if you beg me to burn you."

"Don't you touch her," Maeve gritted out, fighting against her own bonds.

"Shut your whore mouth!" he spat, malice dripping from his words.

A flash of iron caught Mia's eye as it slashed down, cutting into her cheek, splitting the skin to the bone and making her scream, thrash against the rough rope. Her face burnt hot as blood poured over her, soaking into her collar.

Maeve whimpered a name too low for Mia to hear. Her eyes darted to the tree line.

"Now, now, Maeve. We both know she isn't just a child, is she?" a voice crooned—one that slithered up her spine, disappearing into the dark corners of her mind.

No. No, it can't be...

A flicker of fear cut across Maeve's face. "Ophelia isn't who you think she is."

"Oh? So she wasn't born under the Erydaysis stars, then, from two fated enemies? My mistake. You, sir, light the pyre and burn the girl."

The soldier snapped to attention, giving Mia a chance to squirm against the binds.

A lone man emerged from the tree line, made of hulking muscle and sinew. One who seemed to command even the surrounding air. His narrow face was made of lines and angles, framed by the blackest of hair. His golden-hued eyes tracked each squirming movement, like a raven searching for its next meal. He was almost birdlike with the way he cocked his head, folding his arms behind his back like feathery wings.

His face was familiar.

She had stared at it for weeks, months. Seen it in every light, clenched with pain and with pleasure. However, the man she now gawked at wasn't her beloved.

It was Mortias Blackwood, the true vampyre king, and it was his voice she'd had twisted, muttering in her ear.

"She should burn like the rest of your scum kind. But we both know that is not a good idea."

"How did you—"

"Escape? Who said I escaped?" Mortias interrupted, striding across the clearing with his long legs as if it were a throne room, not a place of darkness and death. "I will not bore you with the finer details, Maeve. Not when we have more pressing matters to discuss."

"I will die before I let you take my daughter."

From the corner of her eye, Mia saw a flicker of a shadow slipping between the binds that held Maeve. She bit down on her lip to stop the relieved gasp leaving her.

"Then you will burn, and I will take her anyway. You are not above the gods, Maeve, even if you believe yourself to be. They have woven this thread. Now, we have to follow it."

"She is a child, Mortias. You are not so depraved as to take her as your bride now."

Mortias had the gall to look disgusted. "It is beyond revolting to suggest that. Ophelia will be my bride when she turns twenty-one,

Maeve, not a day younger. When she is a grown woman, ready to bear my children. And I prefer not to even raise her. That will be up to my witches."

Maeve's mouth screwed up. "Those succubants are not witches. They are creatures of your own making."

Mia grunted, shifting her wrists. The rope loosened a fraction. But her wiggling caught Mortias' attention. His eyes fell to the bleeding wound on her face, his expression curling into a snarl, teeth and all. More monster than man.

"Who did that to you?"

The rough-handed human shifted on his feet, not speaking or looking at the seething vampyre in front of them.

"You."

Mortias moved so swiftly that Mia couldn't track him. One minute, the man was standing, looming over her, terrifying, and the next, he was a slackened body on his knees, showering blood over her. Frightened, she screamed and scrambled away from the rolling head, pressing against the solid stake. Mortias put his ruby-ringed fingers to his mouth, licking off the blood as if it were dripping honey, spilt from the hive.

"This simply will not do, little Ophelia. You were created for me, and I dislike broken things."

Mortias dragged a finger over one of his sharpened canines, cutting himself. His black blood bloomed to the surface in one fat drop. He reached over her, making her scramble and fight her bindings. She watched in horror as the blood dripped from his finger, melting into her clotting wound. He whispered an incantation, and then a chilly tingle spread over her face.

"No, no!" Maeve cried out, breaking her brave, stoic mask, shattering it to a thousand pieces. "What have you done?"

"We are destined. What is a bit of my blood really going to do? This is just to keep an eye on my bride to ensure she stays unsullied."

Maeve's wide eyes flashed to her, then to Mortias. Her mother's shadows worked faster, more hurriedly. "If the gods have truly fated you two, then she will be drawn to you, as the prophecy has said."

Mortias' finger popped from his mouth in a sick slurp. "I would rather not leave that up to the gods. And the prophecy mentions nothing of her being drawn to me, only that she is *mine*."

Maeve pleaded, begging for Mia's life, causing his attention to be dragged away from her.

A calming presence settled behind her, hands hovering over her wrists. Mia's gaze flashed over her shoulder, finding her sister untouched by death, radiant and beautiful.

"Kali," Mia breathed, her wrists shifting together.

"You need to get away, Mia. You aren't supposed to be here. This is not where you were meant to be. You were supposed to go to your sisters."

"I am with my sister."

Mia had fought, but she couldn't get free. Her gaze flicked up to Mortias, who was still deep in conversation with Maeve. Something in her cowered, frightened of him. That same thing knew it was wrong. It wasn't how the memory went. Someone was missing. Idris was missing. He would have saved them, cutting their bonds to allow them to escape.

Kali glanced over her shoulder, as if someone were standing behind her. "I cannot leave her—"

Silence cut her sister's words short.

"No. I will not—"

Silence again.

"Fine. Fine. If that's what it will take."

Kali cursed under her breath, her hands reaching out hesitantly and grasping the rope. Her face screwed up in pain, making her glow dim a fraction. She was forcing her light that surrounded her into the darkness that held Mia in the twisted memory. Kali grunted with effort, loosening the bonds enough for Mia to slip out.

Kali clasped her around her cheeks. "You've got to run now. Run like your life depends on it. Because it does."

"I don't want to leave you. Not again," Mia said, shaking her head, tears welling.

Kali's own eyes filled with tears, but pure, undiluted love slammed right into Mia. Her sister dragged her into a tight hug, then pushed her an arm's distance. "I will always be with you, watching, waiting for you to join me." Her hand pressed over Mia's heart. "I will always be here, sister, as you will always be in mine."

"I love you, Kali."

"I love you, too, Mia. Now go!"

Kali faded into nothing but ash, raining down onto Mia's outstretched hands. She didn't feel that sharp stab of grief. All she knew was the warm embrace her sister had left her with.

"Where do you think you are going? I've been waiting for you, my sweet creature," Mortias said in that calm, chilling voice.

Mia refused to turn to him. Her eyes searched the maze of long shadows and the darkness of the forest before her. The trees seemed to beckon her towards them, with swaying limbs. Waving her to safety, away from wherever terrors happened in this clearing.

Without even a glance back, she launched herself into the tree line. Her legs burnt, and with each breath, her lungs constricted. She kept glancing over her shoulder as if she could see whoever was following her. But she saw only darkness approaching, eating away the trees, soil and sunlight, like an undulating mass of nothingness devouring everything in its wake.

"You cannot run from me, Ophelia. Not here, not ever. We are destined."

She skidded to a stop, her hands in fists. "First, my name is Mia. Second, come out and face me, you coward!"

A soot-encrusted hand snapped over her mouth. The other flashed to her throat, dragging her back against a soft, plump body. She fought, struggling against the iron grip. Her hands lashed out to only strike air. A hot, metallic breath cascaded over her ear, sending shivers down her body.

"You are too cocky for someone so fresh, so young. The youth these days are impatient, proud—"

Mia's muffled screams stopped his tirade.

"You will be quiet and listen when your betters are speaking to you, witch!" Mortias commanded, his voice shaking in the darkness.

Mia's vision faded as her air supply became worryingly short. Blackness edged in until she succumbed to it.

Voices called to her through the void, dragging her to consciousness. Mia slumped to the ground, leaves and dirt cushioning her fall. All her strength had seeped from her. Even her muscles felt soft, toneless. She knew Death wanted her powerless, empty to bend to his will.

"Wake up, my heart. You have little time left," Maeve called from the trees.

"I can't fight him. He is too powerful, Maeve, and I feel so weak and tired."

A gentle hand brushed over her face, tucking that annoying strand from her eyes. "You are not weak. A fighter. That's what you are, Ophelia. You battle with claws and teeth, with shadows and magic."

Mia cracked an eye open—even that was difficult. Maeve came into view, the aged twin of her own face. Not blooded and bruised, but radiant, as she would have looked on her obsidian throne.

"Get up, my heart. I didn't pray for you for years, only to see you die in the mud."

"You prayed for me?"

"In every breath, in every heartbeat, in every quiet moment."

"I cannot remember you—"

"But your heart remembers, doesn't it?" Maeve cut in, her eyebrows bunching. "And that will have to be enough for me."

An ever-steady drumbeat filled the air. Idris and their bond were calling for her. A tug in her chest made her push to her hands and knees, fingers diving deep into the dirt. He was dragging her back to him, inch by inch. And she would respond to him with her own broken song.

"Although you are young, you have gone through the Ritus. Your magic must be powerful, above even mine, or any witch in our bloodline."

"I don't know how to use it, or attempt to control it."

Mia heard Sorcha's gentle but firm voice call her name, like a steadying hand on her body.

"Your magic isn't a wild stallion for you to break. You simply let it flow from you as if it were water flowing to the shore. The more you trust it, the more you will feel in control. Now, you must wake up, my heart. You've been dead for far too long."

Benny's voice rumbled through the ground under her, forcing strength into her tired body. Even James, in his utmost serious tone, forced her chin to rise. Each movement seemed slow and painful as if she were trudging through molasses. But what spurred her to her feet was not Idris' heartbeat, but his demand for her to return to him, in that same commanding tone that awoke a fire in her belly. The same one he would whisper in her ear with when she was in his embrace. And she needed to fight something more than a vampyre with a cackling laugh.

She needed to battle Death himself.

Meave slowly raised her chin, brows bunching to the darkening canopy above them. Her hands went to her mouth. "Oh, Idris, you lovesick fool. You will only break your own heart by loving her."

Mia slumped against a bloodred oak. "And what of my heart, Maeve? Will that break when the gods call me to heel?"

Maeve shook her head, hands dropping to her sides. A look of steely determination crossed her face. She looked like that fierce queen who stared down at her approaching doom. "No, Ophelia, you will never be called to heel. You were born of witches who spat in the faces of men who told us we were nothing because of what we had between our legs."

"Why do I feel so soft, so full of emotion?"

Maeve reached out and traced her jaw. "There is strength in that softness. Stay soft, untwisted by this cruel world. We need you. This land needs you. Now, I have to go."

"No, not yet. You can't. I have so many things to ask you."

"All the answers you seek are inside of you, my heart."

Maeve leant down to press a kiss to Mia's forehead. But, as soon as her lips found her, Maeve faded into twisting black shadows, her whispers of love brushing over her.

"Goodbye, Mama."

With each call of her name, by each one of those who tethered her to the waking world, Mia found more and more stability in her legs. Enough to stumble more quickly through the scrub.

When Idris' smokey rumble became louder, more ferocious, she knew she was close to their ironclad tether. Bushes reached out, attempting to imprison her in the darkness. For that man who lurked in these shadows. Away from that pinprick of light that emerged.

"No! No! Stop," Mortias' demands rang through her ears.

Mia snapped branches and yanked plants from the soil, fighting to get to that light. She broke through with a stumble and begged her legs to move faster, pump harder. The ground rumbled under her feet, the earth splitting in two. Trees swayed as roots were ripped from their earthly bindings.

Mortias was tearing the world apart to reach her.

"You are mine! You will never be his!"

Mia whirled around to find Mortias rushing towards her, his bloody hand reaching for her.

She smirked, the warmth spreading on her chilled skin. "You will never have me."

With one step backwards, she fell into the warm light, allowing herself to be engulfed by it, surrounded by it. She realised as she hurtled through the bright, shining void.

It was magic.

Her magic.

And she wasn't afraid.

FIFTY-EIGHT

Mia's head narrowly missed Idris' as she sat up, hands flying to grip anything that would anchor her to the world. With her fists full of his shirt and the soft cotton of Vivan's skirts, she heaved, chest expanding with each desperate drag of the sweaty warm air. Her eyes traced each crack of mortar and exposed brick as a warm hand covered hers, pressing it to hard muscle.

"You survived, Little Witch."

Mia whirled to Idris. Mortias' face flashed over his, twisting and snarling, forcing her sore muscles to tense. She let the image melt away with each moment she searched his features. It was the face of the man she loved and desired, not that snarling monster.

Tears spilt from his emerald eyes, falling with each blink. Relief hung heavily on his face. "I thought I lost you—"

Mia barrelled into him, sending them sprawling to the stone, his arms encasing her. With their bodies tangled, their lips found each other, pressing and turning. A desperate kiss.

"Never, Old Man. Bound in iron, remember?"

A laugh filled the room, then another low rumble of a chuckle. Mia pushed off his chest, sitting up. Sorcha was grinning at Benny, her head resting on his shoulder. Henry gripped his shirt, a mirror of relief on his face. But James slumped backwards, face red and sweaty, not meeting her eyes.

Mia's body ached, and she was damn tired, but that bone-crushing pain was gone. Idris was right; she had survived the Ritus.

"I need a drink," Sorcha groaned. Stretching her long legs out, she cast the witch a shy smile. "What about you, Viv?"

Sorcha's cheeks flushed, and her eyes twinkled. Mia recognised that look—the beginnings of something else brewed between the healer and the witch. What exactly had happened the night she ran into the woods and bound herself to Idris? However, Vivan didn't share her grin. She remained knelt, her hands clenched in her lap, those sharp eyes working in their sockets, piecing something together.

"Vivan?" Mia said, capturing her attention.

Her eyes rose to hers. Something akin to fear flashed. "He knows. Mortias knows you exist. We have failed Maeve."

"How?" James asked, stiffly rolling his neck.

Vivan's gaze hardened. Her hands clenched so tightly that her knuckles pushed against the skin. "I don't know, James, do you?"

As always, joy was fleeting, disappearing in that void of emotion inside Mia.

Her fingers found the rough edge of her scar, remembering the warmth, the tingle of his blood mixing with hers. "He's always known."

Idris' muscles stiffened underneath her. "What do you mean?"

Mia sighed and let her hand drop from her face. She pulled from Idris, finding the stone floor of his bedroom. She drew her knees to her chest as if she could protect herself. "He speaks to me. I thought it was my voice, but he…"

Sorcha gasped. "How can he speak to you?"

"How can he speak to me from the grave is a better question," Mia said, resting her head on Idris' chest.

Silent glances were long and tense. They weren't telling her something—something important. It was Idris who spoke first, snapping the tension building. "Correct. He cannot speak from the pit he is in."

Vivan stood, smoothing her skirts, offering her hand to Sorcha, who took it with a subdued grin. "I think I need that drink now, healer. We shall talk about this more when you've rested. It's time for celebration."

Bodies rose, and subdued chatter filled the room.

Mia glanced up at Idris, who was gazing down at her. She cast him a shy grin. She had an idea for celebrating—one that involved no clothing, his bed and him whimpering her name again. Pulling her up in one fluid motion, right into his arms, he pressed a kiss to her forehead and leant down right to her ear. "Patience, Little Witch. I'll have you moaning soon enough."

Mia flushed, a spluttered giggle falling from her, giddy at the idea.

"She is in no form for what you're disgustingly thinking of, vamp," Vivan objected. "She needs a stiff drink and to go to bed."

Idris' eyebrows pushed together, his head cocked.

Vivan tapped her temple with a long finger. "Stop broadcasting your indecent thoughts so loudly, then. I won't hear them."

"You can hear thoughts?" Mia asked, suppressing the filth that was floating between her ears.

"Unfortunately, yes. A gift and a curse from my coven. Now, drinks!"

Benny cheered, corralling the crowd from Idris' bedroom, leaving Mia and Idris alone. She reluctantly uncurled herself from him. Her eyes found the destruction—mirrors broken, chairs snapped, deep nail gouges in the stone floor, and pools of drying blood. What was once warm and safe, now a ruined battlefield.

"Idris," she whispered from behind her hand. "I'm so sorry"

He shook his head and took her face in his hands. "This can all be replaced. You, however, cannot."

THE HOT WATER PELTED HER SKIN, STINGING FROM THE HEAT of the shower and stripping the sweat, blood and tears from her, vanishing down the drain like it never happened. Mia leant back on the cool wall. The glass of whisky she'd drunk had gone straight to her head, leaving her sloppy and grinning. Idris' muscular arms caged her, blocking the raining water. Water dripped over him, running in thin rivers over sharp cheekbones, parted lips and the scars that lined his body.

Mia's eyes searched every inch of his face, trying to remember each line, every freckle. She wished for nothing but charcoal and paper to sketch him, to create what she saw in the soft glow of the candles and hazy steam. She knew, deep down, that she would struggle to capture the burning gaze he was casting her, or the feeling erupting in her chest. That could never be translated to paper.

Her hand spread over his chest, feeling the rough body hair on her palm. Other women may have been in Idris' bed, but she was the only one who held his heart. *What an honour,* she thought to herself.

"Are you my heart's match?" she whispered, so softly that it was almost swallowed by the pattering of the water.

Idris pressed a kiss to her temple. "What's a heart's match?"

"It's a fae bond of rare, powerful magic that draws two hearts together that were destined to beat for the other. Nothing can break the match. Not even death."

"I can be whatever you want me to be. Blood bond, heart's match, or..." He paused, then breathed the last word, "*Husband.*"

The skin around her eyes crinkled as she grinned at him. "Are you proposing to me, Old Man?"

He laughed, throwing his head back. "No, Little Witch. You'll know when I am proposing."

Instead of heeding Vivan's stern advice, Mia pulled Idris into a soft, unhurried embrace. Her tongue coaxed him open, slipping between his lips. Her hips rolled against his, allowing his hard manhood to slip tantalisingly between the silky skin of her inner thighs.

She needed him. Not in a burning, sweaty lustful way. She craved the connection they shared when they rolled in his sheets. It was something intimate, private and real. As if they were safe to feel there, in the dim warmth of Idris' house.

Idris pulled from the embrace, thumbing her lips open, dragging it down the centre of her throat to swirl over her peaked nipple. With each circled caress, a spark of tingling nerves awoke between her legs, making her gasp. Her hands roamed over him, never tiring of touching him.

"Take me to bed, Idris."

"It would be my pleasure, my Mia."

After the water ceased to rain down on them, and Idris made sure each inch of her was dry, Mia found herself in his bed. Hard flesh pressed into soft. Thrusts and kisses. Blood passed between lips. Their bodies begged to be joined as one, falling together in a panted, moaning release.

FIFTY-NINE

Mia stared at the nondescript house with its sandstone walls and sturdy, thatched roof. She had expected Vivan to live in a wild cottage, with vines holding the mortar up, clucking chickens and all manner of creatures lurking in her overgrown garden. Instead, they stood in the muck of the lower city, with triple-storey homes around them. A raven, glossy and black, circled overhead, searching for its supper. That jumpy, fried nervousness filled her, making her tense and constantly glance over her shoulder—as if Mylo would step out of a shadow and drag her off.

Vivan had commanded them all to come to her home via a brief but concerning letter.

Sorcha had the note scrunched in her hand, brow furrowing. "What do you think she wants?"

Mia leant closer into Idris, yanking her hood down lower. "I don't have the faintest clue, Sorcha, but being out in the daytime is making me nervous. I'm exiled, if you fail to remember."

Sorcha shot her an unconvinced look. "You're being dramatic—"

"Hartwinn has men looking for me," Mia cut in. "They've already gone and searched Rosda Manor, much to Father's displeasure. He meant it when he said he would see me burn."

Idris grunted, resting his hand on the pommel of his skull-headed sword. "And being a stubborn fool who has a death wish, you refuse to leave."

She smirked at him, elbowing him. "You really know how to make a girl blush, Old Man."

"I'm serious. You should have already left."

"I'm not going anywhere until I put Reagan in shackles, Idris, and that's final. Then we can run away into the sunset and find a debilitated cottage in the woods, and have a brood of chickens and a goat."

"How romantic," he muttered, thumb circling the skull. "Vivan has never sent me a letter before. It puts me on edge. We know Luc was forging letters for whoever is controlling the dhampyrs, for what we know, this could be a trap."

Mia rolled her eyes and knocked on the door. "Or, maybe, she is finally trusting you, and not something so dire, Old Man."

Sorcha cocked her head, eyes trained on the star-shaped rune embossed on metal. "That's a witch's mark, correct? What does it mean?"

Idris sighed and hid the sword under his cloak. "It means protection, healer. Now, let's get this over with."

Benny and Alaric, both hurried and breathless, called Idris' name right down the alleyway. He turned with a concerned bunching of his brows.

Mia knocked again.

No answer.

She couldn't even hear movement in the house, only muted stillness. The hairs on her neck rose. She could feel Death lurking. She had become accustomed to his quiet footfalls and bated breaths.

Mia reached for the handle, pushing the door open. She stepped through the doorway, searching for the witch. However, she saw the blood first, sprayed in a fine spatter across the stone floor. Scrambling, she followed the smeared, bloody handprints gripping walls and furniture, heart pounding in her ears.

The sick trail led her right to Vivan—or what was left of her.

Her throat was mangled with such ferocity that her head hung at an unnatural angle, exposing the ripped, torn muscles and the slowly leaking arteries. Her eyes, which held such emotion, were open, vacant. Her now-cold hand reached for Mia as if she could somehow save her. She slumped against the wall, her palm over her mouth to prevent the contents of her stomach from spilling out.

Vivan was dead.

Mia heard footsteps, then Sorcha's voice teasing Idris, and his low chuckle. She moved away from the door, rushing back through the room to protect Sorcha from the same nightmares that made her sheets tangle and her body sweat.

Mia's arm snapped out, blocking her entry. "You don't need to see this."

"What are you doing?" Sorcha blinked at her, confused. "Whatever do you—Mia, is that blood?"

Sorcha pushed past her, forcing her against the doorframe. A scream erupted, filled with horror.

Mia launched herself at her, wrapping her arms around her, yanking her back with such force that she lifted her off her feet. Yet, she fought Mia's tight grip, reaching out for Vivan.

"No, no, no..." she cried, voice cracking with each word. "Let me heal her. I can heal her."

"Sorcha," Mia urged, struggling to hold her. "It's too late. She's gone."

Their legs tangled, sending them to the cold, hard floor. Mia's arms locked around Sorcha's middle, dragging her between her legs. A wallowing sob broke out from her, fingers outstretched. "Please, Oryah. Please. Let me heal her. I beg you. "

Mia glanced up at a pale Idris, slumped against the doorframe. His gaze ran over the massacre, taking in each droplet, each smear. Benny and Alaric were last through the door. Her uncle fell to his knees, inches from the pooling blood. He muttered prayers into his palm, eyes wide. Mia rocked the sobbing Sorcha, her hands still meekly clawing at Mia's forearm.

The sad realisation hit her, causing her to blink back her own tears —yet another witch had been snatched from the earth. Death chuckled as he slipped from the room. She had cheated him, and he returned to take another as retribution for her spitting in his face.

"I thought we killed it, Idris."

His face hardened. "We obviously didn't, Mia. There must be more than one."

"The ring," Mia whispered, almost forgetting its existence. "Where is the sanguis ruby ring?"

"I've locked it away somewhere safe, Mia. We need not discuss it further."

Mia frowned at his tone. "Then, Idris, you have to call for Mylo."

"Alert the Silver? Have you lost your mind?" Idris shook his head, lips pinching. "We don't need one of its lieutenants poking around—especially this close to the witches."

Mia's hand went to Sorcha's curly crown, holding her close. Her tears soaked into her blouse. "Then he needs to be made aware that it's attacked again in broad daylight, and in people's homes, not lurking in the night. He needs to alert the people of Alderdeen that there is danger roaming the streets. Hartwinn's curfew is useless."

Sorcha sniffed, pushing off Mia. Her cheeks were flushed and damp, and her bottom lip trembled. "How do you know this happened in the daytime?"

"Her blood is still warm," Idris answered.

Alaric's gaze rose from Vivan's cooling body, to Idris, then to Mia. His face clenched with confusion, then it relaxed with realisation. He stood and pointed at them. "Both of you, outside. Now."

"I can't—"

"Go, Mia. I need a moment with her alone before I need to return to the tower. I have patients to see," Sorcha said, scrubbing the tears from her face. She pushed to her feet, swaying a fraction.

"Sorcha—"

She held a hand up, cutting her off. "Not yet, Mia. I cannot talk about her yet."

Mia nodded, slipping through the doorway. She glanced back to see Sorcha collapse to the stone, her hands hovering over the body, then the subtle glow of her healing magic—a futile attempt to save Vivan.

Mia sighed and followed the men out of the house and into the alleyway.

Benny slumped against the alley wall, face in his hands. "There have been more murders. It's all the lower can speak of. A fucking heap of them. Six. Well, now seven."

"I cannot believe..." Idris muttered, his thumb finding that skull again. His jaw muscle clenched so tightly that it spasmed.

He failed to keep another witch safe. It must be killing something inside of him, Mia thought, biting down on her lip.

Alaric launched himself out of the house, right at Mia. His hand locked around her shoulder. "Where is it?"

She yanked back, but he had an iron grip on her. "Where is what?"

"The mark."

"What the fuck are you going on about? Let me go."

He shoved up the sleeve of her blouse, exposing the bite mark that saved her life. Alaric's eyes rose to Idris, shoving her aside. His top lip curled, snarling. He launched himself at Idris, slamming him against the closest wall. "You bastard. You blood-bound her."

Idris didn't move to fight him off. "Mia is a grown woman, Alaric. Who she binds herself to is her choice, not yours. I did what I had to do."

"Idris is right. I was dyi—"

"She is barely more than a girl, Idris. Anyone can see that," Alaric cut in. "A young, naive girl, charmed by you. Just like my sister."

Mia bristled. She was a woman, not a girl, and the man—who didn't know she was alive until a week earlier—seemed to believe that he knew what was best for her.

Idris was silent until Alaric slammed him against the wall again and hissed, "Speak, vampyre."

"Alaric, you knew him. If you care about her at all, you know she shouldn't be just given to that monster," Idris pleaded. "Besides, Maeve never wanted it to happen. She never wanted Mortias to have her."

"What do you mean?" Mia asked, eyes flicking between the men.

No one answered her.

"So, Idris, you decided in all your years of wisdom to fuck with a Divine Bride? Is this just another way to mess with your father? Or are you so deluded that you think you can love her?"

"She is *mine*—"

"She is Deus' to give, and you dare to spit in his face while sullying her."

"That's enough, Alaric," Benny said, reaching for the men. "You've gone far enough."

Alaric turned to him, lip curled. "You lost the right to tell me what to do many years ago, Benjamin."

Anger didn't flare in Alaric's eyes. Hurt did. That tear-jerking twist of grief. She knew he wasn't furious about the blood bond. He was simply protecting her—his sister's only child—from a man who couldn't protect his family.

"Alaric, please let us explain—"

"You were born to be given to the true vampyre king. To be his wife, his queen, Mia, and now you've fucked with things beyond your comprehension."

Mia's hand snapped back, the warmth dashing in her chest. "*Given?* I'm not some piece of property to be handed off to a man who is more of a monster. Nor am I putting any faith in a god who has only ripped people I love from me."

Alaric whirled to her, his nostrils flaring. "Yes, you will—"

"And King Mortias is dead. There is no true vampyre king. Not anymore. They executed him."

The distant sounds of the city seeped into the silence that met her words.

She took a step back, her chest tightening as panicked confusion rose. "He's dead, right? Burning in Heylla. You said so yourself, Idris."

Benny sighed, stepping towards her, palms up. "After the massacre, Mortias was too full of blood for them to execute him, so—"

"They had to starve him before he met the executioner's axe?" Mia finished.

Her eyes flashed to Idris, who didn't meet her gaze. "Idris, look at me. You told me he was dead."

He pushed Alaric away, swirling his tongue around his mouth. "Mia, I..."

"Don't you dare try to twist the truth, Idris. Is your father alive?"

"Yes."

Mia stumbled back into Benny, her eyes working in their sockets. "Am I destined to be given to Mortias?"

"Yes."

A dark thought emerged in her mind. She couldn't keep it in; it spewed from her mouth in wavering tones. "You've known all along, haven't you? That's why you approached me at The Cauldron and…" Mia held her arm, covering the scar. She resisted the urge to scratch it from her skin. "That's why you bonded with me. Just to get back at your father."

Idris' eyes finally found hers, his eyebrows knitted so tightly that a deeper wrinkle emerged. He even had the nerve to seem surprised. Her magic flared in her chest at the sick, fiery feeling of betrayal, allowing a gust of shadowy mist to slip from her.

Benny's hand clutched at her elbow. "Mia, calm yourself."

"Answer me, Idris," she demanded. A single shadow curled around her fist, ready to bend him to her will.

"I approached you at The Cauldron to you fuck you, Mia. Nothing more. I was seeking nothingness between a woman's legs to stop whatever the fuck was going on in my head, and you were the first woman I found. It was never to get back at the monster who sired me. Admittedly, the thought crossed my mind, but it was just a thought. I cast it away when I realised who you are—"

"When did you realise who I was?"

"I knew who you were from the moment I laid eyes on you, Mia."

"So what was your plan, Idris? Have me before your monster of a father did? Just so you could rub it in his face that you had me first?"

"Mia, don't be ridiculous. I'm not the only man you've had. Stop acting like I took your virgin—"

"That is Princess Ophelia to you, coward. And you will not soil her name further," Alaric cut in, stepping in closer.

"My name is Mia, and my name is soiled plenty, Alaric. I don't need you to defend me," she snapped, not taking her eyes off Idris.

"Ophei—Mia, you need to calm down, or risk exposing yourself. It's not worth it for this worthless sod," Alaric said, a fraction softer.

Ozul swirled up her arms, seeping from her clenched fists. She shot her uncle a sharp look, making him take a step back. Tears filled her eyes, blurring her vision. "Call him worthless again, and it will be the last words you ever speak. I'll rip that tongue from your mouth and let you drown in your own blood. He is my blood bond, and you will speak to him with the respect he deserves."

Alaric put his hand to his chest, appalled. "You wouldn't dare."

"Say it again, and we shall see."

Her threat lay heavy in the alleyway. No one dared to speak.

Mia's gaze trained on Idris, whose eyes narrowed at her. Benny stepped back, reaching out for Alaric, yanking him away from her. Idris took a step forward, springing Mia into action. Their bodies collided, not in a tangle of lips and limbs, but of fists and swirling shadows. He caught her by the biceps, dragging her to the wall. She fought, kicking. Her boot never found flesh.

Shadows slipped over his straining forearms, wrapping tightly, like bonds not made of iron, but of something stronger—her magic. But she was losing a grip on it, that flash of heat from his lies being replaced with a cold, heavy sadness. She grew tired of the numbness that consumed her emotions, leaving her hollow, empty.

A tear escaped the brimming and rolled down her cheek. "How could you keep this from me? The only thing I ever asked was the truth from you."

"I told you, Mia, that we shouldn't let feelings grow between us. It was clear from the start that this would only result in heartbreak for both of us. I tried to stay away from you, to fight this pull you have on me. I even went as far as to curse Oryah for letting this feeling develop in me, when all I wanted was to feel nothing."

Mia watched as his words spilt from him like an upturned glass, and he wouldn't stop until he was empty.

"I cannot anymore, Mia. I cannot deny it to myself, to you, to the whole fucking world. Not for a single second more." He pressed his hand over his heart. "Each broken, scarred part of me is yours. I will fight for you with all I have, Mia Ashmore."

She sank to her knees right in front of him, shadows slipping in the ripples of her dress, letting whatever filled the divots of the cobblestoned alley soak into her skirts. He collapsed to the stones with her, his hands finding her cheeks, thumbing the tears away.

"I will keep proving I'm worthy of your love for as long as I breathe on this cursed land. Because you are worth the battle, the fight, Mia. You are worthy of love, as you have shown me I am."

She sobbed as if his words were an antidote to the poison Mortias had infected her with. She could whisper it to herself a million times, but hearing it fall from his lips made it ring true.

"Truth?"

Idris' eyes searched hers, then answered, "Truth."

She pressed her lips against his, her palm falling over his ever steady heartbeat. "Fuck fate. I care little about it, nor what the meddling gods have done to force its hand. I weave my own fate, and mine is entwined with yours forever, Idris Blackwood, until the great goddess calls us home, and in every life after that."

Alaric's stare narrowed, crossing his arms. "Then you've doomed us all."

"Wow, very ominous, Alaric," Benny muttered, turning on his heel. He glanced over his shoulder, casting a tight expression at her uncle. "'You've doomed us all' is a touch dramatic—"

"Ben, stop!" Idris ordered.

Mia watched in horror as Benny's leg disappeared down the hole of an open sewer drain. The momentum made him fall, his lower half devoured by the darkness of the tunnel. His hand scrambled over the slick cobblestone, unable to find a grip. Mia launched herself at him, scurrying over the ground, her hands reaching. She firmly held onto the cuff of his shirt. Then, the telltale sound of fabric ripping, mixed with her heaves, filled the tense air.

He glanced at her, fear pinpricking his irises. "Mia—"

His sleeve tore clean off the seam, leaving her with a scrap of fabric and Benny hurtling into the dark, dank sewers of Alderdeen.

Sixty

BLOODY FINGERPRINTS WERE SMEARED ACROSS THE discarded iron sewer lid. Someone had wanted to escape—and quickly. The cobblestones cut into Mia's knees as she stared down into the shadowy abyss. She cried Benny's name down the shaft, only to have it ring back at her. His frightened face burnt into her mind.

Is he scared of the dark? Is he afraid of what is lurking in those tunnels?

Those bloody flashes of ripped skin and gore splattered had returned, along with the sick glee she knew grief was taking from it.

"I guess we know how they are getting around unnoticed," Alaric said.

James stood behind him, arms crossed, a pinched expression on his face. "This is sloppy, even for this monster. I don't think we should go down there. It could be a trap."

"We need to go," Mia croaked, voice hoarse from the screaming. She crawled closer to the edge, swallowing the ball of nerves, and swung her legs over. A dire sense of urgency filled her. Idris' steadying hand gripped her shoulder, stopping her from launching herself down the manhole.

"Benny is a survivor," Alaric assured. "He will survive this."

"But I won't!" Mia's voice cracked, tears rolling down her cheeks.

The truth always found a crack in her to slip free. She wouldn't bear another loss. Grief would drag her to the swirling depths, and she wasn't sure she would fight it.

Alaric squatted and peered into the darkness. "Before we descend into this Heylla hole, we need supplies—weapons, torches and a map. We'd get turned around down there before you could even pray to Oryah."

"We don't have time for supplies," Mia snapped, edging on hysteria. She glanced up to Idris, who hadn't spoken since Benny disappeared. "He's down there alone, Old Man. We have to go."

"Mia, be reasonable," Alaric ordered, shaking his head. "Is his life worth more than yours? For all we know, he is dead."

"Be reasonable?" Mia sneered, scrubbing the tears from her face. "How about I show you reasonable—"

"We don't have time for this!" Idris exclaimed hotly. "My best friend could be dying in a fucking sewer, all alone. We go *now*."

An unsettling feeling had formed deep in Mia's guts, like an iron ball weighing down each step. Something felt off, but she couldn't put her finger on it. *Is this a trap?*

James called out her name, waking her and forcing her to move.

Mia cringed as she lowered herself down to the dark, dank sewer. Idris was there, waiting for her, hands finding her hips, helping her down. A flash of flame and a lantern was lit. The flickering orange glow illuminated a long tunnel. The walls shone with the moist, sickly dampness, catching with each turn of the light. It congealed on her skin, sticking stray hairs to her neck. The rushing of filthy waste filled water ran through the Heylla hole with a strange sereneness.

It stunk. Well and truly stunk.

A puddle of something squashed under her boot, making her stifle a gag. She prayed it was blood, and not what she thought it was. *I would hate to throw away my favourite boots, and Benny's measly bartender wage can't afford to buy me a new pair after I thoroughly throttle him for not watching where he steps.*

Idris yanked a skull-headed dagger from a sheath strapped to his thigh and pushed it into her hand. "Do you remember our lesson?"

"The pointy end is the stabby end," Mia replied softly, staring at the whirling iron. *A drawn blade will call to Death with a soft siren's song.* "I pray I won't need to use it."

Idris pressed a kiss to her temple and whispered, "I hope so too."

"I can't see him," Alaric said, voice echoing. "Or a body."

Idris stepped closer to the sewer's wall, head tilting. His nostrils flared as if he could smell more than the hot, putrid scent of bodily waste. He reached out, brushing over the wet-looking stone, making Mia cringe.

Fresh blood stained his fingers.

"This way," he ordered, striding into the darkness without a second look.

Mia rushed after him, leaving the others huddled together in the light. James and Alaric cursed, racing after her. Their footsteps were loud in the tunnel. But her eyes were glued on Idris' broad figure sauntering through the dark sewer. She reached out and gripped the back of his shirt, knowing she'd be turned around without an anchor.

"I've got you, Little Witch."

Mia exhaled. Fear had already allowed her soft shadows to be freed, circling her trembling fingers. Her other hand had a stranglehold on the leather hilt.

The tightly packed group followed Idris deeper into the sewers in silence. Hands on blades, heads snapping over shoulder at any noise. But Mia's hand never left him, her hold tightening with each passing moment.

"Loosen your grip, lest you mean to rip my shirt from my body."

Mia let out a shaky laugh, forcing the tensed muscles in her fingers to relax a fraction around the crumpled linen. She turned to Alaric, whose face glistened with the same sweat which dripped down her spine. "So, what is going on with you and—"

A body slammed into James, tackling him to the ground, lantern shattering on the stone. She screamed his name, her voice reverberating around the vast corridor and slow-moving water.

She plunged into darkness, only to discover the broken remains of the lantern—and no James.

"James!" Idris yelled. His eyebrows knitted as his eyes searched the darkness wildly.

A raspy, warbling voice came from the shadows. "You took my friend. Now I will take yours, Mia—all of them. One by one. This is going to be so much fun."

A skin-prickling cackle radiated down the corridor, sending the hair on her neck straight.

"Return him, you blood-hungry vermin," Idris bellowed into the dark, taking a step, bumping into her.

A thought slammed into her scrambling mind. *If Mortias made those creatures, and I am to be his bride, they have to bend the knee to me.*

"You will give him back now! That's an order from your queen."

Scampering of footsteps paused, and sharply whispered words were her reply until an unsure voice echoed again, "No, no. Only he can command me."

"I'm your master, by proxy. You will obey me," Mia demanded, full of fake confidence mixed with the rush of bravery.

She met the others' eyes, hoping her desperate gaze would stay their hands. More footsteps and a muffled bellow from James, and the dhampyr slinked out from the darkness, lit by the slatted sunlight from outside, with her friend locked in its arms.

It was Tobias—Reagan's brother.

He wore only rags, exposing the stains of a mix of dried and fresh blood across his skin. A wild, jaw-twitching look crossed his gaunt face. The veins running down over his cheekbones throbbed painfully as his shoulders twitched.

James squirmed in Tobias' brawny arms. He wasn't strong enough to loosen the tight grip.

"Mia," Tobias crooned, sharp claws traced James' bobbing throat. "You're not supposed to be down here."

"Just let him go," she pleaded, taking a step forward. "And we will leave..."

"But Master said—"

"Tobias, I don't wish to see you punished—or worse, executed—for Reagan's evil doings. You don't need to keep cleaning up his mess."

"But he smells so delicious, Mia. Just a little taste," Tobias crooned. His long, wet tongue dragged up James' neck, causing him to scrabble against the iron grip. "Witch? Now, that is surprising."

"Tobias, fight it. Please, fight it."

He glared at her, tightening his grasp. "But I don't want to fight it, Mia. If you ever knew true power, you would never want to give this up. I feel powerful for once in my life."

"This isn't power. This is control. Reagan just controls you, Tobias, and you cannot let him."

Idris stepped forward, hand on his sword. His voice, like icy death, filled the space between them. "Enough of this. Let him go now, or you'll die where you stand. I care not who your father is."

Tobias scrambled back a step, taking James with him. "You're not supposed to be down here. You've angered the master by sullying his bride."

Mia rushed forward, ignoring Idris, her hand still reaching out. "Take me instead. Your master wants me, right? Mortias is waiting for his bride. Take me and let me help you."

"No, Mia," Idris uttered, that icy façade shattering. "You cannot go with him."

"Help me? There is nothing wrong with me. Nothing at all," Tobias hissed. "I refuse to be cast aside for him anymore."

He backed further into the darkness until their outlines were just silhouettes.

"I'm your friend—"

"You're not my friend! You're nothing but a witch slut!" Tobias barked back. "Master told us that you're not pure, but unclean...." His voice trailed off as he delved deeper into the gloom of the sewer.

Mia cried out into the darkness, hand gripping her blouse. With a steadying breath, she did something truly idiotic—or brave. She sprinted straight into the darkness, following the sound of the retreating footsteps. Idris' booming command to stop was a soft whisper over her thundering heartbeat.

She wouldn't let anything else happen to those she loved. Never again.

Mia darted down the dark corridors, skidding around corners. Her heaving breath cut in her lungs just like sharp razor blades, but she never slowed. Ozul slipped loose from the hold she had on them, misting around her.

Mia slammed right into an iron door. Her shoulder took the brunt of the painful impact. She bounced off and fell on her rear, sending a sharp shooting pain up her spine. The mossy, rusted door towered over her as she fought to catch her breath. Unsettling nail gouges clawed at the forgotten metal. Mia scrambled to her feet, ignoring the aches in her body. She felt for a handle, anything. Her fingers came across a cool ring of iron. She yanked it on it as the age-old hinges creaked.

Her mind was silent. Not a whisper of a rational thought settled between her ears.

What she found surprised her; a bedroom of sorts. Bed rolls were strewn across the floor, blankets tossed back carelessly. The glass of the low lanterns was black and stained, as if they had burnt for days, and the kerosene had melted the wick to nothing. The overwhelming stench of sharp copper and rotting flesh filled her nostrils, making her recoil.

Mia forced herself to enter the circular room, her eyes roaming over the unfettered gore left by those monsters. Wet, sloppy patches of innards and blood littered the floor. Flies buzzed, settling on the maroon masses, making her skin crawl. The creeping bile rose in her throat as her stomach flipped, forcing her to slip a hand over her mouth and nose. She flashed the dagger around, allowing the worked iron to glint in the light. Benny and James were nowhere to be seen, and neither was the blood-crazed Tobias.

It was quiet. Too quiet.

All her senses were on alert. Even the wallowing creaking of the walls sent her turning and twisting.

"Benny? James?" Mia called out, barely louder than a whisper.

Only that sad groaning of the metal replied.

Mia bit down on her lip, waving away the flies. The buzzing nuisances searching for fresh meat. *Where could they have gone? The sewers are a complete maze, running under most of the city.*

She cursed herself as she strode up to the lone doorway that didn't appear to be rusted closed. Her gaze fell to the sweeping gouges scarring the stone—the door was open often. She gripped the handle, pulling with all her might, clawing to get out of the room of massacre and macabre.

With the door cracked, Mia slipped through and fumbled backwards into the darkness. Her eyes were glued on the horrors beyond, her breath heaving, waiting for the dhampyrs to return with her friends in tow, alive or dead. She prayed to Oryah that they were alive.

The cramped chamber reeked of a man's body odour and the yeasty, sharp scent of mouldy bread. The rattle of iron chains filled the almost silent air.

She wasn't alone.

"Mia?"

The thing in there with her knew her name.

Mia whirled around, tripping on a taut chain. She fell, but not onto cold slick stone, but rough hay.

"Fuck," she cursed, her knee throbbing from the impact.

"Fuck, indeed," the voice muttered back, harsh and strained from disuse.

Mia glanced up and, illuminated by the sliver of light, was half a gaunt face, a shaggy beard hanging from hollow cheeks. But what made another curse fall from her lips was the pair of bloodshot eyes that were squinting against the glare. Those sky-blue-on-a-hot-summer's-day eyes. She would know that colour anywhere.

"*Reagan?*"

Those eyes clenched as if the name pained him. "The one and only."

Sixty-One

Mia sat back on her haunches, frowning at the figure crouching in front of her. Was he a ghost, or an illusion her mind was projecting into the dark, dank space?

She shook her head, demanding the apparition to disappear. But Reagan stared at her, waiting for her to do something—anything. With a trembling hand, she reached out, poking him firmly in the centre of his chest, feeling hard bone under his thin skin.

Real. He is real.

A small gasp left her as her heart beat a fraction faster.

Who—or what—had been walking, talking and scheming in his body?

She didn't know, but had Kali? Had she discovered what he was? Now, that was a secret worth killing for.

"I presume you're not here to save me," Reagan said drily.

"Not exactly," Mia muttered under her breath. Thoughts were swirling like a hurricane, slamming against the shores, ripping all she knew from their roots. "I will try to get you out—"

Abruptly, the door swung open, and light flooded the chamber—no, it was a prison cell. Reagan scrambled right back to a dark corner.

Rags hung on his thin body, as did a collar of iron that was locked around his scarred throat.

He had been there the whole time. Hidden away.

"What do we have here, lovely Mia?" a familiar voice crooned from behind her.

She froze like a sly fox caught in a chicken coop. But in those desperate moments, she realised she was not the fox, but the squawking chicken, fearful, with wings flapping.

Mia spun towards him, rushing back through the dry hay towards the cowering Reagan. The imposter swaggered through the doorway, hands in his pockets. An unsettling smirk curled on his face, straining and twitching at the corners. His eyes gleamed with that highborn cockiness, but an edge of giddy madness flashed in those blue irises.

"What?" she spluttered. "What the fuck is—"

"What? What? What?" the imposter mocked her with an eye roll. "Gods above, are you really that daft to not be able to connect the dots?"

Mia's mouth opened and closed, like a fish gasping for air. Her thoughts were rushing around too fast for her grip onto, outside of the ones screaming in her skull: *Kali. Reagan. Murderer. Imposter.*

The imposter bent at the hip, cocking his head at an unnerving angle. "Come, now, Mia. You always seem to have something to say."

"I know you're making these monstrous creatures into whatever you are with those rubies."

He snapped his head the other way, leaning forward on his tiptoes. "I'm surprised you didn't catch on earlier, or have you been too busy being ruined by that filth to use the brain between your ears?"

Mia cringed back at the crassness of his words. "How have you made these creatures? Fae magic—"

The imposter spat, cutting her off. "You wound me, Mia. This is true power, not that nature shit the fae use. One gifted from a god himself. Now, pray tell, who do you think that is?"

Reagan whimpered, chains jangling as he pressed against the wall.

"Mortias."

He straightened, and the grin that spread was more teeth than lip, unnerving her.

"Yes, Mia. The one true king. Our saviour."

"Are you him? Is that what you are?"

The imposter's head jerked sideways. He nodded, lips moving as he cast strained whispers over his shoulder. But they were alone. Terrifyingly alone.

A chuckle escaped him when he returned his icy gaze to her. He swung into a low bow. "No, lovely Mia, I am his dutiful servant, Jesper. And King Mortias shall grant me any power I desire after I ensure there is nothing left of Hartwinn."

"What are you going to do to him?"

"What do you think, girl? Good Deus, you think when you sell your soul to Diabolus, he forgets to collect? You get dragged to Heylla eventually. And in Hartwinn's case, it's now."

"And you will instil yourself as the Lord of Alderdeen."

Jesper nodded, eyes widening, urging her onwards.

"And when you marry King Ewan's eldest daughter, you solidify the ties with him and make sure he cannot raise a finger to Mortias. You've also been gifting the sanguis rubies to those in power, forcing corrupted magic into their bodies. Full well knowing what it'll turn them into. Preying on their desire for power, feeding into it."

"And what a delicious meal it has been," he murmured. He continued with a smirk, "The dhampyr are an...unfortunate byproduct of the rubies. Not all those who hold one turn—only those who are truly desperate for power. And my union is to simply ensure that when King Mortias rises to power, he has allies in all reaches of this cursed land, ready to march on his command." Jesper's eyes twinkled as if he was proud, boastful. "The princess, well, she is already growing my seed inside of her, mixed with Mortias' magic. What a creature it will make. If it's a son, he shall sit on Zeroth's golden throne."

Mia glimpsed at the iron door to the circular room sitting ajar—her only exit. But Jesper began rambling gibberish about gods and their divine match. His hands flailed around, working faster as his words became almost slurred.

"You know, they were destined, Deus and Oryah. But she had to be a frigid bitch and refuse him, only to seek safety with his brother,

Diabolus. How dare she! Didn't she realise the honour of being married to a god? But worse, denying him broke the heavens apart."

"Broke the heavens apart?" she repeated, rising slowly to a crouch.

"You think there were just three gods who lived in harmony and that was all? You are fucking stupid. Deus and Oryah ruled the great gardens together. She banished him back to his own realm for taking what a man has a right to."

Mia's hand gripped the leatherbound hilt so tightly that her knuckles whitened. "Oryah was smart to kick that woman-hating piece of shit out."

Jesper's gaze flashed to her, malice boiling in his pupils. He hissed through a clenched jaw, "How dare you!"

Mia sprang up, dragging her skull head dagger from the pool of shadows surrounding her hands. The dull iron glinted in the spluttering lantern light.

A warning.

Jesper strode forward, unfazed. He cracked his neck as if whatever was inside of him was pushing against his skin, demanding to be released. He pressed on further until the sharp tip dug into the plush velvet surcoat. "Have you ever used that little sewing needle before?" he asked, his voice grated against her skin. "Have you felt the life drain from a man? Did it get you all warm and tingly?"

Luc's lifeless corpse flashed in her vision, making the dagger tremble a faction against him.

"Back the fuck up!"

"Now, now, Mia, no need to use such language. It's below a woman of your breeding. And what considerable breeding it is."

Her eyes flashed to him. A question fell off her tongue before she could even stop it. "You had Kali killed, didn't you?"

That smile of teeth cracked across his face as his eyes widened. "She was going to ruin all our plans—all the plans he has for you—with her big mouth. She needed to be silenced permanently."

Mia's eyes filled with tears, falling with each shocked blink. She had found the creature who killed her sister, a monster hiding in plain sight. His hand snapped out, gripping her by the wrist, dragging her forward.

He forced her to sink the blade further in until she cut into flesh. A drop of ink black blood bloomed on the tip of the wrought iron, rolling down to meet her clenched fingers.

"If you hold a dagger to someone, Mia, be prepared to stab them."

"Trust me, you fucking bastard, you'll know it when I stab you."

"Again—*language*. I guess that's what you get for being raised by a fae male and his lover." He paused, leaning in closer until she could feel the sharp whiskers of his stubble brush over her ear. "Your precious sister called out for you when she was dying in that dirty alleyway. Not your mother or father, but you."

With a hard shove, Jesper pushed Mia back, her blade cutting free of his flesh. Her spine hit the door, slamming it closed, sending Reagan bellowing, crying out from inside his prison.

Idris' dagger clanked across the stone.

Jesper sighed, pulling a handkerchief from his pocket. He reached down with a grimace and plucked up the dagger, holding it out as if it pained him to touch it.

"You know where to find me, Mia, if you're still set on revenge. Or if you come to your senses and wish to join Mortias, the true king and your husband," Jesper said over his shoulder before disappearing into a fluttering of wings.

"I'd rather face the fiery pits!" she screamed back.

Mia straightened. Her breaths were ragged pants. Her anger was at a boiling point, simmering, splashing out with flecks of bitter rage. Ozul slipped free, filling the room with a black mist.

Jesper was simply another monster who thought he could take and take until she had nothing left.

No family.

No home.

No purpose.

Nothing.

He thought he could end lives without consequence. That what swung between his legs allowed him to be above whoever he stepped on to reach his bloody goal.

Mia realised she wasn't entirely angry at him, but at the cruel human king, at Luc, at Samuel, at Hartwinn. All the rotten men who had touched her life. She wasn't destined for a world where a man would tell her to watch her language, what to wear, what to say or who to be. She was shadow-blessed, and a godsdamned heir to a formidable coven, born from a line of powerful women. And she refused to take a command from a man ever again.

Sixty-Two

Mia grunted, dumping the heavy chains to the ground. She had been yanking on them for what felt like an age. Even though the iron was rusty and worn, it held strong. Her shadows slipped over, adding an extra layer of strength. The emaciated and weak Reagan was no help. Mia squatted, waving her shadows away. She inspected the padlock, her eyes skimming over the worn, intricate pattern, with deep gouges over the keyhole. Someone—Reagan, she presumed—had tried to pick it.

"Open it now, Ozul. I cannot bear to be down here a moment further."

Her shadows slipped over it, disappearing into the lock.

"What are they?" Reagan asked wearily, staring at the swirling mists.

"They are—"

"*Witch* magic, aren't they?"

Mia's eyes rose to his, pausing. Suspicion grew in her, making her bristle. Her anger had barely settled, and she was ready to spit venom at anyone who strayed too close.

"So what if they are?"

He raised his hands, a half-smile pushing up one side of his face. "I care not what you use to get me out of these, Mia. I've been in them long enough."

A *click* of a lock filled the space between them, and relief poured from Reagan, so much so that his shoulders shook with gentle sobs. With delicate fingers, Mia pulled the manacles from him, dumping them at their feet. No weeping wounds marred his thin wrists and throat, only white, raised scars from where the chains had rubbed, leaving his body scarred.

"How long is long enough?"

"Two years, sixty-three days and a handful of minutes," Reagan replied, pushing to his feet unsteadily.

The rags he wore hung uncomfortably on his frame, but covered enough of him. She slid her arm around his waist, letting him lean on her. He weighed barely anything.

Conflicting emotions arose in Mia as she debated whether to abandon Reagan to rush after Jesper. She knew full well that it was most likely a trap to lure her in—and one she'd sprint into. Those competing demands drew her heart and head into a battle. Steel was drawn, and she didn't know who would come out victorious.

"We take this one to the surface, witchling," Ozul whispered, brushing along her arm.

"You can move without me?"

Her shadows turned their unseen eyes on her. They replied matter-of-factly, *"We have no limit now that you have awoken."*

A strange chill skidded up her spine. Their words did not soothe her, but made her uneasy. She had to have limits. Her magic couldn't be endless. *They must be mistaken,* she decided, calling to more shadows and creating an almost human-like figure to slouch Reagan into.

He grimaced as Ozul slipped over him, holding him up.

"I have to go—"

He waved her away, a weary gaze still on the misty hands which held him. "Go, Mia. I can find my way out with a little help from...."

"Ozul. Their name is Ozul."

"Well, thank you," Reagan murmured, nodding to the misting shadows.

She exhaled, tucking her hair behind her ear. "It's awfully good to see you, Reagan."

His gaze rose, eyes glassy with unshed tears. "You don't know how wonderful it is to see you, Mia."

She opened her mouth to speak, but Idris calling for her rattled through her chest, cracking her resolve. Glancing back meant seeking him and the safety of his arms. So, Mia did what she had been doing for months: she ran.

THE DESPERATE SOUND OF IDRIS PLEADING FOR HER replayed in Mia's ears. His desperation encircled her and kept her company as she sprinted through the darkened cobbled streets of Alderdeen. Past shopkeepers closing up for the evening, past curious eyes who tracked her. Her sweat-drenched clothing shifted against her skin, sticking and pulling with each step.

If Mia slowed or stopped for a heaving breath, she would turn around and find Idris—and allow him to cut down her enemies, tarnishing his soul even further. And she was unwilling to let that happen. She had to do it, not just for herself, but for Kali and every woman Jesper had ripped away. She needed to be the one who sent that monster back to where he had crawled from.

She only paused when she arrived at the crumbling, vine-covered wall of the Valliss castle. Her thudding heartbeat, racing to her fingertips, made her hands tremble. She craned her head, fighting to even out her breath, seeking the cracks and divots Kali used to sneak in.

With an exhale, Mia began her climb, heaving her body up the wall. She swung her leg over, straddling it. Her boot slipped on a loose stone as she lowered herself down, sending her plummeting towards the grass. Mia held in the shriek of panic that emerged. Her hands scurried to find any sort of grip, ripping the skin from her soft palms. Her shadows flared out like black, feathery wings on a raven, slowing her rapid descent and cushioning her as her body hit a flower bed with a heavy *thud*.

"*We got you, witchling.*"

"Thanks, Ozul," Mia murmured, pushing to her knees, crushing more of the delicate petals. Her hands stung, and the watery blood pooled in the webbing of her fingers.

As she stood, Mia swayed, shadows lingering to catch her. The pain in her spine sent a sharp sting down the backs of her legs with each step. Her hips and shoulder would bear dark purple bruises. But they would heal, as her broken heart had done.

Mia lifted her eyes to see the marble castle buzzing with life. Her hands twitched, splattering fat drops of ruby red across the gravel, calling forth her shadows. She cared little for being seen, refusing to sneak through Valliss like a rat in a wall. She would stride through, bloody and rageful, not hiding who she was—what she was—not a speck of fear inside of her.

SIXTY-THREE

Mia ran down the side of the castle, past the shining glass until a sharp, scared scream made her whirl around to a window. A large, meticulously decorated sitting room stared back at her, but the furniture was upturned, vases broken, and books ripped from shelves. A concerning pool of blood seeped from a slumped Hartwinn.

Jesper stood over Sorcha. She was trapped in his grip as he yanked her back and forth. Mia had never seen someone so scared. Her freckled face was pale, tears gleaming on her cheeks. He was snarling at her. Words, though muffled, were enough to make her flinch.

Sorcha's small hand flashed out, slapping him. Jesper cocked his head, his shoulders tensed into a curved hunch. His hand darted out, gripping Sorcha around the throat. Tightly. Her eyes bulged in their sockets as she clawed at his forearm. Her boots scrambled over the slippery marble.

"Help me!" Sorcha's scream shook the glass.

Mia moved before she could even think, sprinting over the crunching gravel. Shadows glided behind her, resembling a cape made of the glittering night sky. She rushed down corridors, searching for the room that held Sorcha, her boots slapping hard against the stone. Past guards, whose commands for her to halt fell on deaf ears. She skidded to a stop in front of a plain, nondescript door.

No one had heard her screams, while Luc thought he could take what he was owed. Mia had listened to that pained, frightened scream enough. She refused to let it settle inside her, making itself comfortable.

With an exhale, she burst through to a surprised Sorcha and a growling imposter.

"Let her go," Mia commanded.

"Now, Mia, this has nothing to—"

"I will not ask again."

Sorcha fought against his tight grip, her eyes flashing between the pair. The sharp stench of fear filled the room, coating Mia's clothing. She knew it would linger on her for days, like a rotten stench. Sorcha's nails still latched onto his forearm, cutting into his skin, black blood pooling from the gouges leaked down her wrist. Yet, Jesper remained, snarling as if he couldn't feel pain.

He tossed Sorcha into a hardwood side table. The sickening *crack* of bone filled the tense air as one of her ribs broke. She bellowed out, scrambling against the wood, her hands knocking free a vase, smashing it to the ground.

Mia's gaze flashed to the shattered porcelain.

A mistake.

Jesper charged at her, that same unnerving smirk on his face. His body crashed into hers, flinging her into the door, slamming shut their only exit. Mia fought, writhing and hurling her elbows into any fleshy part she could reach, but his grip never loosened. He relentlessly slammed her against the door, causing the wood to split. Her shoulder and hip took the brunt of the impact. She could even feel the concerning shift of her brain in her skull.

Mia spat vicious curses at him, her voice dripping in malice. She cast every barbed word she could think of, and he welcomed each with that unnerving grin, seemingly enjoying her foul words.

With a final slam, she swung her head forwards, colliding with his chin, splitting the delicate skin on her forehead. Blood gushed down over her eye, dying her vision red.

"Let us free, witchling. He is powerful, but we are stronger."

"Be free, Ozul."

Her shadows poured from her, dragging the lingering wisps from dark corners to her flexed hands. Black mist circled, whipping at Jesper. A shadowy hand grasped his shoulders, wrenching, making Mia groan with effort. His hold loosened a fraction, allowing her to wriggle free. She darted across the room towards Sorcha, whose eyes were on the groaning, waking Hartwinn. He pushed up on an elbow, only to scurry back from Ozul. His bloodshot gaze met hers, revealing a fierce battle of disgust and adoration.

"Witch," he muttered.

Mia's chin raised a fraction as a smirk curled her lips. "From the Umbra Coven, to be exact."

A muffled scream erupted in the room's corner. Her gaze snapped to the sound. Finding James bound and gagged, a bruise forming on his cheek, but conscious. Her shoulders sagged with relief.

Mia's attention jerked back to Jasper as she heard a bolt latch, her stomach flipping. She beckoned to Sorcha, but fear had frozen her in place.

"He's going to kill us, Mia," she whimpered. "Please, Oryah, save us."

Jesper turned on his heel. His lip curled. Not a snarl, but a slimy smirk, like she had done exactly what he wanted. "Your bitch of a god won't help you here."

Mia cursed under her breath, inching towards Sorcha. "He's locked himself in with us, Sorcha, and I shall meet Oryah swinging."

"Now, Mia, is that how you speak to the new lord of Alderdeen?"

Mia narrowed her eyes at his words, then nodded at Hartwinn. "I'm no healer, but I believe he is still alive. You haven't been crowned yet, monster."

Jesper tapped his bleeding chin with his forefinger. "Oh, he is? Pardon me."

Mia watched with her heart in her throat as Jesper launched himself across the room, jerking Hartwinn off the marble floor.

"Now, father, as the head of a powerful family, you cannot afford to be seen not looking your best," the imposter said, straightening

Hartwinn's tunic and dusting an invisible piece of lint from his shoulder.

The lord of Alderdeen swayed, eyeing the imposter. "Reagan. Son, please, this isn't you."

"Well, you're correct. I am not Reagan. But rest assured, your legacy will die with you."

Hartwinn's eyes widened. "What are you—"

A flash of iron captured the last of the afternoon sun as Jesper swung his arm, stabbing Hartwinn right in the stomach. Not with just any dagger—Idris' skull-headed dagger.

"Mortias sends his regards."

Hartwinn gaped at the imposter. A final cough had blood spattering over Jesper's face. He yanked the blade free, only to plunge it again and again, until his hand stained red and his sleeve was soaked. Hartwinn slumped to the ground, dagger still in his belly, eyes wide, light flickering, then fading to nothing. The man she called *Uncle* was dead.

"No!" Sorcha cried out.

"What have you done?" Mia asked, her voice wavering.

Jesper, with hunger glittering in his gaze, raised his hand to his face. With one long lick, he dragged his tongue up over his palm, then right between his forefinger and middle, smearing blood on his chin.

"Obeying King Mortias' wishes, girl, as you should."

"I will never obey a man who rules with fear and death."

Her gaze dropped to her only weapon, glinting in the afternoon sun, stuck in its fleshy scabbard.

"Ozul—" she whispered.

"*On it, witchling.*" Her shadows crept slowly, inching towards the blade.

She needed to distract the imposter before they could get to it. She took a step towards him, making Sorcha take a sharp breath.

"What's he like, anyway? Mortias?"

Jesper's gaze snapped to her, his teeth-filled smirk widening. A strange glint awoke in his eye. "King Mortias is handsome, charming—"

"And a fucking mass murderer," Sorcha cut in, finding her voice. She struggled off the table, a hand around her ribs. "A madman, drunk with blood."

His lip curled up, snarling at her. "Mortias is a god, destined to rule this land, and you'd be smart to remember that, girl."

"And with me beside him, isn't that right? Am I to be his queen, or just his brood mare, cast to the side when I give him an heir?"

Sorcha's eyes flashed to Mia, confusion written all over her features. But her gaze dropped from her, shadows swirling around Idris' blade, realisation relaxing the muscles of her face.

The imposter nodded. "He wishes for you to rule by his side as his queen. He recognises your power, Mia. If you come with me now, he will forgive you for all the things you have done."

With a sneer, she threw out her hand and yelled, "Now, Ozul. I cannot stand to hear this drivel any further."

The shadows slid the iron across the floor, right to her boot. She scooped it up, and with a scream, lunged for him, dagger held high. He slid to the side, making Mia stumble past him. She whirled around, swinging her arm down in a slashing arch, only to have two hands stop the descent, fingers digging painfully into the flesh of her forearm.

Her eyes glanced behind her, finding that wide, dreadful sneer. Then, he twisted her arm, pulling it at an unnatural angle—until those delicate muscles holding her shoulder together screamed. Mia cried out, her hand spasming, struggling to hold on to the dagger.

"You're not even good enough to cut me," Jesper hissed.

Not good enough.

Not good enough.

Not good enough.

Not good enough.

Iron cluttered on the stone. Tears leaked down her cheeks as a heart-breaking, mournful wail left her. Her boiling rage had morphed into something she had held in since she lit Kali's body alight.

Sadness. Complete and utter sadness.

Shadows blasted from her in black tendrils as each heaved sob filled the room with more black mists. She needed a single lantern in the darkness—something to reach for while the emotion drowned her. Then, that deep, rumbling voice echoed through the door, calling her name. Fists, then a heavy body slammed against the wood.

Idris.

He had come as if she had summoned him. Her light in the dark.

She returned his call through a sob.

Jesper's hand snapped out, gripping her around the face. He forced her to meet his gaze, pure, unfiltered rage flaring back at her. His thumb brushed over her lips, smearing blood and tears across her chin. Her boots scurried over the dagger, dragging it closer.

"Do you wish to burn, witch, like the rest of your scum kind? Put them away."

"Burn me. It means he will never have me."

"Or do you want your lover to be hanged for the callous murder of Lord Hartwinn? You know, that is a fascinating dagger. Rare, some would say. Those blades come in a matching set, called...." He paused, searching the air. "Oh, that's right, the Oath Keeper. Only held by Queen Maeve's guard, Captain Idris Blackwood."

Mia shot a look over his shoulder at the door. The man she loved was still pounding away, the wood flexing with each frantic slam, revealing his yearning to be with her, to fight for her, to protect her.

Mia returned her tear-stained gaze back to the imposter. "You wouldn't dare."

"I have just found you, Mia! Don't let me lose you now!" Idris called out again.

She closed her stinging eyes, swallowing the ball of choking emotion. Her fingers brushed over the dagger slung on Jesper's hip. She wrapped a hand around the hilt, dragging it from the sheath. With one slamming movement, she stabbed him, right in the guts. The blade cut through flesh, finding a home in his squishy organs.

"You will burn in Heylla for what you've done," she viciously spat at Jesper.

But the monster's grip never loosened, nor did he crumble at her feet. He simply pulled the dagger from his belly, stained black with his blood, and stared at it. Mia's eyes widened with shock, her lips parting.

I can't fight him. He's going to get away with it.

"You can, witchling, you just stuck him with the wrong blade."

"You think this little shard will stop me? I'm born from Mortias' own hands. His magic pumps in my veins," Jesper snapped, shoving Mia back against a bookcase. A hard edge caught her ribs, knocking the breath from her lungs. Books rattled with the impact, thumping to the floor. Her vision flashed to Sorcha, who straightened, scrubbing the tears from her face. A look of determination emerged, hot and blazing.

"I thought it would at least hurt, you arsehole," Mia snapped, gaze casting daggers at him.

"You know, it was going to be you I lured into the maid's closet. So desperate to be seen, to be loved. But your sister was a much sweeter catch."

The door bowed at the force Idris pushed against it. "Fight, Mia!"

The venom simmered up her throat, but before she could spray it, his face crumpled in pain. Roaring, he spun around to Sorcha, standing with Idris' blade in her hands. The iron, stained with inky blood, quivered in the air. Even her curls shook with every shudder of her muscles.

"Leave her alone," Sorcha ordered, voice wavering.

"You little bitch—"

"Now, Ozul!" Mia screamed.

Her magic flared, capturing Jesper's legs and ricocheting up his body, trapping him. Her magic was waning, sending a coolness through her chest. But Mia battled through it. Jesper bellowed and fought like an animal caught in a snare. He snarled curses at the women.

Sorcha raised her chin, scrubbing the tears from her face. "I am Sorcha Cirrus, a slànaighear blessed with Oryah's healing light, born from a bloodline far greater than yours. Some human lordling's son will not bring me to my knees."

"You both are the same—filth. Mortias is going to flog the disobedience out of you, girl," Jesper spat back.

Mia wavered. Her body was exhausted, aching in places she never had before. She turned to Sorcha, who stood straighter. Her eyes sparkled, as fire of determination had been lit in her belly. She held the dagger out to Mia, nodding for her to take it. "For your sister. For Vivan."

She grasped the hilt, noticing the heavy weight in her palm. The last time she took a blade to another, it was in self-defence. Her only way out was through blood and pain.

It was for revenge.

Mia knew that the sticky molasses of vengeance coated it, sticking to her and leaving traces over everything she touched. She stared down at the blade, the skull glinting in the fading sunlight.

You've disappointed me, Sweet Creature. You wavier, hesitate to end the monster who killed your sister, when your bloodlust was so delicious, delectable, Mortias crooned, right in the shell of her ear.

With a frown, her eyes flicked up. *I have rid myself of him after bonding with Idris. Haven't I?*

That dark chuckle slithered over her, making the hairs on her neck stand straight up. *No, my sweet creature, you're terribly wrong. You've let me in, and now you will never be rid of me.*

"You hear him, don't you? Your dark husband, your dark king?" Jesper crooned, a smirk growing wider at her, raising the blade. "And what do you think you're going to do—"

Mia lunged forward with a quick movement, the blade burying in his chest. This time, he snarled as pain broke out across his features. Her irises glowed a golden, burning orange, reflecting in his dead eyes. She dragged the blade downward, slicing through the resistant flesh. Blood didn't splatter, nor did his innards gush out like she had expected.

Nothing flooded from the dark abyss, only the strange sound of fluttering feathery wings.

Mia and Sorcha stumbled back as Jesper cackled, sputtering inky blood down his front, unnerving them both.

Idris blasted through the doors, sending splinters of wood across the floor. He searched wildly for her, his movements frantic.

"Over here, Old Man."

Idris stormed towards her, pushing back the loose hair from his face. He was murmuring her name in a soft prayer. Inky black blood covered him, but she couldn't see a single wound. Alaric emerged from behind Idris, with Benny slumped over his shoulders, blood-stained but alive. Tears of joy and relief flooded her eyes as a small smile crept on her face.

They were all alive.

Looking over her shoulder, she glanced at the corner where James had been gagged and bound. He was gone, his bindings discarded. A flare of panic worked its way through her. Mia stumbled a few steps forward, reaching for Idris. Her fingers wrapped around the sweaty, soiled fabric of his shirt as he enveloped her in his arms.

"My Mia," he breathed, lips finding her crown. "I thought I had lost you."

Her eyes didn't move from the empty corner of the room. "James was just—"

The sounds of hundreds of fluttering wings drowned out Sorcha's sharp scream.

Sixty-Four

Ravens.

Hundreds of ravens squirmed and fought their way out of the gaping wound in Jesper's stomach. Their feathery bodies slithered out, taking flight within the room, squawking and cawing. Mia screamed and crouched, throwing her hands over her head. Beaks and talons cut and bit exposed skin.

Jesper's body disappeared under black fluttering bodies, escaping his torn open stomach. Books and trinkets were thrown to the ground as wings fluttered against furniture, attempting to land. Birds slammed against the clean glass in loud *thunks*, seeking the freedom of the late afternoon sky, only to be trapped in that Heylla hole.

A hand seized her elbow, forcing her to stand. Two powerful arms locked around her, dragging her closer to a hard body. However, it wasn't the warm, safe one she knew.

"Got you, witchling," James whispered in her ear.

"Thank Oryah." Mia sighed, relaxing a fraction. "Where is Idris? We have to get out—"

A damp cloth slammed over her mouth and nose. Mia breathed in the sweet, alcohol-smelling fumes in panicked gasps. Her hands snapped to his, fighting for fresh air. All she did was drag more of the toxin into her lungs.

"Now, Mia, stop this bloody squirming at once," James demanded, struggling to keep hold of her.

She stamped down on his toe with the heel of her boot. He barked a yelp, freeing her. She lurched forward, still tasting the poison on her lips, into the squalling ravens. Her head spun at an alarming rate.

The flock converged on a silent order, angling their bodies to create a circling whirlwind of flapping wings and gleaming, silky feathers. In the centre of the blurring void, a flash of lightning cracked, shaking the ground. A black portal split open, revealing what lay beyond it—slate grey basalt stone and threateningly thunderous clouds. Chilled air curled around her, then was lost in the room's heat.

It was a gateway to somewhere else, far from Alderdeen.

A pair of soot-covered hands erupted from the void, then another. Two lithe women slid through, wearing sheer gowns of black and gold. Bizarre markings had been inked into their skin, across their chests and down their arms. Their dark eyes rose to the swaying Mia, whose vision was blurring with each second the poison worked in her body.

"Our queen, his bride," they said in unison, dipping into a low curtsy. "We are here to bring you home."

"Get away from her," Idris demanded from behind her.

The women hunched over, snarling at him. "The cowardly prince has no power here. Does he, sister?"

"No power," the other hissed.

Idris forced his body forward, fighting the brunt of the gale-force winds. Mia reached for him, her hair whipping against her face. All she wanted was to get to him, into the safety of his arms. Black-stained fingers gripped her around the bony part of her shoulder, hauling her back towards the void.

"Idris!" Mia screamed.

"You think I'd just let you have her, son? She is mine," a voice echoed from the portal, causing dread to wash over her. "To have and to hold, until death do us part."

Idris took another determined step forward, straining to get to her. His hair cut across his face, in inky strands over his cheekbones. His emerald eyes never left her, beaming that soft, fluttering emotion at her. At that frantic moment, Mia wished he had asked her to be his wife. That they had run to the closest temple of Oryah and been wed. For her to be his. Forever.

"*Yes*, Idris." She tugged the opal ring from her finger and tossed it across the room. "My answer will always be *yes*."

His eyes widened, and his open palm shot up and caught the gold. "Truth?"

Her jaw shook as a tear rolled down her face. "Truth."

Closer and closer, Mia was being pulled towards the portal. She could feel the sparking electricity flow over her skin. She threw herself forward, scrambling against the forthcoming darkness. Until her hand brushed his.

A desperate final touch.

James stepped in front of her, cutting her off from Idris. A smirk curled on his lip, and he crooned, "Time to meet your fate, Ophelia."

With a strong shove, he plunged her into the portal, limbs flailing. Mia plummeted through the void. Her hands still reached for that dot of light, even as it grew smaller and smaller by the second. Tears spilt into the air, Idris' name on her lips.

Mia was spat from the portal, flying through the air, landing in ankle deep sludge. Her aching hip took the brunt of the fall, splattering mud over her ruined clothing. The rain pelted down on her, stinging her skin with each drop. With a groan, she rolled onto her knees, spitting out a mouthful of bloody spittle—one of her teeth had gouged through her lip.

A person towered over her, sheltering her from the chilly dredging. Tearfully, she raised her gaze to find King Mortias standing tall above her, haloed by burning torches. Those intense amber eyes burnt into her cooling skin. He wasn't the Mortias of her memory. His aged face bore a silver scar that started at his temple, crossed over his nose and ended at the sharp edge of his jaw. A smirk gradually appeared, lighting his eyes.

With a sweeping arm, Mortias bowed and said, "Welcome home, Sweet Creature..."

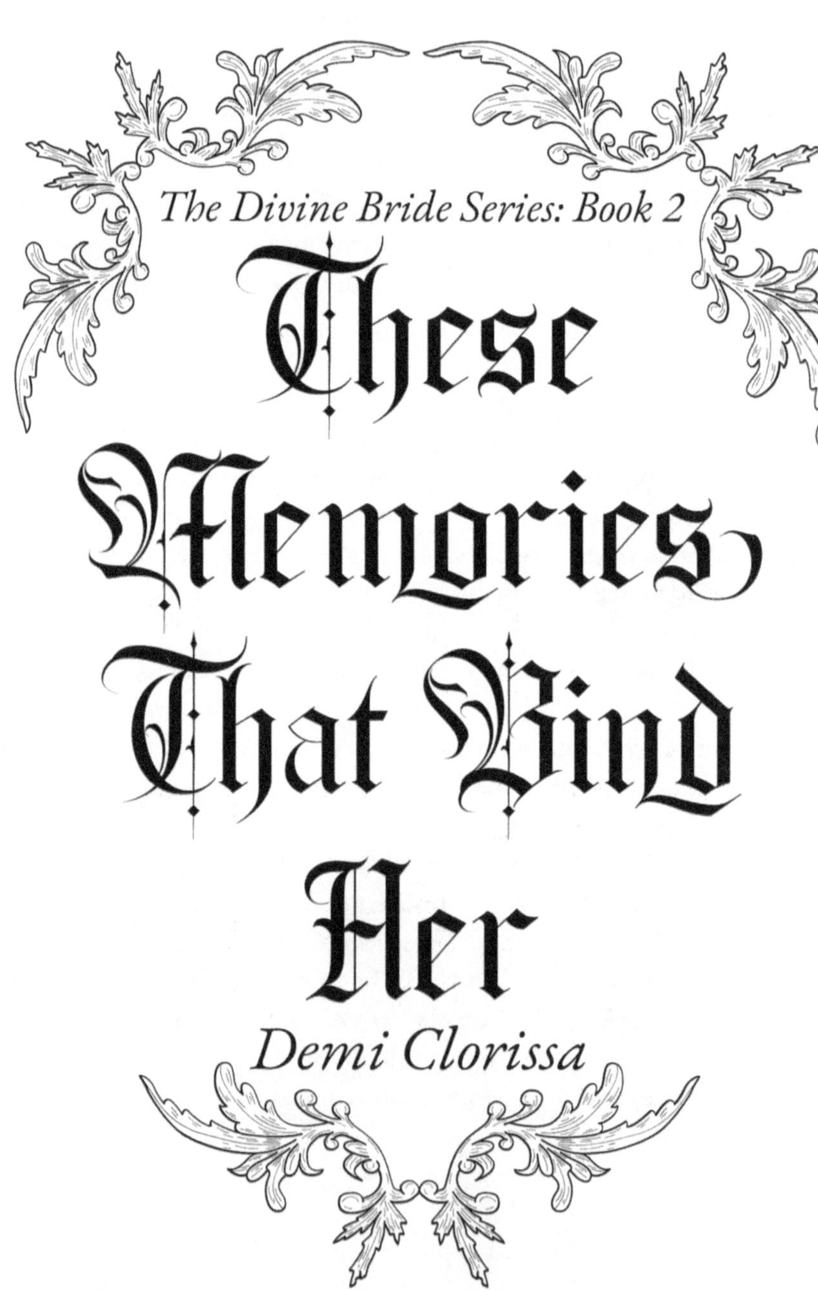

The Divine Bride Series: Book 2

These Memories That Bind Her

Demi Clorissa

Acknowledgments

Well, well, well...we made it to the end of the book, and to be perfectly honest, finding the words to thank every single soul who shaped These Shadows Become Her into the novel is difficult to find—those elusive bastards!

Yet, here are my thanks and immortal gratitude:

To my beautiful, amazing husband, Nathan. Your support has been incredible, and I cannot thank you enough for all the late night brainstorms, wiping my tears away, constant encouragement, snacks and letting me ramble about these fictional characters until we both know them inside and out. You're my inspiration for love, and how to be loved. I love you forever.

To my wonderful, and ever positive, editor, Brittany. You have helped shape this story into what it is today. From your cheerleading, to asking the tricky questions (of whether or not I should keep Wyn!) you've made this process such a smooth, and incredible journey. Here's to more brooding men, and bad (bitch) witches!

Thank you to my found family—*Lauren, Mel, and Kaitlyn*. From countless messages brainstorming ideas, to arguing over pronunciation of characters' names, to being forced into becoming a plotter. You girls have been my rock, my greatest support, and at times, my harshest critic (I *can* do better than that, Lauren!). Shadows, and this incredible world, wouldn't be the same without the love you've shared. It's been a true pleasure to have you in my life.

To my Beta readers, thank you! I appreciate the time and effort you put into making sure These Shadows Become Her shines! I literally couldn't have done it without you. From the kind, encouraging words, to those words which spurred me on to knuckle down and produce this fantastic novel. Thank you, I hope we can share this love for fictional worlds in the future!

And, lastly, you the reader. I could (or literally would not) be here without the love and support you have shown me. You have made my dreams come true, and I will be eternally grateful for it. I cannot wait to bring you more stories full of love, lust, and heartbreak. This is just the beginning.

Lots of love,

About the Author

I'm Demi Clorissa, a proud Wiradjuri woman, who writes heart breaking dark romantic fantasy. You will find body diverse FMCs, men who YEARN, and emotional damage (that will make you reach for the tissues) within the pages. I'm inspired by strong women, and those who they decide to love.

When I'm not writing you'll find me reading anything I can get my hands on (mostly fantasy), watching trashy TV shows, reading BL and spending my afternoons at the cinema. I love food (but I'm a self confessed awful cook!). I'm blessed to have a little dachshund, Della, who is often curled around my feet as I craft my next emotional scene.

ALSO BY DEMI CLORISSA

THE DIVINE BRIDE SERIES:

THESE SHADOWS BECOME HER

THE ROSE AND HER WARRIOR

THESE MEMORIES THAT BIND HER

THESE FATES THAT FORETOLD HER (COMING IN 2026)

THE DAUGHTER OF THE WOOD SERIES:

BLESSED BY THE MAIDEN (COMING SOON)